Strong from the Heart

OTHER BOOKS BY JON LAND

The Alpha Deception

Betrayal (nonfiction)

Black Scorpion: The Tyrant Reborn

Blood Diamonds

The Blue Widows

The Council of Ten

Dark Light: Dawn

Day of the Delphi

Dead Simple

Dolphin Key

The Doomsday Spiral

The Eighth Trumpet

The Fires of Midnight

The Gamma Option

Hope Mountain

Keepers of the Gate

Kingdom of the Seven

Labyrinth

The Last Prophecy

The Lucifer Directive

The Ninth Dominion

The Omega Command

The Omicron Legion

Pandora's Temple

The Pillars of Solomon

The Rising

The Seven Sins: The Tyrant Ascending

Strong as Steel

Strong at the Break

Strong Cold Dead

Strong Darkness

Strong Enough to Die

Strong Justice

Strong Light of Day

Strong Rain Falling

Strong to the Bone

Strong Vengeance

Takedown (nonfiction)

The Tenth Circle

The Valhalla Testament

The Vengeance of the Tau

Vortex

A Walk in the Darkness

The Walls of Jericho

*Published by Forge Books

STRONG FROM THE HEART

A CAITLIN STRONG NOVEL

Jon Land

A TOM DOHERTY ASSOCIATES BOOK
NEW YORK

STRONG FROM THE HEART

Copyright © 2020 by Jon Land

A Forge Book
Published by Tom Doherty Associates
120 Broadway
New York, NY 10271

www.tor-forge.com

Forge® is a registered trademark of Macmillan Publishing Group, LLC.

The Library of Congress Cataloging-in-Publication Data is available upon request.

ISBN 978-0-7653-8470-6 (hardcover)
ISBN 978-0-7653-8471-3 (ebook)

Our books may be purchased in bulk for promotional, educational, or business use. Please contact your local bookseller or the Macmillan Corporate and Premium Sales Department at 1-800-221-7945, extension 5442, or by email at MacmillanSpecialMarkets@macmillan.com.

First Edition: 2020

Printed in Canada

0 9 8 7 6 5 4 3 2 1

For my publisher, Tom Doherty,
and my editor, Bob Gleason, Caitlin's biggest fans.

It is the nature of the strong heart, that like the palm tree it strives ever upwards when it is most burdened.

—Philip Sidney

PROLOGUE

The Texas Rangers were never more than a handful in number, but they were picked men who knew how to ride, shoot, and tell the truth. On the Mexican border and on the Indian frontier, a few Rangers time and again proved themselves more effective than battalions of soldiers.

—J. Frank Dobie, *Guide to Life and Literature of the Southwest*,
University of Texas Press, 1943

SOUTHWEST TEXAS

"There is a house in New Orleans they call the rising sun."
   As the famed song played in the single bud still wedged inside an ear, Tom Santiago found himself baking beneath a sun that had risen hours ago, long before his postal rounds brought him to the town of Camino Pass. The mailbag was still slung over his shoulder, a trail of circulars, bills, and typical junk mail left in his three-mile wake across the desert. His other earbud fluttered by his side, but Santiago noticed that no more than he noticed that the wind had blown his cap off a mile back, exposing his nearly baldpate to the blistering sun.
   His scalp was already scorched red, but neither the pain nor the burn registered with him one bit. He walked purposefully, even though no part of his assigned route awaited him and only bobcats, mule deer, and coyotes were anywhere about to claim the mail he was toting.
   "And it's been the ruin of many a poor boy and God I know I'm one."
   Santiago listened to classic rock through the duration of his route, able to time his delivery schedule by how many songs he'd covered. He could cover an entire neighborhood in the length of one of Bob Dylan's ballads and a whole street in the time it took to listen to almost any pair of Beatles songs that ranked among his favorites.
   Today, though, he didn't register the song playing in one of his ears, or anything else. He walked in an absurdly straight line, as if the desert flora he passed lined his normal route, not noticing the Homeland

Security drone overhead. Homeland maintained a fleet of them in the area of the Texas–Mexico border to watch for immigrants making their way north after illegally crossing the border. But the dispatcher who radioed the nearest patrol vehicle currently coming up on Tom Santiago from behind never had to deal with a wayward mailman before.

The Humvee with the Homeland Security logo stenciled on both sides came around Santiago and banked to the side to cut him off, only to have him skirt the vehicle and continue on as if it were a natural obstacle. So officers Jim Ochoa and Darnell Reavis leaped down from their air-conditioned cab and caught up with the dazed, barely blinking mailman after a brief chase.

"Hey, buddy, what's wrong?" Ochoa said, snapping his fingers in front of Santiago's face, positioned so Santiago could not resume his march through the desert. "You lost or something?"

When this produced no response, Darnell Reavis plucked some mail from the top of Santiago's bag.

"Isn't that a crime or something?" Ochoa asked him.

"I don't think this drunk sack of shit is in shape to care."

"You think he's drunk?"

Now it was Reavis who snapped his fingers before the mailman. "Or stoned. What else?"

Ochoa regarded some of the mail Reavis had handed him. "Looks like he left a whole bunch of mail to Camino Pass undelivered."

"Never heard of it."

"Small town; no more than three hundred residents," Ochoa recalled.

"Maybe one of them can tell us what happened to this guy. Hey, what's that song he's listening to?" Reavis wondered, easing the stray bud into his ear to find out.

"*Well, I got one foot on the platform, the other foot on the train, I'm going back to New Orleans to wear that ball and chain.*"

Both Ochoa and Reavis felt something strange as the town of Camino Pass came into view. Though neither would admit it, both were of a mind not to continue and to call in the highway patrol instead, especially when Tom Santiago's eyes bulged at sight of the town and he began thrashing against the bonds of his shoulder harness.

"*No, no, no, no, no, no, no, no, NO!*"

Santiago finally stopped, with his eyes frozen open on Camino Pass, which was growing in shape before them. The perspiration that had soaked through his blue postal uniform was now gluing him to the Humvee's leatherlike upholstery.

"What do you want to do?" Reavis asked Ochoa.

"Let's see what we can see," his partner replied, even though that wasn't what he wanted to do at all.

They passed by the homes dotting the town's outskirts and continued toward its small commercial center, which was populated by stores that had been around since before either man had been born, some of them closed.

"Hey," Reavis said, his attention drawn to the right, "there's an open door over there. A restaurant, I think."

"Or a bar," from Ochoa.

"That would explain things."

"Want to check it out?"

"I'm thinking one of us should stay with the mailman."

Ochoa threw open his door. "He's not going anywhere. Come on."

Tom Santiago's blank stare followed the men passing through the open door. Little more than the length of a breath passed before they stumbled back outside, both nearly falling in their desperate rush back to the vehicle.

"No, no, no, no, no, no, no, no, no," the mailman repeated, over and over again on an infinite loop, as Ochoa screeched the Humvee around and raced from the town with the accelerator floored the whole way.

Reavis grabbed the mic from its stand. "Central, this is Rover Six! Central, come in!"

"This is Central, Rover Six."

"Central, we've got a potential level one event in the town of Camino Pass. Send . . ."

"Rover Six, this is Central," the Homeland Security dispatcher said, when Reavis went quiet after using terminology reserved only for the most serious of catastrophes. "Rover Six, we read you. Please continue."

Reavis swallowed hard. "Send . . . *everyone.*"

PART ONE

JOHN COFFEE HAYS

Born in Tennessee, Hays arrived in San Antonio in 1837, shortly after Texas won its independence from Mexico. By 1841, at the tender age of 23, he was a Ranger captain. A fearless fighter and skilled leader, Hays won his fame defending Texans from raids and attacks by both Native American (Comanche) groups and Mexican bandits. More than any other man, he would come to symbolize the Rangers of the Texas Republic era. During the Mexican War (1846–48), Hays' Rangers scouted, defended U.S. supply and communication lines from attacks by Mexican guerrillas and fought alongside regular U.S. army troops, earning a national reputation for their bravery. After the war, Hays went further west to California, where he made his name in politics, real estate and ranching and helped found the city of Oakland.

—Sarah Pruitt, "8 Famous Texas Rangers," History.com

I

Caitlin Strong pushed her way through the gaggle of reporters and by-standers clustered before the barricade set up just inside the lobby of the Canyon Ridge Elementary School building.

"Look," she heard somebody say, "the Texas Rangers are here!"

She focused her attention on the six men wearing black camo pants and Windbreakers labeled "ICE" in big letters on the back who were glaring at her from the entrance of the school that they had clearly been prevented from entering. She pictured several more Immigration and Customs Enforcement agents stationed at additional exits in case their quarries tried to make a run for it.

"We didn't call the Rangers," snarled a bald man. The name tag he was required to wear read "Orleans."

"No, sir," Caitlin told him, "that would've been the school principal. She told dispatch you'd come here to collect some of her students."

Caitlin let her gaze drift to a windowless black truck that looked like a reconfigured SWAT transport vehicle.

"Just following orders, Ranger. Doing our job, just like you."

"My job is to keep the peace, sir."

"Ours too, so I'm going to assume you're going to assist our efforts, given that we're on the same side here."

"What side would that be?"

Orleans snarled again, seeming to pump air into a head Caitlin figured might have been confused for a basketball. "United States government, ma'am."

"I work for Texas, sir, and the principal told me all the kids you came for were born on Lone Star soil."

"That's for a court to decide."

"Maybe. And you're right, the both of us are here because we've got a job to do, and I respect that, sir, I truly do. My problem is it's never right, in my mind, for adults to involve children in somebody else's mess."

Canyon Ridge Elementary, located on Stone Oak Parkway, was part of San Antonio's North East Independent School District and featured a comfortable mix of Caucasian and Hispanic students, in keeping with the city's general demographics. The building featured a rounded arch entry, where Caitlin could see any number of faces, both child and adult, pressed against the glass. She also glimpsed a heavy chain looped through the double doors to prevent entry, although numerous chairs, boxes, and what looked like an overturned cafeteria table had been piled into place as well. Caitlin pictured similar chains and barricades barring entry at any of the other doors as well, the eyes of both children and adults alike gaping with hope at her arrival through the glass.

"As a Texas Ranger," Orleans responded finally, "you enjoy a degree of discretion I don't have. I wish I did, but I don't. And as long as I don't, I've got orders to follow, and that's where my discretion begins and ends."

"Where are you from, sir?"

"Not around here, that's for sure. Does it matter?"

"That ICE is about to take six U.S. citizens, all under the age of ten, into custody matters a lot," Caitlin told him. "Some might even call it kidnapping."

"Did you really just say that?"

"Like I said, I'm only trying to keep the peace. Exercise that discretion you mentioned."

"It's not your jurisdiction."

"San Antonio was still part of Texas, last time I checked."

Orleans's spine stiffened, making him look taller. "Not today, as far as you're concerned. You don't want to push this any farther than you already have, Ranger, believe me."

"It's about the law, sir—you just said that too. See, the Texas Rangers maintain no intergovernmental service agreement with ICE; neither does the city of San Antonio. And, according to the city's detainer agreement, a local police officer has to be present whenever you're staging a raid. And I don't currently see an officer on-site."

"That's because this isn't a raid."

"What would you call it then?"

Orleans's face was getting red, taking on the look of sunbaked skin. "There's a local inside the building now."

"Right. The school resource officer. What was his name again?"

Orleans worked his mouth around, as if he were chewing the inside of his cheeks.

Caitlin cast her gaze toward the pair of unmarked black Humvees that must have brought the ICE officials here. "You got assault rifles stored in those trucks, sir?"

"Never know when you might need them."

"Sure, against fourth graders wielding spitballs. Report I got said those and the fifth graders helped barricade the doors."

"So arrest them and let us do our jobs," Orleans sneered, his shoulders seeming to widen within the bonds of his flak jacket.

"Be glad to, once you produce the official paperwork that brought you this far."

"We can give you the names of the students we're here to detain, Ranger."

"What about warrants, court orders, something that passes for official?"

Orleans shook his head. "Not necessary."

"It is for me." Caitlin took a step closer to him, watching his gaze dip to the SIG Sauer nine-millimeter pistol holstered to her belt.

"Don't make me the bad guy here, Ranger. I'm doing my job, just like you. You may not like it, all these protesters might not like it, but I don't suppose they'd disobey the orders of their superiors any more than I can."

"I know you don't make the rules, sir, and I respect that, to the point where I have a suggestion: Why don't you stand down and give me a chance to fetch the kids you're after from inside before somebody gets hurt?"

A skeptical Orleans nodded stiffly. "Sounds like you've come to your senses, Ranger."

"Never lost them, sir. You're right about orders, and mine were to defuse the situation through whatever means necessary. That's what I'm trying to do here. The lawyers can sort things out from that point."

Orleans hedged a bit. "I didn't figure something like this fell under Ranger domain."

"This is Texas, sir. *Everything* falls under our domain. In this case, we can make that work to your advantage."

Orleans nodded, his expression dour. "The doors were already chained and barricaded when we got here, Ranger. That means somebody tipped the school off we were coming, even fed them the names of the kids we were coming to pick up."

"It wasn't the Rangers," Caitlin assured him.

"No, but somebody in the Department of Public Safety must've been behind the leak, after we informed them of our intentions as a courtesy."

"That's a separate issue you need to take up with DPS, sir. For now, how about we dial things back a few notches so the two of us can just do our jobs?"

"That sounds good to me, Ranger. The United States government thanks you for your support."

Caitlin stopped halfway to the school entrance, beneath the curved archway, and looked back. "Don't confuse what I'm doing with support, Agent Orleans. When things go from bad to worse, blood often gets spilled. What do you say we do our best to keep the street dry today?"

2

San Antonio, Texas

Caitlin watched the school's principal, Mariana Alonzo, unfasten the chains after enough of the makeshift barricade had been removed to allow one of the entry doors to open.

"Thanks for coming, Ranger," Alonzo greeted, locking the chain back into place.

"I'm sure your sister would have preferred intervening herself, ma'am."

Alonzo swallowed hard. "Did you mean what you said out there, that you're going to deliver the kids to ICE?"

"I also said I was here to defuse the situation through any means necessary."

Mariana Alonzo's sister, Conseulo, was a former San Antonio police captain and deputy chief, currently climbing the law enforcement ladder at the Department of Public Safety in Austin. She'd called Caitlin immediately after first getting word of ICE's pending arrival at Canyon Ridge Elementary, though not before alerting her sister to what was coming.

"All six of these kids are honor students, Ranger," the school principal noted.

"This kind of thing would be just as wrong even if they weren't, ma'am. I imagine your sister believes that more than anyone. I'm surprised she didn't come here herself, instead of calling me."

Now, an hour after that call, the sister of DPS's deputy police commissioner was looking at Caitlin with the same hope she'd glimpsed on the faces of the kids pressed against the glass.

"She wanted to," Principal Alonzo said, "but I wasn't about to let her throw her career away. Then she told me she had another idea. Nobody messes with the Texas Rangers, right?"

"Your sister and I go back a ways, ma'am," Caitlin told her, not bothering to add that not all their interactions had been positive.

Alonzo steered Caitlin away from the throng of children, who were unable to take their eyes off her badge and gun, to a corner of the hall. They stopped beneath an air-conditioning baffle blowing bursts of frigid air.

"What now, Ranger?"

"Where are the children, ma'am?"

"In my office," Alonzo said, tilting her gaze toward an open door, through which Caitlin spotted a pair of school secretaries busy fielding a nonstop flurry of phone calls. "Be nice to keep as much of a lid on this as possible."

Caitlin weighed her options. "That lid got blown off when your sister called me in on this. I don't figure on ICE breaking down the doors, but they'll wait us out for as long as it takes. Means we need to find a way to take these kids out of their reach."

"Is that even possible?"

"I've got a couple of ideas."

"You want to do *what*?" D. W. Tepper, captain of Ranger Company F, blared over the phone.

Caitlin pictured him reaching for a cigarette. "You heard me, Captain."

"Well, that's a new one, anyway."

"First time for everything."

"Our necks better be made of Silly Putty, if we're going to stick them out this far."

"Not the first time for that at all. And put down the Marlboro, D.W."

"Jeez, Ranger, what are you, psychic now, like that seven-foot Venezuelan giant of yours?"

"Speaking of Colonel Paz . . ."

3

SAN ANTONIO, TEXAS

Twenty minutes and another phone call later, Caitlin inspected the three-page document Principal Mariana Alonzo had printed off an email attachment she'd just received.

"You Rangers sure work fast," she complimented.

"Always been our way," Caitlin told her, folding the document in thirds so the proper section was face out, "long before there was any such thing as email, or even electricity."

"You ever wonder what it was like, ranging in those days?"

"Strongs have been Rangers almost as long as there's been a Texas. I never really had to wonder, since I grew up with all the stories about their exploits."

"I've heard of your grandfather. Your father, too."

"Well, ma'am, my great-grandad William Ray and my great-great-grandad Steeldust Jack had their share of adventures too."

"I'd love to have you back sometime to talk about that history to our students."

"Let's take care of the ones I came here about today first," Caitlin said, pocketing the now trifolded set of pages.

———

"You sure about this, Ranger?" Mariana Alonzo said to Caitlin, after bringing from her office to the main lobby, just out of sight of the barricaded entrance, the six students that the ICE officers had come to collect.

Caitlin ran her hand through the hair of a trembling girl who looked all of ten years old, then used a tissue to wipe the tearstains from the cheeks of a boy who was all of nine.

"As sure as I am that if we don't do something fast, ICE might breach the building."

"What happens then?"

"This is still Texas and I'm still a Texas Ranger, ma'am. Just ask your sister."

"I did, after she told me you were coming."

"What'd she say?"

"To stay out of your way. That everything I'd heard was true."

Caitlin bristled. "I wouldn't put much stock in those stories. The press is prone to exaggeration."

Alonzo nodded. "She told me you'd say that, too."

Caitlin felt the boy whose cheeks she'd swiped clean tug at her sleeve.

"Are you going to save us from the bad men?"

She knelt so they were eye to eye and laid her hands on his shoulders. "What's your name, son?"

"Diego. I'm scared."

"Well, Diego, let me show you what happens to men who scare little kids."

The bald ICE agent named Orleans smirked when Caitlin emerged from the school entrance with the six children in tow, school principal Mariana Alonzo bringing up the rear. Cameras clacked and whirred as she brushed aside microphones thrust in her face.

"That wasn't so hard, was it?" Orleans said, once Caitlin reached him, her charges gathered protectively behind her. "Good thing you came to your senses. If it makes you feel any better, I hate this part of the job as much as anybody."

"I hope that's the case, Agent. I truly do." Caitlin eased from her pocket the document Captain Tepper had just emailed. "Because this is a duly executed warrant naming these six children as material witnesses to a crime, subject to protection by the Texas Rangers until such time they are called to testify."

Orleans started to turn red. Caitlin could feel the heat radiating through his uniform, dragging an odor that reminded her of a gym bag with yesterday's dank workout clothes still stuffed inside.

"You lied to me, Ranger."

"No, I didn't, sir. I told you I was here to defuse the situation, and that's what I'm doing. I said I'd fetch the kids from inside before somebody got hurt, and that's exactly what I did."

"You mean nobody's been hurt yet, Ranger." With that, Orleans snatched the warrant from her grasp. "This is bullshit and you know it," he said, having barely regarded it.

"That's not for either of us to say, sir. It's for a court to decide now."

"You want to tell me what crime exactly these six suspects are material witness to?"

"Did you just call them suspects?"

"Answer my question, Ranger."

"I'm not at liberty to say, sir. It's a confidential investigation."

Orleans turned his gaze on the imposing group of five armed men dressed in black tactical garb behind him, then looked back at Caitlin and smirked again. "So you think we're just going to let you parade these suspects past us all by yourself? You really think we're going to just back down and stand aside?"

The blistering roar of an engine almost drowned out his last words, as an extended cab pickup truck riding massive tires tore onto the scene and spun to a halt between the ICE agents and their Humvees. The springs recoiled as a huge figure with a pair of M4 assault rifles shouldered behind him emerged from the cab, towering over those he passed, including the men with "ICE" embroidered on their jackets.

"This is Colonel Guillermo Paz," Caitlin told Orleans, "an agent of Homeland Security, just like you, sir. He's going to help me parade these 'suspects' past you."

"Colonel G!" a first-grade boy beamed, coming up only to Paz's waist as he hugged him tightly, before Paz could lift him into the backseat of his truck. "You remember me from preschool?"

"Of course I do, Marcus."

"Do you still work there?"

"No, I moved on. I do that a lot. Learn what I can from a place and then try another."

"I miss you, Colonel G. You never finished the story of what you did to those bad men who tried to hurt you when you went home for your mommy's funeral."

"They're not alive anymore, Marcus."

"Really?"

Paz fixed his gaze on the ICE agents, who'd edged closer, weighing their options. "It's what happens to bad men."

"Thank you, Colonel," Caitlin said through the window, eyes even with Paz's in the driver's seat.

"'The purpose of life is to contribute in some way to making things better.'"

"Robert Kennedy?"

Paz's eyes widened. "I'm impressed, Ranger."

"Just a lucky guess."

"Edward Bulwer-Lytton didn't believe in luck. He called it a fancy name for being always at the ready when needed."

"Describes the two of us pretty well, I suppose." Caitlin looked at the four kids squeezed into the big pickup's backseat, Diego and Marcus in the front, staring wide-eyed at the giant behind the wheel. "You know where to take them."

Paz cast his gaze back toward the ICE agents frozen in place fifteen feet away with scowls plastered across their faces. "And if they follow?"

"They won't get very far," Caitlin told him. "Principal Alonzo yanked out the valve stems on their tires while we were loading the kids."

Caitlin's phone rang with a call from Captain Tepper, just as Guillermo Paz was driving off and the ICE agents were discovering their flat tires.

"Now who's psychic, Captain?" she greeted. "Kids are safe and I didn't even have to shoot anybody."

"Good thing you saved your bullets, Ranger, 'cause there's somewhere else you need to be right now. A town in the desert called Camino Pass, formerly with a population of two hundred and eighty-eight, according to the last census."

"Formerly?"

"Looks like they're all dead, Ranger. Each and every one of them."

4

HOUSTON

Cort Wesley Masters braked for an arriving ambulance, then pulled his truck into a no parking zone striped in front of the entrance to the Houston Methodist Willowbrook Hospital. He rushed through the automatic doors so fast he banged into the one on the right, which didn't open fast enough.

"My son!" he blared to the admitting nurse, before adding a name. "Luke Torres!"

Leaving it there.

He'd gotten the call at the Holiday Inn Express a few miles from the Village School on Gentryside Drive in Houston. After watching his younger son play soccer the night before, he'd returned to his room with no plans beyond a room service dinner and watching whatever football game he could find on television. His oldest son, Dylan, was back at Brown University, back playing football for the Bears under their new head coach, James Perry. And Cort Wesley was staying overnight to begin the college-visiting process with Luke at nearby Rice University.

Turned out the hotel didn't offer room service, so Cort Wesley fished a sandwich from the available offerings in a lobby cooler, then fell asleep in his clothes, watching two college football teams he'd never heard of play on a network he found only by scrolling through all the available channels. He was showered and ready to go in the morning, making his way through the motel lobby, when he'd gotten the call from someone at the hospital telling him his younger son, Luke, was currently in the emergency room.

"What happened?" Cort Wesley heard himself ask, his stomach having sunk to his feet.

"Sir, you just need to get down here," the voice attached to a name and a title he'd already forgotten told him.

"Was he in an accident? Is he all right?"

"We aren't permitted to release that kind of information over the phone."

"But he's okay. Can you at least tell me he's going to be okay?"

Cort Wesley had hung up and resumed his stride through the lobby while the man was halfway through his curt rejoinder again. And now here he was, glaring down at the admitting nurse, who seemed to be reading from the same script.

"Mr. Torres?" he heard a voice call.

Cort Wesley turned to see a bearded doctor wearing a white lab coat flecked with what looked like blood. Luke's maybe? Had he been attacked, singled out by one of his father's many enemies yet again?

"It's Masters," Cort Wesley corrected. His boys had always gone by their legal name, which was given them by their late mother and his former girlfriend, Maura Torres. "How's my son?"

"I'm Dr. Riboron, Mr. Masters. Your son is in stable condition and is expected to make a full recovery."

"Recovery from what?"

"My understanding is he hasn't turned eighteen yet."

"Not until the spring," Cort Wesley acknowledged.

"In that case, I can tell you he's recovering from an overdose."

"An overdose of what, Doctor?"

Riboron held Cort Wesley's stare for a long moment before responding. "Opioids."

Cort Wesley's stomach took the same path to the floor. "Say that again."

"He was transported from the Village School by Houston paramedics, who administered Narcan during transport."

"Who called nine-one-one?"

"I don't have that information handy, Mr. Torres."

"Masters," Cort Wesley repeated. "Can I see him?"

"As soon as we finish running some tests. We're keeping your son here under observation and will let you know if we determine admitting him is necessary."

"We're supposed to be visiting colleges today," he said, wondering if that sounded as lame to Riboron as it did to him.

"You're going to have to postpone your trip."

The lights in the emergency room reception area suddenly made Cort Wesley's eyes ache. And there was a buzzing in his ear that reminded him of the sound made by a finicky transformer high up on a telephone pole. He glanced at the fluorescents overhead, wondering if one of them was about to blow.

"The police will want to talk to you, Mr. Masters," Dr. Riboron said over the buzzing. "And your son as well."

"Did anyone from the school accompany him here or show up later?"

"From the school?"

"Teacher, administrator—something like that."

"No."

Cort Wesley looked down to keep the light from his eyes. "No?" he echoed, the buzzing getting louder in his ears.

"I don't have all the details, sir. You should check with reception."

"I want to see my son."

"We're finishing up those tests now. Shouldn't be more than another few minutes."

"Did Luke say anything about how he got the pills?"

"We haven't had the opportunity to ask him about that yet."

"I'm wondering if he volunteered anything on his own." Cort Wesley could feel himself groping for words, speaking with the buzz sounding as a constant backdrop. "You know, like maybe he accidentally took more pills than he should have. You know, from a prescription for a sports injury or something."

Riboron took a step backwards, seeming to disappear into a shadowy zone untouched by the brightness that was blinding Cort Wesley. "Doctors are extremely averse to prescribing opiates to minors without their parents' permission. And . . ."

"And *what*, Doctor?"

The shadows deepened around Riboron. "He didn't swallow the drugs, Mr. Masters. He snorted them."

5

CAMINO PASS, TEXAS

"You mind doing a pass over the town?" Caitlin said to the helicopter pilot through her headset. "Like to see what I can see from the get-go."

"Would if I could, Ranger," he told her. "But airspace over Camino Pass has been closed."

Caitlin knew it must be bad, when Captain Tepper arranged for her to take the Ranger helicopter. But all he had at that point was a report from a Homeland Security border patrol team about a mailman who'd been found wandering through the desert—and what the Homeland agents had found in the last place his route had taken him.

Officers from the highway patrol had rushed to the outskirts of Camino Pass and cordoned off the entire area to await the arrival of a surge capacity force dispatched by the Department of Homeland Security. That force comprised representatives from various federal and local officials attached to DHS in some capacity, including Caitlin, in this region.

The town had been blockaded to a one-mile radius in all directions, and that extended to helicopters. The DHS officers who'd found the mailman wandering through the desert had been placed in quarantine until such time as it could be confirmed no airborne organism was responsible. The surge capacity force currently en route would perform a detailed inspection of the town, going house to house to tally up the dead and to search for any potential survivors. The fact that there had been no sign of life anywhere in Camino Pass since the Homeland Security agents had called in their report didn't bode well for finding anyone still breathing.

Normally, the flight from Stinson Airport in San Antonio would have been routine, but flying of any kind had proven to be a challenge since Caitlin had suffered what doctors referred to as a blast injury, thanks to the percussion of a propane explosion she'd set off several months before. The blast, at a besieged Spanish mission in the desert Southwest, had temporarily ravaged her hearing in one ear, and while the hearing had quickly returned, the rest of her symptoms had refused to abate. Doctors explained that the percussion had caused something called blast overpressurization, resulting in tiny fracture lines along portions of Caitlin's skull, which proved agonizing as they healed. They'd prescribed treatment with low doses of Vicodin so long as the pain persisted. After ridding herself of the fog that had accompanied the initial doses, Caitlin had adapted well enough to function, though she was downing, on average, four pills on a good day and six on a bad one. Unfortunately, there were more bad days than good, as the healing process continued to take its own sweet time.

Caitlin swallowed a ten-milligram pill with water, as the Ranger helicopter landed on a closed-off section of the four-lane highway, just short of the command center, which had been set up far enough away from Camino Pass to hide even the slightest glimpse of the town. A highway patrol captain whom Caitlin recognized as Ben Hargraves was waiting when she jogged up to join him at the makeshift roadblock.

"When I saw the helicopter, I was hoping it was Homeland," he greeted. "As in experts who could tell me what the hell we're facing here."

"Nice to see you too, Captain."

"Forgive my manners, Ranger, but this is as strange as it gets."

"How have you been able to confirm initial indications that whatever happened killed almost three hundred people?"

Hargraves nodded. "Thanks to a thermal imaging machine on the highway patrol chopper. From the looks of things, they died in their sleep, the whole goddamn town."

"Sounds like something in the air," Caitlin said, trying to make sense of what Hargraves had just told her. "Or water maybe."

"That's right. As I recall, you've had some experience with these kind of catastrophic events."

"Unfortunately, you might even call me an expert, Captain. Not a distinction I'm proud of."

Caitlin wandered if Hargraves was facing away from the town to keep fear from stretching over his expression. "That crisis response team, or whatever it's called, is en route now. Our orders are to secure the area in the meantime. So we've closed every access road out a mile and have directed air traffic control to steer all aircraft away from the area."

"I don't think this town lies in anybody's flight pattern."

"If it did, it doesn't anymore, Ranger."

Caitlin turned her gaze in Camino Pass's direction. "What about nine-one-one calls, police reports, any anomalies arising in the past twelve hours that might give us more of an idea of what happened here?"

Hargraves shook his head, his expression tightening anew. "Nothing. Absolutely nothing."

Caitlin took off her Stetson and held it by her hip, just over her SIG. "I'll reach out to the cell phone providers."

"What did I just say?" Hargraves asked, like a man thinking he was talking to a wall.

"I heard you, Captain. I'm talking about contacting them to get a notion as to cellular traffic coming out of the town. See when it stopped, to give us a better notion as to the timeline of whatever happened here."

A heavy *wop-wop-wop* announced the arrival of two more helicopters, barely specks coming in from the north, until they quickly grew into massive june bugs splitting the air. Army Black Hawks, by the look of things, meaning DHS's surge capacity force was now on-site. That explained the presence of the massive SWAT-like RV parked off to the side, straddling the shoulder, likely dispatched from San Antonio in the initial moments of chaos after Homeland's agents had called in what they'd seen.

"Care to tell me what to expect next?" Hargraves said, his voice carrying over the loudening roar of the choppers.

Caitlin's gaze moved from the RV to the choppers just now setting over the scene. "The Homeland personnel land, and I suit up to join them in checking out the town."

6

HOUSTON

"You can see your son now, Mr. Masters."

Cort Wesley practically bounced out of his chair in the hospital's emergency room waiting area. His legs felt heavy, the overly bright lighting around him seeming to have dulled. Dr. Riboron wasn't standing more than six feet away from him, but it felt like a mile.

He'd spent the last several hours cataloging his son Luke's youth, able to count the times on a single hand that he'd disciplined the boy for just the slightest of infractions, which didn't even approach, much less suggest, drug use. Part of him figured he was going to be ushered into a room to find another boy altogether lying there, a mistake having been made. The other part, meanwhile, contemplated exactly what he was going to say to his younger son, because this clearly was no mistake.

"Your son's one of the lucky ones, Mr. Masters," Riboron said, after Cort Wesley had fallen into step alongside him. "Near as we can tell, he ingested the drugs last night. His roommate found him unresponsive this morning. Absent that stroke of fortune, we'd be having an entirely different conversation."

"Stroke of fortune?"

"The fact that somebody was there to find him in that condition. Most of those, the vast majority, who overdose aren't as lucky."

Cort Wesley almost said he didn't consider having a son who'd overdosed on opiates very lucky at all.

"You have any notion as to what it was he took, Doctor?" he asked instead.

"OxyContin or an equivalent generic oxycodone, according to the tox screen. The drug of choice these days," Riboron continued, speaking with an edge to his voice that sounded like resentment to Cort Wesley.

They stopped just outside the curtained cubicle where Luke remained, hours after his initial treatment.

"We'll be doing a psych evaluation of your son soon, Mr. Masters, which is strictly routine in cases of overdose." Riboron hesitated, until Cort Wesley met his gaze. "That same routine also dictates we inform the police. We've done that and filed the appropriate report but have yet to let them know he's regained consciousness, so you can see him first."

"That's not routine, even for a minor?"

"In Texas, drug offenders are considered adults at sixteen, just like with violent crimes."

"You think my son is an offender?" Cort Wesley wondered, taking umbrage at the doctor's use of the term.

"According to the law he is," Riboron said, parting the curtain enough for Cort Wesley to enter the cubicle.

Luke was sitting up, propped by pillows, chewing on crushed ice packed into a plastic cup he was holding. His eyes were narrowed and glassy, lagging between sight and recognition, judging by the languid fashion in which he viewed Cort Wesley.

"I'm sorry, Dad," he managed, voice cracking.

Cort Wesley felt his insides melt as he drew even with the side of the bed on which Luke was resting, safety rails lowered. His mind froze between thoughts, intentions.

"Sorry doesn't begin to cut it, son," was all he could manage.

Luke swallowed hard, worked some more ice from the cup into his mouth.

"I mean, what were you thinking?" Cort Wesley continued.

"Clearly, I wasn't."

"Please tell me this was the first time."

Cort Wesley heard the crackle of Luke chewing on the ice.

"Mostly," the boy said.

"What's that mean?"

"Almost."

"*Almost* the first time you snorted OxyContin?"

The boy's features sank. He sighed dryly. Cort Wesley saw tears forming in the corners of his drooping eyes.

"It was the first time I *snorted* it, yeah."

"But not the first time you've used."

"Everybody at school does, at least the seniors."

"I wasn't asking about everybody; I was asking about you."

"It was a mistake, Dad," Luke said, between a wheezy exhale of breath.

"How many mistakes we talking about exactly?"

"Like a half dozen. Six or so times."

"With oxy or with other drugs too?"

Luke looked past Cort Wesley, toward the curtain that flapped slightly when a nurse or doctor passed by beyond. "Vicodin, I think."

"And you're telling me everyone in your class is using?"

Luke started to roll his eyes but didn't quite complete the motion. "Don't use that word."

"What word?"

"'Using.' It's for addicts, junkies."

"From where I'm standing, that suits you just fine. Now answer my question, son. How many kids in your class are *using*?"

"Some."

"What happened to 'everybody'?"

"A few. Can you back off? My head is killing me."

"You should've thought of that before you snorted oxy, son."

"Like I said, I wasn't thinking." Luke smacked one side of his head and then the other. "Stupid, stupid, stupid. I don't know what I was thinking, all right?"

"There's something else you *do* know you can tell me, son."

"What's that?"

"Where you got the drugs," Cort Wesley told him, feeling cold sweat mat his shirt to his back even as something heated up inside him. "As in who sold them to you."

7

CAMINO PASS, TEXAS

"On whose authority are you here again?" Colonel Samwell Teavens, designated head of the DHS's surge capacity force, asked Caitlin.

"Same authority as you, sir," she told him, fingers looped through a handhold on board the armored RV that came equipped with its own oxygen supply. "That being the Department of Homeland Security. This isn't my first rodeo, Colonel, and it's not my first time in a hazmat suit, either."

Teavens nodded grudgingly. He was full time with the Texas National Guard out of San Antonio and crisis response leader for the region. Like Caitlin, he'd been detailed out to both Quantico and Washington, DC, to learn the ins and outs of managing catastrophic events like this one, specifically when it involved a potential threat to the country, hostile or otherwise. In all probability, some kind of accident had claimed the lives of the residents of Camino Pass, but that didn't mean whatever it was didn't hold the potential to do grievous harm well beyond the town's borders if the cause wasn't identified and isolated.

"All the same . . ." Teavens started.

"All the same *what*, sir?"

"Whatever killed these folks isn't something you're going to be able to gun down, Ranger."

"Really? You sure about that?"

Teavens had been less than enamored by Caitlin's presence on scene, even before she voiced her intention to join his hazmat team in investigating whatever had transpired in Camino Pass.

"We don't need a glory hound getting in the way here," he groused, while inventorying the equipment the personnel accompanying him had carted off the two choppers.

"You think that's what I am?"

"You seem to get your name in the papers a lot, Ranger."

"Not by choice, sir, I can assure you of that. And I'm here on orders, just like you."

Caitlin found herself missing the man she knew only as Jones, the shadowy Department of Homeland Security operative who'd called Texas home until he was unceremoniously relieved of duty six months back, when the government needed a fall guy for an operation gone wrong. She owed her involvement with DHS matters like this to him and had half expected Jones to step out of the lead chopper, until Teavens emerged in his stead. Not that she trusted Jones all that much, but he was a professional who knew his way around a gunfight, which meant the kind of pressures that awaited in Camino Pass wouldn't bother him. Teavens, on the other hand, had the button-down look of a man more used to commanding paper and firing off reports instead of bullets. Kind of man for whom the uniform looked more like a wardrobe accessory than a lived-in garment.

Teavens's eight-man surge capacity force included a pair of communications specialists, one of whom would remain behind and set up shop at the checkpoint. There were also a pair of doctors with infectious disease expertise and two forensic scientists who would be gathering the proper samples for lab study. Since they were not permitted, under any circumstances, to remove any of the bodies from the quarantined town, a task left to a much larger team out of Washington being assembled now, those samples would prove crucial to any initial assessment and analysis as to the cause and potential virulence behind whatever had killed nearly three hundred men, women, and children. The team was rounded out by a pair of specially trained national guardsmen, who'd be toting M4 assault rifles with them instead of sample collection kits.

"Just so we're clear on one thing, Ranger," Teavens told her, after Caitlin had climbed into her hazmat suit with far more dexterity than the rest of his team. "I'm in charge here."

"Wouldn't have it any other way, sir," she told him.

Upon pulling to a halt in the center of Camino Pass, Caitlin helped the doctors and scientists fit their hazmat helmets snugly in place, after which Teavens opened the RV's rear door in the middle of the town's main drag and led the procession outside. She could feel herself baking inside the hazmat suit, as she always did, regardless of temperature. The fabric was stiff and airtight to ensure that no germs or microbes could pass through. And with the helmet securely fastened, she always felt as if she were scuba diving on land, the sound of her breathing resonating in her ears and the light sheen of sweat on her face inevitably swelling into dollops.

"On my lead," she heard Teavens say through her helmet's built-in speaker, as he led the way out of the SUV and toward a squad car complete with revolving light array riding its roof. It was labeled "Camino Pass Sheriff" in letters that looked like they were painted over another marking, as if the vehicle were a hand-me-down from a larger department.

Caitlin's heavy, plastic-coated rubber boots made walking a slog, and she was aware of the two soldiers taking up strategic flanking positions on either side of the group. Defensive, as if anticipating an attack.

Closer to the vehicle, she spotted the body of a man in uniform who'd crumpled just short of the car, eyes frozen open and mouth agape. Out of habit, Caitlin noticed that his gun was still holstered, but his hat lay between him and the driver's door, as if it had been shed as he was reaching for the latch.

"Any thoughts?" Teavens asked, suddenly alongside her.

Caitlin kneeled by the body, another motion made difficult by the confines of her suit. "Whatever hit him, he had time to make a go for his car, out of instinct probably." She looked up, judging the distance from the storefront sheriff's station to the squad car. "Twenty-five, maybe thirty seconds, more or less."

"Meaning he was awake when whatever it was happened, in contrast to the rest of the town."

"On duty, in all probability," Caitlin advanced, "while pretty much everybody else was asleep. Maybe somebody else was awake, too, and they called the station. Looking at it that way, he could've been in the process of responding to a call. That could indicate whatever happened didn't happen all at once."

She watched one of the scientists move off to collect samples of the air and of standing water in a puddle left over from a rainstorm the night before. Eventually, he'd take and catalog samples of pretty much everything they encountered. Everyone else proceeded directly toward the car, where both doctors and the remaining scientist took turns examining the corpse already stiffening on the asphalt.

"Lividity and settling of the blood confirms whatever it was happened fast," she heard one of them say.

"Not so fast he didn't know something bad was happening," Caitlin offered.

"How can you tell?"

"Because he strapped his gun belt on before he went for the car. In a rush or a panic, since he didn't stuff the end of the belt through the loop."

The others nodded, except for Teavens.

"Looks like something in the air to me," the colonel said. "I'd say close to for sure on that."

"Let's not to jump to any conclusions," Caitlin heard another voice say inside her helmet.

"Running a preliminary analysis on the air now," chimed in the scientist off to the side, busy following the LED readouts. "So far, it's clean. No contaminants, toxins, or unidentified chemicals or compounds."

"You mean, not anymore," another voice reminded.

"All the same," said the scientist, leaving it there.

Teavens was running his gaze along the street and then letting it drift to the closest nesting of homes.

"Let's take a walk," Caitlin heard him say.

They checked out six houses right off the bat, breaking off into two teams to better manage the effort, starting with the homes closest to the center of town. The hard stuff, as Caitlin's father or grandfather might have called it, given that they knew what awaited them.

There was something familiar about Camino Pass, but Caitlin couldn't put her finger on what exactly. Probably a case her grandfather or father had worked; there were so many embedded in her memory, it was impossible to keep them all straight. Beyond that, she knew nothing about Camino Pass. It was just another border town, one of literally hundreds that dotted the jagged line dividing Texas from Mexico. The ones closer to the Rio Grande tended to have larger populations, thanks to the surrounding farms and ranches. In these parts, there weren't a lot of either of those; the residents of towns like this one scraped by as best they could, working odd jobs while in search of more permanent employment just to make ends meet.

The furnishings in the three homes Caitlin checked in tandem with Colonel Teavens, an MD, and one of the scientists were testament to that. They were simple, old, or both, likely handed down through multiple generations or purchased at secondhand stores before they could be acquired by other families. The only exception in each home seemed to be the flat-screen televisions mounted on cracked, peeling walls that looked ready to crumble under their weight. One of the sets was still humming, radiating sunlamp-like heat from being on for so many hours straight. A man wearing pajamas and a bathrobe sat in a chair set directly before it, his frozen features identical to the dead town sheriff's. They found his wife in the identical condition in their bed. The couple was too old to still have kids in the house.

There were kids in the next two houses they checked, though. Caitlin walked about the single-story structures that seemed uniform in design and layout. She tried to busy herself by putting her investigative skills and instincts to use, seeking some clue as to what did this. But her observations yielded nothing and her team was left to catalog the bodies and nothing much else.

"You ever seen anything like this before?" Teavens asked her, his lips seeming to move a beat ahead of his voice reaching her.

"No."

She watched him flash a grin utterly devoid of amusement through his helmet's faceplate. "I thought you mixed it up with space aliens once."

"You didn't ask me about space aliens," Caitlin told him, whatever had struck this town having forged an uneasy bond between them.

"How about recent reports of anything odd, out of place, beyond Camino Pass since last night?"

"Nothing like this, Colonel. Not even close."

"So whatever killed these folks is contained," he said, nodding. "That's something."

"For now, anyway."

Back in the street, the guardsmen carrying M4s were nowhere to be found. Teavens tried to hail them, to no avail.

"We don't have a lot of daylight left here," he said, turning his gaze on the sun dropping toward the mesas that climbed the horizon.

"What happened to your men, Colonel?"

"I handpicked them myself. They didn't run off, I can tell you that much. Get back to the vehicle," Teavens ordered the doctors, scientists and communications specialist. "If we're not back in twenty minutes, tell the driver to get out of Dodge."

With that, he gestured toward Caitlin and the two of them set off along Camino Pass's central square, checking the buildings from the outside in search of the missing soldiers.

"You sure about these boys?" she asked him.

"Right now, I'm not sure of anything."

They both, at the same time, caught sight of a screen door flapping in the wind. Over the door was a sign that looked something like the symbol of the Red Cross.

"Local clinic?" Teavens wondered.

Caitlin kept her eyes glued in that direction. "Seems to be. And that door wasn't open when we pulled into town."

Teavens glanced back toward the RV, just as the four men he'd sent back there were climbing inside. Caitlin thought the colonel looked like he wanted to join them. Then she fell into step behind him, moving toward the clinic. They were six feet from the door when a shadow swallowed the light.

And a dark, formless shape burst through the door.

8

HOUSTON

The hospital let Cort Wesley sign Luke out six hours later.

"I need to go back to school," Luke said, not looking across the seat after settling himself in Cort Wesley's truck.

"I was thinking home would be a better idea," Cort Wesley said, as patiently as he could manage.

"Sure," Luke nodded, still not regarding him, "as soon as I pick up some stuff. Books, my computer—you know."

Cort Wesley gunned the engine but didn't drive off. "What I don't know is who sold you those drugs, because you still haven't told me."

"Dad . . ."

"What?"

"It's not like that."

"Like what?"

"Like we bought them from some street pusher."

"We," Cort Wesley repeated.

"Kids steal the pills from their parents, sometimes get scrips themselves."

"'Kids' meaning your friends. Are they soccer players too? Would I know them?"

"Dad . . ." Rolling his eyes this time, just like his brother, Dylan.

"Don't do that, son."

"Do what?"

"Make me feel like I'm in the wrong here." Cort Wesley finally eased his truck from the no parking zone, realizing only then that there was a ticket flapping beneath the windshield wiper. "You talk about snorting oxy like it's no worse than draining a six-pack."

"I don't drink, Dad."

"Right now, I wish you did. I mean, you pretty much grew up in the company of a Texas Ranger. Didn't that teach you anything?"

Luke finally swung his way, fear brimming in his eyes. "We have to tell Caitlin about this?"

"Oh, ashamed now all of a sudden?"

The boy frowned and brushed the long hair from his face with a swipe of his hand, in contrast with his brother, who was more prone to blowing it off. "More like embarrassed."

"You want to add 'stupid' to that, given that you almost died?"

"It won't happen again, I promise."

"You won't snort oxy again or won't OD again—which is it?"

Luke turned back toward the windshield, his reflection elongated like in a funhouse mirror.

"You know I can't let this go," Cort Wesley told him.

"What?"

"I need to find out where those drugs came from."

"I already told you that."

"Doctors aren't prone to prescribing oxy to teenagers. And those friends of yours don't go home often enough to replenish their snorting supply. That means they're buying from somebody local."

Cort Wesley went silent, staring at Luke until the boy turned his way again, then resuming when the boy didn't say anything.

"I'm going to find out who that is."

"Then what?" his son asked, his voice sounding piqued in frustration, eyes aimed straight ahead now.

"I'll find out where he got his supply."

"How?"

"I'll ask real nicely." Cort Wesley could see Luke's eyes flash in the reflection off the windshield glass, as if he were considering that very scene. "And I'm going to keep climbing the ladder until I'm at the top rung."

"You're not a cop."

"No, but I happen to know a Texas Ranger."

"But you're not going to tell her because you want to handle this yourself."

"Now you're telling me my business?"

Luke swung his way again, as Cort Wesley snailed the truck to a halt at a red light. "I'm telling you *Caitlin's* business. You want to handle this yourself but you know she'll take over if you tell her."

"The Seventh Cavalry wouldn't be able to hold her off, and God help whoever's behind selling drugs to kids."

"They'll need God's help if you find them, too. Just as much."

Cort Wesley looked across the seat, and this time Luke held his gaze. "Maybe I'll ask Colonel Paz to ride shotgun on this. Would you prefer that?"

That eye roll again. "He drowned two men in my fish tank a couple years back."

"They had it coming, just like anyone who sells oxy in schools."

"So now he's going to drown my friends in a fish tank?"

Cort Wesley shook his head. "No, only whoever sold them the drugs to spread around campus."

A horn honking alerted him to the fact that the light was green. It stopped, then started in again.

"Dad?"

Cort Wesley didn't drive forward, on principle. A part of him wanted whoever was honking to climb out and confront him. Pictured what his fist would do on impact with the asshole's face.

More honking followed and he checked the side mirror to see an old lady blaring her horn. Seventy maybe, or eighty. Even a hundred, for all he knew.

"Dad," Luke uttered.

And Cort Wesley screeched through the intersection just as the light turned yellow, stranding the old lady behind him, her car shrinking in the rearview mirror.

9

CAMINO PASS, TEXAS

The shape had what looked like a pair of scissors in his grasp, whirling in a blur toward Teavens with the twin blades slicing toward him on a downward angle.

Caitlin angled her left hip in between them, first deflecting the strike and then trying to work her grasp on the shape's wrist to wrest the weapon away. She forgot about the bulky hazmat gloves in that moment, unable to gain firm purchase on the wrist, which left the scissors squarely in the shape's control.

She recorded the fact it was a man, his expression locked somewhere between fury and terror, wearing wrinkled clothes dappled with sweat. He wheeled toward her, seeming to record through her faceplate the fact that she was a woman, which created just enough hesitation for Caitlin to slam a knee into the man's midsection. Then she used a different hold to take control of his scissors, jerking down and to the side to strip the man's feet out from under him and drop him to the street's hot asphalt. She tore the scissors from his grasp on impact and pressed a forearm against his windpipe to discourage any further attacks.

He thrashed for a few moments, then settled as his face reddened, his eyes still gaping with terror.

"Who are you people?" he gasped. "What the hell happened here? Why's everybody dead?"

Caitlin eased up on the pressure but left her forearm in place.

"That's what we're hoping you can tell us," she said, as the missing soldiers burst breathlessly through the screen door in the man's wake.

It turned out the national guardsmen had entered the building after spotting motion flitting by a window. Caitlin left the man in their charge and watched the soldiers jerk him to his feet by either arm.

"What's your name, sir?" she asked him.

"Who wants to know?" he snapped.

"Caitlin Strong. I'm a Texas Ranger."

"Bullshit," the man squawked.

He had rheumy eyes and a bird's nest of hair that was thinning in patches. Caitlin guessed his age as somewhere between fifty and sixty. He had a lived-in face lined by deep furrows and eyes drooping toward bags that looked like overinflated tires. The work clothes swam over his gaunt frame and, from experience, Caitlin made him as a heavy drinker.

"That I'm a Texas Ranger?"

"You're a skirt, ain't you? Skirts don't make Ranger."

"They do now," Caitlin said, still uncomfortable with the tinny echo of her own voice banging around the inside of her helmet. "What's your name, sir?"

"Lennox Scully. This here's my home—what's left of it anyway." He glanced back toward the clinic. "They're all dead inside there, and everywhere else, I'm guessing. When I run out, I figured you people were the devil come to get me."

"You a resident of Camino Pass?"

Scully nodded. "Rent me a room in a house back that way," he said, casting his gaze toward the outskirts of town, one of the houses the other group had been checking. "When I don't sleep it off here in this here clinic, that is."

A drinker all right, Caitlin thought, exchanging a glance with Teavens.

"What do you remember about last night, Mr. Scully?"

"'Mister'? Nobody done calls me mister no more. You can call me what most others folks do: Scull."

"Same question, Scull."

"Don't remember nothing, on account of I was sleeping one off. Last thing I recall before the spins got me was being tucked away in my home away from home inside the clinic there. Had a dream they was space aliens come to kidnap me. Was it them that did this?"

"Sir?"

"Space aliens," Scully said, aiming his words at Teavens this time. "We at war with a foreign race? And I don't mean Mexicans, neither."

"That remains to be seen," Teavens told him.

10

CAMINO PASS, TEXAS

Caitlin would have been more comfortable restraining Lennox Scully, but she had left her handcuffs inside the RV when pulling her hazmat gear on. The presence of Teavens's handpicked national guardsmen comforted her somewhat, though she had no way of telling for sure whether they'd ever fired their M4 assault rifles in a combat situation or, more to the point, had ever seen combat at all. Gun carriers' bravado, as she called it, rose to the most extreme levels in people who'd never been in an actual gunfight.

None of the preliminary DHS security threat assessments pertaining to Camino Pass had accounted for the possibility of survivors, so no isolation procedures had been prepped or readied. The best their ad hoc team could do was discard Scully's clothes into a contamination pack and help him climb into a spare hazmat suit, which would keep him from infecting anyone with some germ or microbe he might have picked up that had spared him while wiping out the rest of the town.

In Caitlin's experience and training, this scenario didn't fit the classic biowarfare incident at all. The initial analyses of the town's air composition suggested no contaminants or toxins present. That indicated that whatever had killed all but one of the residents of Camino Pass was no longer a danger.

For Caitlin, that changed this from a containment issue to more of an investigative one. Something had killed nearly three hundred people, by all indications, in a matter of minutes. Virulence levels aside, whatever it was needed to be isolated and identified ASAP.

Toward that end, the soldiers remained in the RV with Lennox Scully while the rest of the team continued its sweep of the town. Most of the doors were either unlocked or easily pried open. A few required an air gun contraption that Teavens used to effectively blow the whole latch assembly from the door, which was still rattling around the floor when they entered.

The high-tech respirators attached to their three-hour supplies of oxygen blocked all odors, but Caitlin had the odd sense the homes smelled of nothing anyway. No lingering odors of the last cooked meal, stale aftershave or perfume, or human waste. She passed this off as a product of her imagination conjuring the notion that whatever had wiped out the residents of Camino Pass had wiped out anything they'd left behind as well. No residue to suggest the enormity of what had transpired here.

She made it a point to avoid looking at photos collected on tables, shelves, even walls. So too did she ignore small touches like reading glasses left by the side of a chair or glasses still half full of soda in the sink. The last thing she wanted, or needed, was the distraction of her mind dredging up mental pictures of whoever owned the glasses or hadn't finished their soft drinks.

The hardest houses to enter were the ones with bicycles strewn in the driveway; some combination of baseball mitts and bats, basketballs or footballs littering the lawn. In one house, a video game was frozen on a flat-screen television, a dead teenage boy still clutching the controller in his grasp. She found televisions humming or music playing in a few homes, unwelcome in the sense that they suggested life when nothing could be further from the truth.

With sunset fast approaching, they completed their inspection of the homes and outlying buildings, confirming that no one else was alive. The final home Caitlin checked contained a pair of cribs in a corner bedroom. Though she couldn't bring herself to look inside them, the sight conjured by her imagination would stay with her forever.

She stopped halfway back to the RV, alone in very center of the town's main drag. Something had scratched at her spine, like an itch she couldn't quite reach. She swept her gaze about Camino Pass, then toward its outskirts, and finally beyond them, unable to shake the distinct feeling of unease that had set her hackles rising like a dog getting ready to fight.

"Something wrong, Ranger?"

Colonel Teavens's voice shook Caitlin from her trance.

"After what we just saw," she said through that tinny echo of her own voice, "tell me something that's right, sir."

"Your captain's been calling," Hargraves told her, after she'd shed the bulky and stifling hazmat gear back at the makeshift command center. Her shirt and jeans were soaked through with sweat.

"What'd you tell him?"

"That you hadn't shot anybody yet."

"I'm sure he was pleased to hear that." She fixed her gaze on Hargraves. "You notice anything while we were gone?"

"Like what?"

"I'm not sure. Anything that stood out, I guess. Something that made you look or listen twice."

Hargraves shook his head, clearly not grasping what had gotten her dander up. "No. Why?"

Caitlin fixed her gaze back on him. "Because I think somebody was watching us."

II

WASHINGTON, DC

"Thank you for seeing me," Roland Fass said from the head of the conference table. "But I guess that's not exactly accurate, is it?"

"We can see you just fine, Mr. Fass," intoned a voice that sounded like it was rattling around an empty tin can, from in front of one of the table's chairs, all of which were empty except for his. "What we'd like to *hear* is that the situation in Camino Pass is under control."

When Roland Fass got called to a meeting in Washington, he figured there'd be other people in the room, or at least their representatives. Instead, what he got were four talking snow globes, except they lacked the fake, powdery stuff encased in fluid and glowed only when the individual on the other end was talking.

Fass knew each of the snowless globes represented one of the true power brokers he'd partnered with on the project they'd managed to find plenty of money for, measuring into the hundreds of millions. That sum had gone to construct the interior of the facility he'd painstakingly designed, the proposal they'd chartered leaving nothing to chance. He'd developed an actual three-dimensional schematic, complete with every machine and covering the entire manufacturing assembly line. Most of it had been automated from the start, and now, just about a year in, virtually all of it was.

He'd arrived at the office building that sat in the shadow of the Capitol, expecting to be ushered into an ornate, wood-paneled room with a lavish conference table made of mahogany—or a suitable replacement. What he got instead was a barren, windowless square with the feel of an oversize closet. The walls were stark white and bare, the table formed of cheap laminate and the black chairs looking like they were picked up at a flea market.

"The situation has been contained," Fass tried to assure them all.

"We found the video feed of those folks in the Halloween costumes disturbing, son," a thick southern accent crackled through another of the snow globes. "We also got word that the Texas Rangers are involved now, and when they strap on their guns, no one in their right mind can call anything contained."

"Just one Texas Ranger," Fass reminded.

"You ever hear the motto 'One riot, one Ranger,' son? 'Cause it's damn near true."

"Senator—" Fass started, but the first speaker swiftly cut him off.

"You know the rules, Mr. Fass: no names, no titles. I'm sure you understand."

"Of course," Fass agreed, when what he really understood was that two of the snow globes had no names or titles, not as far as he could tell. They were the ones he'd expected to meet in person, as opposed to this vapid conference call he could just as easily have conducted from back home in Texas.

But that wasn't the way these people worked. This was the way power spoke—literally, in this case. Multiple layers of it, of which the participants in this meeting only cracked the surface. Huge sums of money drew a crowd, and the sums involved here involved more zeros than he could count. Money wasn't a function of power; money *was* power. And Fass knew his work would likely elect a president someday. The massive slush fund his efforts had produced for the power represented in the four snow globes before him held the means to topple and install governments the world over. It could finance wars, outfit armies, determine the winners in age-old conflicts. It was a grand plan to remake the world in the image fostered by the faces behind the voices emanating through the snow globe–like speakers.

"Sir," Fass restarted, "my comments pertain to the fact that whatever happened has been contained to Camino Pass. There is no indication of exposure beyond the town's borders."

"Exposure to what?" the southerner drawled.

Fass found himself focusing on the two globes that hadn't spoken yet, waves of soft color rolling around inside them as if they were in sleep mode or something. "We're not sure, sir. Our facility is rock solid—literally. And none of the chemicals we're working with could produce this kind of result."

"What about some combination of them?"

"I've considered that, but my people assure me it's impossible. We have redundant measures for our redundant measures, and the mere notion of looking at that for causation would require an outside stimulus in the form of an explosion or a systemic breakdown of our security measures that never occurred. If it had, you would've heard the alarm bells all the way to Washington. I have no idea what killed that town, sir, but I have every confidence it had nothing to do with our work. We need to look elsewhere for a cause."

"Where?" demanded the southerner. "Outer space maybe? Because nothing on God's green earth could kill an entire town the way this one died, son."

"But it didn't kill everyone, did it?" the original voice noted. "There was a survivor. Can you explain that?" he asked Fass.

"Not at all, sir. Not until we have a better idea of the cause."

"We're concerned this was the result of hostile action, an attack that missed its intended target."

"You think our facility was targeted?"

"I said we were concerned. The alternative is that we caused this somehow, in which case . . ."

Fass waited for the voice to continue.

"In which case," it finally did, "there will be questions, challenges, attention drawn plainly where we don't want it. We don't need that; we can't have it."

"There's nothing that could possibly draw any attention to our work, even from the Texas Rangers."

"You're missing the point, son," said the southerner. "We need to keep whatever did all this killing contained as well. Can't have anybody sniffing around the area. Can't leave any clues for them to follow. You getting my drift here?"

"I believe I am, sir. I'll handle it as soon as I'm back in Texas."

"Make sure you do," said the other talking snow globe. "Our work has produced great results. We are remaking the world, Mr. Fass, and we must continue to remake it, through any and all means at our disposal. No setbacks. That's priority number two."

"And priority number one?" Fass asked, eyeing the silent snow globes as if expecting them to speak at last.

"Right now, we need to uncover what wiped out Camino Pass."

12

SAN ANTONIO, TEXAS

"I couldn't help but notice you were looking for a physical education teacher," Guillermo Paz said to Principal Mariana Alonzo, from across her desk at Canyon Ridge Elementary School. "When I was here earlier today, I mean."

Paz waited for a response, but all he got was a nod.

"Got an application," he asked her, "something I can fill out?"

"Do you have any experience, Mr. . . ."

"Paz. Guillermo Paz. And it's colonel, not mister."

"I'm sorry."

"Don't be. It's not official by American standards. It was my rank in the Venezuelan military and, later, when I was running the country's secret police, aka Dirección Nacional de los Servicios de Inteligencia y Prevención, or the National Directorate of Intelligence and Prevention Services. I wouldn't expect to be submitting any references from those days."

Alonzo nodded, clearly pleased by that.

"My Texas Ranger still calls me colonel. I figure if it's right for her, I should keep the title."

"*Your* Texas Ranger?"

"Figure of speech, and a long story not germane to the subject at hand, meaning my application."

"We were talking about experience."

Paz shifted in the chair, which was much too small to accommodate his size. It creaked in protest every time he moved, so he did his best not to shift positions even in the slightest. Mariana Alonzo looked distinctly uncomfortable in his presence, her gaze constantly shifting to the door or the wall clock—he couldn't tell which.

"As in teaching experience," she elaborated.

"Oh," Paz said, "I've got a lot of that. I always schooled all the operatives who served under me on the finer points associated with their work. Would you like some examples?"

Alonzo leaned forward, seeming to relax a bit. "Yes, please."

"Well, it's important to be able to kill using a gun, knife, or your bare hands. Proximity, lighting, the relative stealth nature of the mission are all factors determining the ultimate choice. Instinct plays a factor here, of course, and that's something that can't be taught. But for men who'd advanced to the special ops level, this is a conscious decision, and I wanted to make sure I taught my men how to make the right one."

Paz stopped, impressed with his answer. Principal Alonzo looked frozen behind her desk.

"Another example," he jumped in. "Back in Venezuela, to be honest, we weren't trying to win any hearts and minds. But when a village misbehaved and required punishment, it was important for me to teach my men restraint. For example, don't kill a whole family, just the oldest son, to teach them a lesson. Don't burn down the whole village, just a building or two. And never touch the crops. That was especially important, because destroying the village's food source would most likely drive them even closer to the rebels, defeating the purpose of our coming there in the first place. I taught my men to understand the geopolitical realities we were facing, taught them that we wanted the locals to fear us but not necessarily hate us. That was an important distinction. You see my point?"

Alonzo tried to nod. "What about experience working with children, Colonel?"

"Well, I already told you about my work at that day care center some of your students attended—you could ask them for references. I taught English to immigrants for a while, and some of them were kids. Oh, and I volunteered to run religious services at a local homeless shelter, but there weren't many children in attendance at those. Occasionally, you'd get a mother with a couple kids hiding out from an abusive spouse. I'd look at her through the whole of the service, reading the fear in her eyes and watching her flinch at every loud noise. A few times I asked these women to tell me their stories, and then I'd pay a visit to the men who abused them. The men in question never bothered those women again." Paz couldn't help but crack a smile there. "So, hey, I guess you could say I taught *them* something, too."

It was hard to tell from Mariana Alonzo's expression whether she agreed.

"But you know who I've taught the most to? Myself. See, jefa, I was a different man when I first came to this country ten years ago. Did I tell you about that?"

"Er, no."

"You need to hear this for some historical perspective. See, I came to America to kill several people, most notably my Texas Ranger. Of course, she wasn't *my* Texas Ranger back then. So we're trying to kill each other and our eyes meet and I see in my Ranger's something I'd never seen in my own. I realized that was what I wanted to see when I look in the mirror, so I entered a kind of transitional period. I thought it would get me where I wanted to be, but now I realize it really isn't the destination that matters, it's the journey. It was Ralph Waldo Emerson who said that, even though a lot of people attribute the quote to Jerry Garcia."

Paz noted that this distinction produced no response from Alonzo.

"My priest, Father Boylston, put up with me until he suffered a stroke. I visited him every day in the long-term care facility and was the only one who could get him to eat. I'm going to tell you something, jefa. The doctors said he couldn't understand things anymore, but I knew he could hear what I was saying, even if he couldn't respond. Nobody asked me to be a pallbearer when he died, and that bothered me, because I thought I owed it to my priest to carry him into his next life after he helped carry me to a new place in mine."

Alonzo leaned farther over her desk, looking like she was glad it acted as a barrier between her and Paz. "Father *Edward* Boylston?"

"The very same. Do you know him?"

"He baptized me, Colonel."

Paz found himself missing his priest, in that a moment, more than any other time since the man's death. "He listened to my confessions, jefa—no easy task, as I'm sure you've figured out for yourself. He never judged me, because he felt that was God's job. But he helped set me on the right path toward finding myself and seemed pleased when I figured out that path was endless, all on my own. Because every time you find yourself, you're already somebody different and it's time to start the process all over again. You see what I'm getting at here?"

Mariana Alonzo nodded as her eyes met Paz's, no longer looking afraid. "When can you start, Colonel?"

PART TWO

SAMUEL H. WALKER

Hays and his men were usually outnumbered in their skirmishes with Comanche and Mexican forces, but managed to hold their own thanks to their highly effective use of a more modern weapon: the revolver. Soon after Samuel Walker joined Hays' Ranger company in 1844, they and 14 other Rangers took on some 80 Comanches in the battle of Walker's Creek. Armed with the first practical revolver, designed by Samuel Colt, the Rangers came out on top in the fierce clash. Walker was seriously wounded, but recovered to become a celebrated Ranger captain during the Mexican War. In late 1846, he made some simple suggestions to improve Colt's revolver design, and the upgraded "Walker Colt" became the deadliest weapon of the war. Walker was killed in a clash with Mexican forces at Huamantla in October 1847.

—Sarah Pruitt, "8 Famous Texas Rangers," History.com

13

"Watching you," Captain D. W. Tepper commented, after Caitlin had finished bringing him up to speed on what had transpired in Camino Pass. "Got anything to support that assertion?"

"Just my gut. I'm thinking it was one of those high-altitude drones, pretty much invisible to the naked eye."

"Is your gut telling you anything else?"

"Yes, sir. Your office smells like cigarettes."

"That's your nose, not your instincts." Tepper pulled a half-gone pack of Marlboros from his top desk drawer and flashed it toward Caitlin. "One of the advantages of you being out all day is I can do as I please in my own office."

"That include chopping years off your life?"

"With you determined to put me in an early grave, what's the difference? Homeland Security's talking about blowing Camino Pass off the map. You want to give me the short version of what you think happened there?"

"It wasn't hostile action, an attack, or anything like that."

"Your gut tell you that too?"

"If this were a bioterror attack, some kind of experiment on a town located in the middle of nowhere, the perpetrators would've beaten us there to check the results of their handiwork. But there was no trace of any fresh vehicle tracks, other than the ones made by the Homeland RV. No sign of anyone entering the homes for some kind of assessment before we got there, either. And if somebody had beaten us to the town, they would've found Lennox Scully ahead of us."

"I hear he made for a great welcoming committee, Ranger."

"If I woke up to find everyone around me dead, I'd tend to react the same way."

"Except you would've come out guns blazing instead of with scissors."

"Give me some credit, D.W. I didn't shoot anybody today."

Tepper stuck a cigarette in his mouth and waited for Caitlin to reach across the desk and pluck it out, resuming when she didn't. "No, but sometimes your words do as much damage as bullets. I've been fielding calls about you going up against ICE all day, press included. One reporter asked me to confirm that you'd shot one of their agents."

"What'd you tell them?"

"That it couldn't be true, because the report said you only put one of them down. Where's your friend Jones when we need him?"

"Working for one of those private security firms, last I heard. Making the big bucks, after Homeland gave him his walking papers. Any leaks on Camino Pass?"

"Nope. News blackout is holding for once. Doc Whatley was waiting at University Hospital when Mr. Scully arrived."

All major cities, Caitlin knew, had designated a level one trauma center as a crisis response center. This entailed, among other things, a ward outfitted with isolation chambers and vacuum-sealed labs where most everything could be handled without coming into physical contact with anything potentially hazardous or toxic. The process made heavy use of robotic instruments and hazmat suits attached to flexible, accordion-like tubing that allowed the examination team to move about the lab without fear of contamination or infection.

"I understand a second Homeland team is currently clearing the bodies," Tepper continued. "Doc Whatley's gonna be a busy man."

He was referring to the longtime Bexar County medical examiner, Frank Dean Whatley. Whatley had been handpicked by Jones for the duty, grousing but secretly happy about taking on the job for the relevance it provided him. A man devoid of outside interests or hobbies, he feared nothing more than his looming retirement and had so far successfully resisted all efforts to force him out.

"I wonder what he'll make of a single survivor to go with those near three hundred dead," Caitlin noted.

"A drunk, right?"

"You think that's relevant?"

Tepper finally lit his Marlboro. "I think it suggests maybe a bad habit's the secret to staying alive."

"I wouldn't count on that, D.W."

"Tell me more about this feeling you were being watched," Tepper said, making sure to blow his cigarette smoke in Caitlin's direction.

"Felt like crosshairs were zeroing in on me."

"You in particular?"

Caitlin shrugged. "I think somebody was waiting to see who showed up. Maybe the ghost of my great-grandfather. I seem to recall a story about him having his own experience in Camino Pass, maybe a hundred and twenty-five years ago."

"That all you remember?"

"Pretty much."

"Then let me tell you want happened when he got there . . ."

14

Camino Pass, Texas; 1898

"Yup, I feel it too, girl," Texas Ranger William Ray Strong said, patting his horse Jessabelle lightly on her hindquarter. "Something sure ain't right."

William Ray knew something was wrong as soon as he'd reached the outskirts of Camino Pass, a Texas town Mexicans could hit with stones from across the border. He'd felt it the moment the church steeple and dusty assemblage of buildings came into view, a gnawing in his gut that almost felt like some spoiled piece of food was working its way through his system. The gnawing tightened into a knot as he'd drawn closer, leaving the Ranger to wonder whether the Mexican bandit he was here to pick up and deliver to the county seat in Presidio, forty miles down the road, to stand trial was somehow involved. That got him figuring that maybe this simple prisoner transport wasn't going to be so simple, after all.

He'd become a Texas Ranger in 1874, the same year his father, Steeldust Jack Strong, had taken on none other than John D. Rockefeller over the lands of an Indian reservation. All of seventeen back then, a mere boy, in stark contrast to what he'd become in the years since, fighting more battles and killing more men than he cared to count. Many of them had been Mexicans, which made William Ray all the warier anytime his duties brought him this close to the border, to the point where he was always leery of a potential ambush. It had happened before with other Rangers, the plotters inevitably ending up on the short end of the stick—literally, in the case of one Mexican gunman who'd been sent back across the border splayed across his saddle with a shard of lumber stuck up his rear end.

But William Ray suspected no such thing here. This was something else, something that made the air feel chalky, with a palpable sense of fear permeating it. He had the name of the bandit he was to escort north stuffed in his saddlebag someplace, forgotten until he sorted out the source of whatever had so discomforted him upon entering Camino Pass.

He reached the small houses that dotted the outskirts of the town, just short of the main drag featuring a building that housed the sheriff's station, saloon, small hotel, and mercantile exchange. Most of the residents were laborers who relied on odd jobs and seasonal work on either side of the border. There were a few farmers and ranchers sprinkled in among the couple hundred residents, none of whom were in evidence until William Ray heard a door crack open. He eased Jessabelle to a halt in order to peer back at whoever was peering out.

"What happened here?" William Ray asked a shapeless figure beneath a thick mane of gray hair.

"You a Texas Ranger?" the older woman said, having spotted the gleam of his badge in the spray of sunlight.

William Ray pulled back his jacket all the way to display the whole of his badge.

"You come to fetch them all back?"

"Who?"

"The children and the men who gone after them. They never came back neither."

William Ray felt something gnaw at his insides. "What happened to the children?"

"Taken."

"By who?"

"Don't know. Men went that way to fetch them," the woman said, pointing south. "That was two days ago. Last we seen of them too."

Toward Mexico.

"Sheriff in town?"

"He led the posse that disappeared when they went out looking."

William Ray could make no sense of the town's children being kidnapped, though he'd put nothing past the Mexican bandits, who were maybe just desperate enough to try out a new crime. He reminded himself of his purpose here in Camino Pass, his dutiful assignment being no more than to serve as escort for a prisoner who was slated to stand trial in Presidio.

"When this happen?" William Ray asked, because he couldn't help it.

"Children were snatched two days back, early in the morning, round the time school started. Sheriff and the others set off later that day. He's been sheriff of both for a time now." The woman's expression tightened in thought. "Yup, it was two days ago for sure, almost exactly now."

Which was long enough for William Ray to figure they weren't coming back, neither the children nor the members of the sheriff's posse that had gone after them.

"Sheriff leave his deputy behind, ma'am?"

"He did, but the man moved on as soon as he was gone, not about to face what he was fearing might come back, that being them that stole the children."

"Well, I got to be moving on myself," William Ray said to the older woman, focusing back on the task at hand.

She finally opened the door enough for him to see the shapeless dress, more like a smock, draped over her frame. "You're going the wrong way. I told you, they went south."

"Let me see what I can see in town first, ma'am," William Ray told her, spitting out a wad of tobacco behind his disgust at forming the lie.

He felt more frightened eyes fixed upon him as he hitched Jessabelle up to a post outside the sheriff's station and entered the single-room building through a creaking door. William Ray smelled stale sweat and unfinished wood, the cloud of dust that coated the air riding him across the floor.

A Mexican man, more of a boy really, but still the prisoner he was to transport, sat up on a tattered mattress atop a single cot inside a cell against the far wall.

"Keys are hanging on a hook by the window, el Rinche," the man-boy told him.

William Ray followed his gaze, the keys jangling when he fetched them. "You're a cooperative one, aren't you?"

"I'll hang if you take me to trial."

"Not my concern, son," the Ranger said, jiggling the key until it sank home in the lock.

"What about the missing kids? That your concern?"

William Ray pulled the cell door open but held his ground. The prisoner didn't look much out of his teens, with a bird's nest of thick black hair and a forehead stained with grime from where the brim of his hat had dripped sweat. He had a small, angular nose, baby-soft features, and smooth skin that combined to make him look pretty in a male sort of way, though he did have the makings of a mustache struggling to ride his upper lip. More boy than man, in William Ray's mind.

I'll hang if you take me to trial.

Not his concern, indeed.

"You're Doroteo Arango," William Ray said, recalling the man-boy's name as he stepped all the way inside the cell and unclasped a set of wrist irons from his belt.

"I used to be," the boy said, making no show of resistance or protest.

"Who are you now, son?"

"Francisco Villa, but you can call me Pancho. And I know what happened to those missing kids."

"So what's your story, Pancho?" William Ray Strong asked the young man, stopping short of fastening the wrist irons on yet.

"What have you heard?"

"Only what I needed to hear to transport you to trial. That you and a bunch of other bandits you ride with have been robbing folks on both sides of the border. That you killed a man when you were fifteen years old."

"For raping my sister. What would you have done, Ranger?"

"Kill him twice, I suppose."

"The man happened to be somebody you don't want to cross. It was either flee to the mountains or watch far worse happen to my family."

"You kill anybody since?"

"No, sir."

"How is it you speak such good English, son?"

"Couple of the bandits I rode with were from north of the border. They taught me. When you're hiding out, there's plenty of time for learning."

"These Americans have names?"

"They did indeed. Pretty bad hombres in their own right. Maybe you've heard of them. Butch Cassidy and the Sundance Kid."

"Those outlaws have had the good sense to stay out of Texas," William Ray noted. "Well, Pancho, we best get a move on."

"What about the missing kids?"

The Ranger readied the wrist irons. "Not my concern."

"You got any kids of your own, Ranger?"

"I'm planning to."

"And if somebody took them from you?"

"It would be the second-worst day of their lives, the worst being when I caught up to them."

Pancho Villa nodded, the light framing his sharp features in a way that made him still look like a boy. "People in this town got nobody to do that in their stead. And since the raiders didn't get all the kids this time, the townfolk are afraid they'll be back for the rest."

"You saw all of this happen?"

Villa gestured toward his cell window, outfitted with a grate of bars over the glass. "I saw enough to know who the men were and where they came from."

"Keep talking," said William Ray Strong.

Pancho Villa lay back down on the cell's wooden cot, pushing more straw through the fabric of the ragged mattress. "Not from inside here."

"You prefer we talk on the way to Presidio, muchacho?"

"I'm no kid, el Rinche," Villa said, again using the standard Mexican derogatory slang term reserved for Texas Rangers.

"Trying to get a rise out of me, boy?"

"Just returning the favor."

"Maybe I should just shoot you and tell the county seat that you tried to escape."

"But you won't."

"Why's that?"

"Because you're a Texas Ranger, meaning justice is your middle name."

"Ray's my middle name, the first being William and last being Strong, son."

Villa sat back up, his bony shoulders pushing the fabric of his shirt up in the corners. "Then I can call you *Fuerte* or *Sólida*. Which would you prefer?"

"I don't give a good goddamn. Now, get on your feet," William Ray ordered, holding the wrist irons out before him.

Villa took his time rising to his feet. "How am I supposed to ride a horse with those strapped on me?"

"You'll figure it out. And they're for your own good."

"How's that, Ranger?"

"Cuts back on the temptation to make a break for it, in which case I'd have to shoot you." William Ray tossed the chains to Pancho Villa who let them clang to the floor. "Now put those on."

Villa made no move to pick them up. "Afraid to do it yourself?"

"Be less painful if I leave the task to you."

Villa retrieved the wrist irons and fastened them in place before him, making sure to hold his hands in easy view of William Ray Strong. "What about those kids, Ranger?" he repeated.

"Still somebody else's problem."

"And the missing sheriff and that posse? Are they somebody else's problem too?"

William Ray conjured up in his mind a vision of what had gone down here. He saw the town's children being rousted from the schoolhouse he'd noted farther down the main drag, dark faceless men pistol-whipping the schoolmarm when she tried to intervene. The mothers and fathers would have been tending to their flocks and crops, doing what ranchers and farmers do. It would have happened early on in the day, in a sleepy town where both the sheriff and his deputy were as far from men of action as it got.

"You got my curiosity up, bandit, I'll give you that."

"I'm not a bandit."

"Then what got you jailed?"

"What I did, not who I am."

"You always talk this way?"

"What way is that, Ranger?"

"So nobody can understand a dang word you're saying."

"I've read a lot of books while holed up in the mountains," Pancho Villa told him. "History and philosophy, mostly."

"Learn anything?"

"That the world is full of evil men."

"Damn, son, I could've told you that without you opening a single page."

"Was evil men that took those kids, Ranger. There's a town over the border, about thirty miles from here. They would've stopped there on the way where they're going."

"And you know where that is."

"I believe I do."

"And you know who's behind this."

"Yes, sir, I believe I know that too."

"Thirty miles, you said."

"Thirty miles," Villa nodded.

"Then we better get a move on, muchacho."

15

SAN ANTONIO, TEXAS

"Pancho Villa," Caitlin said slowly, when Tepper stopped to light a fresh Marlboro. "I remember that now. I must've been eight when my grandfather told me the story."

"Recall the rest of it?"

"It came to guns."

"Doesn't it always?"

"So fill in the blanks."

"You must really be captivated, Ranger. You haven't said a word about me lighting up another one."

Tepper touched his lighter to the edge of the Marlboro and a flame burst shot up, which forced him to cough the cigarette to the floor and stamp it out with his boot.

"Now how do you suppose that happened?" he asked Caitlin, the furrows and creases lining his face suddenly looking as if they'd gotten deeper.

"Looks to me like somebody must've poked out the tobacco and filled the wrapper with something flammable."

"Yeah?"

"Magnesium, maybe. You going to pick up the story, what happened when my great-grandfather and Pancho Villa got to that town they headed out for?"

Tepper checked to make sure the next Marlboro he pulled from the pack was filled with tobacco, but he held it away from his mouth. "Think I'll risk blowing my face up again first, Ranger."

He watched Caitlin ease an orange prescription bottle from her jacket pocket and shake out a small pill that she popped into her mouth.

"Tell you what, Ranger, you leave me to my smoking and I'll leave you to swallowing those pain pills like candy."

Caitlin dry-swallowed the pill down. "The difference being that my pain's going to pass while your smoking's showing no signs of doing the same."

"You sure about that?" Tepper asked her, an uneasy edge to his voice.

"How is it I don't remember my grandfather ever finishing the story, D.W.?" Caitlin said, instead of answering him.

"Maybe it didn't have a happy ending."

"That never stopped him."

"Must've been something else, then," Tepper said evasively.

Caitlin was about to press the issue when her phone buzzed with an incoming call from Cort Wesley, as opposed to a text, and she excused herself to take it.

"To what do I owe the pleasure of—"

Cort Wesley's words ran right over hers and she cut herself off to listen to what came after "Luke overdosed."

16

Shavano Park, Texas

"You waited long enough to call me," Caitlin said, mounting the steps to the front porch, where Cort Wesley was waiting for her in the darkness, the dome light switched off.

She expected him to have a craft beer or a coffee in hand, but she recognized the dark bottle as that of his favorite root beer—his and that of the ghost of his dead friend, Leroy Epps.

"I wanted to get Luke home and settled first," Cort Wesley offered.

"Will you promise me something?"

"No."

"You haven't heard what I was going to say yet."

"I don't have to, Ranger. You want me to promise you not to go after whoever Luke got the drugs from."

"Close enough."

"Okay, I promise."

"Not good enough, Cort Wesley. I was thinking more along the lines of the opioid network across all of Texas."

"Why not include the whole Southwest?"

"I almost said the whole country, but tempered my thinking."

Cort Wesley sipped his root beer. "Not a bad idea."

Caitlin sat down next to him on the porch swing, drawing a creak from its worn springs. "Can I see him?"

"I waited until he was sleeping to call you. Figured dealing with me was enough for one day."

Caitlin turned her gaze toward the front door where Maura Torres, Cort Wesley's former girlfriend and mother to both Luke and his older brother, Dylan, had been shot dead a decade before. Caitlin had managed to save their lives and had served as their de facto mother pretty much ever since, a role she relished in the face of the challenges that came with the scope of that responsibility. It seemed like both boys had attracted trouble ever since, almost as if the proclivity had rubbed off on them from spending too much time around her and their father.

Caitlin knew smells could pass from one person to another, so maybe tendencies could too, including being a magnet for violence and evil.

"So how was *your* day?" Cort Wesley continued.

"Started out with me coming up against ICE agents trying to roust elementary school kids and proceeded to me wearing a hazmat suit in a town where pretty much everybody died in their sleep."

"I'm being serious here, Ranger."

"So was I."

"Oh," Cort Wesley managed, not all of what Caitlin had said fully registering.

"You can't take a flamethrower to the whole drug trade," she told him.

"Why not?"

"You'd have to torch the whole state, the whole country."

"I'd settle for whoever sold the pills Luke and his friends sucked up their noses."

"They might've come from home, Cort Wesley, some parents' medicine cabinets."

"That's what Luke said."

"But you're not buying it."

Cort Wesley drained the rest of his root beer, his expression that of a man who'd just swallowed something sour. "Luke pretty much admitted this wasn't a onetime thing. Maybe not a regular occurrence for him, at least not as regular as a bunch of his friends."

"Too many pills to come from medicine cabinets then."

"You know how it works, Ranger."

Caitlin nodded. "One of the kids was supplying the others."

"Maybe moving enough to cover his tuition money for Village School," Cort Wesley elaborated.

"That's a lot of pills."

"That's my point."

Caitlin let him see the harshness of her glare. "You can't brace a kid, Cort Wesley."

"I'm going to brace whoever it was that almost got my son killed."

Caitlin pushed herself off the porch swing, drawing a fresh creak from its springs. "I'm going inside to see Luke."

17

SHAVANO PARK, TEXAS

"You knew I'd be awake," Luke said.

He was lying on his bed, still wearing jeans and a T-shirt, arms laced behind his head, facing a wall-mounted thirty-two-inch flat-screen television with the sound muted.

Caitlin stopped at the foot of the bed. "I figured you did enough sleeping."

"After I passed out, you mean. You pissed?"

"Surprised."

"Disappointed?" the boy managed, after swallowing hard.

"I guess you could say that."

Luke unlaced his hands and sat up. "You want to sit down?"

Caitlin took a seat kitty-corner at the edge of the bed, keeping her distance. "I'm trying to figure this all out."

"What's to figure? I messed up."

"That all?"

"It's not enough?"

"How many other times we talking about here?"

"That I OD'd?"

"Used."

Luke rolled his eyes, the snide impatience riding his expression making him look more like his older brother. "Do we have to do this?"

"You asked me to sit down."

"It's not like I keep count."

"Of the times you OD'd or used?"

He started to roll his eyes again but stopped, as if catching himself. "Not a lot."

"You want to tell me where you got the drugs?"

"They weren't mine."

"That's not what I asked."

"The pills could've been anybody's, Caitlin."

"*Anybody's* not a name."

Luke hesitated. "You plan on arresting them?"

"If I don't shoot them first."

"That's not funny."

"Neither was getting the news from your dad."

Luke lay back down, careful not to disturb Caitlin when he stretched his bare feet back toward the edge of the bed. He was taller than his brother, almost six feet now, and she was still getting used to looking slightly up at him, even in boots.

"I feel sick again," he said.

"Side effect of the Narcan they gave you at the hospital."

"The stuff they give to addicts?"

"And overdose victims. I carry a dose in my glove compartment. All Rangers do now."

"Just in case you need it yourself?" Luke asked, seeming to immediately regret the harshness of his tone.

Caitlin took the prescription bottle from her jacket and shook it so the pills inside clacked against each other. "Doctor's orders, Luke. You need me to explain the difference?"

"How long have you been taking them now?"

"I don't mark the days off on my calendar."

"You can't take them forever."

"They're for pain. When it goes away, so do the pills. And I swallow, not grind them up and snort them."

His eyes moistened. "I'm sorry."

Caitlin canted her frame to better face him. "What if all those colleges you're applying to found out?"

Those same eyes widened in fear. "Will they?"

"Nope, not unless you tell them. Of course, they might notice the drop-off in your grades."

"I've got a four-point-two-five grade point average and I'm acing all my AP classes."

Caitlin nodded. "That's better."

"What?"

"Hearing you talk about things that matter. You know what else matters? You telling me how regularly you're using."

"Don't say that."

"What?"

"'Using.' It makes it sound like I'm some homeless guy who gets swept off the streets."

"They had to start somewhere, son. And stop changing the subject."

"You think I'm, what, like an addict?"

"Are you?"

Luke answered with his gaze focused on the muted television. "This was like the third time."

"What was the occasion?"

"A friend from the soccer team got into Harvard early decision. We were celebrating."

"Is that what you call it?"

"It's easier to bring pills to school than weed or booze."

"Sure," Caitlin said, feeling the back of her neck heat up, "that explains it." She paused long enough for Luke to meet her stare again. "This friend of yours have a name?"

"You want me to rat him out?"

She remained silent.

"I can't do that, Caitlin. And stop looking at me like that."

"Looking at you like what?"

"Like you don't recognize me. You talk to Dylan lately?" Luke asked her. His older brother had recently returned to Brown University.

"What does he have to do with this?"

"Nothing. I asked if you'd talked to him, maybe checked Instagram."

"You think I do that?"

"Check out his Instagram page," Luke told her. "You got bigger problems with him than me."

"Worse than almost dying?"

Luke rolled his eyes. "I didn't almost die."

"I think maybe you and me should take a little field trip."

"I just came from the hospital, Caitlin."

"I was talking about the morgue, where plenty of overdose victims end up." She hardened her gaze. "You know what the phrase 'setting of the features' means?"

Luke shook his head. "You know what Dylan's been up to?"

Caitlin ignored him. "It's what a mortician does to make a body suitable for viewing—that placid facial expression that gives the deceased that look like he doesn't have a care in the world. You know how they do that?"

The boy shrugged.

"They stuff the throat and nose with cotton and then suture the mouth shut, either using a curved needle and thread to stitch between the jawbone and nasal cavity or using a needle injector machine to accomplish a similar job more quickly. Small spiked cups are also inserted under the eyelids to keep the lids closed and the eyes from caving in. Should I go on?"

Luke looked suddenly queasy. "I think I'm going to be sick."

"You said that already."

He struggled to sit up again. "No, I mean I think I'm going to puke."

Luke pushed himself off the bed, standing up while clutching the front post. Caitlin fought the urge to help him, holding herself down as he staggered toward the door, then through it and into the bathroom across the hall.

Her phone rang as he closed the door behind him, Doc Whatley's mobile number lighting up at the top of the screen.

"I guess Camino Pass has you working late, Doc."

"You busy, Ranger?"

Caitlin looked across the hall toward the closed bathroom door, hearing the toilet flush inside. "You don't want to know."

"How soon can you get down to University Hospital?"

"You mean in the morning?"

"No, I mean now. This can't wait for morning."

18

TEXAS-MEXICO BORDER

"So, what, this is all about making the *Guinness Book of World Records*?" Roland Fass said to the big man who towered over him.

Inside the cramped dressing room that was once a supply closet, Yarak Bone continued looping hand-wrap tape around his fingers and knuckles to cushion the blows he would soon be unleashing. "I ever tell you I had ancestors that could scalp you in maybe a second?"

The dressing room's light came courtesy of a single bulb dangling from a chain overhead. The facility in which tonight's bare-knuckle fights were being staged had once been a waste treatment facility, constructed to make sure raw sewage wasn't dumped into the nearby Rio Grande. Bone figured this converted supply closet must have once contained harsh chemicals of the kind that could choke your breath, based on the pungent, corrosive scent that still hung in the air after so many years.

The actual fights took place in what had once been an underground storage tank, which stank of waste matter mixed with dried sweat that clung to the iron walls like glue. Spectators, bettors all who'd also paid an exorbitant admission fee, watched from one of the three levels that spiraled upward over the tank. Their cheers echoed in hollow fashion through the cavernous facility, the smells of beer, cigarettes, and weed adding to the stale, fetid air that left spectators in need of a shower just for showing up. As a boy growing up in a traditional Comanche family, Bone had skinned and gutted animals from the time he was seven years old, so the stench didn't bother him.

Fass tried not to look frightened. "You didn't answer my question."

"Answer mine first."

"No, this is the first time you've shared that with me."

"I don't think Guinness keeps records on how fast you can kill five men with your bare hands," Bone told him. "You paying them ten grand to take me on was a stroke of genius."

"They only get paid if they last two minutes," Fass reminded.

Bone flexed his hands to make sure he could still tighten them into fists. "You know the best thing? Each of them figures *How hard can it be?*, two minutes being such a short time. Of course, chances are they've never been pounded for two minutes straight. You have any idea how many blows I can land in two minutes? They could make it one, for all I care. If I can't kill a man in a minute, he deserves to walk away rich."

Fass almost told Yarek Bone that ten thousand dollars hardly qualified a man as rich, but quickly thought better of it. "You read what I sent you, check out the pictures?"

"You made a mess you need cleaned up."

"That doesn't answer my question."

"I didn't have to read anything to know that much. But, hey, I'm about to try to kill five men in under five minutes. You killed, what, three hundred in the blink of an eye?"

"There's no proof our facility had anything to do with this."

"And yet here you are talking to me, *chuma*."

"We're just playing things safe here. What's *chuma* mean?"

"Chief."

"I don't think you understand the extent of the problem here. This is coming from your chief."

Bone twisted his head from side to side, loosening his neck with twin crackling sounds. "You're *a* chief, not *my* chief. I don't have a chief."

"Maybe you don't know me as well as you think you do."

"I know you need somebody killed."

"There was a survivor in Camino Pass."

"Not for long." Bone grinned.

They came through an iron door that looked lifted off a submarine, one at a time; five men, naked from the waist up, with chests and jaws protruding, breathing bravado. Until they got a good look at Yarek Bone's towering, muscular figure, by which point the hatch-like door had been sealed behind them. And, hey, if any of them were still standing after a mere two minutes, the ten thousand would be theirs.

The first fighter was thin and wiry, just a few inches shorter than Bone, with knobby muscle and close-cropped hair. Bone hit him with two blows to the face, leaving one eye closed and two teeth spit out onto the slick floor. Then he let the man slam him with a pair of blows flung from clearly trained hands, just so he could smile through them.

"I got this condition," Bone said, as he circled the man, firing off lighter blows just to feel his head snap back upon impact. "It's called CIP, for 'congenital insensitivity to pain.' In other words, I can't feel pain, no matter how hard you hit me."

At which point, Bone snapped off a blinding punch that flattened the man's nose and sent plumes of blood spraying into the air from both nostrils. The crowd roared their appreciation, pumping their fists. Spilled beer showered the air, some of it falling to the tank floor and further adding to the slippery sheen.

"Currently, there are three known genes, with twenty-eight mutations, that can lead to a diagnosis of CIP," Bone told the man, amid a flurry of jabs that left his eyes glassy and his hands hanging limp by his sides, "all of which affect how nerves transmit pain signals. Bottom line being that my wiring is all fucked up, which is bad news for you since you could rip my arm off and I wouldn't feel a thing."

Bone felt the man's spinal cord crack, as he landed an uppercut that snapped the fighter's head so far back he looked like a rag doll. His feet literally lifted off the floor ahead of him, the back of his head breaking the fall when he landed.

Just over a minute, Bone saw from the LED counters strung overhead, the crowd roaring so loud he could feel his ears bubbling. Taped hands were thrust triumphantly into the air as the body was carried out another door. Meanwhile, a second fighter entered the makeshift ring.

"Ever hear of CIP?" Bone asked him.

"Four minutes forty-one seconds. Congratulations," Roland Fass said to Bone, back in the converted supply closet. "Maybe I'll give Guinness a call."

Bone wasn't even breathing hard as he toweled himself off, leaving an equal mix of sweat, grime, and blood from the five men he'd just left splattered on the ring floor.

"Don't bother," Bone told him. "Next time I'm going for ten in ten minutes."

"Let's talk about your next kill first," Fass reminded. "That survivor from Camino Pass."

19

San Antonio, Texas

"I expected more from you, Ranger," Bexar County Medical Examiner Frank Dean Whatley told Caitlin.

"How's that, Doc?" she asked him. They were in a sealed area beyond the isolation ward that the Department of Homeland Security had constructed inside University Hospital.

"Normally, you bring me puzzles that keep me up at night trying to fit the pieces together. This time you brought me one already assembled."

Whatley had shed the hazmat gear he'd donned to perform detailed examinations and preliminary autopsies on a sampling of the victims who'd died the previous night in Camino Pass. But Caitlin still detected the pungent scents of latex and rubber mixed with the stale sweat that came from wearing the airtight suits for a prolonged period. Caitlin could picture Whatley donning the outfit as soon as the bodies arrived at the dedicated DHS area of University Hospital, and then not shedding it until he'd placed his phone call to her.

Frank Dean Whatley had been Bexar County medical examiner since the time Caitlin was in diapers. He'd grown a belly in recent years that hung out over his thin belt, seeming to force his spine to angle inward at the torso. Whatley's teenage son had been killed by Latino gangbangers when Caitlin was a mere kid herself. Ever since then, he'd harbored a virulent hatred for that particular race, from the bag boys at the local H-E-B supermarket to the politicians who professed to be peacemakers. With his wife lost first in life and then in death to alcoholism, he'd probably stayed in the job too long. But he had nothing to go home to, no real life outside the office, and he remained exceptionally good at his job, which he approached with rare pathos and compassion for those who had the misfortune of ending up on one of his steel slabs. Caitlin had run into him at a Walmart once with a cart full of linens. He said he liked refreshing the supply, out of respect for those whose deaths he was charged with detailing.

"You mind telling me what you're getting at here, Doc?" Caitlin asked him.

"Hazmat gear must have kept you from getting a clean scent of the air, Ranger, in which case you would've caught the distinctive odor of almonds."

"Almonds," Caitlin repeated.

Whatley nodded. "It was cyanide that killed the residents of Camino Pass."

"You want to tell me how, exactly?" Caitlin pressed.

"I can tell you how, but not exactly," Whatley told her. "First off, we're talking about hydrogen cyanide here, an extremely toxic gas that forms in combination with, or exposure to, acids. It's among the most rapidly acting of all known poisons, basically shutting down the respiratory system. An oral dosage as small as two to three hundred milligrams can be fatal. But, according to the results of my preliminary examinations of the deceased, I'd say the residents of this town were hit with maybe fifty to a hundred times the gaseous equivalent of that."

"Fifty to a hundred times," Caitlin repeated, as if hoping it would help her make more sense of how an entire town had died in a matter of minutes.

Whatley nodded. "As near as I can estimate from samples taken from the victims' lungs."

"They stopped breathing—that's what you're saying—most dying in their sleep."

"Like I said, Ranger, this was an easy one to figure out, comparatively speaking."

"So where'd this gas come from?"

"Homeland Security has more personnel trying to figure that out right now than the number of residents who died in Camino Pass."

"Homeland's not here right now, so I'm asking you."

"You want to know if this was hostile action. You want to know if somebody was trying out some newfangled weapon in that border town in the middle of nowhere."

"The thought had crossed my mind."

Whatley shrugged. "I suppose it's possible."

"Likely?"

He shrugged again. "As I said—"

"Ask Homeland Security," Caitlin completed for him. "The problem being that, with our old friend Jones no longer on the job, I don't have anybody's number stored on my phone. Any notion as to how it was Lennox Scully managed to survive?"

"I've been too busy with the dead to focus on the living."

"Speaking of which, what's the alternative to hostile action?"

"Something no one's ever seen before, something I'd call unprecedented."

"I'd call it something else, Doc."

"What's that, Ranger?"

"Monday—as in business as usual in these parts. I think I better have a talk with that survivor."

"That'll have to wait, Ranger," Doc Whatley told her. "Homeland Security's with him right now."

And that's when the alarm sounded.

20

HOUSTON

So what are you going to do, Cort Wesley?

Caitlin's question stuck with him through the early part of the drive north back to Houston and beyond. Luke had wedged earbuds into place almost as soon as they set off, tuning his father out along with the rest of the world. Cort Wesley elected not to push things, having said everything he had to say already. And, truth be told, he was glad for the opportunity to be alone with his thoughts and not bear the burden of forcing conversation, once his youngest son drifted off to sleep.

They'd set out at the crack of dawn so Luke would only miss a few classes—driving into the sun, as his father used to put it. Boone Masters wouldn't have cared much if Cort Wesley overdosed on drugs, beyond the fact that it would rob him of his lookout, the role Cort Wesley had played while his father was boosting appliances from warehouses, from the time he was twelve years old. His father had never told him not to drink or smoke, such things being left out of whatever father–son manual he read from. The only time Boone Masters had ever commented about his behavior was when Cort Wesley had killed his first man, who'd gone at his date with a knife in the midst of a robbery. He never did remember what happened between that and looking down at the knife wedged into the guy's sternum. Cort Wesley was covered in the man's blood, which gave him a pretty good idea of what had gone down, though not the particular sequence that had left the guy, who turned out to be a recently released inmate from Huntsville, dead on the sidewalk.

Did it count as killing a man if you didn't remember doing it?

Anyway, he never dated the girl again, and she made her intentions clear by moving to the other side of the high school halls whenever their paths crossed, until she transferred to another school.

Cort Wesley started making a checklist in his head, various approaches he could take going forward, which all had one thing in common: he couldn't let this go.

Someone had pushed drugs onto the Village School campus and Cort Wesley didn't believe for a second it was as simple as kids swiping their parents' prescriptions. No, this was something else, starting with a dealer at the school getting supplied product by some outside source. Lower rungs on a food chain that likely led straight to a wide-scale drug operation with an organized crime element roosting at the top. Defined by the kind of ilk society welcomed being taken off the map, and the police wouldn't even think twice about the circumstances involved.

Ilk, Cort Wesley repeated in his mind, having conjured that word on his own for the first time, given that he owed its usage to someone else entirely.

"*Now, that's a fact, bubba,*" came the voice of Leroy Epps from his truck's backseat.

21

HOUSTON

In the rearview mirror, Cort Wesley could see the spectral shape's lips were pale pink and crinkled with dryness, the morning sunlight casting his brown skin in a yellowish tint. The diabetes that had planted him in the ground had turned Leroy's eyes bloodshot and numbed his limbs years before the sores and infections set in. As a boxer, he'd fought for the middleweight crown on three different occasions, had been knocked out once and had the belt stolen from him on paid-off judges' scorecards two other times. He'd been busted for killing a white man in self-defense and had died three years into Cort Wesley's four-year incarceration at Huntsville's infamous Walls prison. But ever since, he always seemed to show up when Cort Wesley needed him the most. Whether he was a ghostly specter or a figment of his imagination, Cort Wesley had given up trying to figure out. He just accepted the fact of Leroy's presence and was grateful that his old friend kept coming around to help him out of one scrape after another.

Prison officials had let Cort Wesley attend Leroy's funeral in a potter's field for inmates who didn't have any relatives left to claim the body. He'd been the only one standing at the graveside, besides the prison chaplain, when Mexican laborers had lowered the plank coffin into the ground. Cort Wesley tried to remember what he'd been thinking that day, a difficult task since he'd done his best to erase those years not just from his memory but also from his very being. One thing he did remember was that the service was the first time he'd smelled the talcum powder Leroy Epps had used to hide the stench of the festering sores spawned by the diabetes that had ultimately killed him. And, in retrospect, for days after the funeral, Cort Wesley had been struck by the nagging feeling that Leroy wasn't gone at all. The scent of his talcum powder still hung heavy in the air inside his cell, and Cort Wesley woke up at least once every night, certain he saw Leroy standing there, watching over him, grinning and sometimes even winking when the illusion held long enough.

"Where you been, champ?" Cort Wesley asked the ghost, glad Luke was both sleeping and lost between earbuds humming with music, like a mosquito buzzing around his ear.

"*Busy. You wouldn't think such a word would pop up from where I be now, but you'd be surprised. And you aren't the only concern in my purview.*" Cort Wesley could see the ghost's translucent eyes tilt toward Luke. "*You wanna wake your youngest up so I can set him straight on a few things?*"

"Not sure that's a good idea, champ."

"*Oh no? Even given that there's plenty followed the road to where I be now doing exactly what he done to himself the other day?*"

"I'm not sure he'd be able to hear you."

"*You think he heard you, bubba?*"

"Guess we'll find out."

"*What kind of answer you call that?*"

"Only one I've got right now."

"*On account of your thinking being focused elsewhere. Know how I can tell?*"

"I've got a feeling you're going to tell me."

"*Damn straight I am. It's your knuckles, looking like somebody ran them through a meat grinder, you been squeezing that steering wheel so hard. Hell, for a time there, I thought you were gonna break clean through the leather wrap.*"

"I'm working some things out in my head, champ," Cort Wesley told the ghost of his best friend.

"*You think I don't know that? Answer me a question: How is it all the choices you ran through your mind got bad ends written all over them?*"

"You ever hear about this thing called privacy?"

"*Yes, sir, and it's for folks who are where you be, not my kind. Those of us who've moved on to a zip code with no numbers don't cotton to the same kind of behaviors. We got a bigger picture in mind.*"

"And where do drug dealers fit in to that bigger picture?"

"*Wouldn't know. They normally find themselves occupying a lower realm.*"

"There you go."

"*Doesn't make it your job to punch their ticket there.*"

"You think I'm gunning for bear over this?"

"*Aren't you?*"

"Not with an eye toward putting people in the ground."

"*What would you call it then?*"

Cort Wesley realized he was squeezing the steering wheel again, hard enough to make his knuckles feel as if they were going to pop. A glance in the rearview mirror found a grin stretched across Leroy Epps's face that said "I told you so."

"I'd call it making sure the scum behind the drugs that almost killed my boy can't do it again."

"*Dangerous road, bubba.*"

"I didn't go looking for it, champ. It found me."

"*There you go,*" the ghost said, throwing his own words back at him, as if Cort Wesley had made his point for him. "*I never try to dissuade you from your predilections and foibles because they're normally about the bigger picture. But this one's a snapshot, bubba, and no good can come of you rousting the lowlifes who took it.*"

"You want to tell me where you're going with this?"

"*You aim low, all you hit is dirt. You're normally prone to setting your sights higher.*"

"One step at a time," Cort Wesley told the ghost.

"*You just made my point for me, bubba,*" Leroy said, shaking his head in a way that made it look detached from his body. "*Maps exist to guide you to your destination. But this one don't lead nowhere even I can see, and my vision's got wider angles than those dang flat-screen televisions everybody watches these days.*"

"Is there some advice hiding in all that?"

"*Why don't you let the Ranger lady handle this one?*"

"Luke's not her son."

"*Close enough, and I imagine if she heard you say that, you'd be looking down the barrel of her gun a flick later.*"

Cort Wesley rolled his eyes, resisting the urge to check Leroy Epps in the rearview mirror again. "What's it going to take to make you shut up, champ?"

"*Bottle of root beer be nice. Now that would hit the spot. Better get three so your boy can join us. I believe there's a rest stop coming up dead ahead, no pun intended.*"

Before Cort Wesley could angle the truck toward it, though, Luke stirred in the passenger seat, his eyes opening.

"Who were you talking to, Dad?"

Cort Wesley checked the rearview mirror to find Leroy Epps nowhere to be seen, something like a thin mist floating up toward the truck's roof.

"No one," he told his son. "Just myself. But now that you're awake, there's something you need to tell me . . ."

22

SAN ANTONIO, TEXAS

Caitlin rushed through the security door as soon as it opened, straight into the charge of doctors working with Homeland Security, who were still wearing their hazmat gear.

"What happened?" she demanded, as they stopped in their tracks.

"He took a hostage!" one of them managed. "Threatened to kill her if we don't let him out!"

His words emerged through his helmet's faceplate in garbled fashion, leaving a blanket of mist on the plastic.

"Her?"

"We're doctors, scientists for Christ's sake! Security's handling it, okay?"

"Hospital?"

"Homeland."

"Shit," said Caitlin.

The Homeland Security officers the doctor had just referred to were dressed in camo fatigues, sidearms drawn and aimed unsteadily toward the glass wall, beyond which Lennox Scully was holding what looked like a scalpel against the throat of a woman outfitted like an astronaut.

"Texas Ranger?" one of them said. "Really?"

"You're not authorized to be here," the other added.

"You boys think you can solve this from this side of the glass?"

"We're not authorized to enter the chamber," said one.

"Nobody is, without proper gear," said the other.

"Yeah, about that," Caitlin said, moving toward the keypad mounted on the wall to the left of the access door. "One of you want to give me the code, or should we just watch that lady in there die?"

The door sealed behind her and Caitlin entered with her hands in the air, SIG Sauer left in the observation room beyond the isolation chamber.

"Remember me, Mr. Scully?"

The scalpel trembled in Lennox Scully's grip. "I remember the badge. Big chance you took coming in here without a suit."

Caitlin met the eyes of the woman he'd taken hostage through the faceplate of her helmet. "Gives us something in common, sir."

Scully started to smile, then stopped. "Nobody calls me 'sir.' And I want to get out of here, Ranger. I want to go home."

"Not much left there for you, Mr. Scully."

"Nobody calls me that, either."

"That's right. You go by 'Scull.'"

"Along with loser, bum, drunk, asshole—take your pick."

"I've been called all of those, except for drunk, Scull."

Scully's expression turned sad, the scalpel forgotten in his hand for that moment. "My wife died giving birth to a stillborn."

"I'm sorry."

"I don't want your pity. I want to know what happened back home, what killed my town, if it wasn't space aliens or something like that."

"We're still sorting that out, sir."

"You can put your hands down now, Ranger."

Caitlin did just that. "What's the game here? What do you expect to get out of this?"

"Maybe I got all these people figured as space aliens. Maybe I don't want to get taken to the mother ship."

Caitlin again cast a reassuring glance toward Scully's hostage. "Notice I sealed the door after I entered."

"To keep whatever I may have inside me that killed the rest of the town from getting loose."

"That's not going to happen, Scull. Looks like it was cyanide gas killed everybody else in Camino Pass. My great-grandfather worked a case there as a Ranger, back in his day. Met up with Pancho Villa, of all people."

"I've heard that story. You mean it's true?"

Caitlin nodded. "You know what else is true? The fact that you're the town's lone survivor. It sure will help these science types if they can figure out why that is, why you didn't die. It'll also help them figure out why everybody else did."

"I was in the clinic, passed out."

"We know that, sir. What we don't know is what else made you different from everyone else in town. Were there any other patients when they brought you in?"

"I honestly couldn't say, Ranger."

"What about when you woke up? What'd you see then?"

"Nothing, on account of them putting me in what they call the Scully Suite. Used to be a closet or something, so there's no window I can fall out. I woke up hungry, thirsty, and sick to my stomach. Every time I go on a bender, I promise myself it'll be my last, but it never turns out that way."

"That's the case for a lot of folks, Scull."

"Why am I still alive?"

"That's what we need to find out, why you need to let the woman go, so she and her colleagues can get back to their job of helping you."

"They don't give a shit about me. I'm a road crash dummy to them, nothing more. They been poking and prodding me since I got here. I got more tubes stuck in me than an old-fashioned television. Can they really do this?"

"Homeland can pretty much do whatever they want, if it's in the interests of national security."

"How could a drunk like me serve the interests of anybody?"

"First off, by dropping that scalpel and letting the woman go."

Scully's eyes dipped to Caitlin's empty holster. "You left your gun out there."

"Because I don't need it. Because you're not a criminal or dangerous in any way. Because you're going to let the woman go."

Scully looked toward where scientists still garbed in hazmat suits were pressed close to the glass, forming a thick wall. "They'll have me arrested. I don't want to go to jail."

"You won't. You haven't hurt that woman yet and you don't look like the type to have any plans on doing so. You're scared, Scull, and with good reason. Best thing you can do now is cooperate with these folks, so they can determine why you lived when everyone else died."

Scully jerked the scalpel away from the woman's throat but maintained his hold on her. "I'm scared, Ranger."

"So am I, but not of you. I'm scared of whatever killed your town, and you're the only one who can help us figure out what that was."

Scully grew agitated again, flirting with the notion of lifting the scalpel back into place against the woman's throat. "I can't tell you a goddamn thing, because I don't know a goddamn thing."

"You're the only chance we've got. Help us figure out what wiped out your friends and neighbors."

"You said it was cyanide. I just heard you say that."

"But it doesn't make any sense; no plausible accounting for how such a thing could happen. And the only way we can find out what is plausible is to let your body tell these good folks while everything's in working order, when your friends and neighbors didn't end up so lucky."

"Kids too?" Scully asked tentatively, even though he must have known the answer.

"The poison took everyone's life but yours."

Scully angled his gaze downward, his grasp on the woman slackening. She could probably have pulled free, but Caitlin cast her a slight head shake to warn her off such an intention.

"That's a shame," Scully said, "a damn shame. It was an attack, it must have been. Somebody attacked our town and left everybody dead but me. You need to find them. You need to see justice done. Isn't that what Rangers do?"

Caitlin nodded. "That's why I'm here talking to you, sir. Now, let the woman go so we can continue sorting this out."

Scully finally pulled his hands away and sank back to the bed, eyeing Caitlin's empty holster again. "You can't shoot whatever did this, Ranger."

"I guess we'll see about that."

23

HOUSTON

"Mind if I have a word with you, Ben?" Cort Wesley asked the boy who'd just finished running laps around the Village School track.

The kid did a double take, surprised that a stranger knew his name, and then looked about as if hoping to find someone else in the area. But they had the track to themselves.

"I've got to get to class," the boy said, picking up a gym bag emblazoned with the school logo.

"I'm Luke Torres's father. This won't take long."

The boy named Ben looked around again, not noticing Cort Wesley had positioned himself to block his only route to the gate in the fence that enclosed the track. His last name was Brussard and, according to Luke, he was from right here in Houston, the River Oaks section, where homes went for more than two million on average. Luke said Ben had taken him to eat at River Oaks Country Club several times and had stood up for him when the student population of the Village School had learned he was gay. They were the same height, Ben a bit more wiry and sporting similar floppy hair that he kept trimmed tighter.

"How's Luke?" Ben asked him. "I heard what happened."

"He's fine. I just dropped him off. And I'd like to talk to you about what happened."

The boy swallowed hard but said nothing, seeming to realize that Cort Wesley's stance had blocked his exit.

"Luke told me you were there."

Ben's eyes wavered.

"Congratulations on getting into Harvard, son."

"Thanks," Ben said, looking down.

"Hell of a school. My oldest is at Brown."

A single nod.

"That's definitely an occasion worth celebrating, Ben. Luke told me you're the one who brought the pills to commemorate the occasion."

"I really need to go," Ben said, coming up just short of swiping at his eyes, which had darkened with moisture.

Cort Wesley seemed to recall that Ben's father was in the oil business, but that was hardly unusual in Texas, particularly in the Houston area.

"Could you answer a question for me first, son?"

"If I can."

"Where'd you get the drugs?" Cort Wesley asked, sounding as gentle as he could. He'd despised bullies so much in high school; the irony that this could be perceived as him bullying a kid now wasn't lost on him.

Ben swallowed hard again, his eyes shifting about as if in search of an answer. "I swiped them from my parents. They got so many bottles, they never notice. You're not going to tell them, are you?"

"No, son, I won't, not about that anyway, because it's a lie. See, I've done a bit of work for Homeland Security, which has left me with some contacts. And according to one of them, neither of your parents has filled a prescription for anything even approaching an opioid since your mom had dental surgery five years ago. So you mind telling me how you stole something that wasn't there?"

"Mr. Torres—"

"It's Masters. Torres was Luke's mother's name. Maybe you heard he witnessed her murder."

Ben's features seemed to have frozen. Cort Wesley thought if he waved a hand in front of the kid's face, there'd be no reaction. He reminded himself to back off, dial it down a bit.

"My point being that he's been through a lot. But he makes it a point to tell me you always had his back after he came out, and that means a lot to him so it means a lot to me, too. You had his back then, son, and what I'm asking is that you have his back now. I mean, if you saw someone try to gun him down, you wouldn't hold anything back, right?"

"No, sir," Ben said, sounding as if he was using the word "sir" for the first time in his life.

"Same thing here. Somebody almost killed him with pills instead of bullets, and that somebody is the guy you bought the drugs from. Just give me a name and I'll take it from there."

"*Mr. Masters . . .*"

Cort Wesley twirled his head around to find the head of the Village School, Julia De Cantis, striding across the grounds toward the school track. He figured Ben Brussard would be uttering a sigh of relief over being granted a reprieve from the pseudo interrogation. Instead, though, the boy had pulled a phone from his gym bag and was scrolling through his contacts.

"Guy calls himself Cholo Brown. Here's his phone number, sir."

24

Houston

"Get to class, Mr. Brussard," Julia De Cantis said to the boy, her high heels clacking against the track's surface.

Ben dropped the phone back in his gym bag. "Yes, ma'am."

The head of the Village School waited for the boy to jog out of earshot before she looked back at Cort Wesley. She was wearing a fashionable skirt and form-fitting blouse that showed off her figure. Her bronze complexion was somewhere between Latino and Mediterranean, and Cort Wesley thought he recalled from her bio that she was the daughter of immigrants, though he couldn't recall their specific nationality. Her front teeth were stained with lipstick, residue from her tongue and likely a habit bred of nerves. The sun made her skin look bright and shiny, a light sheen of perspiration rising up through the thin coat of makeup Cort Wesley figured came complete with sunscreen.

"I'd thank you not to address our students in a threatening fashion, Mr. Masters," she said firmly, swiping her tongue across her upper lip and leaving a dent in the coloring.

"What makes you think I was threatening him?"

"Given your history—" De Cantis started, before he cut her off.

"Let's talk recent history, starting with two nights ago when my son overdosed on drugs he ingested on school grounds."

"I assure you that we're conducting a thorough investigation into the matter."

"Starting with where Ben Brussard got the drugs that almost killed my son?"

She didn't respond.

"I didn't think so. And I wasn't threatening the boy, just appealing to his better nature. You don't want to see me when I'm threatening."

"If you had given me the courtesy of returning my calls, I would've provided an update on our investigation."

"Not interested, if that doesn't include the name of the dealer in question."

"You should let the police handle this, Mr. Masters. And I'd respectfully ask you not to enter school property without checking with me first."

Cort Wesley pitched his gaze downward. The track was a bright clay color, the lane markers freshly painted with white paint that was almost blinding. He could feel the heat radiating off the hard top, detected waves of superheated air dissipating like mist into the ether.

"Any of those calls include an apology, Ms. De Cantis?" he asked, looking back up again.

"I said I was sorry for what happened. I asked if there was anything I could do."

"I don't believe you ever said you were sorry that it happened at your school, under your watch. Where I come from, that makes you as guilty as Ben Brussard and whoever sold him the drugs that almost killed my son."

"I assure you, Mr. Masters, Ben will be dealt with. To be frank, expulsion is a very real possibility."

"Just one semester before he graduates? You'll ruin his life, ma'am."

Julia De Cantis suddenly looked as if she didn't recognize Cort Wesley. "I'm confused, Mr. Masters. You don't want the boy responsible for your son's overdose to be punished?"

"He's a good kid. Ben was the first to stand up for Luke when he told his friends he was gay. He made a mistake. It shouldn't ruin his life when what you're really trying to do is relieve your own guilt."

De Cantis's lower lip quivered. "I could have you arrested for trespassing."

"Ben Brussard is a spoke in a much larger wheel. I imagine if you start expelling students who bring drugs or alcohol onto school grounds, you'd lose about a third of your student body. I know you want to make an example of Ben, but there's better and fairer ways to do it than destroying his future. He owned up to what he did, ma'am, and that's a heck of a lot more than I can say for most in a similar situation."

Julia De Cantis's eyes widened, suddenly curious. "How's that exactly?"

"Let's leave things there."

"What'd you ask him, Mr. Masters?"

Cort Wesley started past her for the gate. "I better leave before you have me arrested for trespassing."

"What did he tell you?"

Against his better judgment, Cort Wesley stopped and turned back around when he reached the gate, letting De Cantis see him study the track. "Maintenance did a real good job on this. Cleaned it up nice and neat. That's what I'm going to do for you, too, ma'am. Clean this mess up all nice and neat. You cut Ben Brussard a break and I'll make sure nothing touches the school. I owe you that much for all you've done for my son. We square?"

De Cantis looked as if she was about to nod, but then changed her mind. "No, Mr. Masters, we're not square. I don't want to be a party to whatever it is you're going to do. I don't want to hear about it, I don't want to know about it, and I don't want you tarnishing the school name in the process."

Cort Wesley nodded, weighing her words. "A bunch of your seniors held a pill party to celebrate one of them getting into Harvard. I don't think it gets much more tarnished than that, ma'am."

25

SAN ANTONIO, TEXAS

With time to kill until Lennox Scully awoke from being sedated, to help him calm back down, Caitlin stopped at the Magnolia Pancake Haus, where she went occasionally with Cort Wesley. The Texas Ranger badge and the mystique about her conjured by the media normally led Caitlin to forego public places like this due to the unwarranted attention she drew. But the Pancake Haus was roomy and populated with enough tables that she normally could find one out of reach of prying eyes. Interesting how this usually led her to choose a seat with her back to the entrance, in stark contrast to the typical gunfighter mentality, a compromise necessitated by the place she too often had occupied in the twenty-four-hour news cycle.

She opened her phone and jogged it to Instagram, where she'd created a fake account because, strangely, so many criminals and suspects maintained pages on the site. She hesitated briefly, thinking of closing the app as quickly as she'd opened it, until Luke's words chimed in her head.

Check out his Instagram page. You got bigger problems with him than me.

She hadn't been able to chase Luke's warning about Dylan from her mind, and she couldn't stop herself from logging in and then going to his feed. Dozens of pictures from recent days at Brown University popped up, none of them particularly noteworthy, until Caitlin's scroll reached photos from three days ago.

Her eyes froze on a single candid shot that was slightly out of focus, the kind of picture that gets posted randomly among a bunch of others. She felt her skin crawl and prickle with heat, and she was dialing Dylan's number before she could stop herself.

"Jeez, Caitlin, do you know what time it is?" he greeted groggily.

"Just after nine a.m. in these parts. You sleeping in today?"

"Shit, I must've overslept. Is everything okay?"

She realized Cort Wesley hadn't informed him about his brother's overdose and decided this wasn't the time to do so, not with something else on her mind.

"Is she there?" Caitlin asked instead.

"Er, who?"

"Put her on, Dylan."

A pause followed, muffled words exchanged on the other end, before a female voice replaced Dylan's.

"What's the haps, sis?"

Caitlin had known the young woman first as Selina Escalante, a pharmaceutical rep who'd picked Dylan up in a bar. But her real name was actually Nola Delgado and she was Caitlin's half sister, thanks to a brief affair between her father and Luna Diaz Delgado, the most powerful criminal figure in all of Mexico and known as the Red Widow for good reason.

Nola Delgado had also stepped into the shoes of a legendary assassin known as el Barquero, named after the mythological ferryman, for her expertise in taking people to their deaths. They had met for the first time several months back, and the fact that Nola may have saved her life twice had little bearing on Caitlin's orders that she never see Dylan again, Caitlin left recalling their first conversation:

Dylan's been through a lot.

I get that impression.

He's gotten hurt.

I got that impression, too.

And here we are, celebrating, what, the anniversary of your third night together?

Something like that.

I believe you get my point.

I think he's looking for a woman like you. Someone strong as steel, who can't

get hurt the way his mother did. Who can stand up for herself, take no prison-
ers, and take no shit. Go toe to toe with him, no matter what.

We talking about me or you, Selina?

Both. At least, that's what I'm hoping.

"Don't call me 'sis,' Nola," Caitlin said, suddenly chilled by cool air pumping through the air-conditioning vent directly overhead.

"That won't make it any less true."

"I'm guessing it was you who posted that picture of you and Dylan on Instagram. I'm guessing you wanted me to see it."

"And why would I do that, sis?"

"To get a rise out of me."

"In which case, it would seem I've succeeded."

"You're putting him in danger," Caitlin said, through what felt like icicles breaking up in her mouth.

"He doesn't need me for that, Ranger. He's got you."

"Go home, Nola."

"America not a free country anymore?"

"Not when it comes to Dylan. One gunfighter in his life is enough."

"I'll take that as a compliment."

"I didn't mean it as one."

"My feelings for him are genuine, sis."

Caitlin bristled again at being called that. "Is that why you posted that picture on Instagram for me to see? So I'd know your feelings were genuine?"

"Maybe I just missed you. Thought we could do Thanksgiving to-gether, so you could tell me about my father, since I never met him."

"He never even knew you existed, Nola, and I wish I could say the same."

"In which case, you'd be dead."

"You think I couldn't have handled the shooters you gunned down?"

"Guess we'll never know now, will we, sis?"

"Put Dylan back on," Caitlin said, realizing she was getting no-where.

"Hey," Dylan's voice returned.

"What are you doing?"

"Right now, putting my pants on so I can get to class. I'm late."

"She's using you, son."

"I can take care of myself."

"She show up at your door or call first to ask you to take her back?"

"I called her, Caitlin. And it was me who posted that shot of us on Instagram. I didn't mean to, but I did. My bad."

"And now you're making it worse," Caitlin said, wishing she'd never placed the call.

"Can Nola really come for Thanksgiving?"

"This isn't a joke, Dylan."

"I was being serious. Why do you hate her so much?"

"It's not that I hate her, it's that I don't know her, and neither did you."

"She's your sister."

"Half sister," Caitlin corrected, "and you just made my point for me."

"What's that?"

"It takes one to know one."

"As in killers? Difference being I'm sleeping with her, not you."

"You don't want the likes of Nola Delgado in your head or your life, Dylan. She should come with a warning label like you see on a cigarette box, that her company could be hazardous to your health."

"Like you said, Caitlin, it takes one to know one. Look, I gotta go. Bye."

The click left Caitlin staring at her phone, which immediately lit up with an incoming call. Hoping it was Dylan calling back, she was ready to answer it when she saw JONES lit up in the caller ID instead. She laid the phone on the Pancake Haus table, only to have it start ringing again right away. She ignored it for a time, then glanced at it and saw HEAD-QUARTERS.

"Can you squeeze a visit to the office into your busy schedule, Ranger?" Captain Tepper asked her.

"Any specific reason?"

"You'll see when you get here."

26

San Antonio, Texas

"Okay, muchachos," Guillermo Paz said to the young charges gathered before him, "who wants to go first?"

A slew of tiny hands shot up in the air, forming a blur with their waving.

"Let's go over the rules first."

Paz didn't believe in wasting time. So, first day on the job at Canyon Ridge Elementary, he'd set up an obstacle course in the cramped school gymnasium, using up all the space it gave him and making do with the limited equipment he'd found tucked away in a storage closet. He'd dragged the gymnastic parallel bars out, along with some orange cones, a tarpaulin, steel folding chairs, and two sets of stanchions, with the limbo sticks that belonged to them. He'd also lugged in some old truck tires he'd poached from a junkyard.

"This is a version of the obstacle course I designed to train my men back in Venezuela. Of course, when they were going through it, I was firing live rounds at them. Only winged a couple, which was far preferable to watching them fall in battle. Nothing's more important than training, because it's what keeps you alive."

A small hand extended into the air.

"Yes, muchacha?" Paz said to a second-grade girl.

"What's 'live rounds'?"

"Real bullets."

"You shot your friends with real bullets?"

"They weren't my friends, they were my men. It was my responsibility to keep them alive, just like I'm doing with you."

"We have to do this to stay alive?" a boy asked, sounding confused.

"We never know when the shit's going to hit the fan, do we?"

"You said a bad word," another little girl scolded.

"That's right. *Lo siento.* I'm sorry. Now, watch me demonstrate how to run the course."

A second boy raised his hand. "Can I go first?"

"After me."

"I want to go first."

"Benjamin Franklin once said, 'By failing to prepare, you are preparing to fail.'"

"Who's Frank Benjamin?" the same boy asked.

"Benjamin Franklin," Paz corrected, "and he was a very smart man. You ever hear of Abraham Lincoln?"

The boy nodded. "He was president."

"That's right. And he also said, 'Give me six hours to chop down a tree and I will spend the first four sharpening the ax.' What we're doing right now, we're sharpening the ax. Watch."

With that, Paz effortlessly mounted the parallel bars, squeezing the slick wood with his hands and pulling himself along over a blue wrestling mat.

"First thing," he explained, "you need to get across the water without getting your feet wet."

"Where's the water?" another kid asked.

"It's the blue mat."

"But it's not wet."

"Use your imagination. Albert Einstein once said, 'The true sign of intelligence is not knowledge but imagination.'"

"Was he president?" the boy who knew about Abraham Lincoln wondered.

"No. He couldn't be president because he came from Ulm, Germany, an immigrant like me."

"I'm an immigrant too," a little girl said.

"Good."

"But I'm not from Germany."

Paz dropped off the parallel bars, having cleared the imaginary water. "Then you drop down and crawl through the tube," he said, doing just that along the makeshift tunnel he'd formed by wrapping the tarpaulin around four steel chairs on either side. "Then you bounce back up and hurdle this branch and duck under the next one."

With that, Paz bounded over the lower limbo stick, then bounced up and rolled under the higher one set before it. Next, without breaking stride, he weaved through the orange cones and jumped into the center of one truck tire after another, four in all.

"Last thing," he told his gym class, "you grab hold of the rope here and swing over the minefield."

"Where's the minefield?" a familiar voice asked.

"The basketball lane."

"Oh."

Paz followed his own instructions and dropped lightly off, back near his young charges. "See, that's not too hard, right? Well, it might be the first time you do it, but that's okay so long as it gets easier the next. Like Helen Keller once said, 'We can do anything we want to do if we stick to it long enough.'"

Paz could see the kids fidgeting, eager to get started.

"Any more questions?"

Before any of them could answer, Paz felt a cold, shrill wind hit him like a battering ram, nearly toppling him from his feet. He looked toward the heavy gym doors that opened onto the playground, expecting a sudden tornado looming outside to have blown them open. But they were still sealed. Next, he felt a searing heat chasing the chill, following the same path through him. It left his skin unmarred but seemed to singe his insides and superheat his blood. He looked back toward his class to see the lot of them turned to ice that melted right before his eyes, leaving nothing but bloodred puddles atop the gym floor.

"Colonel G?" he heard inside his head.

Paz realized his charges had risen back from the puddles, bouncing with eagerness to start their turns on the obstacle course, the message to him effectively delivered.

Something was coming, something bad. Close and getting closer, sure to be set upon the world before too much longer.

"Now," Paz said, shaking off the spell, "who wants to go first?"

PART THREE

BEN MCCULLOCH

McCulloch followed his neighbor and family friend Davy Crockett from Tennessee out to Texas in 1835. He came down with the measles and didn't make it to the Alamo before its fall, but joined Sam Houston's army for the Battle of San Jacinto. After joining the Rangers, he fought courageously against Comanches at the Battle of Plum Creek and other engagements and was named Hays' first lieutenant. During the Mexican War, McCulloch earned the distinction of chief scout for General Zachary Taylor's army. In 1849, McCulloch joined many other fortune-seekers who headed to California during the Gold Rush. By the time the Civil War broke out, he was back in Texas, and in May 1861 became a brigadier general in the Confederate Army. Assigned to defend Indian Territory in Texas, he contributed greatly to the Confederate victory at the Battle of Wilson's Creek in August 1861. In March 1862, McCulloch was killed in the Battle of Pea Ridge in northwestern Arkansas.

—Sarah Pruitt, "8 Famous Texas Rangers," History.com

27

SAN ANTONIO, TEXAS

"Hey, look who it is!"

Caitlin stood in the doorway of D. W. Tepper's office, looking at the man who'd just greeted her. He was seated, with his shiny cowboy boots propped up on the captain's desk. "You my new boss, Jones?"

"I work in the private sector now. It's not 'Jones' anymore."

"Oh, what is it?"

"What's the difference?"

"And how's the private sector treating you?"

"Money's great. Everything else sucks. Too much accountability."

"Meaning you can't send Paz to kill somebody who gives you the stink eye at a board meeting."

The man Caitlin knew as Jones smirked. "I've been under the radar so long, it's awfully tough living between the lines. First week I drew an actual paycheck, I realized I needed to open a bank account in my real name. There's something to be said for cash and having credit cards you never have to pay down yourself."

"Right. Sounds like a regular utopia."

Jones had become a top operative for Homeland Security by way of stints with the Special Forces and then the CIA. Caitlin had first met him when his name was still "Smith" and he was attached to the American embassy in Bahrain. Enough of a relationship had formed for the two of them to remain in contact and to actually work together on several more occasions. Sometimes Jones surprised her, but mostly he could be relied on to live down to Caitlin's expectations.

Caitlin couldn't say exactly what Jones had done during his years with Homeland Security, and she doubted that anybody else could either. He'd operated in the muck, among the dregs of society who were plotting to harm the country from the inside. Caitlin doubted he'd ever written a report or detailed the specifics of his operations in any way. He'd lived in the dark, calling on the likes of Guillermo Paz and the colonel's henchmen to deal with matters, always out of view of the light. When those matters brought him to Texas, which seemed to be every other day, he'd seek out Caitlin the way he might a former classmate.

The office's dull lighting kept Jones's face cloaked in the shadows with which he was most comfortable. Caitlin tried to remember the color of his eyes but couldn't, as if he'd been trained to never look at anyone long enough for anything to register. He was wearing a sport jacket over a button-down shirt and pressed trousers, making him seem like a high school teacher. But he was back to the tightly cropped, military-style haircut that had been one of his signatures until he'd let it grow out. He had never seemed comfortable with so much more to comb.

"Where's Captain Tepper?" Caitlin asked him.

"Said he needed to go out to pick something up. Said you'd know what."

"More cigarettes, on account of the fact that I found all of his hiding places over the weekend."

Jones pulled his boots off Tepper's desk and rested them on the floor. "How do you wear these things, Ranger?"

"It's an acquired taste, but you need to break them in."

"Kind of like you and me."

"I have no idea what that means, Jones."

"You didn't pick up my call," he said, sounding genuinely hurt.

"Maybe I was busy."

"That didn't stop you before, when I enjoyed an official capacity."

"Doesn't mean I enjoyed working with you," Caitlin told him, hands planted firmly on her hips now.

"Come on, Ranger, cut me a break. For old time's sake."

"Did you really just say that?"

"We don't have enough history between us?"

"Yours is the revisionist version." She gave him a closer look. "You're not carrying."

"That's what the private sector will do to you," Jones sighed. "Wearing a shoulder holster tends to make my colleagues uncomfortable. Sometimes you have to compromise."

"Unlike your days at Homeland."

The last time they worked together, a mistaken assessment of the situation had left Homeland looking for a fall guy, and Jones had found himself gone, just like that. With the explosion of private security operations, though, he wasn't out of work for long. Caitlin couldn't say exactly what he was doing in the private sector, but she figured it probably didn't differ all that much from his work for the government, except for extra zeros in his yearly take-home pay.

"Maybe I want back in with them, in which case I've got to prove myself all over again. Work my way back to the majors. You know how it is."

"Not really."

Jones gave her a long look, as if trying to reacquaint himself with their relationship—or lack thereof. "I heard about Camino Pass, Ranger."

"What's that?"

Jones snickered. "Border town where the residents went to sleep and never woke up a couple nights back, save for one survivor you paid a visit to at University Hospital a few hours ago."

Caitlin held to her calm, not wanting to appear riled by Jones's intimate knowledge of her movements.

"You following me?" she asked him.

"I'm following whatever it is you're after, as in what killed that town."

"You want to keep playing dumb, we can end this meeting now, Jones."

"All right, all right. I know all about the cyanide gas. There was a reason why hydrogen cyanide was the primary killing agent used in gas chamber executions, but last time I checked, nobody executed nearly three hundred people at once in Camino Pass. That definitely piqued my curiosity."

"So, what, you register on Google Alerts for mass deaths?"

Jones didn't answer, which Caitlin took for an answer in itself.

"How's Paz?" he asked instead.

"You mean you're not keeping tabs on him too?"

"I heard he's working as an elementary school gym teacher."

"Next step in his spiritual transformation."

"I also heard there was an incident involving ICE at the same school yesterday. Nice way to treat a fellow law enforcement body, Ranger."

"Rangers don't enjoy a cooperative agreement with ICE, Jones. We like to keep to ourselves."

"Guess I'm lucky you made an exception in the case of Homeland Security."

"Don't make me regret it."

Jones rose to his feet, standing on his toes to stretch out his feet in yet another new pair of boots. Caitlin figured he swapped them out every time one got a scuff mark.

"However that cyanide gas got deployed could be my ticket back to Homeland."

"Deployed? This was an accident, not hostile action."

"That's a matter of perspective."

Caitlin met his focused stare, starting to increase in intensity. "You already know everything I do, Jones. What do you need me for?"

"Thought we could ride on this one together, like the old days."

"You ever even been on a horse?"

"It was a metaphor, Ranger."

"Oh."

"So, do we have a deal?"

"Not even close."

Jones studied her briefly, like a card player who knew he had a winning hand. "How about if I sweeten the pot a bit?"

"How's that?"

Smiling now, the way the same player flips over his cards before claiming the pot, he said, "I happen to know you're not the first member of the Strong family associated with Camino Pass."

"You're talking about my great-grandfather, William Ray, and how he ended up riding with Pancho Villa."

Jones nodded. "And I also happen to know where your captain left off in the story . . ."

28

MEXICO; 1898

"You make a run for it, I'll shoot you 'fore you finish your next thought," William Ray said, mounting his horse after helping Pancho Villa atop one he'd borrowed from the local stable, leaving a hastily scrawled note in its place.

"You haven't asked me why I'm doing this, Ranger," Villa said, the sun already heating up the iron lashing his wrists together with maybe a foot of links between them.

"Maybe I don't care."

"But you're curious."

"I figure you're gonna try pulling something and that I'll shoot you when you do."

Villa's expression turned pained, bordering on disappointment. "It's because of my sister."

"The one who got raped."

Villa nodded. "The man who did it, the one I killed, worked for the same man as those kidnappers. He's the one I had to go on the run on account of. We find those kids, maybe I get my chance at him, too." He turned to the front, then swung from the sun back around. "How many Mexicans you killed in your time, Ranger?"

"Got a feeling the tally's about to rise a bit, muchacho."

"Is that a fact?"

"At least by one, if you don't shut your trap."

William Ray Strong and Pancho Villa came upon the bodies three hours into their ride, attracted by the buzzards circling overhead.

"Looks like they been dead around a couple days now," the Ranger pronounced, kneeling downwind over another of the bodies.

"Then the ambush would correspond to the time the posse rode out of Camino Pass after the kidnapped children."

William Ray looked up at Villa, who was still seated atop his horse with irons lacing his wrists together. "You talk pretty good for a bandit. Best English I ever heard a Mexican speak."

"Like I told you, I became a bandit by necessity, not choice. I assure you, I have far grander ambitions for both myself and my country."

"This little trip we're going on have anything to do with that?"

"I guess we'll see, Ranger," Villa said evasively.

"Well, amigo, here's something I *can't* see: tracks, anywhere in the vicinity. An ambush by the bandits in question would have left plenty of them. And you ever seen an ambush where no horses got themselves shot dead too?"

"I don't have a lot of experience in ambushes. Like I said—"

"I know what you said," William Ray interrupted. "And the jury's still out on how much I believe of it. I've got a sense you're holding plenty back."

He stood up, knees cracking, and walked about the perimeter in which the dead had fallen. An even dozen by his count, a number of whom had managed to crawl behind rock formations and natural boulders before death claimed them.

"How many you figure set out in this posse?" the Ranger asked Villa.

"The same number of dead we're looking at here."

"Got them all, then."

He continued his survey, doing a fresh reconnoiter of the bodies and focusing on the weapons this time.

"At least half never even drew their weapons. And, except for those four shotguns, not a single one of them managed to get their carbines or Winchesters out of their saddle holsters. What's that tell you, amigo?"

"That the ambush hit them fast."

"I already told you, this was no ambush."

"Then what was it?"

William Ray gazed up at the mesas and hillsides looking down on the flat clearing from the east. "What say we take that there trail up a ways and see what we can see."

"Ever seen one of these before?" the Ranger asked Pancho Villa, holding up a big brass shell casing for a rifle bullet.

Villa squinted from atop his horse. "Can't say that I have."

"Comes from a carbine rifle called the Gewehr 98, made by Mauser and manufactured in Germany. But don't let that fool you, because it's been shipping all over the world, though I never seen an indication that included Mexico. Takes a five-round stripper clip loaded into an internal box magazine and comes complete with iron sights that makes it the best shooting weapon in the world for distance."

"*Tiradore,*" Villa said under his breath.

"What's that mean?"

"Sharpshooter."

William Ray kicked at one pile of expended shells and then another. "Better make that plural, amigo, because by my count we got a half dozen ter-doors."

"That's tiradore, Ranger."

"What's the goddamn difference? They made camp here and had a grand old time while waiting for the posse coming after the kidnapped children to ride right into range."

"I don't know about these rifles making their way to Mexico or not. But I've never come across a single Mexican sharpshooter in my life," Villa noted.

"Me neither. And next time you gaze off into the distance contemplating making a run for it, I'll strap irons on your ankles too and make you ride sidesaddle."

"I was looking for some sign of the shooters, Ranger."

"And I'm a monkey's uncle. I know you got your share of secrets, amigo, but I got no intention of prying them out of you so long as you stay true to your word and lead me to the sumbitches who took those kids. Them being killers now, too."

"You plan on bringing them back to Texas?"

"Haven't got that far in my thinking yet, just like you're not gonna get much farther down this trail unless you find me something worthy of the effort soon."

Pancho Villa gazed into the distance again, ignoring William Ray's warning. "We've got two more hours of riding ahead of us, Ranger."

"'Til we reach what, exactly?"

"A town where you don't want to be seen."

"What's this town called, Pancho? Maybe I've heard of it."

"Sal Si Puede."

"That's beyond the limits of my Spanish, son."

"It means 'Exit if you can.'"

"This the place where we're gonna find the kidnappers, like you told me?"

Villa looked at William Ray as if the Ranger were speaking to somebody else. "Did I say that?"

"You said it."

"I meant we'd find clues to where we could find them. Sorry for the misunderstanding."

"Next time we have a misunderstanding, amigo, I'm gonna leave you tied to a tree for the buzzards."

The two hours turned out to be closer to four, and the sun was starting to bleed out of the sky when they reached the outskirts of Sal Si Puede. There was no way they could have handled the chore of burying all the bodies of the dead posse from Camino Pass, or even covering them with rocks. The best they could do under the circumstances was drag them to the shade provided by the nearest boulders and rock formations. Then William Ray could either cable Austin about what he'd found or deliver the news to the town personally upon his return from Mexico.

Sal Si Puede was situated in what would have been the middle of nowhere, if not for the train depot a mile to the west. The town owed the bulk of its business to the fact that it was often the first stop for those getting off the train. That kept its hotel and restaurant open, along with a sprawling saloon that featured gambling.

But the town had gained its name, and infamy, from the days prior to the railroad moving in nearby. It was one of the first vestiges of civilization Mexican bandits and bushwhackers would encounter upon crossing the border and fleeing whatever pursuit was coming from the Rangers, the army, or somebody else. So it had enjoyed a well-earned reputation as a place to be avoided for ordinary, law-abiding Mexicans. While that had changed somewhat with the coming of the railroad, Sal Si Puede still laid claim to being a respite for any number of bad hombres. Their number, though, was mostly limited to the south side of town and a nameless cantina that was rumored to be frequented by the Hole-in-the-Wall Gang.

The dirt streets were sand colored and darker in patches where thick puddles from a storm the day before hadn't yet dried. The flat-roofed buildings were constructed of adobe that had once been uniformly white but now was stained an ugly urine color in the worn areas that drew the most sun. Some of these stains had been covered by colorful paintings or tapestries hung from the eaves, where canvas awnings set over doors didn't get in the way.

Rolling hills rose to the east, the combination of their beauty and rugged, imposing nature forming an odd juxtaposition that made them look painted over the scene. The main road that cut through the center of Sal Si Puede stretched on beyond the town itself, seeming to reach into the foothills before shrinking from sight amid earth that looked red and scorched in the glow of the setting sun.

At the center of Sal Si Puede, a fence post rose from the ground, topped with the impaled head of what William Ray at first thought was a man. Drawing closer, he realized it actually was a wild boar, which was some comfort.

"You should wait outside, Ranger," Pancho Villa advised, when they reached the cantina in question. "Let me go in and at least get the lay of the land."

"So you scamper out the back door, amigo? No way in hell. We walk in together."

Villa let William Ray see him regarding his badge. "Suit yourself. But Texas Rangers are about as welcome here as malaria and there's probably more wanted men than not inside."

"How 'bout I promise not to arrest anybody?"

Villa extended his hands. "You should take these off. I walk in there as your prisoner, it won't be a good day for either one of us. They'll figure you dragged me in to eyeball men you're tracking."

"Good point," the Ranger said, drawing the key from his pocket. "Just remember, I speak Spanish well enough to know if you pull something."

"At least take off your badge."

"Might as well go in naked. Come on, amigo, I'll lead the way."

Many of the men inside, several wearing bandoliers and with squat-looking shotguns not far out of reach, recognized Pancho Villa immediately.

William Ray figured this must be the gang the young Mexican had been riding with, leading him to similarly figure he'd walked straight into a trap and things would be going to guns soon.

But he resisted the urge to draw when those closest to the door noticed his badge and lurched up from their chairs, fumbling for their weapons. It seemed like William Ray hadn't even taken his next breath before two dozen guns were poised his way, held by men who need fear no repercussions this far south of the border.

Instead of going for his gun, the Ranger let the men see his eyes. This was far from his first experience being vastly outnumbered and outgunned, and that experience had taught him that nothing stops the first man from beginning a fusillade better than fearing he might get shot himself. With only six bullets in his Samuel Walker Colt, all twenty-four of the men behind the guns aimed at him knew he couldn't possibly shoot all of them. But the question of which six would ultimately fall to his bullets was argument enough to preserve the stalemate long enough for Pancho Villa to intervene.

"*Tranquilizarse! Tranquilizarse!*" Villa yelled out, urging the gunmen to stay calm, as he moved in front of William Ray. "*Todo está bien! Está conmigo!*"

Hearing the young bandit say they were together was a welcome relief for the Ranger, while soothing whatever reservations he held about the man's intentions. William Ray knew that Pancho Villa was after something himself in all this. He just didn't know what that was yet.

"What are you doing with this el Rinche?" a bearded man with a stomach hanging well over his belt asked Villa in Spanish.

The young bandit stole a glance at William Ray before responding. "He agreed to keep me out of an American prison if I agreed to help him."

The fat man had a full beard that stretched down to his chest and a depressed scar across the bridge of his nose that made his face look like it had a hole on it. His bulbous cheeks were bell-shaped and seemed to merge with the drooping jowls hidden by the fall of his beard. His eyes looked to be different colors. William Ray was left to wonder whether the lighter one might be made of glass.

"Help him what?" the fat man asked Pancho Villa.

"Children were taken from the town where I was jailed. I told him I could help him get them back."

William Ray felt something in the dusty cantina change in that moment, a heaviness filling the air, as if this gang of bandits had found something else to be scared of besides him.

"Dile que te equivocaste, chico."

"I'm not a kid," Villa told the fat man. "And I'm not going to tell him I was wrong, because that would be a lie. I might steal, I might kill, but I won't lie. If you know something about whoever took those kids, just tell me so we can be on our way on their trail."

"I never kill a man lightly," the fat man told him. "And if I tell you that, I will be killing you. What kind of friend would I be then, chico?"

"We came upon a posse from the town that set out after the stolen children, all of them dead. Shot from the hilltops above by sharpshooters." Villa turned to gesture at William Ray Strong. "I want the Texas Rangers to know we weren't behind all those killings, that we are many things but not sharpshooters who gun down innocent people who've done us no harm."

The fat man looked genuinely sad, his jowls drooping to the point where they appeared ready to slip off his face. "If you leave here still on their trail, you will die too, you and your new *Tejas diablo* friend."

Villa swallowed hard. "Maybe that's a chance I'm willing to take."

The fat man nodded in resignation, looking toward his men, who took that as an unspoken gesture to finally lower their weapons. "When you ride with the Texas devils, chico, don't expect God to be by your side."

"Speaking of which," William Ray interjected, in the best Spanish he could muster, "you look familiar. Maybe our paths have crossed before, jefe."

The fat man shook his head. "I never forget the face of a man I kill or want to."

"Well, in my case there's been too many of those to keep track of in my head. You sure we haven't met before?"

"What did I just say?"

"Maybe I didn't hear you right. Guess my Spanish is a bit lacking."

"Eres un pedazo de mierda."

"Not the first time I've been called a piece of shit, jefe."

The fat man grinned broadly. "Maybe your Spanish isn't as bad you think, el Rinche."

"Who are we looking for, exactly?" William Ray asked him.

"If I tell you that, I might as well shoot you myself."

"Like I said," Villa told him, looking toward William Ray Strong, "that's a chance we're willing to take."

The fat man uttered a raspy sigh. "Los Chinos."

29

SAN ANTONIO, TEXAS

"The Chinese," Caitlin translated. "You sure you got that part of the story right, Jones?"

"Have you ever known me to be wrong, Ranger?"

"I've known you to be a liar and an asshole."

"That's not what I asked you."

"Okay, so what did these Chinese want with the kids from Camino Pass?"

"Uh-uh," Jones said, shaking his head. "My turn. Tell me more about that cyanide gas that wiped out the same town a hundred and twenty years later."

"You want to know where it came from."

"Do you blame me? Almost three hundred people getting killed in less time than it takes me to tie my shoes tells me this was no accident."

"You're wearing boots, Jones."

Jones chose to ignore her. "Could be somebody's already figured out how to weaponize this cyanide, the alternative being that whatever did this is *waiting* to be weaponized. Either way, I want in."

"In on what, exactly?"

"The party, Ranger. And it's in your best interests to cooperate, because you're going to need me before this is over."

"Just how do you know that?"

"Because this is Texas, the lowest point on the planet where all the shit comes to settle. And you, Ranger, are a person with a true gift for attracting that same shit. All your ancestors had it easy by comparison; all they had to deal with were criminals, instead of every aberration the devil can throw at the world."

"What were the Chinese doing in Mexico in 1898, Jones? What was it my great-grandfather really latched on to?"

Jones shook his head, smiling wryly, instead of responding. "Your grandfather mixed it up with J. Edgar Hoover. Your great-great-grandfather took on John D. Rockefeller, and your great-grandfather ended up running buddies with none other than Pancho Villa, not to mention Judge Roy Bean."

"What's your point?"

"I'm wondering if maybe your father solved the Kennedy assassination and didn't bother telling anybody. What is it with you Strongs?"

"Just lucky, I guess."

"I want in on this, Ranger," Jones repeated. "Whatever wiped out Camino Pass is my ticket back to Washington. I'm making more money than I've ever seen in my life and I hate every single minute of it. I hate bureaucracy and accountability. I hate wearing a tie and having to suck up to people I'm never going to see again. I hate shareholders, stakeholders, and cup holders. I hate finding somebody eyeballing me every time I turn around."

"That's quite a mouthful, Jones."

"I don't like being on the outside, Ranger."

"Give me something I can use to help you back in."

Jones smiled like a man who'd just found somebody else's wallet stuffed with cash. "I knew we could do business, just like we always do."

"Except you're accountable now and don't have an army backing you up."

Jones weighed her words. "I'm accountable, but the company I work for has ten thousand mercenaries on speed dial. You bet I've got an army."

Caitlin gave him a longer look, realizing he was slowly morphing into the very man she didn't trust at all but had often found common ground with. "What did the Chinese want with those children they kidnapped?"

"Beats me."

"What were they up to south of the border?"

"Your guess is as good as mine, Ranger."

Caitlin pulled her gaze off him, the distance between them lengthening in a figurative sense. "If you want back in, Jones, you'll have to do better than that."

He flashed that smirk she knew all too well. "Keep asking the questions, Ranger, and sooner or later you'll get the answers you're looking for."

Caitlin was about to continue pushing him when her phone rang, with CORT WESLEY in the caller ID.

"How's Luke?" she said, by way of greeting.

"Just dropped him off at school."

"Well, that's good. Why do I think you called for a different reason entirely?"

"Because I did. I need you to run a name for me, somebody I need to have a sit-down with."

"Please tell me this has nothing to do with the drugs Luke over-dosed on."

"You want me to lie?"

"Your definition of 'sit-down' varies from the rest of the population, Cort Wesley."

"I'll be on my best behavior. Promise."

Caitlin knew there was no way to talk him out of this, searched for a compromise instead. "Why don't we do this together?"

"Because I'm in Houston and you're not."

"Whoever this guy is, we can just as easily find him tomorrow."

"Guy's name is Cholo Brown, Ranger. Call me back as soon as you've got something."

30

HOUSTON

"Think this is a good idea, bubba?" Leroy Epps wondered from the passenger seat, as Cort Wesley pulled into a southwest Houston parking lot, past a sign that read "TAKE YOUR VALUABLES."

"No, champ, but it's all I've got. I'll buy you a root beer as soon as I'm done."

"They serving root beer in hell these days?"

"Cholo Brown is an alias," Caitlin had told him when she called back, an hour after they'd spoken. "The guy's real name is Frankie Ramos and he's got a rap sheet that would fill a shoe box."

"Sounds like the man I'm looking for."

"He seems to specialize in selling dope to minors. There's a couple notations on his sheet that suggest middle schools are right up his alley. I probably shouldn't have told you that, Cort Wesley."

"My blood's already boiling, Ranger. That just keeps the steam rising."

"Here's something to bring it down: Ramos cut his teeth with MS-13 before he went to jail, where the mob took a liking to him. The word is he's connected to greaseballs running smack through the projects of cities all through the South. Even the gangs don't mess with him, on account of his association with the old Branca mob, your former employers."

"I've since seen the light."

"Good thing. Maybe you should take Paz along for the ride," Caitlin suggested.

"He's not available. That school you got him hired at doesn't get out until three thirty."

Cholo Brown used a bodega two blocks from the parking lot as his headquarters, and Cort Wesley figured he'd wandered into a different world. The neighborhood was just a ten-minute drive south of the Galleria shopping mall, one of Houston's most famous landmarks. In the seventies, the area had been known as "Swinglesville." Dozens of sprawling apartment complexes, some of them a block long, had been built here, one right beside the other, to accommodate the horde of young, single white adults who were then coming to the city to begin their careers. The complexes were given such sophisticated names as Chateaux Carmel, Napoleon Square, Villa Royal, Sterling Point, and the Turf Club. The owners had planted crape myrtles by the front gates and offered free VCRs to renters who signed yearlong leases. At one complex, a two-story disco was built next to a swimming pool.

Today, the crape myrtles continued to bloom, but there were no more free VCRs—and no disco. The walls of almost all the complexes boasted large banners, many written in Spanish, offering ninety-nine-dollar move-in specials, with no credit check required. In the court-yards, where the young singles once played sand volleyball in skimpy bathing suits, young mothers in faded dresses held babies against their hips, watching their other children kick soccer balls. Old men sat in plastic chairs on tiny balconies, drinking beer and looking down over rusting cars that had become part of the scenery.

The corner bodega out of which Cholo Brown based his operation featured outdoor tables set mostly in the shade of an awning. A pock-marked, acne-scarred face that matched the picture Caitlin had texted him sat under that awning, drinking from a bottle of fruit punch–colored liquid that Cort Wesley took as the kind of wine cooler that had been popular back when Leroy Epps was still alive.

"Wish I could help you bust some heads, bubba," he heard, from some-where close by.

Cort Wesley looked to the side but found no trace of his old friend's ghost.

"I be here, even if you can't see me."

"How's this going to end, champ?"

"With you buying me a root beer, either on this side or the other."

31

Houston

"Cholo Brown," Cort Wesley said, when he was close enough for the man seated in the shade of the awning to hear him.

Two other men were seated at the circular, rusted metal table, atop folding chairs that looked salvaged from a junkyard. Cort Wesley had spent enough time with men like Cholo Brown to know that they were almost never alone, at least not in public, as if they detested their own company or considered sitting alone at a table to be a sign of weakness.

Maybe I'm no one to talk, Cort Wesley thought to himself, *considering I keep company with a ghost.*

Brown's hair was twisted into dark, shiny dreadlocks, and the tint of his complexion left Cort Wesley thinking he was of mixed race.

"Tell me, Cholo, what would your friends and associates think if they knew you were selling drugs to kids?"

The man's eyes narrowed, the muscles in his neck tensing. "You must have me mistaken for somebody else. Be a good idea to get yourself gone before damage gets done you won't be able to undo."

"That's quite a mouthful. You practice saying it in front of a mirror?"

Cort Wesley watched Cholo smirk toward his henchmen. *"Dios mio, que olor a culo hay ahi afuera."*

"The only thing that smells like ass here is you, Cholo. That's what cowards smell like, and only cowards sell drugs to kids."

Cholo looked like he wanted to stand up, but he stopped short of doing so. *"Cree ud que soy una cobarde?"*

"I don't think you're a coward. I *know* you are."

Cholo Brown kicked his work boots up onto the table and interlaced his hands behind his head. "I'm gonna give you one last chance to run away. Then I'm gonna snap my fingers and have you driven out of here in the trunk of a lowrider."

"Do it," Cort Wesley told him, feeling the blood boiling inside him.

"What?"

"Snap your fingers."

"You're a strange kind of crazy, brah."

"What happened to snapping your fingers, Cholo?"

Brown stretched a hand from the back of his head and creased a finger and thumb together. The resulting snap sounded more like a crack to Cort Wesley. He studied the man he was hovering over, Cholo's eyes telling him everything he needed to know for starters. His hearing and the shadows flitting at the edge of his vision picked things up from there.

Before Cort Wesley could record the motion, he'd picked up a metal chair one of Brown's lackeys had just vacated and slammed it across the face of a beefy, onrushing thug. The metal dented, literally dented, on impact, leaving Cort Wesley to wonder if any of the man's nose was left recognizable.

The next guy coming had a pistol out, and Cort Wesley flung the dented chair through the air at him. It spun like a Frisbee and clipped him hard enough to take his feet clean out from under him.

In that moment, the two guys sharing the table with Cholo Brown launched themselves at Cort Wesley from opposite angles, close enough to each other for him to slam both with the upturned table he'd hoisted off the sidewalk, before tossing it through the bodega window at a man steadying a shotgun. The shattered glass flying inward stunned the man enough to lose the trigger, and by the time he found it again, Cort Wesley was already through the jagged hole, grabbing hold of the thug by the lapels and tossing him out through what remained of the pane.

He followed in the thug's wake and had his pistol palmed in the next moment, steadying it on a final trio of thugs coming fast from around the corner, big fancy guns held absurdly to the side in the best gangbanger tradition.

Cort Wesley fired off ten shots in rapid succession, the bullets impacting low by their feet to kick up a storm of concrete shards that stung like needles on impact. Two of them managed to get off feeble, poorly aimed shots before turning and hightailing it from the area, freeing Cort Wesley to lurch back toward Cholo Brown's table.

He had his own hand cannon tilting for Cort Wesley in that moment, his eyes bled of the bravado he was desperately trying to recapture.

"Make the call, white boy."

And Cort Wesley did, by kicking Brown's chair out to send him tumbling. Cholo got off a single wild shot, pistol still clutched in his grasp when Cort Wesley planted a boot over his neck.

"Drop the gun or I'll crush your throat."

Cholo Brown tossed his hand cannon aside.

"Now, we're going to have a little talk, you and me, about you pushing drugs, opiates especially, at the Village School."

"What's it to you, man?" Brown rasped.

"My son's a student there," Cort Wesley said flatly. "He OD'd on your drugs and almost died."

"I got nothing to do with that!"

Cort Wesley pressed his boot down more firmly. "You want to rethink your answer?"

Brown's eyes watered, filling with hate. He was breathing in short, rapid heaves that made Cort Wesley wonder if he was about to pass out.

"You some kind of tough guy, a real badass? You try cleaning house in these parts, it'll be your own clock ends up getting cleaned."

"Where'd you get the pills that almost killed my son?"

Fear replaced anger on Brown's expression. The dreadlocks had been tossed back from his face, revealing a receding hairline.

"I tell you that, we're both dead men."

"A chance I'm willing to take."

"I don't shit where I live, puta."

"Give me a name, Cholo. If he's mobbed up, chances are I know him."

Sirens wailed in the narrowing distance, Brown not looking relieved by the sound. "Mob? What, were you born yesterday or something?"

Cort Wesley pressed his heel down a little harder. "A name, Cholo."

"Don't have a name for you. Just an address. Knock yourself out, puta. Just make sure you got your affairs in order first."

32

San Antonio, Texas

For Yarek Bone, looking the part made for the best disguise of all. With his target technically being held at University Hospital by Homeland Security, he knew the protective forces he'd be facing would be made up of national guardsmen drawn from a rapid response team formulated as part of an emergency action plan. Troops not used to working with each other and comfortable carrying weapons but not much more. He doubted all but a very few of them had ever seen real combat—not a requirement to manage this particular protective vigil.

Bone dressed in the proper regalia, wondering how long it would take him to kill the entire team assigned to the hospital. More than five minutes for sure. The irony of that location, the fact that people came here to be treated for the kind of pain he couldn't feel, wasn't lost on him.

He figured there'd be at least a half dozen of them on site, the first two of whom cast him nothing more than nods as he passed through the main entrance, their M16s held in the same fashion. So Homeland couldn't even provide their men with the updated M4 model, figuring the antiquated M16s to be more than adequate for this particular mission.

Bone knew he'd have to show some ID as he drew closer to the isolation ward where his target was being held. Dealing with them would be no harder than peeling off a self-stick postage stamp.

No call for subtlety here, this assignment being the murderous equivalent of a smash-and-grab robbery. Yarek Bone didn't care why the lone survivor of Camino Pass needed to die, just wondered how many more lives he'd have to take before getting to him.

33

SAN ANTONIO, TEXAS

"What are we missing here?" Caitlin asked Doc Whatley from across the University Hospital cafeteria table.

"Icing," the Bexar County medical examiner said, looking up from his danish sprinkled with nuts and what look liked cinnamon drizzle on top. "You know, like the kind they sell at La Panadería."

"That place serves the best baked goods in the city, Doc, but the lines are ridiculous."

"Depends when you shop, Ranger."

Caitlin watched him cut another slice of his danish with a knife and fork. "So why's Lennox Scully still alive?"

"I'm working off the theory that the cyanide had a limited dispersal range. And sometimes what something *isn't* provides a clearer notion as to what it *is*."

"You've lost me, Doc."

"Well now, that's a first, isn't it?"

"Sounds like you're gloating."

"I've been stuck here for two straight days now and this is my sixth danish. It feels good to do something besides eat."

"So tell me what it is you're gloating about."

"How is a typical bio attack waged?"

"Airburst," Caitlin said, recalling a rudimentary lesson she'd learned at the FBI's Quantico training facility. "That maximizes spread, potency, and overall saturation effectiveness."

"Thanks to Lennox Scully, then, Ranger, we can rule out airburst. Because if this toxin was dispersed that way, he'd be dead and gone with the rest of the town."

"So he's in a room upstairs instead. The question being, what made him different from everybody else, Doc?"

"Well, for starters, the vast majorty of the town's population died in their sleep."

"Scully claims he was asleep, too."

"Passed out drunk, to be precise, Ranger."

"You think the distinction is important?"

Whatley shrugged, seeming to have forgotten his danish. "Being passed out as opposed to asleep means different blood levels, different breathing cycles, pulse ox levels, heart rate, potential arrhythmia . . . You want me to go on?"

"No, you made your point. Scully said he was sleeping it off inside a converted supply closet."

"I'm aware of that."

"So what makes a supply closet different from the kind of bedroom where almost all the residents of Camino Pass died, Doc?"

Whatley shrugged again, suddenly looking very old. "No windows would be the first thing that comes to mind."

"You pin that as important?"

"You asked me what comes to mind, Ranger, not what's important."

"Scully's alive while almost three hundred other folks are dead. We find out why that is, we're that much closer to figuring out how it was cyanide gas wiped a town clean off the map."

Whatley pushed his chair back, looking like he wanted to be some-place else. "Please tell me you're not suggesting this was some kind of experiment, attack, or both."

"Old friend of ours is thinking along those terms."

"Jones?" Whatley wondered, as if it hurt to say the name.

"None other."

"I thought he was out of the picture."

"Nope, just slightly out of frame. He picked up a scent that brought him out of the woodwork."

"Like an old bird dog," Whatley said, shaking his head. "Just can't let go of the hunt."

"Jones wants back in with Homeland. He sees this as his ticket."

Whatley went back to his danish. "I swear that man won't be happy until the rest of the world is as miserable as he is."

Caitlin rose from her chair. "Think I'll head back upstairs to have another talk with Lennox Scully."

34

San Antonio, Texas

Caitlin knew something was wrong as soon as she found the guards missing at the security checkpoint set up before the entrance to DHS's isolation ward. There had been two on duty here yesterday and there was no obvious explanation for why they wouldn't be on duty today as well.

She had memorized the four-digit key code that had allowed her access on the day before, but she saw the red light flashing and then noticed that the windowless double doors were cracked open. She eased her way through them, hand on the butt of her holstered SIG Sauer, which she promptly drew at what she saw next: the bodies of four of the national guardsmen attached to the Homeland Security team, the two she'd just noted were missing to go along with two more who'd been posted here. All shot in the head at close range, by the look of things.

A pro, then. Somebody who enjoyed a knowledge and particular willingness when it came to killing. A stone killer, in other words.

Caitlin yanked the glass off a fire alarm–like station, depressed the red button until she heard a click, and a high-pitched wail began to shriek. With that sound pounding her eardrums, she charged through the next set of doors and headed on toward the isolation ward.

The entire medical team, two men and a woman, was dead, their bodies splayed in the laboratory outside the ward where Lennox Scully was the only patient. Scully lay half on, half off the hospital bed, beyond the thick wall of glass. Caitlin imagined his screams going unheard as someone pumped what appeared to be four bullets into him, the blood both soaking the sheets and widening into pools on the floor.

She could still smell cordite in the air, indicating this had all gone down just minutes before. Likely not enough time for the killer to flee University Hospital before the sounding of the alarm led to the hospital being sealed. No one allowed in or out.

And that meant she had a chance to catch up with whoever had done this.

Yarek Bone took the stairs to the basement level, where the hospital morgue was located, then used a separate stairwell to reach the sub-basement, in keeping with his planned escape route. That subbasement housed the works and controls of the hospital's heating, cooling, filtration, and ventilation systems, in huge steel cases, producing sounds from a soft rumble to a deafening roar.

Bone had never served in the actual army, had cut his teeth instead as part of a Native American resistance group called Fallen Timbers. The group took its name from the battlefield where, in 1794, General Anthony Wayne had defeated confederated Indian tribes under the leadership of the famed Chief Tecumseh. The battle became more or less typical of that era and in more modern times had given way to such causes as the American Indian Movement, which was responsible for the occupation of Alcatraz Island in the early 1970s and the 1973 Wounded Knee incident at the Pine Ridge Indian Reservation in South Dakota.

Fallen Timbers had manifested as a more radical offshoot of the American Indian Movement, made up of Natives like Bone, committed to seeking economic justice for their people, who were often being ripped off by unscrupulous energy companies. Those companies were adept at stealing mineral rights for Native American lands, then laying pipelines and constructing fracking operations with little or no compensation to any number of tribes. Fallen Timbers dedicated itself to fighting in court and, when that failed, beyond.

Yarek Bone specialized in the beyond.

The group neither received nor sought publicity or attention. They preferred flying under the radar, where men like Bone could do their murderous work unencumbered by media. And when work dried up on that end, he had made himself available on a paying basis, along with his like-minded associates, who saw nothing wrong in using their skills to turn a profit.

For his part, Bone sent most of the money he made back to the Comanche Nation in Lawton, Oklahoma, not needing to be paid much to do what he loved to do the most. Roland Fass had proven to be his most lucrative, and frequent, employer yet. No shortage of work corresponding to the cause that had led to the death of all but one of the residents of Camino Pass, who had now joined his neighbors in the great beyond.

The sudden wailing of a shrill alarm through the hospital told him his work had been discovered. He picked up his already rapid pace down the stairs, emerging in the building's mechanical subbasement, just as he heard an elevator chime nearby.

Caitlin surged from the car, SIG held with one hand bracing the other. The elevator in University Hospital's isolation ward constructed by Homeland accessed this level directly, the only level the killer could escape through once the security alarm had been triggered. She couldn't be sure, of course, but she knew well enough to trust her instincts, which had brought her down here like a dog picking up the scent of the man who'd left eight bodies in his wake upstairs.

The mechanical subbasement was neither as cluttered nor as noisy as older versions with which she was more familiar. Gone was the hissing and rattling of pipes, the clanking of exhaust baffles dumping out heat sucked from the vents. Instead, white PVC piping ran in labyrinthine fashion up the walls and along the ceiling, pulsing with life and dripping moisture onto the shiny finished flooring. Huge machines Caitlin took for heat pumps and air exchangers colored royal blue climbed the walls, humming softly and then rumbling slightly louder when kicked up into the next gear. Exhaust fans with huge metal blades spun at various intervals to prevent the air from stagnating or superheating, and space-age turbines hummed, routing power through the complex.

Caitlin slid along the darkest path she could find, off center of the walkway that sliced down the center of the subbasement and past various heavy fire-retardant security doors that housed the hospital's various HVAC controls. It might not have been as voluminous down here as she'd expected, but there was still more than enough noise emanating from the slew of machines to drown out any footsteps that might have clacked ahead of her.

She kept peering forward, figuring the man who'd killed eight people upstairs with the ease of doing his laundry was ahead of her, when shots echoed to her rear, puncturing the PVC piping overhead and pouring steam everywhere.

Yarek Bone couldn't say how he knew it was the Texas Ranger, the same one from the photos lifted from video footage captured by a drone over Camino Pass. He'd spotted her as soon as he'd watched that footage, knowing a gunfighter when he saw one, even through an orange hazmat suit. Maybe it was something in the blood, the generations of battles fought by his ancestors against hers.

Her...

The legends of female Comanche warriors notwithstanding, Bone had trouble reconciling that this Texas Ranger was a woman. He wondered if his initial shots had been steered awry by his subconscious, the fact that in his long history of killing he'd never shot a woman before today, just a few minutes earlier, upstairs. Strangled or stabbed more than his share, yes, because he respected women enough to believe they should be killed up close, not with the impersonal distance wrought by bullets.

This Texas Ranger, this woman, deserved that much, too, Bone deemed, before her bullets punctured plastic steam pipes all around him, forcing him out into the open, amid their crisscrossing spray.

To find the Ranger standing before him.

The figure looked ephemeral in the steam, more phantom than man. Caitlin emptied the last of her SIG Sauer's magazine toward his massive shape and, amid the pistol's slight kick, registered that he was a Native American. He gave the impression of floating before he dropped out of sight and fired a dozen shots her way, rapidly enough to make it seem as if he were firing on full auto.

Caitlin had hit the floor by then, rolling across the smooth surface as she tried to track him through the gushing steam. Fresh magazine jammed home, she was ready to open fire as soon as he came into view again. She just needed to right her position to better steady her aim.

But her left boot had lodged in the gap between the housing of one of the big turbines and the floor. That left her squarely exposed, like a target on a shooting range.

Caitlin thought she glimpsed the huge figure rushing her, then wasn't so sure. His shape was there, and then it wasn't, reappearing somewhere else with a swiftness of motion that defied reason. It was almost like this man could will himself someplace else, action and thought one and the same. He was closing on her snared, still form, there until he wasn't, while drawing near enough to make his next shots count for sure.

Caitlin fought to pull her foot from her jammed boot, to no avail. She needed to find a way to neutralize the big man, at least flush him out amid the steam that was providing her only cover for the time being.

She could feel his presence, knew he was close and taking his time in full awareness that she had fourteen fresh bullets. A shadow danced amid the steam, silhouetted by it briefly. Gone as quickly as it had appeared, only to reappear closer to her. He was baiting her to aim erroneously, at which point he'd stage his attack.

So she fired. Erroneously. On purpose. SIG barrel tilted upward, toward the traffic jam of iron piping that formed the base of a network of ductwork running all the way through the building.

Twelve shots, the resulting muzzle flashes carving through the mist, just as her nine-millimeter shells cut through the piping and sent a torrent of steaming oil lubricant spraying downward.

Yarek Bone felt something hot coating him, as if he'd stepped into a scalding shower. It wasn't pain, of course, more like the sensation of his skin being superheated. For a brief moment, he actually thought it was starting to hurt, that he was about to understand what pain was for the first time.

Thanks to this woman, this Texas Ranger . . .

He could feel his skin already blistering as he clawed the oil free of his face with his hands, the palms puckering from the thick fluid right before his eyes. Bone had been shot twice and stabbed a whole bunch of times. Once he strangled a man to death while the victim kept jabbing a blade into him again and again. Bone still wore the scars across his stomach.

But this was different; this he could feel—actually *feel.* Not quite pain, but a sensation that stopped just short of that, even as the heat coating him started to feel like somebody had turned up the oven.

Caitlin glimpsed the shadowy shape freeze briefly, then jerk about in the manner of some crazed dance. She heard grunts, gasps, groans as she pictured the oil soaking the Native American's National Guard disguise. A retching sound followed, evidence that at least some of the oil had made it into his mouth.

If only I had a match . . .

She wondered what D. W. Tepper might make of her wishing for the first time that she was a smoker. Caitlin thought she caught two glowing eyes glaring at her from behind a dark mask of dripping oil, and she fired off her final two shots.

As the mist began to dissipate, though, she could see no fallen body. The big man had vanished with the steam, leaving in his wake a black, viscous trail of footprints through the hospital's subbasement.

Part Four

WILLIAM "BIGFOOT" WALLACE

The 19-year-old Wallace (whose more-than-six-feet, 240-pound stature earned him the nickname "Bigfoot") was at home in Lexington, Kentucky, in 1836 when he learned that his brother had been killed by the Mexican Army in the massacre at Goliad. He headed to Texas looking for payback, but the war was over by the time he arrived. Wallace decided to stay on in the new Texas Republic, and eventually moved to San Antonio. After joining the Texan Army to repulse a Mexican invasion in 1842, he was captured and spent two years in a notoriously brutal prison at Vera Cruz. Upon his return to Texas, Wallace joined the Rangers, and would serve under Captain Jack Hays; in the 1850s, he led a Ranger company of his own. An opponent of secession, Wallace stayed in Texas during the Civil War, continuing his defense of the frontier against attacks by Comanches, Union soldiers and deserters. In his later years (he died in 1899), Wallace regaled friends and neighbors in South Texas with tales of his wild frontier life, earning a reputation as a Texan folk hero.

—Sarah Pruitt, "8 Famous Texas Rangers," History.com

35

Washington, DC

Senator Lee Eckles held the microphone stand down to make sure that it didn't rattle as he spoke.

"You can see why I insisted we hold this hearing in closed session, I believe. I'd like to open things up with some general questions I invite any or all of you to answer. Since this is a closed session, you should speak freely, with the assurance no transcript will be made available to the press and entered into the Congressional Record only under seal. I will now continue with my opening statement but reserve the right to pose questions amidst my words. Any of you have a question you'd like to pose or concern you'd like to raise before we go on the record?"

The men sat rigidly at the table, mirror images of one another, down to their matching dark suits.

"Very well then," the senator resumed.

He was a bull of a man with a squarish head topped by gray-black stubble that was just starting to grow out. The back of his neck was perpetually red, as if someone had spilled paint on it, and his neck was thick, fleshy, and lined with a wrinkled depression down the middle that started just under his chin. His eyes were too small for his face, set way back in his head as if God had inserted them as an afterthought. They were so small that they seemed to be bled of white, dominated by the dark pupils that looked black even from close up.

"America is in the middle of an epidemic like none it has ever seen before," Eckles began. "The opioid crisis knows no bounds. It is affecting individuals and families in every congressional district. Its consequences, ranging from personal health to the economy, are devastating. Tragically, more than eighty thousand Americans died from drug overdoses in 2018. This year, more than two million Americans will suffer from addiction to prescription or illicit opioids. I'm going to repeat that to make sure you gentlemen heard me clearly. Two million."

Eckles stopped and ran his eyes from one CEO to another, the five men representing the five largest pharmaceutical companies in the world, all of which counted prescription narcotics as crucial to their bottom lines.

"Mr. Oswell, are you aware how many opioid prescriptions were written in 2012, for some historical context?"

"I am not, Senator," said the man at the end of the line on the right.

"The answer is more than two hundred and fifty-five million, or just over eighty-one scrips for every hundred people in the United States. Does that seem excessive to you?"

Oswell leaned in closer to his microphone. "That is a matter for the patient and his or her doctor."

"I see," Eckles said, turning to the man seated to Oswell's left. "Mr. Barthwell, are you aware that in 2007 Purdue Pharma pleaded guilty in federal court in Virginia to misleading doctors and patients about OxyContin's safety and paid a record six-million-dollar fine in penalties?"

"I am, sir."

"Then are you also aware, for the record, that between 1995 and 2015 the same company made thirty-five billion dollars from OxyContin sales alone?"

Barthwell leaned forward again, his motions as casual as his words. "I am not."

"Let's move on to Mr. Jenks, then," the senator said, continuing down the line to the thin man in the center. "Are you aware of the law passed several years ago entitled the Ensuring Patient Access and Effective Drug Enforcement Act?"

"I testified in open hearings in support of it," Jenks said smugly.

"Of course you did, since it required the DEA to warn anyone involved in the drug industry, in virtually any capacity, if they are in breach of any regulations, in order that they are given a chance to comply before their licenses are withdrawn."

"I believe that's the case, yes, Senator."

"Do you also believe, as many of us do, that what this bill really did was take away the DEA's ability to go after a pharmacist, wholesaler, manufacturer, or distributor they suspect of wrongdoing?"

"That is not my understanding," Jenks said.

"Let's move on, shall we?" Eckles asked rhetorically, focusing his gaze on the fourth man in the row, who kept dabbing at his nose with a handkerchief. "Mr. Flood, I'm going to quote some statistics. Please stop me if you find yourself in disagreement with any of them. Let's start with the fact that there are two point five million Americans suffering from substance abuse disorders related to prescription opioid pain relievers. . . . No argument, Mr. Flood? How about that over the past three years, deaths by synthetic opioids increased by over five hundred percent, from three thousand to twenty thousand. . . . No argument again, Mr. Flood? Let's try the fact that each day, nearly two hundred Americans die from opioid overdose. . . . Nothing? Okay, how about the fact that, in the past decade, your five companies combined have spent nine hundred million dollars on lobbying efforts. Putting that in context, it's eight times the amount spent by the gun lobby."

Eckles waited for Flood to mount an argument, then moved on to the final CEO when he didn't.

"Your company produces a version of the overdose-reversal drug Narcan, called Remeo, is that correct, Mr. DePrete?"

"It is, Senator."

"And it is also true that two years ago your company sold two dosages of Remeo for five hundred dollars but today that price now approaches five thousand?"

"I don't have the records in front of me," DePrete said into his microphone.

"Then it's a good thing I do," Eckles followed, flapping a ream of pages in the air before him. "Let's proceed, shall we?"

36

Washington, DC

His fellow committee members gave Lee Eckles a standing ovation when he entered the hotel suite where they'd gathered at the hearing's conclusion. Eckles smiled, trying to appear humble though inwardly relishing their praise and, in conjunction, the power he held over them. That power was furthered by a performance earlier in the day that had served only to enhance his credibility on the subject.

Indeed, the fact that Washington's top drug crusader was the mastermind behind a multibillion-dollar scheme to flood the country's streets with all manner of opiates was known only to a select few, none of whom were present in this room, which meant that Eckles would have to maintain his guise.

"Thank you," Eckles said, still in humble mode but genuinely meaning it. "Thank you."

Their laudatory comments went in one ear and out the other. Eckles's attention focused instead on a man standing by himself off in the suite's darkest recesses. After exchanging sufficient pleasantries and accepting back slaps to go with all the praise, he made his way over to Roland Fass, pretending to greet him warmly like an old friend.

"You want to explain why I'm looking at you up close and personal?" Eckles asked sharply, his back to the room so no one would see the anger stretched across his features. "What part of 'We are never to meet in person' don't you understand?"

"I don't trust the phones, especially anything with a two oh two area code."

"Can't say I blame you there, but this is a serious breach of protocol. Need I remind you what the people we're both on the hook to might make of it?"

"I don't know, tell them we're lovers or something."

"That wouldn't bother them a lick, but if they found out about this, us meeting in person, we'd both be looking to change our identities tomorrow."

"Couldn't be any worse than today."

"This about Texas? Mission accomplished, I thought."

"The survivor from Camino Pass is out of the picture, if that's what you mean."

"What else would I mean?"

"Our man had it out with a Texas Ranger."

"That's bad."

"It gets worse, Senator. The Ranger's still alive."

"How is that possible?"

"You tell me."

"I've lived in Texas my whole life and never met a single Ranger."

"And you don't want to meet this one. That's why I'm here. To tell you we need to do something about her and we need to do it fast."

"Did you say *her*?"

"The name Caitlin Strong doesn't ring any bells?" Fass asked him.

Eckles nodded his head. "I'm the senior senator from the state of Texas, son. So, yes, that name rings a whole bunch of bells, like the church ones that ought to be playing at her funeral after she went up against this hired gun of yours. Maybe he's not as good as advertised."

"He killed eight people before he ran into her."

"So you're telling me it's Caitlin Strong who's investigating Camino Pass."

Fass nodded. "As part of some Homeland Security detail."

Eckles was about to respond, but then he greeted with a wide grin and a celebratory slap on the back an overweight man with shiny skin who was passing by.

"We ate their lunch," he said, the grin holding, "and left the fork stuck in their mouth."

The overweight man sauntered off to freshen his drink, leaving the corner all to Eckles and Fass again.

"Now, what is it you crashed the party to tell me?" Eckles said.

"The cause of death in Camino Pass was exposure to hydrogen cyanide."

"The stuff they used in the old gas chamber?"

"The very same."

Eckles could see something squirrelly lurking behind Fass's eyes. "You didn't need to come all this way to tell me that."

"No, I didn't. After Camino Pass, we did a detailed check of the inventory for contamination. Turns out we've got a problem."

"How deep we talking, Fass?"

"If you don't mind killing a whole lot of people, not deep at all."

Eckles found himself intrigued by what he was hearing, overcoming whatever anger he felt over Fass's presence in the room. "Tell me more."

37

SHAVANO PARK, TEXAS

Caitlin was almost to Cort Wesley's house when her phone rang.

"Perfect timing," she said, figuring it was him calling now.

She'd spent the last six hours at University Hospital, interviewing witnesses and being interviewed herself as FBI and Homeland Security officials tried to make sense of the murder of three medical personnel and four national guardsmen, along with the subject responsible for their presence. Caitlin labored through the first few hours just trying to convince them it was the work of a single man, going through another ten milligrams of Vicodin to take the edge off the pounding in her head, which had returned in all of its original intensity in the ordeal's wake.

"No one man could do this," a procession of investigators insisted, one after the other. "It's not possible."

"It is in my world. Business as usual."

"I'd listen to her if I were you," D. W. Tepper's voice chimed in as he strode onto the scene. "You have now experienced the winds of Hurricane Caitlin firsthand."

Without asking for permission, Tepper brought Caitlin with him into an empty room and closed the door behind them.

"Heard all the initial reporting, Ranger. If I didn't know better, I'd say you were describing your friend Paz."

"Except he was Native American."

Tepper rolled his eyes. "So on top of everything else, you've mastered time travel. Revisiting old Ranger battles."

"This guy didn't come from the past, Captain. But you can bet whoever sent him had something to do with those near three hundred victims in Camino Pass."

"Man you're describing has to be in somebody's database."

"Paz isn't," Caitlin reminded.

"I'm sorry, Caitlin," Dylan's voice, instead of Cort Wesley's, began in her ear. "I couldn't stop her."

"You want to tell me what you're talking about?"

"I thought I had, but when I woke up there was a note on the other pillow that read 'Family is everything.'"

"Got a feeling I know who wrote it," Caitlin said, pulling into the driveway to find Nola Delgado seated on the front porch.

She was drinking one of Cort Wesley's craft beers, rocking the swing casually as she sipped from a can of Freetail Brewing Company's Original American Amber Ale.

"Come on, sis, take a seat."

"I'll stand, if you don't mind."

"Hey, suit yourself. At least get yourself a beer or something."

"I'm fine."

"I heard you could've used my help earlier today. Is it true the guy was an Indian?"

"Native American," Caitlin corrected.

"We still call them Indians down in Mexico."

"You're in Texas right now, Nola."

Just a few months ago, Caitlin hadn't even known she had a half sister, the product of a brief affair between her father, Jim Strong, and the infamous Mexican crime boss Luna Diaz Delgado, aka the Red Widow. They'd fought on the same side against forces both her mother and Caitlin's father had battled before in what became known as the second Battle of the Alamo. Caitlin had known a lot of people in her time, true gunfighters to the core, like Guillermo Paz and Cort Wesley, who were good at killing, but she'd never met anyone who enjoyed it as much as Nola Delgado.

Nola smelled of something sweet and soft, jasmine or sandalwood. Her complexion was dark, though a few shades lighter than her mother's, neither of whom saw the need to wear makeup, just like Caitlin. Nola was wearing black leather leggings tucked into scuffed black boots, her shirt tight enough to show off her muscular arms and shoulders. Caitlin pictured her spending lots of time in the gym, very much the equal of men who grunted and groaned their way through heavy lifting routines. She imagined the men staring at her across the mirrored room, while Nola paid them no attention whatsoever, secure in the notion she could wipe the floor with every single one of them without breaking a sweat.

Nola looked across the porch to where Caitlin was standing against the railing, seeming to read her mind. "Hey, sis, you know what I was thinking before you got here? Which of us has killed more men."

"I don't keep count."

"Me neither. And notches in the gun belt always seemed a bit tacky."

"What do you want, Nola?"

"Is that any way to talk to family?"

"I'll let you know if any shows up."

Nola hesitated, eyes continuously sizing Caitlin up from one second to the next. "Dylan told me what happened to his brother."

"Is that why you're here?" Caitlin asked her, figuring Cort Wesley must have finally spoken to Dylan about Luke.

"Maybe I just want to help."

"Maybe it was your mother's drugs that almost killed him."

"He OD'd on opioids. We're not into that."

"That's comforting to know."

"Tell me about the gunman in the hospital."

"Why?"

"Because maybe our paths have crossed."

"On the same or different sides?"

"Could be both, sis. Did you really shower him in oil by shooting out the overhead pipes?"

"Your mother tell you that?"

"She does have her sources and, it turns out, she's taken a particular interest in you."

"Why's that?"

"Because you saved her life. In my mother's code, that makes her responsible for yours now. Might say you've got another guardian angel, one with an army at her command."

"And a daughter she can't control."

Nola drained the rest of her beer and winked. "Guess it runs in the family, doesn't it?"

"You promised you'd stay away from Dylan, Nola. You remember that?"

"I remember nodding when you asked me to. Why don't we just say I changed my mind?"

"You came all this way to tell me that?"

"Along with a story your father once shared with my mother. Something I thought you might want to hear."

"What makes you think that?"

"Because it involves your great-grandfather, what he and Pancho Villa found after they partnered up . . ."

38

Mexico; 1898

"Is this really necessary, Ranger?" Pancho Villa asked William Ray Strong, as the Ranger clamped his leg irons in place.

"It's for your own good, amigo," William Ray said, going to work on his wrists.

"I don't understand."

"The less you're tempted to run off, the more chance there is I won't have to kill you."

The wrist cuffs clacked into place.

"After today, I thought I'd gained your trust."

"You have, amigo. That's why I didn't chain you to a tree."

William Ray Strong and Pancho Villa made camp in the foothills beyond Sal Si Puede, the town's lights flickering and fading as the night wore on. The descent of darkness made continuing on a fool's errand, given where the bandits told them they could find los Chinos that those same bandits insisted were behind both the murder of the posse from Camino Pass and the kidnappings that had preceded it. The Las Bajadas country beyond this stretch of rolling hills was as lawless as it got, populated by Mexican cutthroats and criminals, along with, occasionally, the American outlaws who rode with them. William Ray had heard it said that Mexicans and Americans got along better in Las Bajadas than anywhere else, given that they shared an indelible bond forged in blood and crime.

"What do you make of your friends telling us it's Chinese we're after?" the Ranger said, after getting a fire going.

"They're not my friends," Villa told him. "Take these irons off my wrists and I'll tell you."

"Those irons are staying where they're at whether you tell me or not, amigo."

"I don't know a lot about los Chinos, anyway. They came to my country in the 1870s as part of the same flood of Chinese immigrants who built your railroads. They found other work south of the border and have grown into a community that's spread from their original settlements in Sinaloa mostly to the cities that dot my country's northwest border. Today the majority of them are bilingual in Spanish and Mandarin and have Mexican Christian names."

"A fine tale," William Ray nodded, "but last time I checked we weren't anywhere near Sinaloa or your northwest border. And I've never heard, not even once, of Chinese gunmen stealing kids and gunning down Americans."

"No, because you've pretty much enslaved them."

"Last time I checked, they signed up to build the railroads. Nobody forced them to do a goddamn thing."

"What other work could they have done?"

"Can't say I've given the matter much thought."

"If you had, you'd realize your country's traditions of slavery didn't end with your Civil War."

"And that's why you figure they stole kids and shot a posse clean off their horses?"

"That's not what I said."

"What did you say?"

"You're conflating two different things, Ranger."

William Ray worked some more wood into the fire. "*Conflating?* Maybe I was wrong about how good your English is, amigo."

The Ranger watched Villa studying his every move.

"Am I conflating something else, amigo?"

"That's a pretty big fire you're building."

"It's a pretty cold night in these parts. Never liked the desert, either here or back north of the border. Weather can never make up its mind what it wants to do. I can handle heat, I can handle cold, but getting both thrown at you so quick twists me into knots."

Villa continued staring into the fire, its glow shining off his smooth complexion, reminding William Ray that he was still a kid. Hell, the Ranger couldn't even tell if he'd started shaving yet or not, given that wispy mustache he was trying to grow.

"Get some sleep, amigo," he advised Villa. "We're up at dawn."

It was actually an hour or so before sunrise that the sounds of Colts being cocked and shells racked into the chambers of both Winchesters and pump action shotguns woke both men up. William Ray Strong's eyes opened to the sight of the fat man from the cantina grinning down at him with a long-barreled pistol angled on his face.

"For a Texas Ranger, you're awfully stupid."

"Everybody makes mistakes . . . Jesus. It is Jesus, isn't it, as in Jesus Arriaga?"

The fat man's mouth dropped, a black hole opening amid his beard. "Maybe you're smarter than I thought . . ."

"Of course, you're better known as Chucho el Roto, 'Chucho' for short. The subject of all kinds of books and magazine articles. You're even a folk hero in some circles, given the legend says you shared the spoils of your crimes with the poor and downtrodden. Problem being that both Jesus Arriaga and Chucho el Roto supposedly died in 1885. So tell me, am I looking at a ghost?"

Jesus Arriaga held his pistol in place, in direct line with the Ranger's eyes. "Too many books, too many articles, and you didn't even make mention of the stage plays. You know, I actually played myself once. People criticized me because they didn't think I looked the part," Arriaga said, grinning and slapping his considerable stomach. "Of course, I was thinner back in my folk hero days."

"Since when do folk heroes steal children from their families to enslave?"

William Ray could see Arriaga stiffen, a glint of fear flashing in his eyes. "That wasn't me, el Rinche," he spat hatefully.

"Then who was it? I'd love to meet him."

"That's good, because he wants to meet you too. Said he's never killed a Texas Ranger."

Arriaga's men unlatched the chains from Pancho Villa and fastened them around William Ray's wrists instead.

"You're free to go, muchacho," Arriaga said to Villa.

Villa held his gaze on the Ranger. "If it's all the same to you, I'd like to see this through. Nowhere else I need to be right now."

"Suit yourself."

Villa positioned himself to ride alongside William Ray Strong through the foothills leading up into the higher peaks and mesas that formed Las Bajadas.

"You want to tell me what you're up to?" the Ranger asked him.

"You trusted me back in Texas. I owe you this much, to do what I can to keep you alive."

"Seems to me that's a foregone conclusion."

"I'm going to make sure you don't run off. I know that's what you're thinking of doing, but it will get you killed."

"Appears I'm gonna get killed either way, then. So if you got something to say, just spit it out."

"It's better you see for yourself, Ranger. Besides, you never told me the truth of why you built that fire so high. You *wanted* Arriaga to find us. You wanted him to take you prisoner."

William Ray shrugged, not bothering to deny it. "I figured he'd take me to the man in charge."

"A man like that works for no one."

"Even los Chinos?"

Villa grinned. "You're a smart man for an American."

"Why don't you tell me what you left out of the story last night?"

"Tell *me*," Villa said, staring straight ahead as if the Ranger wasn't there at all, "what's it like needing the help of a Mexican?"

"I've helped plenty more of your people than I killed, amigo. I don't keep count of such things, but I'd wager I've killed more Indians and even Texans in my time than Mexicans."

"Any Chinese?"

"Not yet," William Ray told him. "But I believe that may all change today."

39

Shavano Park, Texas

"And did it?" Caitlin asked Nola Delgado.

"My memory's foggy on what happened next. Give me a few days to let my thoughts settle."

"You can fill me in from Mexico."

"I leave town and you'll never know. Want to know the funny thing? I'm the last blood relative you've got left in the world."

"Why's that funny?"

"Because I'm half Strong and got as much of your father inside me as you do."

"You're not worthy of sharing the name, Nola."

"Ouch, sis. Is that what I get for saving your life on a regular basis?"

Caitlin watched her rocking gently back and forth on the swing. Nola Delgado seemed to be ten seconds ahead of the rest of the world, knowing exactly how to respond to any moment because she already knew what was coming. That was the best way Caitlin could describe the cocksure swagger that defined her. She owned every situation in which she had a part. Caitlin figured that, more than anything, described the stone killer whose blood she shared.

"You need to stop using Dylan to get to me," she heard herself say, as if it were someone else's voice.

"You think that's what I'm doing?"

"Tell me I'm wrong."

"You're wrong. No, worse than wrong. Why is it you can't accept the fact that I like being around Dylan because he's Dylan? It might not have started out that way, but that's the way it is now."

"And I'm supposed to just accept that?" Caitlin asked, resisting the urge to stick her foot out to stop the swing from rocking.

"You need to talk to Dylan about these conflicted feelings of yours."

"My feelings about you aren't conflicted at all, Nola."

"I'm talking about your feelings for him, sis. In your mind he's still the fourteen-year-old kid whose life you saved after he witnessed his mother being gunned down. You don't want to face the fact that he doesn't need your protection anymore." She seemed finished, then resumed. "You're not his mother."

"And what's your mother think of the whole thing?"

"We haven't discussed it."

"Maybe I should have a talk with her."

"The two of you having so much in common and all."

"I think you're missing my point."

Nola stopped the swing on her own. "No, sis, you're missing mine. My mother managed to achieve everything she has while raising three children."

"While grooming one of her grandkids to take her place."

"Keeping it in the family; something you can't do because you don't have one. We all make our choices and then life makes us live with them. My mother with hers, you with yours, and me with mine. You want to think me following Dylan to school in Providence, Rhode Island, is all about you, go ahead."

"Really?" Caitlin said, feeling her heart starting to hammer against her chest, the heat building up inside her. "Then why leave him to come back to see me?"

"Maybe I figure you're going to need me again."

"Know something, Nola? You're starting to sound like—"

Caitlin broke off her thought, realizing something.

"He called you, didn't he? Guillermo Paz called you, and now here you are."

"He said he had one of his visions."

"With you as a part of it?"

"He didn't say, sis. I get the feeling it was more general in nature, real end-of-the-world type shit. You know, the world tearing itself apart, starting in Texas." Nola paused and tightened her gaze, seeming to look through Caitlin more than at her. "Looks like I almost got here too late. You want to tell me what it was like going up against that Indian, go tit for tit now that I've told you a story?"

"It's 'tit for tat,'" Caitlin corrected.

Nola teased her with a smile. "Sure. Whatever you say, sis. Just don't hate me because we're related, same blood pumping through our veins and all."

Caitlin nodded, her thoughts settling again. "You ever hear of Medusa, Nola?"

"The Gorgon from Greek mythology? The woman with snakes for hair whose look turns men hard as stone—and I'm not talking about their *penii* either."

"That's the one."

Nola grinned almost playfully again. "I guess I can see what you're getting at."

"No, you don't. Everyone considers Medusa a monster, but that's not entirely accurate. Many elements of the myth suggest her tragic nature. There's an epilogue to her story, telling of how Athena gave two drops of Medusa's blood to Asclepius, one of which has the power to cure while the other kills on contact."

"You think that describes me?"

"Go back to Mexico, Nola."

"You don't think it describes you just as much—no, even more? Maybe you're the one who turns men to stone, sis. That would explain why it took so long for you to find one."

"Beats robbing the cradle, Nola."

Caitlin's phone rang and she answered it, her eyes never leaving Nola Delgado, who had resumed rocking on the porch swing.

"You're not going to believe who I'm talking to, Captain," she answered, after glimpsing D. W. TEPPER on the caller ID.

"Nola Delgado?"

"Am I the only one left in the world who's not psychic?"

"I'm not reading the future, Ranger, just the security bulletins.

Camera flagged her coming into San Antonio airport. Anyway, I'm sorry to break up the party, but Cort Wesley Masters is in jail up in Houston. I've arranged for him to be released into your custody. How soon can you leave?"

40

HOUSTON

Cort Wesley sat in the corner of the holding cell, leaning his head against the cold concrete and doing his best to block out the stench of urine, which was battling with the vomit for supremacy. Reviewing the chain of events that had landed him in here.

A name, Cholo.

Don't have a name for you. Just an address. Knock yourself out, puta. Just make sure you got your affairs in order first.

Cort Wesley had gone straight to that address, his intention being to get the lay of the land before returning the following day with a plan in place and his emotions contained. What he found when he got to 7231 FM 1960 in the Houston suburb of Humble, though, changed all his intentions.

He checked three times to see that he had the right address, since he'd found himself in a strip mall of slab-style buildings colored an ugly turquoise shade. The office suite in question belonged to the Uptown Medical Clinic, a facility not unlike the ones he was more familiar with closer to home around Shavano Park. He'd gotten there just as the sun was setting and found the reception area packed with patients—literally, standing room only.

He checked the address yet again, searching his memory to make sure he'd entered the right street number into the app on his phone. This was the place, all right, he was sure of it.

After watching yet more patients arriving as others left, Cort Wesley decided to have a closer look. He angled his features downward to avoid any security cameras and found a seat in a darkened area of the lobby that afforded a clear view of the single door through which clinic patients both disappeared and emerged in a steady stream. Based on the building's size and patient traffic, he figured there were at least four exam rooms beyond that door, and as many as six. Probably two hundred patients crammed into the waiting area with him, most standing in what looked like lines you'd see for a bank teller, the place packed solid with bodies except in the back where he'd snared a seat.

The patients seemed to have virtually nothing of substance in common, other than that none of them appeared to be sick. They passed through the single door as soon as their number was called, many re-emerging either holding a prescription bottle in hand or tucking one into their pocket. That alone struck Cort Wesley as strange, given that so many prescriptions were phoned into pharmacies these days, not treated like take-out food by a walk-in clinic.

What struck him as stranger, though, was the presence of not one but two armed security guards, who had the look of men with more experience than typical rent-a-cops. They stood off to the side in respective corners, doing their best not to stand out, and, to that point, none of the clinic patients seemed to be paying them any heed at all.

He remained in his seat for an hour, the clinic traffic showing no signs of slowing. He had a sense of what he was witnessing here, but that didn't make it any easier to believe. He was doing a mental count and some rough multiplication to answer a single question: What if all the "patients" of this clinic left with a hefty supply of opioids tucked in their pocket, backpack, or handbag?

Cort Wesley figured he'd need a calculator or even a computer to come up with the right numbers. He continued running the math in his head, sitting there stewing as he considered the very real possibility that the drugs that had nearly killed his son had originated here, if the claims of Cholo Brown were true.

He read the clinic's hours backwards through the glass door and saw that they closed at ten o'clock. Shortly after that, he was one of the last people in the waiting room, and he chose that moment to approach the reception desk, which was tucked behind a sliding glass partition.

Drawing closer, Cort Wesley saw that it was thick enough to be bulletproof, complete with a thin gel layer between two matching panes of glass. He waited as patiently as he could manage for the woman wearing a lab coat to slide the glass partition open, his heart slamming against his rib cage nonetheless.

"How can I help you, sir?"

"I just realized I forgot my insurance card."

She started to reach for a clipboard preloaded with some kind of blank form. "Did you fill out our patient questionnaire yet?"

"Guy who referred me said that wouldn't be necessary. Patient of yours named Cholo Brown."

Cort Wesley had hoped mention of the name would get a rise out of the woman, perhaps because Cholo had called ahead to warn the clinic that Cort Wesley was coming. But she didn't so much as flicker an eyebrow at mention of the name, handing over the clipboard in casual fashion instead.

"Fill this out, sir, and I can get the number from your provider."

"It's ten o'clock, though."

"We stay open until the last patient is seen," the receptionist said, as one of the armed security guards threw back the locks and took up vigil, arms crossed, directly inside the glass door, to bar further "patients" from entering.

"That's good, because I'm in a lot of pain. Car accident."

"Just take a seat and fill out the form. You will be seen tonight before we close."

Cort Wesley pretended to check the boilerplate questions, quickly tiring of the whole charade. He wished he'd asked Colonel Paz to accompany him—not Caitlin, since she had a way of talking him out of the impulsive responses to which he was prone. And, as he stood in front of the glass partition the receptionist had neglected to close while waiting for the return of his form, he felt one of those responses coming on, as impossible to impede as a sneeze or cough. For Cort Wesley, violence had long been a natural bodily function. He figured he could thank his upbringing at the hands of his criminal father for instilling such a trait in him. It had served him well a few times, while getting him in a boatload of trouble, including a dishonorable discharge from the army, far more often.

"That won't be necessary," Cort Wesley said, returning the clipboard and its blank form to the receptionist. "I changed my mind."

The words sounded as if someone else was speaking them, as close as he'd ever come to what felt like an out-of-body experience.

The woman reached up to close the partition, regarding Cort Wesley again with a forced smile. "You can always come back tomorrow."

"I've got business here tonight, ma'am. Can you tell me who's in charge?"

"Tonight, that would be—"

"Not tonight; all the time. Who pays the bills? Who finds doctors willing to dispense pain meds to patients with no intention to use them to treat pain?"

In the glass, Cort Wesley could see the reflection of one guard approaching, the other falling into step behind him. Both men had their hands atop their holstered pistols, the way ex-cops might.

"I think a drug dealer named Cholo Brown got his hands on drugs prescribed in this place and sold them to students at the Village School. My son was one of those students. He almost died."

It took all his will, and a picture of Caitlin flashing in his head, to not react when the security guards brushed against his shoulders on either side.

"Sir, you're going to have to leave."

"But I haven't seen the doctor yet," he said, his eyes remaining locked on the receptionist, without moving an inch.

Cort Wesley could feel the hands closing on his elbows.

"Don't make us call the police, sir," the other guard said.

"Would you really do that?" he asked the receptionist, still paying the armed men no heed. "Would you call the police? I don't think so, given what you're up to in this place with the likes of Cholo Brown. Want to tell me how many of the pills dispensed here end up on the streets? I'm guessing some of the 'patients' I watched go through that door are shilling for him. Think he pays them more than you clear every week?"

The security guards started tugging him backwards, Cort Wesley making no effort to resist while keeping his gaze fixed forward.

"You know what," he said to the receptionist, "I think I will come back tomorrow."

41

HOUSTON

It had taken all the self-control he could muster to stop Cort Wesley from dropping the two security guards and feeding them their pistols. He saw himself doing it, frame by frame and blow by blow, as they led him toward the glass door and he watched their reflections growing in the glass.

As it was, just picturing himself putting them down provided enough of a calming influence to see him through the door without further incident, even when they shoved him hard off the curb. He pretended to stumble, letting perceived weakness be enough of a weapon to make the men, ex-cops for sure, pay him no further heed.

But he couldn't make himself leave the scene, unable to chase from his mind the phone call that had brought him to the hospital where Luke had been rushed by ambulance, recalling how close his son had come to meeting the Grim Reaper. Cort Wesley shared the bouts of acid reflux his father had suffered, another piece of unfortunate DNA, and right now he felt bile pushing up his throat while he eyeballed the now darkened Uptown Medical Clinic from the other side of the parking lot. He'd moved his truck there after driving out the exit while the two guards were watching, only to pull back in when they weren't.

He knew the smart and obvious thing to do was to leave, whether he came back tomorrow or sent more formal authorities in his stead. The mere thought of that, though, made him cringe. He continued to steam and seethe, boiling in his truck and refusing to cool himself with a blast from the air-conditioning, as if not wanting to disturb his discomfort. He could no more stop himself from climbing back out of his truck than he could stop himself from breathing.

Cort Wesley figured that, like many patient-centric facilities throughout storm-prone Houston, the Uptown Medical Clinic had installed a generator, and sure enough, he found a commercial model, manufactured by Kohler, at the rear of the building, connected up to the office suite in question.

Thanks to the robberies he'd done with his father, locked doors posed no impediment whatsoever. Security alarms were something else again, but given the response time in this part of town, he figured he'd have all the time he needed, even with it triggered.

He entered through the rear, which had the same antiseptic smell that had greeted him in the front. Since no bells and sirens began to shriek, Cort Wesley assumed it must have been a silent alarm, so he figured he had enough time to do what he was certain he'd probably regret later.

He found the interior feed line connecting the emergency supply of propane to the office's heating, cooling, and electrical systems. The system was rigged to automatically kick on in the event of a power failure, and locating the line was as simple as following its origins in the rear of the building through the walls. He found a trio of access hatches high up on the walls, which he reached by climbing on a chair. He popped those hatches and, one at a time, sliced the rubber tubing.

By the time Cort Wesley finished, the coarse stench of propane filled the clinic. His impulsiveness and commitment to finish what he started kept him from considering the damage that might be done to the adjoining structures. In that moment, he didn't care. What pushed his buttons was the fact that the drug dealer who'd nearly gotten his son killed had identified this as the place where he'd gotten his supply. A pill mill, by all appearances, where anyone with a pulse could get a supply of prescription opioids to use recreationally.

In high school, he'd been forced to give up playing football because he couldn't contain himself on the field. He'd hit a kid and keep hitting him well after the whistle had stopped play.

"You don't have an Off switch, son," his coach told him in dismissing him from the team after his fourth ejection in five games. "Turning you on is like unleashing the hounds of hell, and I'm tired of getting bit."

Nothing had changed since—not in the army, not while serving in Desert Storm, not while working as muscle for the Branca crime family, and not during the years afterward. Cort Wesley pushed until whatever he was pushing went off a cliff.

Being a nonsmoker, he didn't carry a lighter or matches. As expected, though, he found a lighter in a drawer belonging to one of the receptionists. With the stench of propane starting to make him nauseous, Cort Wesley exited the building through the glass front doors and poached a rock from a garden that rimmed the single floor of storefront offices. Around the rock, he balled the remains of a newspaper he'd found on a chair inside the waiting area, backed up to what he considered a safe distance, and lit the newspaper ablaze.

Cort Wesley could feel it starting to singe his hand. He threw the paper-wrapped rock forward in line with one of the windows, which would shatter more easily than the thicker glass forming the entry's double doors. He heard the crackle of the glass shattering in the same instant that he became aware that the sirens belonging to police speeding to the site of a suspected break-in were fast reaching a crescendo.

That was all drowned out by the rippling blast that followed, accompanied by a surge of superheated air that buckled Cort Wesley's legs and nearly toppled him off his feet. The parking lot felt cushiony beneath him, as the whole of the Uptown Medical Clinic was swallowed by a bright, white-hot fireball that lent daytime brilliance to the night sky.

For a moment, he thought the colors splashing off him from the flames had morphed into a rainbowlike sparkle, maybe from all those pain pills going up in flames, but then he realized that the kaleidoscope was spawned instead by the trio of police cruisers that had sped into the parking lot.

"Hands in the air! Freeze where you are!"

Cort Wesley stuck his hands in the air and froze. Felt his legs being kicked out from under him before he hit the pavement hard, where his hands were jerked behind his back. Through it all, he never took his eyes off the raging flames, even when a pair of the cops jerked him to his feet.

"What the fuck did you do?" one of them asked him, shaking his head.

"Your job, hoss. You want to read me my rights, go right ahead."

42

Houston

So now here he was in lockup, nose pressed against his own shirt to ward off the dueling stenches of urine and vomit. The booking officer who'd formally processed him wrote down D. W. Tepper's name and phone number and promised to contact him.

"What are you, a Ranger or something?" the man asked.

"Something."

"And what you did to that medical clinic, how'd that involve the Rangers?"

"I'm not allowed to say. That's why you need to call Captain Tepper."

Cort Wesley knew it would still be several hours before Caitlin arrived to pick him up, once Tepper had made the proper arrangements to secure his release. He figured the captain's authority and rank would carry more weight with the Houston PD, and, besides, Cort Wesley was too embarrassed to have Caitlin find out first.

"How is it, bubba, that you're prone to doing so much shit you end up regretting later?"

He was glad it was only Leroy Epps's voice in his head right now and not the ghost himself appearing up close and personal, which would have necessitated a response. Yet Cort Wesley still made one, muted and under his breath, as he raised a hand and pretended to stifle a cough.

"It's a gift, champ, what can I say?"

"Well, I'll be looking forward to what you got to say to the Ranger lady about all this."

As if on cue, a uniformed Houston officer appeared at the cell, calling out Cort Wesley's name as he jiggled a key in the old-fashioned cell lock.

"Get a move on, Masters," the officer continued. "Your ride's here, and you don't want to keep him waiting."

"Him?" Cort Wesley questioned.

43

HOUSTON

"What do you mean he's gone?" Caitlin asked the desk sergeant at the Houston police station located in Kingwood, where Cort Wesley was being held, instead of by the locals in Humble, where he'd been arrested.

"Someone else secured his release."

"Without posting any bail, on an arson beef?"

"The man who signed him out is owed lots of favors by this department, Ranger. Kind of guy you'd make the rain stop for, if you could. He was Ranger once, before he joined the DEA. Maybe you've heard of him: Doyle Lodge."

"I've heard of him, all right," Caitlin said, having a pretty good idea what Doyle Lodge's stake in this was. "Must be pushing ninety now."

"But still sharp as a tack and looks like he could still mix it up with the likes of John Wesley Hardin or Sam Bass."

"His Ranger career straddled my dad's and granddad's," Caitlin told the desk sergeant.

"Why does a man leave the Rangers for the Drug Enforcement Administration?"

"Beats me," Caitlin lied.

At that point, after a tortuous drive from San Antonio spent ruminating about what had moved Cort Wesley to torch a medical clinic, the last thing Caitlin wanted to do was turn around and drive straight home. She always carried a kind of go bag with her, and she decided to make use of it to spend what remained of the night in Houston, checking into a chain motel between the jail where Cort Wesley had been held and the Village School.

The clerk didn't raise an eyebrow over what Caitlin needed a room for at three a.m., not after he glimpsed her Ranger badge, and he refused to take the credit card she tried to hand over.

She called Cort Wesley from the clean, functional room but didn't get an answer. Tried texting him, with the same result. A former Texas Ranger who'd become a legend in the DEA had bailed him out of jail in the wake of Cort Wesley torching what must've been a medical pill mill for the illegal distribution of narcotics. Caitlin didn't need a program in front of her to figure he'd somehow uncovered the source of the drugs that had almost killed Luke.

Luke . . .

For more than a day now, she'd been questioning the tone she'd taken on what had already been the most miserable day of his life. He'd never gotten into as much as a speck of trouble before, and now this. Caitlin wasn't sure what frightened her more, that fact alone or another undeniable truth—that this was hardly an isolated incident, from a nationwide standpoint. The young opioid users of today were on a road that led to heroin and, further down, fentanyl, with all its deadly dangers.

She slept hardly at all, stirring from a doze to find the television playing but with no memory of turning it on. On a whim, she tried Luke's phone, half surprised when he answered.

"You decide to arrest me?" the boy greeted.

"Let's have breakfast this morning, just you and me."

"Er, you know I'm at school, right?"

"I'm not too far down the road right now. I'll pick you up."

She heard him take a deep breath on the other end of the line. "I'm kind of confined to campus; nothing unsupervised."

"I'm a Texas Ranger. That should qualify me."

"I don't want to push it, Caitlin."

"Okay," she said, thinking fast, "we can have breakfast in the school cafeteria. What time do they start serving?"

She called Dylan over her SUV's Bluetooth on the way to the Village School.

"Do you know what time it is?" he asked groggily, leaving Caitlin with the feeling that this was a replay of her call to him yesterday, when he'd put Nola Delgado on the line.

Caitlin pictured him chasing the sleep away, just past six in the morning out in Providence.

"I didn't figure you'd be sleeping in with no one to sleep with."

"Very funny," he said, pushing the words through a yawn.

"Your girlfriend and I had a little talk."

"She's not my girlfriend."

"A few other words come to mind, but we'll leave it there. Anyway, I think maybe I was a little hard on Nola."

"Is this really *the* Caitlin Strong talking?"

"I don't know about *the*, but it's Caitlin Strong all right. What I mean is, I think I'm confusing whatever relationship you've got with Nola with my own issues. I think it all goes back to me having trouble accepting that she's my half sister, that my father had a whole other life I never knew about."

"Your father never even knew Nola existed, Caitlin. I don't know where you're going with this."

"I'm trying to figure what I'd think of Nola if it wasn't for all her baggage. I think she used you to get to me a few months back, here in Texas, but that's got nothing to do with her following you to Providence. So, I don't know, maybe I've got her wrong."

"You haven't even mentioned a word about her being a psychopath."

"I've been accused of the same thing often enough, and I imagine Nola doesn't look at herself any different that I look at myself."

"I think you're softening on her," Dylan said, sounding once again like an adult. "I think this sister stuff is starting to grow on you."

"She mentioned she was the only blood relative I've got left in the world," Caitlin told him.

"You can't choose your relatives. But I'd say you've more than made up for it."

44

HOUSTON

"What are we looking at here exactly?" Cort Wesley asked Doyle Lodge, as they sat inside Lodge's truck in a mostly empty parking lot of an industrial building on Rankin Road, maybe five miles out from the center of the city.

"That there warehouse across the street was vacant from the start of the big recession all the way through last year, when all of a sudden it got filled up again," the old man said in a leathery drawl.

Cort Wesley gazed across the grassy knoll cut in half by a low-lying ditch to catch rain runoff. "You plan on telling me with what?"

The series of buildings in question was nestled in what looked like a hive of industrial structures, Cort Wesley figuring it for maybe a hundred thousand square feet or so.

"Petrochemicals, as near as I can tell. The real dangerous stuff that goes into making fertilizer bombs and the like. Explains all the security, on the surface anyway, given there's still a big need for the same ingredients that killed all those folks in Oklahoma City, the population of a day care center inside the building being foremost among them. How did that make you feel, partner?"

"I think I was overseas at the time."

"And now you and Caitlin Strong are quite the item, from what I hear told, which is the primary reason I'm taking you under my wing."

"Taking me under your *what*?"

"I spent a good part of twenty years with her father and grandfather. Fact that a Strong has given you the stamp of approval is good enough for me."

"But that's not why you bailed me out."

Doyle Lodge turned from the warehouse across the front seat of a truck that seemed as old as he was, the upholstery living on duct tape, with an old, worn smell no dangling deodorizer could remedy. He had a baldpate dotted with brown freckles and liver spots, his ears stretching out from his head like an old-fashioned TV antenna.

"Caitlin never mentioned my name?" Lodge asked, turning back toward the warehouse.

"Why would she?"

"Because there's a story associated with it, but I don't suppose she shares all the bad ones with you, mine in particular. See, Mr. Masters, you and me got something in common most men never have to face."

"What's that, Mr. Lodge?"

"How you almost lost your son a few nights back. Word travels fast about such things, sir."

"You had a similar experience," Cort Wesley concluded.

Doyle Lodge neither nodded nor shook his head. "Except for that 'almost.'"

As Doyle Lodge told it, his Ranger days ended in a bourbon bottle–size despair when his son's life was claimed by an opiate overdose eerily similar to the one that had nearly taken Luke's. The son was in his late twenties, out with his friends, celebrating a promotion to parking lot manager at Arlington Stadium, when one thing led to another.

While the old lawman tried to give that part short shrift, it was clear that his son had been using for years, had been what was generally called a functional addict. Doyle Lodge's plunge into the bottle had led to his unseemly parting with the Rangers; by his own admission, he had embarrassed himself and the department more times than he could count.

"My son might have been a functional addict, Mr. Masters, but I was no functional alcoholic. Rangers had the courtesy to let me resign instead of get fired, which allowed me to get help and then get into the DEA."

"Call me Cort Wesley, Mr. Lodge, and you still haven't explained why you bailed me out of jail."

The old man kept his gaze fixed out the windshield, though he no longer appeared to be studying the warehouse surrounded by heavy fencing topped with barbed wire.

"While I was in the bottle, I found out where my boy was getting his drugs from, just like you did. And I went there, just like you did, only I didn't have the guts to do what you ended up doing. I must've gone back there a hundred times fixing to, but I never did. Guess I didn't have the balls. So when a Houston police officer was kind enough to inform me of your story, I thought maybe, just maybe, I'd found my guy. What is it they say, kinder spirits?"

"Kin*dred*, but I get the idea." Cort Wesley joined the old man in gazing toward the warehouse down the street. "Now, tell me about that warehouse, Mr. Lodge."

"Call me, Doyle, and let's get us some breakfast. This is a tale better told over coffee, since I don't do nothing stronger anymore."

"Sounds good to me."

The old man snapped his eyes toward him across the seat. "The coffee might be, but the story I got to tell you is as far from good as it gets. You're about to hear things you can't unhear, no matter how hard you try. I need to be sure you're okay with that."

"I'm craving some bacon and eggs, Doyle."

Lodge seemed to be looking more through than at him now. "One thing I learned when I fell into the bottle, Cort Wesley, was that when you dance with the devil, the devil don't change—he changes you."

"So why bother dancing at all?"

"Because I know his tricks, partner, and it's about time I showed them to somebody else."

45

Houston

"I owe you an apology," Caitlin told Luke. The two of them were seated alone at a cafeteria table that could accommodate four or even six chairs.

Of course, this was like no school cafeteria she'd ever seen. The Village School seemed to pride itself on what looked, even to the casual observer, more like a restaurant. Both day students and residential students, like Luke, dined together, enjoying scrambled eggs, buttermilk pancakes, French toast, bacon, sausage, and breakfast potatoes as well as specialty offerings such as Asian eggs and rice, breakfast tacos, an omelet bar, and a make-your-own-waffle bar. There was also an assortment of bagels, cold cereals, and breakfast pastries, and a fresh fruit bar that included low-fat yogurt.

"I might come here more often," Caitlin resumed, as Luke kept picking at his eggs.

Around them, the eyes of just about everybody else in the dining hall lingered to some degree on their table. Caitlin had spoken at the school's graduation a few years back, and her Ranger badge would have attracted attention all on its own.

"Maybe they think you're interrogating me," Luke said, finally breaking his silence. "After what happened the other night and all."

"Remember Rafiki in *The Lion King*?" Caitlin asked him, referring to a character in a stage production of the Disney film that she and Luke had attended years ago, just the two of them. "The baboon?"

"Actually, he was a mandrill, but same general family of monkeys."

"Remember what he said every time he hit Simba with a stick?"

"'It's in the past,'" Luke quoted.

"Just like the other night."

"Does that mean you're not interrogating me?"

"Like I told you, I wanted to apologize."

"For what?"

"I think I was too tough on you the other night."

"You weren't tough at all. My father was tough. He barely said a word through the whole drive home and then back to school. That's tough."

"Another reason why I wanted to see you."

"Dad?"

"He found the place that sold the drugs to the dealer in question. He found the dealer, too," Caitlin said, leaving it there.

Luke looked back down at his eggs. "He squeezed the info out of a friend of mine."

"The one who brought the drugs to the party, no doubt."

"Isn't that the kind of thing you wanted to apologize for saying?"

"Anyway," Caitlin resumed, instead of responding, "you may hear mention of a medical clinic not too far from here that got torched last night."

"My father?"

"I wanted you to hear it from me. He let propane gas fill the place and then tossed in a match."

"Boom," said Luke, looking up from his eggs.

"And then some."

"He get arrested?"

"That's what I'm doing up here. I was supposed to pick him up. But somebody else beat me to it."

"My dad doesn't exactly have a long Christmas card list, Caitlin."

"He never met the guy who beat me to it in his life. Another Texas Ranger, believe it or not, only retired for around thirty years. He worked at the DEA for a bunch of those."

"DEA?"

"This man lost his own son to an overdose, Luke," Caitlin finished.

"And they didn't meet up until after my dad torched that clinic?"

Caitlin nodded. "By all indications."

Luke took a deep breath and blew the hair from his face just like his brother. "That can't be good."

Then his eyes strayed over Caitlin's shoulder, out the window, toward the area where she'd parked her car.

"You better have a look at this, Caitlin."

46

Houston

"You're kidding, right?" Caitlin asked Nola Delgado, who was leaning against Caitlin's SUV in the parking lot. "What are you doing here?"

"My job, sis: keeping you alive."

"I can do that all by myself."

"Is that how you'd describe what happened at University Hospital yesterday?"

"I'm standing here, aren't I? So tell your mother I appreciate the consideration."

"She doesn't know I'm here. Like I told you last night, I'm doing this on my own."

"I spoke with Dylan," Caitlin said.

"He told me."

"I meant what I said to him, Nola. Don't make me regret it or give me a reason to change my mind."

"Compared to his other girlfriends, I'm kind of a stabilizing influence on his life."

"He said you weren't his girlfriend."

"Boy doesn't like labels. It's one of his strong points."

"That's right, Nola, he's a boy. Something you should keep in mind."

"Maybe you haven't spent any time with Dylan lately, but he's no kid. He'll always be one to you, the same kid you saved from his mother's killers. You like freezing time, sis, keep things stuck just where they are, where you like them. Dylan might as well still be fourteen and this might as well still be nineteenth-century Dodge City with the O.K. Corral."

"That was Tombstone."

"And you're Wyatt Earp, Doc Holliday, and Bat Masterson all rolled into one. I keep thinking that if I check out enough pictures from those days, I'll see you in a few of them."

"What do you want, Nola?"

"Nothing. The big man asked me to watch out for you today because he was tied up. Working or something."

"Right," Caitlin said, not bothering to mention that Guillermo Paz was now teaching gym to elementary school students.

Nola crossed her arms, smiling smugly as she leaned in tighter against the SUV. "So here I am," she said, extending her hands outward.

"The matter's under control, Nola."

"What matter would that be exactly? You don't know what's really going on here any more than Paz does. So how it could be under control?"

"Figure of speech."

"I looked into the man you described at the hospital, the one you doused in oil. You sure can pick 'em, sis."

Caitlin edged a bit closer. "You mind stepping away from my car?"

"I haven't told you about that man yet."

"Text or email whatever you've got. I'm in kind of a hurry now."

"If he's involved in this, we're probably looking at an army, not just a man."

"And that would suit you just fine, wouldn't it?"

"Colonel Paz wants to spend some more time with me. Says I'm in need of some serious spiritual healing."

"Maybe he's right, Nola."

"I think his exact words were something to the effect of 'Violence is the last refuge of the incompetent.'"

"Yup, sounds like Paz. That's a quote from Isaac Asimov. His book *Foundation*."

"You read it?"

"Paz has. He quotes from it a lot."

"He also quoted something from the Bible, something like 'When you follow the desires of your sinful nature, your lives will produce these evil results.'" Nola Delgado finally stepped away from the SUV. "You think I'm evil, sis?"

"I think you're a victim of your upbringing, Nola."

"How's that exactly?"

"Your mother turned you into el Barquero, and now you've taken almost as many to their deaths as the ferryman from Greek mythology."

Nola smiled smugly again. "You'd like to believe that, wouldn't you?"

"It's the truth."

"One version, sis. The other is that I'm just following my nature. I think you're afraid that nature comes from the Strong side of me and not my mother's."

Caitlin climbed into the driver's seat but didn't close the door right away. "We're not the same, not even close."

"You're going to need me, sis," Nola said, after Caitlin had finally closed the door. "And it won't be long now."

47

Houston

"Who's the root beer for?" Doyle Lodge asked, when the server at Denny's set it down atop a third place mat, which Cort Wesley had stopped her from taking away.

"In case I get thirsty later."

The old man let his gaze linger on the empty chair, as if he could see Leroy Epps in it, even though the ghost was nowhere to be seen or heard at the time.

"Sure, partner, whatever you say," Lodge said, his shriveled lips coming as close to a snicker as they could manage.

"Tell me about that warehouse, Doyle."

"What I've got to say is sure to be of prime interest to you."

"I figured that much out for myself. But what do petrochemicals have to do with drugs killing your boy and almost killing mine?"

"Because those chemicals are just a front for what's really being stored there. This all goes back about a year."

"Right . . . to when the warehouse reopened," Cort Wesley nodded, figuring Doyle Lodge needed to be reminded about what he'd already shared. "After it closed during the recession."

"You don't have to do that," Doyle Lodge told him.

"What?"

"Repeat things I've already said. I may be old and been in more than my share of scrapes, but my mind's as sharp as a tick."

"You mean tack."

The old man winked, both his eyes encased in beds of wrinkles. "Gotcha, didn't I?" he grinned.

"You did at that."

"You keep looking toward that empty chair."

"Maybe I'm waiting for somebody to take it."

"Like who?"

Then Cort Wesley surprised himself by letting the truth spill out. "Old friend of mine, a prison cellmate who died inside the Walls prison. His ghost has been known to show up from time to time."

"And this ghost likes *root beer*?"

Cort Wesley shrugged. "Would it surprise you to hear I think he actually drinks it?"

Much to his surprise, Doyle Lodge didn't shake his head or cast him a disparaging glance. "Son, I'm damn near ninety years old. Fought in both Korea and Nam, then served as both a Texas Ranger and DEA agent. I've seen enough shit in my time to have lost the ability to be surprised a long time ago." Lodge settled back in his chair, twirled his coffee cup around on the edge of the table. "Anyway, I'm glad to hear my sources were correct."

"Sources?"

"I asked around about you and learned enough to figure there's plenty nobody can see. The obvious stuff is all out there, and one of the three people I contacted mentioned he'd heard you talked to ghosts."

"Just one."

"We got eighty thousand of them in 2018 alone, thanks to overdose deaths."

"They don't all come back the way Leroy does."

"Leroy?"

"My ghost," Cort Wesley said.

"Only around a quarter of those were the direct result of opiates," the old man told him. "Of course, a big chunk of the deaths were the result of heroin or fentanyl, and it's a safe bet plenty of those gravitated there from illegally obtained prescription narcotics."

"Thanks to places like the medical clinic I torched last night, right?"

The server came to take their breakfast order but Lodge asked her to give them a few more minutes and returned his attention to Cort Wesley.

"Knowing your history," he said, "my bet is you got that location from the drug dealer responsible for the oxy that almost killed your son. It's an equally safe bet that a number of people who frequented that clinic sold the pills they left with to him at a profit, taking their slice of the pie. Dealer like that can probably move around a thousand pills a week. That's around a hundred and seventy prescriptions at two pills per day."

"You've done your homework, Ranger."

That drew a smile from Doyle Lodge. "I haven't been a Ranger in a long time."

"Retired doctors are still 'Doctor' to me, too."

"Okay, I ran some numbers for you. Now you run some for me. How many so-called patients you figure that so-called clinic you blew up sees every day, seven days a week?"

Cort Wesley had already done some figuring on that in his head and did some more before responding. "I'm thinking maybe thirty patients an hour, fifteen hours per day."

"So, four hundred and fifty."

"Give or take, but that would be at minimum," Cort Wesley acknowledged.

"Plenty of them make use of the pills themselves, but plenty more are part of the underground process that pumped enough pills into Mingo County, West Virginia, for every single one of the twenty-five thousand residents to take four hundred and fifty pills per year."

"Wow."

"That only scratches the surface, soldier."

"Did I mention I served to you?"

"You didn't have to, on account of everybody else I talked to about you did. And you did mention you were overseas for a time. Given you don't look much like the touristy type to me, what else would account for that?"

"Why don't you tell me why our government, your DEA included, lets clinics like the one I took a match to operate under their noses?"

"Isn't it obvious? The government is complicit in it," the old man told him. "My DEA included."

48

HOUSTON

"I don't necessarily mean that literally," Doyle Lodge continued, "but close. You need to picture a three-legged stool."

Cort Wesley watched the man prepare his spoon, fork, and knife as visual aids atop his place mat, the spoon dripping coffee onto the paper. Lodge pushed the knife out first.

"The first leg of the stool you already saw for yourself: doctors operating clinics that are effectively pill mills. The second leg is the pharmaceutical companies themselves, who have known about the dangers associated with opiates for almost as long as the tobacco companies knew that their cigarettes caused cancer. They purposely overproduce prescription narcotics in full awareness of how they're going to be dispensed and where they're going to end up. The profit margin is just too great to turn away from."

"Sounds familiar."

"Right. Corporate America at its very best."

"Just like the tobacco companies, as you said, Ranger."

Lodge beamed at being called that again. "And don't forget that car company that decided not to fix a design flaw because it would cost less to pay out damages to the dead and injured."

"Ford," Cort Wesley recalled. "And I think the car was the Pinto. I almost bought an old one when I was a kid. The owner was practically giving it away."

"I can't imagine why. You buy it?"

Cort Wesley nodded. "It died a month later, but at least the gas tank didn't blow up. What about the third leg?"

"Drug distribution companies, maybe the worst of the bunch. See, pharmaceutical companies don't ship directly to pharmacies; distributors hired by them do. The more pills they ship, the more money they make—big money in the case of opiates. Dig deep enough and, at best, you'll find connections between the distributors and pill mill clinics like that one you torched in Humble. At worst, you'll find direct links that go as far as the distributors forming shell companies that actually own the clinics. We're talking names like Cardinal Health, AmerisourceBergen, and McKesson. Anyway, son, those three companies are responsible for shipping eighty-five percent of all prescription drugs in the United States. That helps make McKesson the seventh biggest of all U.S. companies. Cardinal must be slacking, because they lagged behind at fifteenth."

Cort Wesley sipped some of his coffee, running all that through his head. "But there's a fourth leg of the stool, isn't there? You already said so yourself: the government."

"Including the DEA," the old man said, then nodded.

"How's that work?"

"We're supposed to be a country of laws."

"Emphasis on *supposed*," Cort Wesley said through clenched teeth, thinking of Luke.

"But laws are only as good as the people who enforce them. And these pharmaceutical and drug distribution companies maintain armies of lobbyists to get those laws written as they want them to be written. Care to guess where the bulk of those lobbyists come from?"

"The DEA?"

Doyle Lodge nodded. "The administration's own lawyers, hopping the fence to join the other side."

"In full awareness of the DEA's capabilities and weaknesses."

"Especially the weaknesses. It's a massive bureaucracy riddled by turnover and politics. The best friend the pharmaceutical industry ever had is our political system, since everything resets every four years or so on average. A new administrator comes in and starts from scratch."

"While the bad guys just keep at it," Cort Wesley elaborated, "their ex-DEA lawyers getting the laws written in language that best serves their interests. But what does that have to do with that petrochemical warehouse you showed me this morning?"

"Political pressure is finally forcing the government to chip away at all three legs of that stool, shave them down a little at a time, but plenty enough to make a sizable dent in their profits. Add to that newly passed safeguards regarding the numbers of pills manufactured, shipped, and prescribed and you've got a host of Armani-clad drug pushers who work out of corner offices instead of street corners running scared."

"So that warehouse . . ."

"I think it's one of a whole bunch, but I haven't been able to get anywhere in tracking that down, finding the link, because digging deeper I hit rock I can't blast through. All I can tell you for sure is that it's clear somebody at the top of the food chain has found an alternate means of getting their narcotics onto the streets. And the top of that food chain might as well be the Washington Monument, if you get my drift."

Cort Wesley did, and it was stealing his appetite. "How much of this can you prove?"

"Almost nothing, partner. It's all circumstantial, and whoever's behind it knows how to game the system because, my guess, they're part of the system." The old man's tired, dull blue eyes sought out Cort Wesley on the other side of the table. "That's why I bailed you out of jail, because I need you."

"To do what exactly?"

"I've heard told you got friends in law enforcement who can help us."

"Us?"

"We got something in common all too many share. Difference being my boy didn't make it while yours did. This time."

Those final words got Cort Wesley's dander up. But the worn, sad look on the old man's face induced sympathy more than anything else and the warning implied by "this time" was valid, like it or not.

"Okay, Doyle, let's go with *us*."

"Well, hell, I feel like I accomplished more in the last five minutes than I have in the last five months."

"What do you need exactly?"

"Everything your Ranger lady friend can get us on that warehouse in particular, and any connection to those others I'm sure are out there but can't get a handle on. She still hooked up with the Department of Homeland Security, son?"

In that moment, Cort Wesley couldn't think of another man who'd called him "son," except for his own father. "Caitlin can still make some calls," he said, missing Jones in his old role for the first time. "She can be rather persuasive when she puts her mind to it."

"I'd expect nothing less from the granddaughter of Earl Strong and daughter of Jim Strong."

Cort Wesley looked to his right to see the root beer he'd set out for Leroy Epps remained untouched. Of course, that didn't mean the ghost wasn't sitting there listening.

"I'm going to need some more details, Ranger."

"Happy to provide those while we eat," Doyle Lodge told him, signaling for their server to come over, then looking toward the empty chair with the still-full glass set before it. "Why don't you order your friend breakfast, too?"

49

Livingston, Texas

Yarek Bone couldn't chase the memory of the woman Texas Ranger from his mind. She was there when his eyes were open, but especially when he tried to close them. Like a phantom, some kind of spirit sent to either set him on a new path or just blow up the one he was on.

He hadn't been able to shake the stench of oil from his body since his encounter with her yesterday in the hospital's subbasement, amid the building's mechanicals. Being doused with the noxious, steaming fluid had blistered his skin and left him with a patchwork of second-degree burns. He'd retreated to the Alabama–Coushatta Indian reservation outside of Houston, between Livingston and Woodville, where old-fashioned medicine men practiced the old ways of healing. Actually, it was a medicine *woman* who applied to his wounds a homemade salve that smelled worse than the oil.

"This is going to hurt," she warned him.

Bone had smiled up at her. "Not me," he said, not bothering to elaborate further.

This 4,593-acre reservation in Polk County just off U.S. 190 was the oldest in Texas. It featured recreational campgrounds, a smoke shop, a souvenir stand, and a truck stop—all of which were also open to non-natives in order to raise much needed revenue. But the reservation's vast lands were similarly home to the headquarters of Fallen Timbers, the reactionary Native American group that preached violence, often as a first resort. When he needed to get right, this was where Bone came and lingered for a time.

And yesterday he had needed to get very right indeed, both physically and spiritually. Because something had happened during his encounter with the woman Ranger: he had felt pain. Not his own, but hers. It rode his being with as much prominence as the oil that scorched his flesh and gave him a new insight into the ways of the world, as if he could suddenly know the pain of others, even if he could not know his own.

Who was this woman?

Maybe this had somehow been caused by his burning. Maybe that experience had reformulated his nerve endings so they could reach beyond the borders of his own body to experience the pain he inflicted upon others. An exquisite, glorious, metaphysical experience, to feel what they felt as he hurt them, killed them.

But Bone feared the new sensation might be transitory, that it would vanish with the blistering of his skin, once the medicine woman's salve did its job. He had to know whether this new gift, new blessing, would be his for all time forward, had to know it wasn't just a fluke spurred by the burning and this woman Texas Ranger.

So Yarek Bone wandered into the deep woods, where the greatest concentration of the reservation's wildlife resided. As a boy, his father had taught Bone, on different lands, how to "thump" a deer, to stalk it from the rear and slam a hand down on its hindquarters to make the animal rush away. His father, like all traditional Comanche, believed in hunting only for food.

When he spotted the big antlered buck today, though, food was the last thing on his mind and he wasn't interested in hunting, either. Bone stalked the big buck, as he had thumped deer as a boy. Instead of slapping its hindquarters, though, he skulked closer to where it was feeding on some grass. When the buck raised its head to sniff at the air, Bone grabbed the animal's antlers and twisted with a force sufficient to snap its neck, the resulting crack as loud as a gunshot. He felt the animal's legs collapse, its eyes bulging in terror and then in realization as it hit the ground with a thud, clinging to the last of its breath. He felt it struggling, felt it heaving, felt it dying.

But most of all, Bone felt its pain. The feeling was indescribable in its primitive nature, as if he had known the simple ecstatic delight of early man. In that sense, what he was feeling was the ultimate reward for killing, for hurting others.

The things Bone did best.

He stood over the buck as it clutched for its last breath. He wanted more than anything, in that moment, to feel that same sensation not with another deer or with just any human victim. He was going to feel the Texas Ranger's pain.

He was glad the medicine woman's salve was doing its job, because it would allow him to return to the world and hurt Caitlin Strong in a way he would feel forever.

50

SAN ANTONIO, TEXAS

"We've had some complaints, Colonel. Some parents are voicing . . . concerns about your teaching."

"There's no accounting for taste," Paz said to Canyon Ridge Elementary School principal Mariana Alonzo, on the morning of only his third day on the job. "And everybody's entitled to their opinion."

"Is it true that you fired something at the children as they were negotiating this . . ."

"Obstacle course," Paz completed for her.

"And you were actually *shooting* at them?"

"Soft rubber bullets that resemble those Nerf things. I make them myself. And I made sure all the kids were wearing goggles. Safety first, right?"

"Right, Colonel, yes."

"Want to see one?"

"What?"

"One of the soft rubber bullets, since that's the subject of our conversation." Paz fished one from inside a side pocket on his tactical pants. "Here you go. See?"

Alonzo rose to take the squat, oblong object that was maybe an inch long from Paz's grasp. She grasped it almost reluctantly. Paz figured that since it looked just like the real thing, the woman might have thought he'd reached into the wrong pocket. But then she ran the soft rubber bullet between her fingers, squeezing it and watching as the sponge-like material eased back into its original shape.

"Impressive," the principal of Canyon Ridge Elementary said.

"Thank you, jefa," Paz said, again referring to Alonzo as "boss."

"Looks just like the real thing."

"I know. That's the point." Paz leaned forward in the armchair that was barely wide enough to accommodate his bulk. "I'm teaching the kids what to do if they're shot at, facing gunfire."

"That was the source of the parents' complaints," Alonzo said.

"What'd you tell them?"

"That I'd look into things."

"You could have quoted some of the statistics from school shootings, jefa. This school has active shooter drills, doesn't it?"

Alonzo nodded. "A requirement of all public schools in the state of Texas."

"You could've told those parents my live fire obstacle course is just an extension of that. Because, let's face it, the only thing active shooter drills teach kids is to run and hide. Problem is, that doesn't always work. Just ask the victims at Parkland or . . ." Here, Paz crossed himself as he knew his priest, the late Father Boylston, would have wanted. "Sandy Hook. There's no substitute for feeling what it's actually like to be shot at. If this were high school, I would've been tempted to use real bullets."

Alonzo handed the sample toy bullet back across her desk. "This is a problem for us, Colonel."

"The problem's already there, jefa. A bigger problem is ignoring it. I think Friedrich Nietzsche put things in a nutshell when he said 'Examine the life of the best and most productive men and nations, and ask yourselves whether a tree which is to grow proudly skywards can dispense with bad weather and storms. Whether misfortune and opposition, or every kind of hatred, jealousy, stubbornness, distrust, severity, greed, and violence do not belong to the favorable conditions without which a great growth even of virtue is hardly possible.' You familiar with that quote?"

"I'm familiar with Nietzsche," Alonzo said, evasively.

"That's what I miss most about my priest. He understood the notion Orwell championed when he said that we 'sleep peacefully in our beds because rough men stand ready to do violence' on our behalf. We need more rough kids, to go with the rough men and women. We need to fully prepare them to survive the school day and get home to their parents, not just teach them to hide in closets, behind desks or locked doors. Because, believe me, none of those are going to stop a person with intent to do them harm."

"With all due respect, Colonel, that's not a decision best supported in physical education class. There are channels you need to go through, and I'd like to head this off before it reaches the school board. On the bright side, no one has voiced any problem with the notion of an obstacle course. The problem lies in what you call the live fire simulation."

Paz squeezed the soft rubber bullet so hard and compressed it so tight that it showed no signs of returning to its original contours. "Let me ask you a question, jefa. How did the parents find out about all this?"

"From their children, of course."

"And what did their children say?"

"That it was the most fun they ever had in school."

"Boys or girls?"

"Both, especially the girls," Alonzo admitted.

"Did they mention to their parents that, through the day, not a single kid got clipped by one of my bullets?"

That seemed to get the principal's attention. "Is that true?"

Paz nodded. "And maybe it would translate into an active shooter situation, now that they know what that's like. You should tell the parents, and the school board, what Thomas Sowell once said: 'Rhetoric is no substitute for reality.'"

"You raise an excellent point, Colonel."

Paz leaned forward.

"But my hands are tied here."

Paz leaned back.

"All Texas public schools have a strict policy against the presence or use of any firearms, and that includes your rubber bullets."

"I was going to teach marksmanship next."

Alonzo rose, comfortable with the desk acting as a buffer between them. "I know you're only trying to do what's right, and I appreciate that."

Paz nodded as he joined the principal on his feet. "It was Kafka who said, 'Start with what's right rather than what's acceptable.'"

"In education, I'm afraid the opposite is normally the case. I'm sorry that this didn't work out, Colonel," Alonzo said, extending her hand across the desk.

Paz swallowed it in his grasp. "That's okay, jefa, because it looks like I'm gonna be going to war again anyway."

51

Washington, DC

Senator Lee Eckles made the call from his private office, not the one in the Russell building but the one off the Senate floor, down a dimly lit hall lined with unmarked rooms, where ranking members like him could hide out when necessary, unburdened and unbothered by their constituents or the press. His was the third one down on the right.

"Placing a call" was the wrong way to describe a procedure that, upon dialing a key code, activated technology that was aimed to maximize security and keep the identity of the call's participants impossible to discern. Participants would speak into their phone and an app, designed by the State Department for use in foreign embassies where spying was constant, would transfer spoken words to text.

"An opportunity has arisen that requires our immediate attention," Eckles began, picturing his words being transcribed for the other six participants, to whom he was beholden, to read on their phones, "an opportunity specifically related to our Texas-based operation."

Eckles had never bothered to add up the net worth of all the men on this call, who had bankrolled this operation from the beginning, after the senator had laid out for them the facts—along with the potential. The thing about rich people was that they always wanted to get richer. He knew, of course, that this was more about power than money, although in his mind they were pretty much the same thing. They'd ask him what he wanted out of all this and Eckles's answer was simple: to be president of the United States.

They hadn't responded, which he took to be a response in itself. And as pleased as they were with the results so far, they were going to be even more pleased after this phone call.

DOES THIS HAVE SOMETHING TO DO WITH THAT TOWN WHERE EVERYBODY WENT TO BED AND NOBODY WOKE UP? appeared on his screen.

"Camino Pass. And the answer is yes."

OUR TEXAS OPERATION HAD NOTHING TO DO WITH THAT, RIGHT? a second participant wondered. NOTHING THAT COULD LEAD BACK TO US.

Eckles thought of the Texas Rangers being on the case. "Nothing that can lead back to us, no. But the opportunity we need to discuss has *everything* to do with Camino Pass."

I DON'T FOLLOW YOU, from another member of the exclusive club.

"We all know how the world works. There's above the surface and below, and the factor all of us had in common before we even convened our first meeting was that we're equally comfortable functioning in both. We're upholding a long-standing and glorious tradition to do what needs to be done, without anyone knowing we're doing it. That's what the Texas operation is all about and always has been, taking the traditions started by those who came before us at tables like this to the next stage."

Eckles waited for the transcription process to catch up with his words before continuing.

"We now have the opportunity to go to another level entirely, beyond anything we or those who came before us were ever in a position to consider."

AND HOW MIGHT YOU DESCRIBE THIS OPPORTUNITY?

"As potentially securing the future."

OURS?

"The country's."

OURS, THEN. AND JUST WHO IS IT WE HAVE TO KILL?

"Anybody we want," Eckles said, watching his words transcribed in real time, "any number we want, anywhere we want."

The silence in his private office became palpable. Eckles took the lack of response from the others as permission to proceed with his plan. That was the way it was with these people: no answer could be taken as a response in the affirmative, as with the promise of him ending up in the Oval Office because of this operation, which he had built himself.

"I'll report back within forty-eight hours," he finished, his transcribed words again standing alone.

PART FIVE

JOHN B. ARMSTRONG

Yet another Tennessee native, Armstrong clashed with Reconstruction-era authorities at home and ended up moving to Texas in 1872 at the age of 22. He joined the Austin militia unit known as the Travis Rifles before moving on to a company of Texas Rangers led by Captain Leander McNelly. Armstrong's most famous exploit as a Ranger by far was his capture of John Wesley Hardin in the spring of 1877. Hardin, Texas' most infamous gunfighter, was said to have killed at least 20 men in the decade following the Civil War; some said the total reached as high as 40. By 1877, he was on the run, wanted by the Rangers for the killing of Comanche County Deputy Sheriff Charles Webb. Though he was recuperating from a gunshot wound, Armstrong sought and won permission to work the Hardin case. He and his team tracked Hardin to Pensacola, Florida, and confronted the gunfighter and his gang in a train car. Though various versions exist as to what happened next, the most commonly told story is that Hardin's gun snagged on his suspenders and Armstrong was able to hit him over the head, knocking him out. Armstrong then sent Hardin back to Texas to stand trial for Webb's murder.

—Sarah Pruitt, "8 Famous Texas Rangers," History.com

52

SHAVANO PARK, TEXAS

"I didn't like seeing Nola Delgado sitting in our spot when I got home last night," Caitlin said, sipping a take-out coffee she'd warmed up in the microwave.

"She does have a way of making herself feel at home, Ranger," Cort Wesley said, working on one of his craft beers instead. "Speaking of which, I notice she helped herself to a couple of my favorite Freetail brand, the amber ale. I'm blaming you for that."

"Me?"

"She's your half sister."

"You can't choose your relatives, Cort Wesley, no matter what the percentage is."

He took a hefty sip, his eyes never leaving her. There was something different, unusual, about his expression, a mix of resignation and uncertainty. Caitlin figured Luke's overdose had given him a new understanding about how little a parent actually knows their kids. Just when you think it's time to let go, you want to reel them in tighter than ever. He'd always preached about letting Dylan and Luke live their own lives, but now one was living with a psychopath and the other had come close enough to death to feel the breaths of angels.

"How's your head feeling?" Cort Wesley wondered.

"Worse than ever, after chasing down that killer at University

Hospital," Caitlin told him. "Feels like there's a hole in it as big as the one he must've slipped through to escape."

"So take a pill."

"Already had my fill for the day."

"Which is how many exactly, Ranger?"

"'As needed,' the prescription says, which seems a whole lot more often lately."

Cort Wesley smiled slightly. "Since bullets can't kill you, I don't think you've got much to fear from pills."

"I'm thinking of going back to the doctor, maybe a neurologist this time."

"What for?"

"To figure out why that blast whatever-you-call-it seems to be getting worse instead of better."

"I need your help with something in the meantime, Ranger. Does the name Doyle Lodge ring any bells?"

"Sure, although I was still a little girl when he drummed himself out of the Rangers."

"On account of falling into the bottle after his son died of an opiate overdose."

"Propelling Lodge into a legendary career at DEA, starting at the ripe old age of sixty-three. He became such a legend, first they waived the mandatory retirement age and then called him a special advisor or something in order to keep him on the books. He tell you they had a nickname for him over there?"

"No."

"The Terminator. The second film in the series had come out around the time he was busting as many heads as dealers."

"Taking a Ranger approach to things, in other words. Lodge reached out to me, sees us as kindred spirits."

"What do you, and he, need?"

"Lodge has been eyeballing a suspicious petrochemical warehouse just outside of Houston."

"Eyeballing? He's damn near ninety. And where do petrochemicals fit in with Luke and his son?"

"The warehouse opened for business at almost the very time a new flood of drugs hit the streets."

"Sure," Caitlin nodded. "About a year ago. I've seen the reports, looked at the data. Sixteen cities have seen a spike that's off the charts when it comes to availability."

"Lodge smells a connection."

Caitlin remembered her coffee and took a fresh sip. "Seems pretty tenuous to me."

"No more than the basis for plenty of your investigations."

Caitlin laid the big Styrofoam cup down on the porch floor. "You want him to be right."

"I want to put everyone behind the likes of Cholo Brown in a box. Whether that's a jail cell or a coffin is up to them."

"And you think Lodge can help you?"

Cort Wesley nodded. "That's why I hope his gut is right on this."

She flashed her phone before him. "Homeland Security is open twenty-four seven, Cort Wesley. I'll make the call and have it stamped priority. We'll have something on that warehouse by morning."

"Glad to hear the doors Jones opened for you there haven't closed in his absence."

"Well, he's itching to get back in."

"You saw him?"

"He rolled in like the bad penny he's always been."

"Don't tell me: Camino Pass."

"Jones may be out of government service, but when it comes to mass deaths he's like the old firehouse dog who springs back to life when the alarm sounds. Sees whatever caused this particular one as his potential ticket back to Washington."

"Well," Cort Wesley groused, "there's no accounting for taste."

"What's Doyle Lodge like?" Caitlin asked him.

"You've never met him?"

"Not for more than thirty seconds."

"In a word: old."

"About the same age as my dad would be if he'd lived."

"The Strong legend is not lost on him, Ranger. He speaks of you with the same reverence he does about your father or grandfather."

"I don't belong in their company."

"That's not an opinion shared by many, least of all Doyle Lodge."

Caitlin hesitated briefly. "It's kind of like old home week, Cort Wesley, me running into Nola Delgado on top of Jones."

"You didn't run into her; she was waiting for you."

"I spoke to Dylan about her," Caitlin admitted, leaving out mention of her breakfast with Luke, during which she had told him his father had set fire to the pill mill behind the drugs that almost killed him.

"Doing my job, in other words."

"I'm sorry."

"I didn't mean it that way. I'm glad you spoke to him, because I just can't talk to him on the subject of women."

"Well, you are his father."

"How do you get away with it?"

"I wasn't talking about Nola Delgado as his girlfriend, or my half sister. I was talking about Nola Delgado as a man killer."

Cort Wesley ran his tongue from one side of his mouth to the other, his cheeks puckering one after the other. "I'm surprised he didn't hang up."

"I get the feeling he thinks Nola is there to protect him."

"From what?"

"Dylan was home for over a year. I think it was harder to return to school than he let on. I think he's scared."

"Dylan?"

"Hard to believe, I know, Cort Wesley, given who his father is."

"Sure, Ranger, I'm scared of nothing besides losing my seventeen-year-old honor student to an opiate overdose."

Caitlin gave him a long look, trying not to appear harsh, caustic, or judgmental, given her own proclivities. "What happens when you catch up with whoever's behind Cholo Brown and that pill mill in Humble?"

"You mean the pill mill, one-stop drug shop that *used* to be in Humble?"

The breeze picked up, blowing the light fixture dangling from the porch ceiling back and forth. The light splayed against Cort Wesley in a way that made him look like he was cut down the middle, one side light and the other lost to the shadows, the illusion intensified by his not realizing what Caitlin was seeing.

"I don't know, Ranger," he said. "And that's the God's honest truth."

"You can't burn down the whole world, Cort Wesley; there aren't enough matches."

"Maybe not, but you know that won't stop me from trying."

53

San Antonio, Texas

"Thank you for seeing me without an appointment, Mr. Fass," Caitlin said, sitting down before the big wood desk.

"Well," the jittery Roland Fass said from behind it, seeming to have trouble getting settled in his chair, "you know what they say about the Texas Rangers."

"No . . . What do they say?"

She watched Fass jiggle himself one way and then the other, making her wonder if he was suffering from hemorrhoids or something. "Figure of speech, that's all. I haven't had my coffee yet. Would you like some?"

"I've had my morning fill already, but please feel free."

"No, I can wait. Don't want to waste any of your valuable time, do we?"

"Your time is valuable too, sir, given that big warehouse you own outside of Houston," Caitlin said, getting to the point by reciting part of the intelligence she'd gathered from Homeland Security. "Tell me: how'd you get into the petrochemical business?"

"I'm not actually, Ranger. In fact, I couldn't tell you a petro from a chemical. I just own the building, not its contents. I lease the space to a consortium or something."

"And that's kind of why I'm here. See, I'm kind of an agent for the Department of Homeland Security, representing Texas. When I get the scent of something that doesn't feel right, with links here, it's my duty to follow it up."

Fass looked even more uncomfortable. "Are you still talking about my warehouse on Rankin Road?"

"Along with the sixteen other warehouses spread all over the country, all owned by a shell company that leads straight back to you," Caitlin told him, paraphrasing the information Homeland Security had provided earlier this morning. "That, and the fact you bought all sixteen of them going back between twelve and eighteen months. A good businessman would never do something like that, unless he had tenants—a whole consortium maybe—already lined up. Are you a good businessman, Mr. Fass?"

Caitlin felt his eyes boring into her while he tried to appear casual, his expression trapped between the beginnings of a smile and nothing at all.

"I'm guessing you already know the answer to that question is a bit complicated," he said softly.

"You mean, on account of your business license being revoked because of that embezzlement beef? Your own engineering design firm, wasn't it?"

"I was one of five partners. The others conspired against me, tried to cut me out of the profits."

"The court must not have taken your extenuating circumstances into account."

"I pled out for a lesser sentence."

"From what I've seen, sir, nobody pleads out unless they're guilty."

Fass tried to hold her stare but failed. "You ever deal with the feds, Ranger?"

"Our paths cross from time to time."

"You can't beat them, even if you're in the right."

"In my experience, they're just out to do their jobs. Aside from that, you know what I find interesting? How you invested that money you embezzled. Your trades were confined to a single sector: the pharmaceutical industry, 'Big Pharma' as they say."

"That's not me anymore," Fass noted stiffly. "You're looking at a changed man."

"You could have skated, if you'd given up the name of whoever fed you the information. Maybe you were fronting for him or her."

"Who said I was fronting for anyone, Ranger?"

"Because the trades came out of nowhere, timed to coincide with the record profits turned in by Big Pharma. You know where the bulk of those profits originated, sir?"

"I'm going to guess prescription narcotics, since they've become the industry's cash cow."

Caitlin studied him across the big desk. "There's some derision in your voice, Mr. Fass."

"I got involved in something that destroyed my career, Ranger. That's on me, all of it. But that doesn't make the men I was involved with any better. They sweat acid, I tell you."

"I'm sorry to drag more baggage into your life, but there've been some concerns raised over that warehouse you're operating just outside of Houston proper."

"Are we talking concerns or complaints?"

"One often leads to the other, sir. That's why I'm here, what with large increases in cancer occurrences regularly showing up within close proximity to facilities like the ones you own. Maybe I can help you avoid a lawsuit, at least in Texas."

"I keep my nose in the day-to-day operations when it comes to oversight, and I can tell you that facility has passed every inspection. We run tests on the groundwater on a weekly basis and have reinforced the walls and floors way beyond what the building code dictates."

"That's good, sir, just fine, because if I can reassure your neighbors to that effect, we may be able to avoid further complaints being lodged."

"They're baseless, I'm telling you."

"Could you be a bit more specific as to the contents?"

"It varies from location to location, but for the most part those warehouses store the raw chemicals that go to make fertilizers, pesticides, industrial solvents, even space-age polymer—anything that's not the finished product. You know, the stuff nobody else wants to touch. You want to climb back up after you hit rock bottom, you stake your claim someplace nobody else wants to get near. You asked about the chemicals being stored in my warehouse on Rankin Road? I can have a list generated before you leave."

"I'd appreciate that, sir, along with any inspections the state has conducted, and all your licenses."

"That's a big ask, Ranger. Might take some time to put all that together."

"I'm just trying to be thorough here and save both of us the bother of getting the state involved. If we can get this sorted out between us, life would be a lot easier. I'll take you at your word that you've got no stake in this consortium or whatever that filled all these warehouses with petrochemicals. But it was something else that caught my eye in

Homeland's report and that I just can't make sense of, sir. Specifically, the fact that all sixteen cities in which your warehouses are located have seen a dramatic spike in illicit drug distribution and use, particularly prescription opiates, from right around the time each of them respectively opened their doors. Can you offer an explanation about that?"

"How about coincidence?"

"That's always a possibility."

"Especially given that the opioid crisis in this country isn't limited to these cities my warehouses happen to be located in."

"No, but they have shown some of the biggest spikes in drug use for large population centers. And I would've thought, Mr. Fass, that more out-of-the-way locations would have been better suited to house such petrochemical facilities."

Fass looked like a man trying to figure out what a player was holding in Texas Hold'em. "Those warehouses were all empty when I bought them. I could just as easily have put in a church choir, if they could make the monthly nut. But, since you know my background, I'm going to assume you know my engineering firm was no stranger to the petrochemical industry, since we specialized in building manufacturing plants. And safety was always our first priority," he added, in what sounded like an afterthought.

"I did figure that's where you became such an expert on the topic. But, tell me, does making your 'monthly nut,' as you call it, require you to be in Washington frequently?"

"What makes you ask?"

"Well, sir, the complaint against you Homeland's investigating also alleges you've got friends there, partners maybe," Caitlin said, reciting what she'd actually learned from Homeland Security about travel charges pulled from Fass's credit cards. "Would that be true? Or maybe you were just meeting with your congressman or something."

"Are you spying on me?"

"The person who filed the complaint might be. I'm only going on what I was told. I can do my best to assuage their fears, if you tell me who you met with in DC."

"None of their business, or yours. This is harassment, on both your parts."

"I'm sorry you feel that way, Mr. Fass. I meant what I said about seeing if we could get this sorted out between just the two of us. I hope we can still do that."

Fass looked at her, seeming very far away, even though only eight feet separated them. "And me as well, Ranger."

"I would appreciate that inventory, too, before I head out of the office, if at all possible. And I hope you won't mind if I pay you another visit before I write up my report."

"Not at all," Fass said, standing, a clear sign he was ready for Caitlin to be gone.

As if on cue, her phone rang and she took it from her pocket to check the caller ID.

"I need to take this," Caitlin said, rising from her chair and moving to the window. "Good morning, D.W."

"Nothing good I can see, Ranger. You and I are taking a field trip back to Camino Pass."

"Somebody find something else there?"

"It's not what they found, it's what they didn't. Full accounting of all the bodies is finally complete, but guess what? There's somebody missing. That was determined yesterday. This morning, Homeland sent in a search team, and guess what?"

"They disappeared too."

"Is there anything I can say you don't already know?"

"How about the rest of the story about my great-grandfather teaming up with Pancho Villa?"

"Chopper's ready and waiting, Ranger," Tepper told her. "Let's get a move on."

54

HOUSTON

Cort Wesley and Doyle Lodge sat in matching wooden lawn chairs set on the plank boardwalk outside his modest, garden-style apartment, which was through the screen door behind them.

"Caitlin Strong came up with all that in less than a day," Lodge said, shaking his head. "Man oh man, she's Jim Strong's daughter and Earl Strong's granddaughter, all right."

"She's pretty good in a gunfight, too."

"So I've heard. Also like her daddy and granddaddy. Man oh man," the former Ranger repeated. "Sixteen warehouses from coast to coast— seventeen when you include the one here—concentrated in areas with the biggest boosts in opioid traffic, all connected to a single man, this Roland Fass."

"Fass is a front for something bigger, Doyle. I think that's a safe assumption to make, as is always the case."

"Didn't used to be, son," Lodge told Cort Wesley, with a combination of regret and nostalgia lacing his voice. "Used to be a bad guy was a bad guy. He didn't need to be fronting for anybody else at the time, like some straw man. We got us a world now where the food chain's so high you can't see the top, new and more powerful links sprouting up all the time."

"Crime has become big business, Ranger."

"It always was, in the minds of those doing it. Difference being they didn't need to report up to the next link if they were fixing to rob a bank or knock off a jewelry store. What we got today is a whole new kind of bad." Something changed in Lodge's expression. "Tell me about your son."

"Why?"

"Because he's the reason you're doing this, climbing a chain you can't see the top of."

Cort Wesley actually liked hearing it put that way, just as nothing gave him greater pleasure than discussing his boys, although this case made for an exception. "What happened shocked the hell out of me."

"It's that way for just about all of us," Lodge said, his eyes moistening. "People are under the impression that drug addicts give you plenty of warning signs that they're in trouble, when that's often as far from the truth as it gets. Difference being, son, you got lucky because your boy lived."

"I always bought into the stereotype of the drug addict."

"The dregs of society?"

Cort Wesley nodded, beginning to feel the heat of the day building.

"Kind of people you cross the street to avoid when you see them coming."

"All itchy, pale, and emaciated. Looking as if they're walking to their own funeral."

"Those are the ones."

"Doesn't describe your boy or mine, though, does it?"

"I have no idea how many times Luke got lucky before he didn't."

"You didn't ask him?"

"It wasn't the first. And it doesn't matter, because all I really care about is that it's the last."

Doyle Lodge looked like he wanted to laugh, but he just shook his head. "You're avoiding the real issue here, son."

"What's that?"

"The possibility that your boy is a full-fledged addict just like mine was. There's no hard-and-fast rules to such things, except for the fact they never admit to that being the case."

"Well, shit . . ."

Lodge pushed his lawn chair closer to Cort Wesley's. "You need to get your boy some professional help before you're calling the coroner instead, son."

Cort Wesley wanted to punch the old man in that moment, pictured himself knocking out his teeth—or dentures as the case may be. Lodge had just confronted him with a reality he had chosen to avoid, even though Leroy Epps had hinted at the very same thing.

Look at me, relying on a ghost from the grave and a man who may have one foot in it.

"But you're a lucky man for another reason entirely," Lodge was saying.

"What's that, Ranger?"

"You've got the skills needed to get back at the people who killed my son and almost killed yours."

"Maybe I'll stuff them all in a meat grinder."

"A worthy pursuit, son, but they don't make a grinder big enough to fit them all."

"Then it's a good thing we've got a place to start." Cort Wesley realized Lodge's eyes had lost their sheen, no longer wet with unspilled tears. "That warehouse we eyeballed yesterday."

The old man grinned, showcasing the still-white teeth Cort Wesley no longer felt like knocking out, dentures or not. "I was hoping you'd say that."

"We need to have a look inside, see if petrochemicals are the only thing being stored there."

"There's no 'we,' in this case, son, given that I'm sure you've noticed it's an effort for me to get out of the car without losing my breath."

"Then I'll have to pull backup elsewhere," Cort Wesley said, taking out his phone.

"What are you doing?"

"Texting my other son, the one in college."

"Why don't you just call him?"

"Because he never answers or listens to his messages."

Cort Wesley kept the text message short and sweet, the way Dylan liked: TEXT ME NOLA DELGADO'S CELL NUMBER.

55

SAN ANTONIO, TEXAS

Caitlin and D. W. Tepper arrived at the Stinson Airport on Mission Road, where the Ranger chopper was based, climbing out of their vehicles to find Guillermo Paz leaning against his massive pickup truck.

"I didn't call him, Captain, I swear," Caitlin assured Tepper.

"I called him, Ranger."

"You . . ."

"A trained Homeland Security team vanished while looking for a missing kid in a town where everybody else died. I thought this might be right up your friend's alley."

"I appreciate you recommending me to the principal of that school, Ranger," Paz told Caitlin, as they walked toward the chopper.

"I'm sorry things didn't work out."

"Oh, but they did, for a couple days anyway. You would think schools would place more emphasis on training their students to prepare for the inevitable."

"School shootings aren't inevitable, Colonel."

"I was talking about the bigger picture. First thing that happens when you get on an airplane, they tell you what to do if something bad happens."

"The passengers don't really listen."

"My students listened. I knew I was saving lives. That's what made my two days there so special. I felt like my priest, the late Father Boylston, showing those children the way just as he showed me."

"Literally as opposed to figuratively."

"Is there really a difference, Ranger?"

They reached the chopper, the engine just starting to warm. "Let's go, Colonel."

"What do we know about the missing kid, Captain?" Caitlin said into her headset, once they were airborne.

She and Tepper were seated next to each other; Guillermo Paz sat on the floor of the hold, immediately behind them. Though cramped, it provided him more room, enough to stretch his legs all the way out.

"Well, let's see," Tepper said. He pulled a crinkled piece of paper from his pants pocket and squinted for lack of reading glasses. "Andrew Ortega, mother a native-born Texan and father originally an immigrant. In and out of trouble to the point where the family moved to Camino Pass to keep the kid from running with the same gang his father did. Father's no angel either, by the way. He fought his way through prison in the boxing ring. Highway patrol has been called to the family home on multiple occasions on domestic abuse calls for damage done to both his wife and Andrew. Told the officers he had a right to toughen his kid up."

"He have an explanation as to why he hit his wife, too?"

"How about the fact he's just an asshole, now gone to an early grave with his wife and the rest of the town, except for the late Lennox Scully and maybe Andrew Ortega."

"If he didn't just up and run away, you mean, D.W. Kid sounds like a prime candidate for it."

"Maybe you're forgetting those three missing Homeland Security officials."

"You think a bullied kid could be responsible for that?"

Tepper shrugged. "Until three days ago, I didn't think the population of a whole town could die in their sleep, either."

56

CAMINO PASS, TEXAS

The Ranger chopper landed in the same spot it had on Caitlin's first trip here, with an equally tight security perimeter erected extending out to a one-mile radius. Although the town had been declared safe, no further threat looming anywhere within it, there was now the press to consider, along with the curious. The last thing they needed was a tourist attraction on the scale of the Marfa lights. It wasn't hard to picture, given the macabre sense of entertainment, people driving for miles and miles just to see the ghost town that had sprung up overnight.

A standard SUV was waiting for them at the command center. Highway patrol captain Ben Hargraves, who'd been in charge during Caitlin's first visit, handed the keys to Tepper.

"Have you even gone home?" she asked him.

"What do you think?" Hargraves said, his voice scratchy and raw. "Maybe we're all dead and this is purgatory."

"That's not as far-fetched as it seems, given that hell is just a mile or so down the road, Captain. Anything on thermal imaging scans or motion detectors?"

"No movement, no heat, and no sound, Ranger."

"And when did the Homeland team go missing?"

"Three hours ago now. They searched his house and came up empty. Then they started a house-to-house, building-to-building search, checking in at five-minute intervals."

"They obviously had phones or communicators. What do the GPS signals say?"

"You think we would have called in the Texas Rangers if they'd said anything at all?" Hargraves asked her, frustration washing the fatigue from his voice for at least the moment. "Did I tell you I grew up in these parts?"

"No, sir."

"Well, I did. And the area's been the capital of weird and strange for as long as I can remember. I can recall hearing a train rumbling past my house when I was little boy. I'd run to the window, but there was never any train, never mind any railroad tracks."

"Boys do tend to have pretty active imaginations, Captain."

A look somewhere between whimsical, nostalgic, and uncertain crossed Hargraves's features. "That's kind of what my parents told me. But funny thing, Ranger, they were lying, because I remember thinking that they could hear that train, too."

Caitlin passed off his reflections as the product of a tired mind. "Let's get back to the missing DHS team. You got a notion as to where they were the last time they checked in?"

Hargraves handed over a sheet of paper folded in two. "I marked it on the map for you."

The map was a shrunken version of a detailed structural schematic of Camino Pass, each residence marked with a blue number and the remaining buildings with a red one. The map had been divided into lightly shaded grids to denote areas divvied up by the Homeland Security teams that had spent the past three days removing bodies and searching for any clues, hoping to get a better fix on how the cyanide gas had inexplicably struck so suddenly and lethally.

Hargraves had made an X on the last known location where the missing search team had been before they'd gone dark: the lone municipal building, by the look of things, housing all the local departments, including police. Caitlin parked the SUV nose in, the other four angled spaces taken by a pair of police cruisers and two municipal vehicles. A fancy RV that looked like their vehicle on steroids was parked another ten yards ahead, the doors left open, clearly empty of the Homeland Security personnel who'd driven it here from the checkpoint.

Climbing out of the vehicle felt strange, given that the last time she was here she had been confined by a hazmat suit. But the air felt just as dead and empty, to the point that Caitlin was almost surprised that she could breathe freely. She looked toward Paz, who was circling his gaze about, and could sense his tension and discomfort as well. It was more than just her firsthand recollection and awareness of what had happened here. Something had grasped her gut the same way it did when she was searching for a shooter or a suspect. A sense of something threatening, danger and menace, as if a predator were about to pounce.

"Colonel?" she posed, when her eyes met Paz's.

He was hanging back, seeming to sniff the air. "Nothing, Ranger. It was Voltaire who said, 'It is not known precisely where angels dwell whether in the air, the void, or the planets. It has not been God's pleasure that we should be informed of their abode.'"

"Sounds like we've stepped square into that void, Colonel."

"No sound, no heat, no movement, Ranger," Tepper said, standing next to Caitlin now. "What's that tell you about this void?"

"If the search and rescue team is still alive, they're in a basement somewhere. Andrew Ortega too, Captain. That's the only explanation for how Ben Hargraves can't pick up any of their thermal signatures."

"Well, we got a problem there, given that not a single building in Camino Pass has a basement. You ever try digging down into the desert bed?"

"So what's that leave us with, exactly?" Caitlin asked herself as much as him.

"That," said Guillermo Paz, who had come up right behind them, his finger pointing straight ahead.

"I haven't seen one of those for years," Tepper said, squinting toward an old logo, above them, that read "Fallout Shelter." "Then again, this town has been here awhile."

"Dating back to at least 1898, when my great-grandfather pulled Pancho Villa out of jail, right, D.W.?"

He ignored her raising of the story that had started here but still lacked an ending. "I believe towns were required to build fallout shelters during the Cold War."

Following the sign's arrow, Caitlin realized that, instead of building an actual fallout shelter, Camino Pass had simply adapted a storm shelter for that use. Tornadoes weren't uncommon in these parts, a far more likely occurrence than nuclear bombs raining down. It would have saved a ton of money and effort while satisfying the instructions of the state.

"They probably shored it up a bit," Caitlin said to Tepper and Paz, when they came to the angled steel double doors with a faded fallout shelter emblem still stuck in place. "These doors were likely wood originally."

"Explains why, if anybody's down there, their phones wouldn't give up their positions, any more than body heat would."

"Somebody's down there," Paz said, unshouldering an M4 assault rifle with a shaved-down stock.

"You think we're going to need that, Colonel?"

He smiled at her, his grin blinding in a ray of sunshine that looked like a spotlight. "Don't we always?"

"I'm going first, Colonel," Caitlin said, after Paz had hoisted open the heavy steel doors as if they were made of papier-mâché.

She looked toward Tepper.

"Andrew Ortega was an abused kid, Captain. Being that he was beaten by his father on a regular basis, this could have been where he went to escape."

"You saying he was down there the whole time, Ranger. Since the night in question?"

Caitlin frowned. "I can't say how that explains his surviving, but it makes sense. Homeland Security team goes down there looking and never comes back out."

Tepper shook his head. "So, for survivors, we've got a drunk and an abused kid."

"Just an abused kid at this point," Caitlin said, recalling all the bodies she'd come upon at the hospital and her battle with the big Native American man.

"You want to tell me something they've got in common, all the same?"

Caitlin moved toward the black hole beyond the steel blast doors Paz had just hoisted opened. "Let's hope we get to ask Andrew Ortega that question."

Caitlin clambered down the ladder under the spray light from a flashlight that had magically appeared from one of the pockets of Paz's tactical pants. She was glad Tepper had called him, since she'd been thinking of doing the same. He was a creature of fate more than a man, it seemed at times, which made his presence reassuring, to say the least, in an airless town where that same fate had struck a brutal blow.

At the bottom of the ladder, she waited for Paz to drop the flashlight to her before she continued on into the depths of the fallout shelter. Maybe Paz was wearing off on her, because Caitlin thought she could actually feel the fear that had collected down here, mixing with the dry rot and must that smelled of rank perspiration.

She had never been in a fallout shelter before. The short hallway widened toward a mouth, beyond which she glimpsed a lantern flickering. Kerosene, she thought, as opposed to batteries.

Reaching the mouth of the sprawling, rectangular shelter itself, she spotted two men and a woman, bound and gagged, with their own belts, socks, and jackets serving as bonds.

"Drop the gun," a young, terrified voice wheezed.

57

Camino Pass, Texas

Caitlin crouched to lay her pistol on the dirt-encrusted plank floor, careful not to shine her flashlight at the boy who was holding a twelve-gauge shotgun in a trembling grasp, his lips quivering and eyes swimming with fear.

"Andrew Ortega," Caitlin said calmly, in what had started out as a question. "I'm glad you're alive."

"That's what *they* said," the boy managed, stealing a gaze at his three captives. "What happened? What's going on? Tell me!"

"I'm a Texas Ranger, son. I'm here to help you, just like these folks are. You've done nothing wrong and have nothing to fear. I want you to lower that shotgun so it's not pointed directly at me. Do you mind doing that?"

The boy swallowed hard and complied, dipping the barrel even lower than Caitlin had asked him to. She looked toward Homeland Security's search and rescue team again; their bonds were indicative of a victim who likely had been held, and tormented, in similar or even identical fashion. Caitlin wished she'd had the opportunity to meet Andrew Ortega's father up close and personal, wished the boy or his mother had called the Rangers instead of the highway patrol to report him.

At first glance, Andrew Ortega hardly seemed the type to fight back against a brutal, bullying father prone to letting the bottle get the better of him. He looked thin to her, with the kind of slight frame that struggled to hold up a pair of jeans even with a belt. His arms were scrawny, his face gaunt, with hollowed-out cheeks and black hair the same color as his eyes. She could hear slight sounds of movement behind her, indicating Captain Tepper and Paz were following in her wake, sure to stay back when they realized her intentions.

"I lowered the gun, now tell me what happened up there," he managed, his voice cracking through lips that continued to quiver. "Is it true what they said? Is everybody dead?"

"I'm afraid so, Andrew."

"Then why did I live?"

"I don't know. Almost surely because you were hiding down here. I can't tell you why, but that's got to be it." Caitlin paused just long enough. "You were hiding down here from your father, weren't you?"

"Do you know him?"

"Wish I did, so I could lay him out for the way he treated you. If you know anything about the Texas Rangers, you know I'm telling the truth."

"But you're a woman."

"A lot has changed in the three days you've been down here."

The boy seemed to relax a bit, Caitlin's light comment achieving its desired effect.

"I didn't know what to do." He tilted his head toward the bound DHS team. "And when they showed up, I didn't know what to do then, either. I thought they were looking for me. They weren't making any sense."

"Would you mind laying the shotgun on the floor, Andrew?"

"Are you going to arrest me?"

"You haven't done anything wrong."

The boy gestured toward the Homeland Security team. "I took them hostage. I didn't know what else to do."

"But they won't be pressing charges." Then, with her eyes trained on the three people, she added, "Will you?"

Three heads shook resolutely from side to side.

"Smart move, because that way we can keep the fact that they let a kid get the jump on them from getting out. That's not something they'd want to become common knowledge."

"What about me?"

Caitlin turned back to Andrew Ortega. "We need to get you checked out, see how it is you survived. Get you some food. I'll bet you're starving."

The boy shed the shotgun from his grasp like it weighed a ton. She could see the boy's throat expand as he tried to swallow but failed.

"How'd everybody else die?"

Caitlin decided to leave out mention of a second survivor to avoid questions she didn't want to answer. "They were poisoned. We're not sure how exactly."

"Killed?"

"It was an accident, Andrew, and if we can figure how it was that coming down here saved your life, we'll be able to fill in a bunch of the blanks. Can you stand up?"

"I've been sitting here a long time."

"You want me to help you?"

The boy nodded, his doe-like eyes widening. "I'm sorry for what I did to those folks over there. But they were talking crazy, like my father. I thought maybe he sent them. I couldn't be sure. You believe me, don't you?"

Caitlin made sure he could see her nod.

"I'm scared again. I guess I never stopped being scared."

"You can now, son," she said, reaching down to help the boy to his feet.

58

CAMINO PASS, TEXAS

Captain Tepper and Paz worked the Homeland agents free of their bonds while Caitlin tended to Andrew Ortega in the flickering lantern light.

"They'll be waiting to tend to you up the road at the command center," she told him.

"You gonna leave me with them?" the boy asked, as if terrified by the prospects of that.

"I'll check on you soon, Andrew, and regularly. That's a promise."

The boy managed the thinnest of smiles before the hatch-like door closed behind him.

The Homeland agents returned to their vehicle, and then Caitlin followed closely as they headed back to the checkpoint.

"Any thoughts, Colonel?" she asked Paz, while D. W. Tepper worked awkwardly through some emails on his phone, swearing under his breath when the one finger he was using refused to cooperate. Then he remembered Andrew Ortega was sitting next to him and apologized.

"This, what happened in this town, was an accident."

"We've already figured out that much."

"There's more. The residue remains. What happened here opened a door. I understand my actions at the school now."

"You mean doing live fire exercises with elementary school kids in gym class?" she said, drawing a rise from Tepper.

"I knew I was preparing them for something, but I didn't know what. I could feel it, Ranger. I could smell what was coming, and I smelled it again in that town."

"You're saying we need to stop somebody bad from turning what happened here into a weapon, Colonel."

"If they haven't already, Ranger."

A windstorm had kicked up by the time they made it back to the checkpoint manned by the highway patrol. Caitlin personally escorted

Andrew Ortega to the RV-size Homeland Security mobile medical unit, which would soon be tending to the three Homeland agents the boy had held hostage for several hours as well.

"This is Colonel Guillermo Paz," she said, by way of introduction, when Paz entered behind her and Andrew Ortega, ducking to clear the doorway. "He's an agent of the Department of Homeland Security, attached here in Texas, and the boy will be remaining under his protection. Anybody have a problem with that?"

A few gazes tilted toward Paz's intimidating shape. No one offered any protest.

"Glad we're all agreed, then," Caitlin said and retraced her steps out of the mobile unit.

Outside, the sandstorm had already picked up in intensity. Dust and gravel swirled about the air, stinging her skin like pinpricks and forcing Caitlin to retreat back inside the Ranger chopper, which was already encrusted with a thickening blanket of grime.

Captain Tepper climbed in next to her and slid the door closed after him.

"Any objections voiced about King Kong's involvement?" he asked, gazed tilted toward where the mobile unit was parked.

"Not a one. Those folks know what happened to Lennox Scully at University Hospital. They don't have much grounds for an argument."

Caitlin hadn't bothered clearing the windshield of dust and grime, leaving only dim patches of light to penetrate the cab. Tepper continued clumsily returning some emails and text messages, fighting his own thumbs and occasionally staring at the windshield as if he could see straight through the sand-colored coating that continued to thicken.

"It's gonna be a while before the chopper can take off, D.W."

"So?" Tepper asked, even though it was clear he knew what she was getting at.

"So we've got time for you to pick up the story of my great-granddad and Pancho Villa . . ."

59

Mexico; 1898

The ride continued, the heat pouring out of the blazing sun seeming to pick up degrees with each yard they covered. The trail thinned, steepened, and the parade of horsemen led by Jesus Arriaga was forced to take a single-file procession. The brush grew sparse, then strangely thickened again as they approached what William Ray took for a thin gully cut out of the Las Bajadas by the years and the elements.

Suddenly, gunmen who hadn't seemed to be there a moment before appeared amid a nest of boulders, one of which was blocking the trail, keeping the group from advancing farther. They wore strangely shaped hats to keep the sun from their faces, enough of a disguise to keep William Ray from noticing they were Chinese until they drew to within a few yards. He was too far away to hear the conversation between the lead Chinese gunman and Arriaga, and he focused on the rifles they had stripped from their shoulders instead: Mausers, the very model used to kill the Camino Pass posse from upward of five or six hundred feet away.

William Ray watched Arriaga tap his horse to make it reverse, opening up enough space for a pair of the Chinese gunmen to ease the big boulder blocking the trail aside like it weighed nothing at all—because it didn't, or close to that anyway. It must have been some kind of model, replica, or something, made out of paper or cardboard, with a tin facing colored to look just like the real thing.

The horses started on again, this time led by the head Chinese gunman, with a second trailing the pack slightly. The grade of the trail slackened, leveling off as they reached the ridge, and then William Ray figured he had to be seeing things. Before him, layered along the rocky ridge, was a town made of tents and open-sided structures formed of logs from trees harvested in the foothills where they'd made camp. There were roads and alleys and outhouses, even a bar and what William Ray would've bet next month's salary was a brothel, given that it was built of logs and was one of only two structures to boast walls.

The other such structure was much more elegant and ornate, painted a majestic red and topped by a sharply peaked roof of the sort William Ray had seen in magazine articles about Chinese culture. It looked entirely out of place here, and he was at an utter loss to figure out how a structure this complex and sophisticated could have been built this high up in the mountains. He'd never been to this part of central Mexico before, but he had heard tales of how the desert ended on one side of the mountains forming Las Bajadas, and some of the country's most fertile lands could be found on the other.

Arriaga's men waited for him to climb down from his horse before they dismounted. Pancho Villa beat William Ray to the ground and moved to help him manage the effort while wearing wrist irons, but pride made the Ranger manage the effort all on his own. This, even as he couldn't for the life of him figure out how a place like this might be connected to a whole bunch of children kidnapped just over the border.

"You ever fixing to tell me what it is you're after in these parts?" William Ray asked him softly. "Or why you came along for the ride? I'm guessing it wasn't to see the sights."

Villa smiled slyly, looking older than his years. "I have no idea what you're talking about, Ranger, and if I did have something to tell you, right now you'd take it to the grave."

"We'll see about that, amigo. I've been in tougher scrapes than this. My daddy's regiment in the Civil War beat back a Northern brigade ten times their number. Nobody would've given them a chance, neither."

Villa turned his gaze down on William Ray's empty holster. "But at least they had guns."

The Ranger was about to respond when he caught Pancho Villa's gaze tighten on that structure that looked lifted from another place and time entirely. William Ray turned to follow his gaze and spotted the figure of an average-size Chinese man wearing woolen suit pants and matching vest into which a perfectly knotted tie had been tucked. He looked like he was going to a wedding or some fancy office somewhere, thumbs hooked inside his vest pockets as he scanned the riders before settling on William Ray.

He seemed to float down a set of stairs from the porch, which enclosed the whole of the fancy structure, and walked, absent fear or thought, straight toward William Ray. Jesus Arriaga and his men fell into step behind him, one after the other, making for quite the crowd by the time he stood before William Ray.

"A Texas Ranger, in the flesh," the Chinese man said in English lacking any accent whatsoever. "I've waited for this moment for a long time, ever since I came here."

"And when would that have been?" William Ray wondered.

The man looked toward Pancho Villa. "Before he was born, surely. Probably a few years prior."

"It appears you have the advantage on me, sir."

The man bowed ever so slightly as he extended a hand. "Felipe Wong, Ranger."

William Ray took the hand, wrist chains clanging, and found it dry and smooth. Wong's grip was like a vise. "William Ray Strong."

"The Rangers have made inquiries as to my whereabouts. I'm surprised you've never heard of me."

"There's others of us more familiar with these parts."

"Would you like to see the source of their interest in me? Would you like to see the great commerce I've brought to this country?"

"Right now, all I'd like to see is those kids I'm guessing you had snatched."

"In time, Ranger."

"No time like the present, Mr. Wong."

Wong stepped back and moved slightly aside so as not to have the sun directly in his eyes, to better size William Ray up. "Your genuine show of respect and manners are much appreciated, Ranger."

"I respect all men, sir, even the ones I have to kill."

Wong's expression stretched into a smile, coming up just short of a laugh. "It's really true, isn't it?"

"What's that?"

"All the legends, the bravado of the mighty Texas Rangers."

"Well, sir, I'm not learned enough to know the precise meaning of 'bravado,' but if it means the willingness to tell a murderer he's full of shit, then I'll take that as a compliment."

Wong looked as if he wanted to laugh. "My enterprise here requires much labor."

"You trying to tell me that's what you needed the kids you took for?"

"It's better I show you, Ranger. I'll have my horse brought round."

Wong's horse was a magnificent steed; thick-legged, as tall as any William Ray had ever seen, and broader at the shoulders than any he'd ever crossed before. Perfect dimensions to cover the difficult mountain terrain that would snap the legs of a lesser animal. It snorted as Wong climbed on, blowing out hot breath in a manner that made the Ranger think of a fire-breathing dragon.

Wong positioned himself next to William Ray, who was back atop Jessabelle, towering over him, thanks to his horse's comparative size. A trio of what the Ranger took to be Wong's personal bodyguards rode close behind them, followed by Jesus Arriaga.

"Where we going, sir?"

Wong kept his gaze fixed ahead, not regarding William Ray when he responded. "Immigrating to Mexico was not a random decision, Ranger. Me and others came here with a plan, and we didn't come empty-handed."

"You talking about those Mauser rifles your men used to gun down a bunch of farmers and ranchers?"

"That bothers you."

"You bet it does. I don't abide the slaughter of innocents, Mr. Wong. No Ranger does. You might even say it's what's kept us together for going on seventy-five years now. I've seen what marauding Indians have done to entire families and settlements. I've seen Mexican bandits shoot up towns with a man who can't find his dentures serving as sheriff. I've seen dreams dashed, good intentions wasted, and lives ended for no other reason than they happened to be standing somewhere at a particular time. So if you truly are responsible for the murder of those folks who went out looking for their kids, I'll have no choice but to kill you."

Wong smiled at William Ray and signaled the procession to stop before he summoned Arriaga up to the front.

"You have the key to those wrist irons?"

Arriaga flashed it.

"Take them off," Wong ordered.

Arriaga looked at the Ranger, then back at the figure atop the tall horse.

"Now," Wong added.

Arriaga removed the cuffs circling William Ray's wrists and laid them before him on his saddle.

"Now you can make good on your word," Wong said to William Ray.

The Ranger smiled. "Time and a place for everything, Mr. Wong, and neither of those is the case right now. But they will be, you can count on that."

Wong smiled back at him. "Old Chinese proverb: 'If you are patient in one moment of anger, you will escape one hundred days of sorrow.'"

"Well, I'm not sure what that means exactly, but I seem to remember another Chinese saying that goes something like 'Talk doesn't cook rice.'"

"It would seem you're a more learned man than your demeanor suggests."

William Ray's eyes widened, then narrowed. "Demeanor? What's that mean?"

The terrain was rocky, the grade uneven to the point where, for the final stretch through Las Bajadas the riders dismounted and walked their horses, clutching the reins tight. Something seemed to have made the animals uneasy—a smell or a sound, William Ray didn't know which.

The sun had reached its peak in the sky when a rocky, downward-sloping ridgeline revealed oddly fertile lands rich in flora and growth in a valley beyond, with a similarly graded, sloping hill guarding its far side as well.

"Behold, Ranger," said a beaming Felipe Wong, sounding like a father showing off his newborn child. "I believe you know what you're looking at."

60

CAMINO PASS, TEXAS

"That's as far as I want to go right now," Tepper finished. "You got enough on your mind already."

"How is it that Andrew Ortega survived, D.W.?" Caitlin posed, putting the tale of William Ray Strong's exploits in Mexico aside for the moment. "What is it he's got in common with the late Lennox Scully?"

"You want to run the math for me and see what adds up?"

"Scully was sleeping one off in a converted supply closet and this kid was hiding out in a fallout shelter. Nothing in common there that strikes me off the bat."

"As in why the cyanide didn't kill them."

"Because it didn't spread to where they were. We figure out why, maybe we figure out where it originated in the first place."

It was three more hours before their chopper settled over the jet-black helipad back at Stinson Airport, where the chopper provided by Homeland Security was housed twenty minutes from Company F headquarters.

"So we're ruling out hostile action, an attack or something?" D. W. Tepper asked her.

"I am. Jury's still out at Homeland, and Jones is champing at the bit to weaponize however the deed got done, to clear a path for him back to Washington."

"That man is a walking enigma."

"I don't believe I ever heard you use that word before, Captain."

"I've been doing a lot of reading. Distracts me from the winds of Hurricane Caitlin constantly blowing up a storm."

"I didn't go looking for this one."

"But it found you anyway, didn't it? You're like human flypaper, Ranger, and wherever you go, the worst of the worst just sticks to you."

61

Washington, DC

"Slow down," Senator Ben Eckles said to Roland Fass, "and tell me what's got you so spooked. Calmly."

"That's easy for you to say," Fass spat out. "You didn't have a Texas Ranger in your office."

"Another Texas Ranger?"

"Actually, it's the same one, the very last person on the planet we want messing in our business, especially with its expanding nature and all."

"Did you just say that *over the phone?*"

"I'm using a burner I picked up at the drugstore around the corner."

"Good, that means what I'm about to say will stay between us. I picked you up off the scrap heap because you impressed me as a man who'd stop at nothing to get something done. That burned you in your former life, but both of us know there were another hundred things you did that could have gotten you nailed six ways to Sunday. I know about a few of those, and it's a discussion we don't need to have. The discussion we do need to have is that you're starting to make me regret my decision, Roland. I served you up a second chance on a silver platter you're now doing your best to tarnish."

"You think I'm spooked? You think I'm gonna end up spilling to this Texas Ranger?"

"I *know* you're spooked. I'm afraid you're going to end up saying more than you should. You know that second chance you got? Well, fate has served up an even bigger one for the good ol' U S of A. A chance to right a whole bunch of wrongs, wipe the slate clean as they say. You don't want to get in the way of that, you hear me?"

"Loud and clear."

"Good. Now, you need to make yourself useful. I've got a job for you to do. Something I know you're good at because it's about numbers. How high can you count up to, Roland?"

"What's the difference?"

"Because if luck's on our side, it's going to reach the millions."

62

HOUSTON

"What's the haps, Pops?" Nola Delgado said, climbing into Cort Wesley's truck, which was parked in the shady part of the Walmart parking lot where he'd told her to meet him. "You actually shop here?"

"Don't call me that, Nola. And the phrase 'What's the haps' is better fit for the Big Easy than Texas. You need to work on your English."

"Dylan thinks I speak it just fine. What happened to 'Like father, like son'?"

"Don't make me regret calling you," Cort Wesley said, already doing just that.

"I'm glad you did. I was getting bored. Watching people's backs really isn't my thing."

"Is that what you're doing in Providence? Watching my son's back?" Cort Wesley said, rolling the driver's side window all the way down to let more air into the truck.

"Dylan doesn't need me for that, Pops. He can take care of himself."

"What did I say about calling me that?"

"Would you prefer 'Dad'?"

"I'd prefer we weren't having this discussion, but 'Cort Wesley' should do."

Nola frowned. Looking at her in the shadowy half light of the lot's shaded portion made him think of Caitlin. Nola didn't sound like her, held herself in an entirely different way. But every once in a while, when he looked across the seat, for an instant he thought he was looking at Caitlin. Same long hair, same strong features and, most of all, the same eyes. A gunfighter's eyes, the eyes of Jim Strong, who'd fathered them both.

"Yeah, about that. We're beyond a simple first name basis, don't you think?"

"No, I don't."

"You really don't get it, do you?"

"Since I have no idea what you're talking about, I guess not, Nola."

"Dylan and I are a couple."

Cort Wesley cringed. "You ignored Caitlin's warning to stay away from him."

"You mean my *sister's* warning?"

"Half sister."

"Blood is blood, Pops, and the heart wants what the heart wants."

Cort Wesley regarded Nola Delgado closer, trying to forget that a woman who'd taken as many lives as lung cancer was living with his son.

"So, what do you need?" she asked him. "And how many do we have to kill to get it?"

63

Houston

There were four guards, two outside the warehouse and two inside. Nola nailed their positions, with the help of a pair of night vision binoculars, from the roof of a building down the street.

"Give me ten minutes to clear the field."

Cort Wesley grasped her forearm, feeling the tight strands of banded muscle that felt like pliable steel. "Nobody dies, Nola."

"Don't be a killjoy."

"Was that supposed to be a pun?" Cort Wesley asked her.

"You asked for my help and here I am. Gotta have a little fun in return."

"By killing."

"Come on, Pops, lighten up. I'm just trying to ease the tension here."

Lots of thoughts scurried through Cort Wesley's mind, but one rose above the others for his attention: his oldest son was dating a psychopath. Or maybe it was a sociopath; he always got them confused. Hell, maybe Nola Delgado was both.

"Hey, thank the Ranger," she said, as if reading his mind.

"For what?"

"Dragging me into your lives. Here's the plan," Nola continued. "I'll work my way onto the property and take care of the guards inside. Give me ten minutes and then the two outside are yours. How's that sound?"

"Don't kill them, Nola."

"Whatever you say, Pops."

Cort Wesley worked his way to the perimeter of the fenced-in property containing the warehouse, careful to cling to the darkness so as not to be spotted by any cameras they may not have spotted. Of course, cameras these days could be easily concealed and remain utterly unobtrusive. Better to take other precautions, which in this case meant donning a neoprene mask still fancied by special operators. Not something particularly conducive to the Texas heat and humidity, even at night, but he wasn't about to risk being captured on video for all interested parties to see.

As he approached the fence line, Cort Wesley reviewed the specifications of what he and Nola were likely to find inside. Since the Texas economy remained dependent on the oil industry, there was no shortage of petrochemical facilities throughout the state, although he'd never heard of one located this close to a population center. Cort Wesley recalled a plant explosion that took a dozen lives, caused by chemicals that remained inert on their own but were stored close enough together to shed vapors that ignited the blast and resulting fire. The fact that a petrochemical storage facility had been permitted within the Houston city limits told him the fix was in, the stench of whatever was inside these walls reaching all the way to Washington.

By the time Cort Wesley, clad entirely in black, melded into the night and reached the fence line, he could no longer spot either of the perimeter guards. He located the spot in the fence where Nola had popped the lock to a towered gate, then slid inside the exterior yard in what he imagined was her wake.

Still no guards, though, which left Cort Wesley wary as he approached a rear security door Nola was supposed to have entered through. She'd left the door open just a crack, and Cort Wesley opened it just enough to slip inside and close it all the way.

Turning all the way around brought him face-to-face with a grinning Nola Delgado, who stood between the downed frames of the two guards he was supposed to have taken out.

"What took you so long, Pops?"

64

HOUSTON

"Hope you don't mind I decided to finish what I started," she continued.

"What I mind is how much you seem to enjoy it."

"And you don't?"

"I don't go looking for opportunities to finish what I start, if that's what you mean."

"Hey, they're still breathing, aren't they? Now, are we going to stand here and argue or are you ready to check this place out?"

The warehouse beyond was sprawling and cavernous. A single level was subdivided by rebar-reinforced concrete walls to form separate storage units for the individual chemicals stored here. Cort Wesley had read that, in Texas, storage of hazardous, potentially dangerous and toxic chemicals had pretty much gone away from the old-fashioned fifty-five-gallon drums to be replaced by what were called intermediate bulk containers. These steel, rectangular units, which resembled basement furnaces, had a 350-gallon capacity, equal to six drums. They could fit on a single pallet and be handled by a single forklift. Because of the new units' superior and more secure construction, the older drums could now be replaced by far fewer IBCs, which were designed to be reusable. Further, they were designed to put safety first; all were outfitted with a bottom drain, which eliminated any need to turn them on their sides to empty their contents in the event of an emergency. It would have made the residents of Texas sleep a lot better, had they been aware in the first place of how many dangerous chemicals were stored from one side of the state to the other.

Sure enough, the steel intermediate bulk containers were the only kind in evidence, not a single old-fashioned fifty-five-gallon drum anywhere to be seen. The IBCs were stacked up to a dozen high in what looked like a tower. Cort Wesley couldn't say what each of them contained specifically, only that the amount stored here was incredible in scope, too much to even estimate in terms of gallons.

"Notice anything?" he said to Nola.

She tensed, scanning the sprawling floor with focused intensity. "I miss somebody?"

"I was talking about the storage containers."

"There's a lot of them."

"Look closer."

Nola did. "They all look exactly the same."

"As in brand new."

"Yeah. So?"

"Intermediate bulk containers aren't a new concept," Cort Wesley explained. "They shouldn't *all* be new."

Nola nodded. "Think I'm reading you now, Pops. You're saying this Fass guy had them all manufactured from scratch, like a special order or something."

"Or whoever's behind him did. Either way, that would allow a custom design to be employed, specific to what might be the real purpose of this place."

"Just enough real chemicals to pass muster and not attract attention," Nola concluded.

"How about we have a look?"

But that initial look proved disappointing. Cort Wesley tapped the steel exterior shells of dozens of IBCs with a thin-headed ball-peen hammer. The resulting sound, a pinging, told him they did in fact contain the liquid or granular petrochemical they were supposed to contain, as opposed to the opioid pills he'd been expecting to find here, based on the conclusions he'd reached with Caitlin.

"What now, Pops?" Nola asked him.

"That was the easy way. Now we have to try the hard one."

Cort Wesley had learned to operate plenty of heavy machinery while pulling jobs with his father, particularly loaders to lift the refrigerators and ranges clipped from warehouses like this into the back of similarly stolen trucks. Fortunately, he found a bucket loader with controls almost identical to a set he was familiar with, which allowed him access to the topmost IBCs upon the stack.

It took him a few moments to get the hang of things again, but as soon as he was being raised into the air inside a bucket, he thought of the old Glen Campbell song "Wichita Lineman."

Closer to the top of the stack, Cort Wesley repeated the process with his ball-peen hammer. Modern forensic techniques would have employed X-rays or ultrasound to confirm the actual contents, but this was all he had, his technological limits reached with managing the controls of the loader.

At first, the results disappointed him; the sound produced by tapping the steel shell was identical to the IBCs at floor level. He'd hoped for false bottoms in the containers to conceal the opiates stored inside, in which case the ping from the ball-peen hammer would have been slightly different. But there was nothing, no difference at all.

And then Cort Wesley felt something like a feather scraping up his spine as he realized why, realized he'd had this part of whatever Roland Fass was involved in wrong. This wasn't where illicit opioids were being stored at all. These canisters really did contain chemicals, almost surely one chemical in particular. He saw that now, still fitting the pieces together when the bucket extension thumped on impact with the floor.

Nola Delgado was nowhere in sight, but Cort Wesley heard the onrush of at least four sets of feet before he could step from the bucket.

"Freeze! Don't move!"

One figure was speaking while three others, garbed in black tactical gear, raced ahead of him with assault rifles steadied, fingers tensed on the triggers.

PART SIX

JOHN B. JONES

In 1874, Jones—a distinguished veteran of Texas forces in the Civil War—was chosen to head the Frontier Battalion, a newly created organization composed of six large Ranger companies and tasked with protecting the Texas frontier. Under his firm hand, the Rangers reached new levels as a state police force, helping preserve law and order in the chaotic period following the Civil War and Reconstruction. Train robber Sam Bass, one of the most notorious outlaws of the time, eluded capture until July 1878, when one of the members of his gang turned informer, writing to Jones of Bass' plans to rob a small bank in Round Rock. Jones' Rangers met the robbers there, and in the ensuing gunfight Bass was fatally wounded. In 1879, Jones was given even greater responsibility as adjutant general of the state of Texas; he died in service in 1881.

—Sarah Pruitt, "8 Famous Texas Rangers," History.com

65

HOUSTON

"You boys don't want to be doing this," Cort Wesley said, hands in the air, a different picture coming together in his head.

"Come out of there real slow like and keep your arms where I can see them!"

Cort Wesley had to lower one of his hands to pop open the latch, keeping that hand in plain view as he did so and started to emerge from the bucket. "Listen to me. Get out of here. Leave now, while you still can."

The four men looked like they found that funny.

"What," another of them started in, "you got invisible friends or something?"

Yes, Cort Wesley almost said, thinking of Leroy Epps, *but that's not your problem.*

"This isn't on me, if you don't get your asses out of here."

"Okay, boss, whatever you say," the biggest of them said. "When we dump your body in a hole somewhere in the desert, it won't be on us either."

The lights went out in that moment, Cort Wesley dropping low just as the first familiar spits of sound-suppressed gunfire sounded. A series of muzzle flashes, a half dozen maybe, followed by another three, blew light in thin swatches that faded as quickly as it came. Cort Wesley heard the thumps of bodies hitting the floor, accompanied by grunts, groans, and the airless wisp of men taking their final breaths.

Then a flashlight pierced the darkness, silhouetting the lithe figure of Nola Delgado, who reached his side as Cort Wesley climbed back to his feet.

"You can thank me later, Pops."

"For what?" he asked, as they retraced their steps toward the building's rear entrance.

"Saving your life."

"You set those men up. You must've purposely tripped a silent alarm so you could enjoy some target practice."

"Well," Nola said, not bothering to deny it, "I haven't been to the range in a while. Gotta stay sharp, right?"

She was close enough for Cort Wesley to feel her breath on him. "You executed them. That's not target practice."

"I go up against four assault rifles and you call that an execution?"

"They never had a chance."

"They were ex-army. I could see that plain as day, even in the dark, and so could you while I was saving your life."

"You dropped them in a barrel and plugged them like fish. And don't say you did it for me. Don't lay this on my doorstep."

She slowed, snickering at Cort Wesley as they neared the door. "Come on, lighten up, Pops."

"I just watched you murder four men, Nola. You might as well have tied their hands behind their backs and blindfolded them."

"Except I didn't. And it was their own fault, not considering the likelihood, at least possibility, someone else was in the building."

"They had me figured as a reporter, maybe a cop," Cort Wesley persisted.

"You heard what the head guy said. You were dead meat, headed for a hole in the desert. A little gratitude would be nice, Pops—just a little." A new look danced across Nola's expression, something hot and cold at the same time, amorphous in the light that made her features look more liquid than solid. "How about we call Dylan and give him an update?"

They stepped into the steamy night air.

"Leave him out of this," Cort Wesley warned.

"You think he wouldn't want to hear? You don't think he eats this shit up?"

"I was there when he killed a kid about his own age a while back. He did it to save my life. I saw the look on his face and, no, I don't think he eats this shit up."

"Ease up and look in the mirror," Nola Delgado told him with chilling assurance. "Because you like the taste as much as I do. That's why you don't want to call him, because you'd have to admit that."

"I apologize for calling you a psychopath before."

"Thanks."

"Because you're something worse, Nola, the kind of a person they don't have a term for. The kind the world wants to believe doesn't exist, just like the monsters that live under the bed."

"Doesn't mean they're not there, does it?"

Cort Wesley stopped and faced her. "I don't want you seeing Dylan anymore. I don't want you going back to Providence."

"He tells me to go, I'm gone."

"I just did."

"But you're not him, Pops. The way I feel about Dylan is why I saved your bacon. Along with something else."

"What's that?"

She smiled like a kid reaching the tree on Christmas morning. "Because I know when you and my sister go to guns, there's a whole lot of fun to be had."

Cort Wesley looked down at the bodies again. "Except we do our best to avoid collateral damage."

"Wake up and smell the gun smoke, Pops. We're at war, and war always brings collateral damage with it. I need to tell you that, after what happened to Luke?"

"You've never even met him."

"But he's family to Caitlin, which makes him family to me. That means I intend to keep an eye out his way, stop him from ending up collateral damage too," Nola said, glancing at the men she'd dropped in their tracks as if to better make her point.

"Thanks, but no thanks."

"I wasn't asking for permission. Like I said, I'm doing it for Caitlin.

I told you I was the only blood she's got, but that's not really true, is it? She's got you, and Dylan and Luke. Think about it. One of the four of you is my sister, and I might be in love with one of the other three. So I figure looking out after Luke isn't a favor, it's a duty."

"Knock yourself out," Cort Wesley told Nola Delgado, no longer able to argue the point.

66

SAN ANTONIO, TEXAS

"You're saying he was underground the whole time?" Doc Whatley said to Caitlin, after listening to her brief description of how and where they had found Andrew Ortega.

"In a fallout shelter, of all places," she told him across his ever-cluttered desk.

"Might be the first time one of those actually saved a life. It took long enough, I suppose."

"The question is how, Doc. What is it this kid has in common with Lennox Scully?"

"Had," Whatley corrected. "And maybe nothing."

"You don't believe that any more than I do."

"I believe it until I find a firm indicator, as in actual proof, otherwise. Run the numbers for me, Ranger. Let's think this out."

The Bexar County Medical Examiner's Office and morgue was located just off the Loop 410, not far from the Babcock Road exit, on Merton Minter. It was a three-story beige building that also housed the county health department and city offices for Medicaid. The office inevitably smelled of cleaning solvent, with a faint scent of menthol clinging to the walls like paint to disguise the odor of decaying flesh. The lighting was dull in the hallways and overly bright in the offices, except for in Whatley's, thanks to lesser-strength bulbs he'd placed in the hidden ceiling fixtures.

"Okay," Caitlin started, "the late Lennox Scully was sleeping off a bender in the local walk-in medical clinic, something he'd done before.

Kind of like it was his own personal Holiday Inn. Maybe the fact that he was drunk is what ended up saving his life."

"How's that compare with this kid?"

"Andrew Ortega fled to that bomb shelter because he was scared as hell of his father beating the crap out of him. Add to that the guilt over leaving his mother to face his fury alone, and his heart must've been going a mile a minute. And, when I saw him anyway, he was breathing so fast I thought he was about to hyperventilate and pass out."

"So now you're in the diagnosis business?"

"You asked me a question, Doc, and now I want to ask you one. Given what I just said about Andrew Ortega's condition, is there anything that jibes, in a medical sense, with a drunk passed out in what used to be a supply closet?"

"Now you're on the right track, Dr. Strong."

"Does that mean you've got an answer to my question?"

"Being on the right track doesn't necessarily mean the right line. Because the answer, in general anyway, is still nothing." Whatley hesitated, tapping a pencil atop his desk blotter until the tip broke. "Can you get me a copy of the results of whatever tests Homeland runs on this kid?"

"I can try. Anything in particular you're looking for?"

"Something maybe with no connection to where you found him. Could be in the blood work, or some congenital issue that somehow rendered them immune to cyanide poisoning."

"Is that even possible?"

"I said 'somehow,' didn't I?" Whatley snapped. "And the answer is that I have no idea. We're operating in totally uncharted territory here."

"And from where I'm standing, we still have no idea where the cyanide gas that killed an entire town originated."

"An entire town minus two, Ranger."

"What are we missing? Like any gas, cyanide disperses through the air. And last time I checked, Andrew Ortega and Lennox Scully were breathing the same air as the three hundred or so others who weren't as lucky."

Whatley's eyes snapped alert. He started to look toward Caitlin, then stopped.

"What, Doc? What's on your mind?"

"How quickly can you get me those test results on this kid, Ranger?"

"Why?"

"Because I've got a notion of how Camino Pass got wiped off the map."

67

HOUSTON

"What's wrong with your face?" Roland Fass asked Yarek Bone. The two of them were standing where all four bodies of the security team had been found on the warehouse floor earlier that morning.

"Ask me that again and there'll be something much worse wrong with yours."

Fass cleared his throat and looked away. "This is where it happened," he said, no longer wanting to meet the big man's gaze.

"I know," Bone told him. "That's why I'm standing here."

Bone could see the bodies, even though they weren't there anymore. They had been removed long before he got to the warehouse, with the so-called authorities being none the wiser. But he more than just saw them; he could also feel the residue of their pain. Not quite as pronounced as what he'd felt in the hospital basement or when he'd killed the deer, but it was there, tweaking his reality with a pleasant euphoria beyond even that of the peyote he'd done as a kid.

No matter how pleasant it might be, though, he couldn't shake from his mind the experience with the Texas Ranger that had left him with his newfound ability. No matter how many showers he took or how many times he washed himself, he couldn't rid himself of the oil smell that rode his flesh like paint. Bitter and sweet at the same time and making him feel like he'd spilled gasoline on himself at the self-serve.

Bone's Comanche ancestors had had more than their share of run-ins with the vaunted lawmen who, back in those days, shot first and shot second, too. A quirky turn of events, then, that his path should cross with a Texas Ranger who'd similarly gotten the jump on him. Bone was left fleeing on foot, the same way his ancestors had on horseback. He wasn't used to running, even less used to failing. But he knew he'd get another chance at the woman Ranger, felt it somewhere down deep, where the pain of others radiated outward. And he couldn't wait to feel the woman's pain again, only magnified a hundred times.

"Are you listening to me?" Roland Fass was asking him, voice raised.

Bone looked down at the man who was at least a head shorter than him, even at almost six feet tall. "You need better security."

"That's not what I asked you."

"It's what you need, all the same. I can bring in some men from Fallen Timbers who've been off the grid for years. All of them have spilled real blood—not just trained to do it, like the ones who died here."

"That nose of yours tell you anything else?"

Bone didn't bother telling Fass that, lately, the only thing his nose had been telling him was that he stank of oil. "They didn't get a single shot off."

"Did I tell you that?"

"You didn't have to. It's obvious from how the bodies fell in such a tight cluster."

Fass looked up at the bigger man, suddenly hesitant. "Can you see them?"

"Feel them. Same thing really. And I can feel something else, too: whoever did this enjoyed it. They considered it sport."

"You don't think they were trying to send us a message?"

"That is a message," Bone told him.

"Because maybe somebody's wised up about our business. Like maybe the cartels south of the border don't like us cutting into their market share."

"The cartels would've burned the place down, Fass. Whoever did this was scoping the place out instead. I can have my people here by nightfall. They come with an ironclad guarantee that you won't be finding any more bodies on the floor unless they put them there."

Fass hesitated. "You think this was the work of that Texas Ranger, the woman?"

Bone sniffed the air. "She wasn't here, but . . ."

"What?" Fass prodded.

"Nothing," the big man said, not sure of what he was feeling. "Tell me about the kid."

"What kid?"

"The one who OD'd, got this whole mess started."

"He's an honor student or something. Kind of like this Texas Ranger's son."

"Yeah?"

"Yeah. She's involved with the kid's father, who happens to be the guy who burned down the one-stop pill shop where the dealer got the oxy that almost killed his boy."

"I see." Bone nodded. "We need to change the game here."

"What's that mean?"

"It's better to have thunder in the mouth and more lightning in the hand. My people have been masters of psychological warfare since before the white man ever got here. I think it's time we started to employ some of that here, make Caitlin Strong hurt in a way she never has before."

"Sounds personal."

"Take another look at my face. There's no worse pain than what follows a loved one dying on your watch."

"You talking about this kid?"

"I'm talking about finishing the job that overdose started."

Fass's phone rang and Bone watched him step aside to take the call.

"You confirmed this?" Fass said into the phone. "You're sure? . . . No, don't do a goddamn thing until you hear from me."

Fass ended the call and put his phone back absently, as if he were sliding it into somebody else's pocket.

"Something good?" Bone prompted, noting the smile breaking out over Fass's expression.

"Good doesn't begin to describe it, kemosabe," Fass said, the smile stretching into a broad grin. "Not even close."

68

Marble Falls, Texas

Caitlin remained silent after Cort Wesley finished, twisting another napkin into knots before shredding it.

"You want me to arrest her?" she asked him finally.

"I watched her gun down four men."

"Who might've been fixing to do the same thing to you if she hadn't."

"Maybe you didn't hear what I said, Ranger. She set them up. Lured them into showing up just so she could enjoy a little target practice."

"'Lured' isn't a legal term, Cort Wesley."

"So you're taking Nola Delgado's side?"

"I'm here, aren't I? But what's the point? The charges won't stick and Nola's sure to skate even if they did."

Cort Wesley looked down at the Bluebonnet Café menu, then up again across the table. "I just want her out of my way."

"This, after you called her in. Have I got that right? I mean, correct me if I'm wrong about who's to blame here."

"You think this is about guilt?"

"I think it's about Dylan."

Cort Wesley picked up the menu set before him. "Which pie you going to get?"

The Bluebonnet Café was known for its wide selection, in addition to offering a Pie Happy Hour every afternoon, during which slices were two for the price of one, mix and match.

"Hey," Cort Wesley said suddenly, "they've got key lime today."

"Stop trying to change the subject."

"It's anger management control, what I do to stop from reacting in a way I may regret later."

Caitlin tightened her stare. "You brought Nola Delgado into this. What did you think was going to happen, exactly?"

"I didn't think she'd punch holes in four shooters like they were cardboard cutouts at the range."

"What'd you tell Doyle Lodge?"

"Same thing I told you about those storage containers. Same thing I'm going to tell Jones as soon as he gets here."

Caitlin leaned back. "We should talk to Dylan, both of us together."

"Now who's trying to change the subject? Nice to see that the kid dating a serial killer actually bothers you."

"Nola Delgado's a lot of things, but she's no serial killer."

"How about a mass murderer?"

"I'm not any happier about them being together than you are, Cort Wesley."

He leaned back in the chair, fanning his arms to the side. "Nola's obsessed with you, Ranger."

"Well, I am the sister she never knew she had."

"Which cuts both ways. But in Nola's case I think it's more the fact that you can match her every step of the way. Her big sis with a bigger gun."

Saying it that way made Cort Wesley tighten his gaze across the table. Caitlin looked different to him and it had nothing to do with the lighting or mood. He figured he was looking at her through a different lens, one filtered through the sensibility of her half sister, Nola Delgado. He knew Caitlin Strong better than he knew anyone in the world but, in that singular moment, wasn't sure he really knew her at all.

"Nola pushes things to the limit because that's where she's most comfortable. For her, going to the extreme is the only way to go."

"Well," Cort Wesley started, leaning forward and laying his arms on the table, "it does take one to know one."

"I'm going to pretend you didn't say that."

"I think you and Nola should have your DNA tested, see if the two of you have an extra chromosome or something. I think you're protecting her, maybe because the same thing corrupted the gene pool that spawned the two of you. You look at her and see an extreme version of yourself, what you'd be like if you embraced the same limits she does."

Caitlin's eyes looked past Cort Wesley and toward the entrance. "Jones is here."

69

MARBLE FALLS, TEXAS

"Why do I think this isn't a coincidence?" Jones asked the two of them, reaching their table but stopping short of sliding in.

"Take a seat, Jones," Caitlin said. "We need to talk."

"That's supposed to be my line."

"Used to be, when you had the world at your feet with the Department of Homeland Security."

"Pull up a chair and maybe you can punch your ticket back in," Cort Wesley added.

Jones slid in on Cort Wesley's side instead. "How'd the two of you know I'd be here?"

"Your expanding waistline would be at the top of the list," Caitlin told him. "Force of habit would be a close second."

Jones glanced down at his belt and at the paunch that had begun to grow over it, in stark contrast with the washboard stomach he'd long prided himself on. "Pie's better than booze to drown my sorrows, Ranger."

"Maybe you should try opiates. Word is they're in especially plentiful supply these days, like somebody opened a spigot law enforcement has no idea how to close."

"What the Ranger's saying," Cort Wesley picked up, "is we just might be able to make those sorrows of yours go away. What would you say to that, Jones?"

"That I'm buying."

Cort Wesley laid it out for him, leaving nothing out, from Luke OD'ing, to Cholo Brown, to torching a pill mill clinic, to getting sprung from jail by Doyle Lodge. Not surprisingly, Jones seemed most interested when he got to the warehouse itself, to what he and Nola Delgado had discovered inside. The only thing Cort Wesley left out was mention of the four dead gunmen they'd left behind.

"And what was it you realized?" Jones asked when Cort Wesley got to the end.

"My original thinking was that that warehouse and all the others being operated by Roland Fass were acting like self-storage units for illegal drugs."

"A reasonable assumption even for you, cowboy."

"I don't know what's in those fancy storage units, but it's not petrochemicals—that's for just about sure. My guess is we're looking at piperidine."

"An organic compound that's used in the manufacture of numerous pharmaceuticals," Caitlin elaborated, "most notably opiates in general and fentanyl in specific."

"I know what piperidine is," Jones said, sounding as if he needed to prove himself all over again. "Tell me something I don't know."

"I think this warehouse serves as the manufacturing base of whoever's behind an increase in opioid distribution all over the country," Cort Wesley told him. "I think all these drugs, including maybe the ones that almost killed my son, are being made right here in Texas."

Jones looked from Cort Wesley to Caitlin before letting his gaze settle on both of them. "Tell me what I'm missing here, unless we're just having a nice, friendly conversation over pie."

"You want your two oh two area code restored," Caitlin told him. "We can help you with that, if you help us with this."

"Okay." Jones nodded. "I'm still listening."

"A second survivor got pulled out of Camino Pass earlier today."

Jones couldn't stop his features from freezing solid. Caitlin tried to recall another time when she'd told him something he didn't already know.

"And Doc Whatley, the Bexar County ME, has a notion as to how it was this kid and Lennox Scully managed to survive the cyanide."

"I appreciate the heads-up."

"I thought you'd appreciate being on the inside, once he confirms his findings, which should give you a leg up on the competition when it comes to figuring out how to weaponize the stuff."

Jones tried to conceal his excitement over the prospects of that, but he couldn't stop fidgeting in his seat as he pretended to regard the pie selections on the menu.

"And what do you want from me in return for such a courtesy, Ranger?"

"I think those warehouses, and the man named Roland Fass who's fronting them, are protected, Jones. I think this whole operation is the work of somebody or somebodies who can pull the kind of strings most folks don't even know exists. And I think you may have a notion as to who they might be."

Jones started to look down at the menu again, then stopped. "Hypothetically speaking?"

"Nothing's hypothetical with you, so cut the bullshit," Cort Wesley snapped at him.

"True enough, cowboy," Jones said, managing to flash his old cocky sneer. "And it just so happens I do have some theories on the subject. But that's all they are, theories."

Caitlin waved to a nearby server. "Love to hear them, Jones. Let's get our order in, so you can get started."

70

Houston

"You took your goddamn time calling me back," Fass said, not bothering to disguise the anger in his voice.

"I know you have trouble comprehending that once in a while I need to attend to the nation's business, son," Senator Lee Eckles told him. "So what's got your britches wedged so far up your ass? Did another four of the men you hired get gunned down?"

"You said you wanted me to do some counting. So I did. Much more of our stock than I anticipated has been contaminated with hydrogen cyanide, the same stuff that wiped out that town."

Eckles remained expressionless. "How much we talking, exactly?"

"First off, we've confirmed that the contamination, for reasons yet unknown, has only affected the current lot."

"How much of it we talking about?"

"A representative sampling indicates somewhere around half."

Dead air filled the line on Eckles's end this time.

"You still there, Senator?"

"How many pills are we talking about here?" Eckles asked finally, his voice cracking with an edge of excitement.

"Enough to dump a whole lot of people in the grave, boss."

"Can you just answer the question?"

"A few hundred million."

"Did you say *hundred* million?"

"As much as two hundred and fifty. Half the current stock on hand. I told you, I've been doing a lot of counting."

More dead air.

"I've got another job for you," Eckles's voice returned, breaking the silence. "Contact the lab quick as you can. Talk to the chemists, the ones who uncovered the contamination."

"About what?"

"How to replicate the same results, on purpose, in the production process."

"We're not set up for that. We'll need to bring in experts, construct new labs. That'll take lots of time and even more money."

"We have plenty of both, Roland. Tell me the experts you need and I'll see that you get them. Send me the specs of what you need built within our existing facility and I'll make the necessary arrangements."

Eckles heard Fass sigh deeply on the other end of the line.

"This is an entirely different operation. We'll basically be starting from scratch, Senator."

"Who do you think said 'Both the man of science and the man of action live always at the edge of mystery, surrounded by it'?"

"I have no idea."

"Robert Oppenheimer, while he was building the bomb for the Manhattan Project. A fair comparison, don't you think?"

71

MARBLE FALLS, TEXAS

They ordered three different flavors, in order to better mix and match the slices, even though Caitlin knew that Jones was loath to ever share his selection. Given his expanding waistline, she had no reason to expect that wouldn't be the case today.

"Remember my old life, before Homeland, when we first met and tried to work together?"

"CIA." Caitlin nodded. "You were a spook."

"'Shady' wouldn't begin to describe plenty of the stuff I did, pretty much par for the course in overseas assignments. They give you a job to do and never ask how you did it."

"What's this have to do with that warehouse in Houston, pill mill in Humble, and the big spike in opioid distribution nationwide?" Cort Wesley asked him.

"Only everything, in another time and place that serves us well here. Before I met the Ranger, I was working as a Company liaison with drug interdiction efforts in the Golden Triangle."

"That sounds like an oxymoron to me," Caitlin noted.

"And, in large part, it was. The efforts were mostly bullshit, window dressing to hide the true nature and history of the cozy relationship between the CIA and Burmese and Thai warlords. On the surface, we were turning a blind eye to the biggest drug pipeline into the United States. Below the surface, we were running one of the biggest drug operations in modern history."

"Air America," Cort Wesley muttered, just loud enough for Jones to hear.

Jones nodded. "Only the CIA wasn't just involved with the transportation of the drugs. Back in the day, as in Vietnam and its immediate aftermath, heroin was refined in a laboratory built at the CIA headquarters in northern Laos. And, as a result, a decade after supposed U.S. military intervention, Southeast Asia represented seventy percent of the world's opium supply."

"You want to explain how this history lesson is relevant to what we're looking at today?" Caitlin prodded.

"Isn't it obvious?" Jones asked her. "What you called 'Air America' never really stopped operating; it just stopped flying."

"Why can't you just answer my question?"

"You've got to understand the context here, Ranger. Right, cowboy?" Jones continued, looking toward Cort Wesley as if for support. "All those Company men back in the Vietnam days believed that what they were doing was in the best interests of America, that their cause was just."

"The ends justifying the means and all that shit," Cort Wesley interjected.

"Context, cowboy, remember? The CIA genuinely thought communism was headed to the U S of A and that it was the Company's job to stop that from happening. They needed to stop the Red threat at all costs, and if that meant making a deal with a lesser devil in their view, then so be it."

"In other words, men like you turned the local population into your drug mules," Caitlin said, shaking her head as if not believing what she'd just said.

"I know this may come as a shock to you, Ranger, but the world is bigger than Texas. We didn't take advantage of anyone and we didn't turn anyone toward the drug business who wasn't already there. Growing opium was a natural agricultural enterprise for these people and they had been doing it for a long time before the Americans arrived. When we got there, they continued to do it, only, thanks to the air support services we provided into and out of the areas in question where the product originated, they were actually able to improve their lifestyle, provide better for their families. Much better."

"What you're saying," noted Cort Wesley, "is that Air America was good for the local economy and you were just doing a good deed here."

"Well, not me personally," Jones corrected. "My mother was still wiping my ass at the time, believe it or not."

"Could I choose not to think about it?" Caitlin asked him. "And how's this relate to all those warehouses we believe are stockpiling product that it now appears is being manufactured right here in Texas?"

"Have you listened to a word I said, or have those pills you've been living on turned your brain to mush?"

"That's right, Jones, you weren't there when I blew a hole in the world."

"From what I hear, you've fallen in."

Caitlin could feel her skin heating up, like she'd strayed too close to an oven burner. "Heard from who?"

"When someone with a rep like yours gets hooked on pills, word spreads, reaching even the new circles in which I move now."

"I'm not hooked."

Their server arrived with their slices of pie, and Jones went right to work on his first piece of strawberry rhubarb, speaking through his first mouthful. "I'll bet that's what the cowboy's son said, too, after he OD'd. Right, cowboy?"

Cort Wesley hardened his stare, said nothing.

"Anyway," Jones continued, looking back at Caitlin, "if you'd listened to what I've been saying, you'd have figured out that a new cabal of power brokers, from Washington and parts unknown, must have followed the Air America model. Filling a void that appeared at the perfect time for them."

"What void is that, Jones?" Caitlin asked him.

"Believe it or not, the government's efforts have begun to put a sizable dent in the practices that have allowed the illicit prescription narcotics trade to flourish. Pill mills like the one the cowboy here took a torch to are going as extinct as dinosaurs. Big Pharma, meanwhile, is under tremendous pressure from Congress to clean up their act. Having already made their billions on the rampant overproduction of opioids, they're starting to adhere to systems and protocols aimed at reducing the flood of the drugs that made them as easy to get as aspirin in some places. The distributors who are equally responsible for this unadulterated mess have had no choice but to play follow the leader. Need I go on?"

Caitlin decided to do that for him. "The end result is a shortage of the pills, which have become far less readily available. A void, like you said, leaving this reconstituted version of Air America to fill that demand with a fresh supply."

"Hey," started Cort Wesley, "at least the CIA's goals made sense, however ridiculous the domino theory seems in retrospect. What exactly are the goals of this new Air America, at least in principle?"

"Isn't it obvious?"

"I wouldn't have asked if it was."

"Money, cowboy, billions and billions of dollars of it, maybe even hundreds of billions, to do with whatever they see fit. Maybe to get candidates they support elected. Maybe to influence foreign elections or, taken to an extreme, to finance regime change when the current regime was acting against American interests."

"In other words," Caitlin said, shaking her head, "as long as it conforms to the catchphrase 'against American interests,' anything goes. Both during the Vietnam War and today. Does anything ever change in your world, Jones?"

"My waistline, apparently," he said, although that didn't stop him from digging into his second piece of strawberry rhubarb.

"You think a reconstituted version of Air America might be running the biggest drug operation in the entire country," Caitlin concluded.

"I think that's what you're describing, to a tee."

"How do I find the men responsible, Jones?"

"Jesus, Ranger, get a clue, will you? You can't get to these people; nobody can. Even a gunfighter like you would get smoked if you tried to flush them out."

"Not the first time I've heard the bull I'm riding at the rodeo will get my skull crushed."

Jones's gaze bored into Caitlin, all of his attention fixed on her as if Cort Wesley wasn't even at the table. "What about your great-grandfather, Ranger?"

"What about him?"

"He rode that bull in the rodeo a long time before you did."

72

Mexico; 1898

The sun still burned blistering hot in the sky, when a rocky, downward-sloping ridgeline revealed oddly fertile lands, rich in flora and growth, beyond.

"Behold, Ranger," said a beaming Felipe Wong, sounding like a father showing off his newborn child. "I believe you know what you're looking at."

William Ray Strong had only limited experience with the bright red flowers growing in the field below, which seemed to stretch forever. But he'd seen the results of opium addiction firsthand, a scourge that seemed to show up in Texas overnight, without explanation, and showed no signs of receding. If ever there was a time and need for the old days and methods the Rangers had used while chasing Comanche raiding parties and Mexican bandits, it was over this. The only judge those druggers needed was a Colt, and the only jury the shovel used to dig their graves.

"When we emigrated from China twenty-five years ago," Wong continued, "we brought the seeds with us. Most thought this to be a random act undertaken in the hope of replicating the success of growing poppies in our new land."

The Ranger watched Wong stiffen atop his horse, his expression curling as if he'd bitten into something sour. His pride at displaying the product of his ambitious efforts was replaced by regret and bitterness over the circumstances that had brought him to Mexico in the first place.

"Most of us worked those fields back home, Ranger, little more than slaves, deemed easily replaceable. Just like the Chinese who built your railroads," Wong added, with a fresh twinge of bitterness lacing his tone.

"I had my own experience with that, going back a few years. Worked with the famous hanging judge Roy Bean."

"I know of that experience," Wong told him. "You served my people well when no one else would bother. You stood up for them when no one else would, against powerful forces who wielded many guns."

"Well, that's true enough."

"I heard a few of those the railroad brought in were famous gunfighters who started killing in your Civil War and never stopped. I heard you faced them down."

"That was a long time ago, mister."

"It's why I wanted to meet you, all the same." Wong patted his horse, then continued. "It's why I'm sorry I have to kill you."

William Ray remained unmoved. "Plenty of men have come at me with that same intention, including those gunfighters you just mentioned, who had me outnumbered by a bunch. You'd be wise not to follow them."

"I admire your system of justice, your laws, for the contrast they pose with China's, where those of a lower caste have no rights. I told you before how the common belief is we immigrated here randomly, but that's not the case at all. We came to Mexico because we already knew the land and climate were ideal for growing poppies. We came to Mexico because we knew we could own it, instead of serving as slaves the way our brethren have, north of the border."

"Don't sell them short, Mr. Wong. I've heard told of them operating brothels, saloons, and opium dens, establishing communities in cities like San Francisco and beyond."

Wong's face wrinkled in what looked like revulsion again. "Fitting in, assimilating, forging communities of their own in darkened corners because the light will not have them. Not so here, Ranger. We have begun something that's going to last for a very long time, built something that's going to endure just as long."

"I'm guessing you're not alone in this, sir."

"Not at all," Wong said, smiling thinly. "Luis Siam controls the trade to the northwest, in Sinaloa and the general Sierra Madre, and Patricio Hong controls the south, leaving me with the center, stretching all the way to the Rio Grande."

William Ray knew about the towns Wong was referring to, all too well. Mexicali, Nogales, Nuevo Laredo, Reynosa, and Metamoros, to name just a few. Population centers that dotted otherwise vast stretches of wildland running through the Mexican deserts and arid hills. Over the years, he'd heard, everything from ceremonial Aztec skulls to Browning machine guns to white tigers had been smuggled over that line in the sand, well before opium began slipping through like water through a sieve.

He cast his gaze down further through the red flowering fields below, squinting to better make out the army of Chinese workers tending to the crop. Virtual slaves themselves, obviously, though William Ray didn't raise that particular irony with Wong, given the priority that had brought him down here.

"I don't see the children you stole from the town of Camino Pass anywhere about, Mr. Wong. If you'd be willing to turn them over so I can bring those boys and girls home, I'd be willing to go on my way and call us square."

Wong couldn't help but smile. "I've never met a Texas Ranger before, but you're exactly as advertised."

"What's that mean, exactly?"

"Bold, strident, relentless, impetuous, brave, and deadly."

"Well, I agree with the deadly part. Don't know what 'strident' or 'impetuous' mean, exactly, and I don't know if I can rightfully claim 'bold' or 'brave.' But, like I said, I'll take 'deadly' anytime, and you'd be well advised to give that strong consideration."

Wong looked at William Ray Strong as if seeing him for the first time. "Would you mind answering a question for me, Ranger?"

"If I can."

"All this, coming south of the border on your own, it was about *kids*?"

"Those kids have rights too, Mr. Wong, and last time I checked, their ages didn't make them any less Texans. And I didn't come alone. I had the company of that bandit I sprung from jail instead of delivering him to Presidio to face trial. Calls himself Pancho Villa now."

Wong's expression went cold amid the heat of the day. "He's a dangerous man, Ranger."

"He's not much out from still being a boy."

"Danger knows no age, and this one has a look to him I know all too well."

"How's that, sir?"

"Because it's what stares back at me when I look into the mirror."

"I'm going to give you a choice of how you want to die," Wong told William Ray Strong, when they got back to the settlement. "Firing squad, hanging, poison, burning . . . It's the least I can do."

From atop Jessabelle, his wrist chains back in place, William Ray swung his gaze about the Mexicans under Jesus Arriaga, who'd grabbed him and Pancho Villa from the foothills that morning. Villa himself stood off to the side, reluctant to meet his gaze. Their eyes finally met, and Villa's passed some unspoken message that the Ranger couldn't quite read and that the young man must have been afraid would be glimpsed by others.

"There's still the matter of those kids, Mr. Wong," the Ranger said. "You hand them over to my possession to be returned to their homes and in return I promise not to kill you."

"That's very generous of you, Ranger, but as you've seen, they're not here."

"One of the other guys have them, then? This Luis Siam or Patricio Hong? Wouldn't mind making their acquaintance, either."

"We were discussing the means of your execution, Ranger."

"You were; I wasn't. Don't see the need, given it's not gonna happen. I'd offer you the same deal, Mr. Wong, but truth be told, a bullet from my Colt is the best I can do."

Wong let his gaze linger on William Ray's empty holster. "You don't have your Colt anymore."

"A formality, sir. And if those kids ain't here, where are they? Tending to another of your fields?"

"Something like that," Wong said smugly. "The territory of my particular *jiéhuǒ* happens to include other good fortunes."

"What's *jiéhuǒ* mean?"

"'Gang.' But there's another Chinese word we've adopted we feel better describes the business we came to do here."

"What's that, Mr. Wong?"

"*Kǎtè ěr.* It means 'cartel' in English."

"Last chance, Mr. Wong."

"I was just about to say the same to you, Ranger, before I choose your means of execution."

"How 'bout you shoot me yourself?"

Wong's face wrinkled in disgust. "A bit crass, don't you think?"

"Maybe, but I'm used to looking a man in the eyes when I kill them. Figured you deserved that courtesy, in return for your hospitality and all."

Wong nodded. "As you wish, Ranger. And you made me think of a most fitting tribute for your passing."

He whispered something to one of his men standing nearby. The man rushed off, returning seconds later with William Ray's Colt in hand.

"A fine weapon that is, Mr. Wong, although I figure it would take more man than you are to use it. Gun's got a kick to it, even from close range."

Wong steadied the Colt on William Ray across the ten feet separating them and fired straight at him. The bullet went wildly askew, just as the Ranger had predicted.

"Need a hand there, sir? Maybe a shooting lesson?"

The Colt looked less steady in Wong's hand. He lowered it to his hip, forcing a smile.

"We have a proverb that, in English, might be taken to say that courage is often caused by fear."

"Yeah, you Chinese are sure smart that way. Personally, I prefer the one that says something like a man who stands straight doesn't fear a crooked shadow." William Ray paused just long enough to let his point sink in before resuming. "Doesn't appear to me that you're standing very straight, Mr. Wong—not a man who steals children."

Wong's expression flattened, his skin looking porcelain smooth. "Be aware, *gwailou*, that even the dragon struggles to control a snake in its native haunt."

William Ray took off his hat and rubbed his scalp with the hands that had been manacled again. "Yeah, about that. Like I said, Mr. Wong, I've had me some experience with your culture and your language. *Gwailou* means 'foreign devil,' but you're as much a foreigner in these parts as I am."

"Not anymore," Wong said, his expression cracking into a smile.

As if on cue, William Ray Strong heard the thunder of hoofbeats, dozens of them, coming fast and hard. At first, he thought whoever was coming had been summoned by Felipe Wong. Then he saw the perplexed expression on the well-dressed man's face, his uncertainty giving way to fear when a flood of riders mounted the plateau, shooting wildly in all directions from horseback.

William Ray ducked low. Wong seemed to look for him briefly, before tearing off upon his majestic horse to rally his own defenses. The Ranger had no idea what was going on here, exactly, but one name clung to his consciousness like mud: Pancho Villa.

And, in that moment, the young man galloped to his side on horseback, brandishing a badly rusted key.

"Stick out your hands, Ranger."

"What are you doing?"

"Saving your life, just like you probably saved mine."

Villa clanked the key into one manacle Wong had clamped back in place, and then the other, making good on his word.

"I'm talking about *this*," William Ray said, hunkered as low as his saddle would have him, as bullets crisscrossed past them. "I'm guessing these guns were following us all the way. I'm guessing you knew who you were after and used me to find him for you."

Villa grinned, firing off some shots from a long-barreled pistol, tearing a pair of Wong's men off their horses. One of them got his boot wedged in the stirrup and ended up being dragged across the plateau, his head bouncing off the hardpan like a ball.

"My men needed something that Felipe Wong has."

"*Your* men?"

Villa reloaded and resumed firing before reloading again; he handed the Ranger a twin pistol that had been wedged into his belt. "Join the fight, amigo."

"So I'm your friend now?"

"I owe you this much."

"Don't make me regret not delivering you to Presidio to stand trial, Pancho," William Ray said, firing at a pair of Wong's men who were coming straight for them and knocking both off their saddles.

"How about you let me take you to where Wong has those kids stashed, first?" Villa asked him.

73

Marble Falls, Texas

They'd all finished their pie by the time the ringing of Caitlin's phone interrupted Jones's tale, just before William Ray Strong rode off with Pancho Villa on the trail of the missing kids.

"Aren't you going to take that, Ranger?" Jones asked her.

"It can wait."

"In that case, getting back to our deal. . . ."

"What deal is that?" Caitlin asked him.

"I get you the skinny on this reconstituted version of Air America operating stateside and you cut me in on whatever comes out of Camino Pass."

"Oh, that deal . . . You must want back into Washington awfully bad."

"I think I've already made that clear."

Caitlin exchanged a glance with Cort Wesley. "Enough to give us a name?"

"None that I can state for sure, but I can run the math for you. The cowboy's theory about that Houston warehouse being a way station for the ingredients needed to manufacture opioids makes a whole world of sense, because who better to fill the void left by cutting the opiate balls off Big Pharma than whoever's holding the scissors?"

"Air America again," Caitlin said, picturing the likes of Roland Fass packing warehouses nationwide with illicit drugs manufactured somewhere in Texas.

"I can't give you all the names, Ranger," Jones resumed, "but I can tell you some of them are splashed all over the news and front pages of the major daily papers. You want to know who's behind Air America, the sequel? Look toward the loudest crusaders taking a hammer to Big Pharma, because lining their pockets was no longer enough. These days they're looking to own the whole pair of pants."

Caitlin nodded. "Looks like I'm headed to Washington, then, doesn't it?"

Part Seven

CAPTAIN BILL MCDONALD

Bill McDonald was one of the most visible Rangers to emerge in this new era. As a Ranger captain from 1891 to 1907, McDonald took on numerous high-profile criminal cases, including illegal prizefights, bank robberies, murders and riots. He earned a reputation for his marksmanship, as well as for being the source of one of the most famous Ranger sayings: "One riot—one Ranger." Though McDonald probably never said exactly that, it's a pretty good statement of his attitude. As one story goes, McDonald arrived in Dallas to stop a prizefight, and when community leaders asked when his fellow Rangers were arriving, he said "Hell! Ain't I enough? There's only one prizefight!"

—Sarah Pruitt, "8 Famous Texas Rangers," History.com

74

"Washington?" D. W. Tepper repeated. "Please tell me I didn't hear that right."

"Want me to lie?" Caitlin said, from the single chair poised in front of his desk.

"You and Washington makes for a dangerous combination, Ranger, oil and water being the first comparison that comes to mind. That said, ammonia and bleach would probably be a more accurate description of what's coming."

Tepper popped a Marlboro red into his mouth from a box he kept hidden in the back of his drawer. Much to his surprise, a lighter flashed in Caitlin's hand, as she leaned across the desk to light it for him.

"Did you rig this butt to blow up or something?"

"No, sir."

"What'd you do to it?" Tepper asked, reluctant to take a puff.

"Nothing."

He held the Marlboro over the ashtray he'd chained to his desk with a computer lock and let it smolder.

"Making enemies in Texas is one thing," Tepper warned. "Playing the Lone Ranger in Washington could make you the kind of enemies you can't scare off and cause you the kind of problems you can't shoot your way out of."

"I wasn't born yesterday, Captain."

"Neither were they, Ranger."

"What do you know about Lee Eckles?"

"Besides the fact he's the senior senator from our great state and the chairman of the Senate health committee? How about that he's a crusader against the pharmaceutical industry, a pain in their collective ass."

"Maybe I'm looking for an ally."

Tepper started to raise the cigarette to his mouth, then stopped. "And maybe I was Davy Crockett in a past life. You never go anywhere to see anybody about anything, unless you're planning on taking them down for something."

"Maybe you didn't read my report."

Tepper feigned feeling about his desk. "Well, it must be here somewhere . . ."

"I meant the oral version I just provided."

"Oh."

"Especially the part about a pharmaceutical lab big enough to fill sixteen warehouses nationwide with opioids being located somewhere in Texas."

"I don't recall any proof being provided in that report."

"That's what I intend to find in Washington."

"You plan on pistol-whipping Eckles until he talks?"

"I won't be allowed to carry a gun inside the Capitol."

"Since when did you let the law stop you?"

Tepper finally raised the Marlboro to his mouth, looking relieved as he took a puff and sucked in the smoke, before coughing it out in a spittle-drenched burst of smoke.

"Goddamn, Ranger," he said, retching as he tamped the cigarette out in his ashtray, "what'd you do to this thing?"

"Nothing."

"Bull*shit*!"

"It's an organic cigarette made of wheatgrass. Guaranteed not to give you cancer."

"Sure. Can't cause cancer if it tastes too awful to finish."

"The price of having no tar or nicotine."

Tepper sniffed at the cigarettes remaining in the pack, nose wrinkling over the fact that it contained only the wheatgrass variety. "I like tar and nicotine. I like Jack Daniel's too. And I'm seriously considering heroin."

"Knock yourself out, D.W.," Caitlin said, standing back up.

Tepper studied her as if seeing her for the first time. "When was the last time a hurricane hit Washington, Ranger?"

"Isabelle, in 2003, but that was only a category one."

"Well, somebody better warn them that Hurricane Caitlin is headed their way and she's a category ten."

75

HOUSTON

"So what do we do next?" Doyle Lodge asked Cort Wesley.

Cort Wesley had recounted everything that had transpired with Jones, and the plan going forward, once again leaving out mention of how Nola Delgado had summarily executed four hired guns who might have been planning to do likewise to him.

"Based on what we've been able to put together, I'd say Caitlin Strong's headed to take Washington by storm."

"She's not us, Masters."

"She's *one* of us, Doyle."

Lodge's eyes brightened, suddenly those of a younger man. His spine looked more erect and there was a harshness to his glare that was consistent with the Texas Ranger of lore he'd once been. It was as if the whole experience had shaved twenty years off his age.

"I want to sit down with her 'fore she leaves," he said to Cort Wesley. "Or, better yet, soon as she gets back. Got a few stories I think she'd enjoy hearing."

"About Earl and Jim Strong?"

The old man grinned proudly. "I once met a man claimed he was Wyatt Earp."

"He died in 1929," Cort Wesley recalled. "Wasn't that the year you were born?"

"That's why I said 'claimed.' I was just a boy at the time, and if he wasn't Wyatt, he sure believed he was. Gave me a whole new perspective on Doc Holliday and the O.K. Corral. My point being that maybe he wanted to live out his final years without the notoriety, so he planned his own funeral around ten years ahead of time."

"That would make him around ninety when he really did pass, Doyle."

Lodge fingered his chin. "Right. Can't expect any ninety-year-old to still have his wits about him, can you? My other point being that the reason I believed that old man really was Wyatt Earp was because I knew he was a gunfighter. Maybe the smell of gun oil clings to them like a second skin. He wasn't carrying at the time, but you could tell by the way he carried himself and held his hand just over where his holster would've been that he knew his way around a gunfight. Just like that girl of yours—and all the Strongs, for that matter."

"Others see Caitlin that way, but that's not the way she sees herself."

"What's she going to Washington for again?"

"Rattle some cages for starters, Doyle, something she excels at."

"Know what that man claiming to be Wyatt Earp told me the day we met? That his first order of business upon reaching Tombstone was to push the Clantons into the fight he wanted. You thinking your girl's gonna do the same when she hits Washington?"

"Well, I've seen Caitlin Strong do her share of provoking, to the point where the only difference between her and Wyatt Earp was that the O.K. Corral would've happened a lot sooner if she'd been marshal."

Something changed in Doyle Lodge's expression, his eyes growing distant and moist. "How's your boy, Masters?"

"I don't know, Ranger, and that's the God's honest truth."

"You think he's still using the pills?" the old man asked, the concern in his voice genuine.

"No, I don't. But I also don't know what I can do to make sure he never does again. I can't watch him twenty-four seven, but I get this hollow feeling in my stomach whenever I'm away from him for too long."

Lodge nodded, looking past Cort Wesley. "I wish I'd gotten the opportunity to worry. As it was, I never got the chance, because my boy was alive one day and dead from drugs the next. I never got the chance to do a goddamn thing about it. You should consider yourself fortunate. By the way, Masters, that ghost friend of yours, is he a colored man?"

"Yes. Why?"

"No reason," Doyle Lodge said, looking away.

76

Washington, DC

"Thank you for seeing me without an appointment, Senator," Caitlin said to Lee Eckles.

"Well," he said, flashing a grin that looked preprogrammed to appear on a regular basis, "I'd do anything for a resident of Texas, but for a Texas Ranger I'd do even more."

"I appreciate that."

Eckles's lean face was weathered in a way that made it look like part of his persona. His leathery, patchwork features had the appearance of someone who wanted to appear at home working in the outdoors, on a ranch or farm or something. Caitlin could picture him fitting those features into place after shaving. Or maybe he'd purposely exposed himself to too much sun to make him appeal to the down-home constituency he best courted. He had the look of a man desperately trying to seem as comfortable sharing a glass of milk in a voter's kitchen as a glass of top-shelf whiskey at private clubs more expensive than that voter's mortgage payment. His corner office suite in the Russell Senate Office Building across from the Capitol came courtesy of both seniority and the glad-handing he'd mastered at every level of politics, fueled by a relentless ambition he didn't bother to hide.

Eckles was a political legend in Texas who'd risen from the bottom of the heap up, from small-town councilman and mayor to state rep, which was followed by a stint as state agriculture commissioner, from which he built the base that sent him to Washington. He was known for skewering potential rivals from his own party and taking a blowtorch to the lives and reputations of opponents from the other. He was currently serving his fourth term in the Senate, having vanquished four different opponents, each of whom had emerged from their respective bruising and bloody campaigns with reputations tarnished and futures sullied beyond repair.

One opponent had been exposed as a serial philanderer, including a dalliance with an assistant that defined the very notion of sexual harassment. Another was revealed to have covered up an accusation of child molestation in his past, while a third had run a red light while drunk and struck a van carrying disabled adults. A woman who'd most recently run against Eckles was revealed to have paid for her law school education with money made by prostituting herself. Of the four, that was the tale that actually carried a modicum of truth; the others were the result of carefully orchestrated smear efforts, to which Eckles's opponents spent the bulk of their campaigns responding. Caitlin had heard that his entire political philosophy came down to a version of the final line from the great Western *The Man Who Shot Liberty Valance*, where the newspaperman famously utters, "When the legend becomes real, print the legend." Eckles had once been overheard saying "When you don't have any shit, make your own asshole."

The senator checked his watch robotically. "So, what can I do for you?"

"I was in town for some meetings at DHS and wanted to thank you for the great work you're doing with the war on drugs," Caitlin said. "Real progress is being made, something those of us in law enforcement are hardly used to seeing."

"Why, thank you, Ranger."

"No thanks necessary, sir. I especially enjoyed your recent hearing with Big Pharma. You tore those boys a new one"—Caitlin grinned—"didn't you?"

"I did at that." Eckles beamed. "Know what those men are at their core? Bullies. They take advantage of people because they're stronger and more powerful, and no one has the guts to put them in their place."

"That wasn't the case at that hearing I watched the other day on C-SPAN. I can understand your motivation, given your own regrettable experience with alcohol."

Eckles looked down at his desk. "You're talking about the accident, when I was just a kid. My best friend was driving drunk, killed himself and a family of four in a head-on."

"You were twenty-four, almost twenty-five, sir," Caitlin said, having trouble reconciling that with being labeled a kid. "Happened on the Sam Houston Parkway, just after it opened as a toll road in 1989. You walked away, I believe."

"A few cuts, scrapes, a broken arm and broken nose. I never should have let my friend get behind the wheel."

"Except you were drunk too."

"There was that," Eckles admitted. "If it means anything, I haven't taken a drink since."

"It does, sir. Just because a man can't undo the past doesn't mean he shouldn't try to make the future better."

The senator nodded, pleased by Caitlin's response. "And what brings you to Washington, these meetings at DHS you mentioned?"

"Well, sir, as you may be aware, I'm an official liaison between law enforcement in Texas and Homeland Security . . ."

"I hadn't heard, actually. Congratulations."

"And I've also got business at the Drug Enforcement Administration."

"What might that be, Ranger?" Eckles asked. Caitlin's words had yet to produce any rise out of him.

"Can this conversation be kept between us, Senator?"

"Of course."

"Good, because I got to thinking you should be made aware of something I'm looking into back home and intend to discuss with the DEA."

"What's that, exactly?"

"I can't give you 'exactly,' because I haven't gotten that far yet."

"What *can* you give me?" Eckles asked her next, his voice losing a slight measure of its processed cadence.

"I believe there's a major drug manufacturing operation going on in our state, specifically pertaining to opioids."

"You don't say, Ranger."

"I do, even though I'm not at the proving stage yet. It was watching that hearing the other day that made me think I should bring it to your attention, because I believe you may want to involve yourself in that effort, you and your Senate health committee."

"Whatever I can do. You know that."

"You know a man named Roland Fass?"

"I don't believe I do."

Caitlin took her phone from her jacket pocket and switched it on, turning the screen for Eckles to see. "Then can you explain how this picture of the two of you together got taken the same day as that hearing, Senator?"

77

Washington, DC

Eckles fumbled for his glasses atop his cluttered desk. Caught by surprise, Caitlin knew, he was trying to buy time to rework his processed script, and she gave him all he needed.

"It was taken in a suite at the Mayfair Hotel, sir," she said, holding the phone closer to him. "One of our tech guys who's looking into Fass brought it to my attention."

The senator took off his glasses. "I do remember meeting him, but not his name. Nor do I recall the subject of our conversation, since he'd forced his way into that reception specifically to confront me."

Caitlin laid the phone down on her lap. "So you remember being confronted, but not what the confrontation was about."

"I didn't mean it that way, Ranger."

"Then how did you mean it, sir? Take your time, please."

"Fass is a subject of your investigation?" Eckles posed, again stalling to form the proper thoughts into the right words.

"Right now, I'd call him a person of interest. Man's got a shady past behind him and did a stretch in prison for defrauding his own engineering company. We believe he's involved in a chain of those so-called one-stop pain shops where people can see a doctor, get a prescription, and fill it, all in the same place."

Eckles nodded. "As fast as we put them out of business, new ones pop up. I heard for a time there was someplace these one-stop shops were more common than McDonald's."

"That would be parts of Florida, sir, which used to be the pill mill capital of the country. Law enforcement's been chasing them out, so they've relocated elsewhere, including Texas."

"We need to do more about that, Ranger."

"I was hoping you'd say that, Senator. That's why I came by," Caitlin told him.

"I am confused about one thing, though," the senator said, starting to scowl before stopping himself. "You mentioned your visit to Washington was about the illegal production of opiates. But this Roland Fass seems to be mixed up on the *distribution* side of these drugs."

"That's the thing, sir. It may well be both. See, these one-stop pill mills started sprouting up," Caitlin said, using just enough truth to better form the lie she was composing, "at the same time we began to get word about a massive manufacturing operation. We've got nothing firm linking Fass between the two, but right now he's the primary focus of our investigation."

"You came to see me because of that picture showing Roland Fass and me together?"

"That's correct, sir."

"But you didn't raise that fact from the beginning of our meeting."

"Also correct."

"Some would call that deceptive, Ranger. What would you call it?"

"Another day at the office, Senator. Does any of this jog your memory about what you and Fass talked about at that reception?"

"Nothing. He talked. I pretended to listen."

"And you'd never met him before?"

"I believe I already answered that question."

"To the extent that you're certain there are no more pictures out there of the two of you together?"

"What did I just say?"

"Ever hear of Air America, Senator?"

Eckles looked at her as if he didn't understand the question, then canted his head from side to side. "Sure. Took place mostly during the Vietnam War, then later in South America. I've held hearings on the fact that the CIA was in league with informant drug dealers the agency thought were serving their cause, by enabling their efforts and protecting them from prosecution."

Caitlin nodded casually. "That's quite a mouthful, Senator, but your hearings must've neglected the fact that it cut a lot deeper than that. Elements of the CIA, in Southeast Asia as well as South America, were using the proceeds to fund illegal, off-the-books operations. A lot of the spies doing the country's business also managed to line their pockets so thick they needed another pair of pants."

"What does this have to do with your visit here today, exactly?" Eckles asked her, starting to lose his patience.

"Well, sir, seeing you in the company of a man suspected of being involved in a major drug operation raises some similar questions, don't you think?"

"No, Ranger, I don't, not at all," Eckles said, straightening in his chair and checking the time on a cell phone resting on the blotter before him. "As much as I've enjoyed talking to you, I have another appointment I'm already late for."

"I understand, Senator. We're almost wrapped up here. Just a few more questions, if you don't mind."

Eckles nodded grudgingly.

"We've also linked Roland Fass to a number of warehouses scattered across the country, believed to be storing huge amounts of opioids. These warehouses are all situated in areas where there's been a significant uptick in drug distribution and abuse, as witnessed by a spike in overdose deaths and suicides. Does that ring any bells for you?"

The senator took a deep breath and let it out slowly. "If it did, I wouldn't be able to comment."

"I was asking because the investigation is ongoing and we haven't been able to confirm our suspicions yet."

"I'm assuming that you have a source who's been feeding you this information, Ranger. Perhaps you should let my committee question him in closed session under seal. I can guarantee his or her safety."

Caitlin held his stare. The leathery lines and creases seemed to have flattened out, as if the subject of their conversation had stripped off his costume.

"I'm sure you can, Senator, but we're not there yet. Like I said, the investigation is at the earliest of stages and may not lead anyplace that would merit a committee as important as yours wasting your time. We don't even have enough probable cause yet to seek warrants to search all those warehouses. That said, when and if we've got something concrete, you'll be among the very first to know."

Eckles rose, his chair creaking beneath him. "I understand. What do you intend to do about Roland Fass, in the meantime?"

"Right now he's no more than a person of interest. And I'm sorry if my mention of you being caught in a picture with Fass cast any aspersions."

"I'm sure it didn't."

Caitlin joined Eckles on her feet. "After all, we're in this together. That's right, isn't it, Senator?"

"Wouldn't have it any other way, Ranger."

78

Houston

The regular season for the Village School boys varsity soccer team had been canceled, but competing in the district and private school playoffs hadn't been ruled out. So the team had started practicing at Matzke Park on Jones Road, far enough away from campus to fly under the radar but close enough to be a manageable drive. The senior captains had come up with an idea to keep the team sharp, and the players had voted unanimously to make the commitment to show up every other day at the nineteen-acre park, which featured a butterfly garden, playing fields, a playground, and walking trails.

It had been a show-of-hands vote, and Luke Torres wasn't sure how he would have voted if it had been secret ballot instead. Not that he could possibly have declined, given that his overdose had made this mess in the first place, and he hated that the senior-dominated team had lost its season, thanks to him. Sure, you could say it wasn't his fault, that maybe ten other seniors had ingested the same amount of drugs he had. The difference, of course, being that they didn't end up in the emergency room needing a shot of Narcan to save their lives.

The thing he'd learned with crystal clarity from his father, brother, and Caitlin was how quickly things in general could turn to shit. How easy it was to be knocked from your pedestal when you figured you were at the top of the world. He'd never experienced it personally until four nights ago, but now he realized it was the very basis of why his dad and Caitlin always warned him to be careful.

Be careful . . .

What did that mean, exactly? He'd never understood the substance behind the statement. And the last thing he wanted to be doing right now was thumbing his nose at the school's formal suspension of the team. He didn't have any strikes left, and, under the circumstances, he could see his ass getting tossed if the team's disregard of the school's orders came to light.

How would that look on my transcript?

He'd made an excuse for missing the first practice, but he knew he couldn't skip out on the second as well. So here he was, running drills, even though he was pretty much a scrub off the bench, here, as much as anything, to avoid being the only one on the team who wasn't.

Luke's practice uniform shirt felt a little big on him, resisting all efforts to remain tucked into his shorts. *That's what you get for overdosing,* he could almost hear his dad say. Then Caitlin would chime in about emaciated junkies with shrunken stomachs and protruding ribs that made them look like walking skeletons. He was lucky to be alive, to have gotten out of this with a mulligan, and here he was risking it all to practice for games the school team might not even get to play. For years he'd watched from afar, pretty much, as trouble continued to find his brother, never figuring that he was going to be the one to go looking for it.

But he had to admit that it felt good to be out in the sun and the fall heat, ebbing now in the late afternoon. It felt good to smack the ball with his cleats and do something that felt normal enough to make him forget, however briefly, how close he'd come to dying, like, ninety-six hours before.

That would have sucked, Luke thought as he hammered a kick past midfield, right onto the foot of Ben Brussard, who launched it high into the net for a goal.

79

HOUSTON

The kid had done Yarek Bone a favor. Taking him out on school grounds would've posed a formidable challenge, even for Bone, especially since he figured that a guy like Cort Wesley Masters wouldn't have left his son on his own. Fass had gotten the man's file from his Washington sources, and Bone found himself focusing more on what was missing than what was there. Because when there was this much stuff clearly missing, indications were the dude was one bad hombre. Bone's kind of guy, in other words.

But there was one thing Masters's file didn't need to mention: the fact that he and the woman Texas Ranger Bone had gone up against were lovers, that she was surrogate mother to the guy's son, who had just slammed a foot into the soccer ball on the field clearly in his view.

Bone was perched in a tree a cool hundred yards from the soccer field where the kid was practicing. He'd heard the legends about how his Comanche ancestors could make themselves invisible to their prey. He wasn't sure he believed that, but he definitely could have used that particular skill now.

As it was, the dark camo gear he was wearing was more than sufficient, since the park wasn't all that crowded and a person could look straight up into the elm tree in which he was hidden and not see him— like he was indeed invisible, for all intents and purposes.

Plenty of men he'd encountered, on both sides of the scale, detested the notion of killing a kid, to the point where it became the one indelible line they refused to cross. These men were capable of far more heinous acts than he would even consider, but they clung to that one exception, as if it might maintain at least a semblance of their humanity.

It was different for a true Comanche warrior, who understood that knocking off the young eliminated your future enemies even as it did the same to your enemy's future. Long before the white man came to town, you raid a village, you don't just kill the chief and his best warriors but also their heirs, so there'd be nobody to come for you when they got older. Or, if they were young enough, you'd kidnap and then indoctrinate the kid to your ways.

But this was about more than just tradition and legacy. This was about inflicting pain on the woman Ranger named Caitlin Strong, a delicious, tormenting pain that would never fade and that Bone would be able to feel emanating from her forever like a rechargeable battery. He should probably be thanking the bitch for this new gift she'd somehow delivered to him in that steaming pool of oil, and his thanks would come in the form of a lifetime of heartache, the worst pain of them all.

Bone's fondest memories of his difficult youth growing up on the reservation were the stories his mother would tell him of the old times. Some of these had sad endings, the hero falling in the end. On that, his mother would comfort him with the old proverb that they are not dead who live in the hearts of those they leave behind. As he grew older, though, Bone came to realize that was bullshit. Dead was dead and there was no coming back from it in anyone's hearts or minds. The kid he was about to kill wasn't going to live on in the hearts of his father or the Texas Ranger who'd left Bone smelling like a gas station. The kid was going to have his insides scrambled by a high-velocity bullet the size of a finger, finishing the job the drugs had started four nights back.

Bone raised the sniper rifle into position, settled his breathing, and searched the scope for a jersey with the number thirteen stenciled on it. While hunting, he'd once heard, the Cherokee would pray to the wind, rivers, and mountains for success. After killing an animal, Comanche hunters would ask the gods' forgiveness for taking its life. After killing a deer, the hunters would throw the tongue and some of its meat into the fire as a sacrifice. While Bone didn't believe in the practice of such rituals, his mother had made him promise on her deathbed that he would always recite the most hallowed of Comanche prayers before knowingly taking a life. And so he did, while he followed Luke Torres through the sniper rifle's crosshairs, waiting for him to be still.

"*Ga lu lo hi gi ni du da* . . ." And then in English, "Sky, our grandfather . . ."

The target was still in motion, a virtual blur. No reason to risk a shot, even as Bone's finger pawed the trigger.

"*Nu da wa gi ni li si* . . . Moon, our grandmother . . . *E lo hi gi ne tse* . . . Earth, our mother . . ."

The soccer team was gathering in front of the far goal on the field, setting up to practice penalty kicks. This was more to Bone's liking, since it was the goalie versus the shooter, mano a mano, not unlike the parameters that defined his life.

"*Ga li e li ga* . . . I am thankful . . ."

But the kids, who looked like a blotch of blue as they milled about in front of the goal, kept covering his target like a cloud covers the sun. Bone willed himself to be patient and continued with his prayer.

"*Si gi ni gé yu* . . . We love each other . . ."

Finally, Luke Torres was captured alone in his crosshairs, number thirteen lit up so big and bright that Bone thought he could reach out and touch it. He briefly held his eye closed in a last, silent moment, opening it again, ready to fire, with the boy locked squarely in his sights. Once again close enough to touch, with the barrel aimed between the one and the three on the back of his jersey.

"*O sa li he li ga . . .* We are grateful . . ."

Bone felt the slight smack of the superheated gases propelling the shell forward, the bullet exploding from the barrel, before he even realized he'd fired. Through the scope, it looked like the kid had been punched in the back. A frothy blood burst exploded from the front of his chest as the back of his jersey darkened in a widening blotch that spread outward from between the numbers.

Dead center.

Bone had squeezed his eyes closed by the time the boy fell, feeling his pain, a single explosive burst of it accompanied by a flash brighter than the sun. In Bone's mind, that moment lingered, stretched into something eternal that would remain forever indelibly imprinted on his consciousness. A souvenir to be pulled from a shelf of memory to be enjoyed again and again. Feeling his own pain was nothing compared to that of others; he had Caitlin Strong to thank for delivering this new gift to him, and he knew just how to thank her: by taking the Ranger's own pain from her and storing it on a shelf all its own.

When he killed her too.

80

Shavano Park, Texas

"That's Caitlin's spot," Cort Wesley said to Leroy Epps, who'd taken her place on the porch swing.

"*Since she's currently taking Washington by storm, I figured you could use the company, bubba. You mind handing me that root beer you were kind enough to fetch from the fridge?*"

Cort Wesley leaned over to pick up the bottle of Dad's Old Fashioned Root Beer and laid it down on the bench between him and the ghost.

"*New brand?*"

"Sorry, champ. I couldn't find the Hires you like. I don't think they make it anymore."

"*Nothing changes for the better, does it?*"

"Not much, anyway."

Leroy's eyes regarded the bottle closer. "*Means we can only do our best and make do with the results, right?*"

"I suppose," Cort Wesley said, and sipped from his bottle of craft beer.

"*Maybe it's time you gave me one of those.*"

"Can ghosts get drunk?"

Leroy flashed his big toothy grin. "*Won't know until we try, bubba.*"

"Can I ask you a question?"

"*Since you're buying, fire away.*"

"Doyle Lodge asked me if you were a colored man."

"'*Colored man'? I'm surprised he didn't say 'Negro.'*"

"I never told him you were African American."

"*You haven't asked me your question yet.*"

"Did he see you, champ?"

"*You ask him?*"

"I didn't know how to."

"*Without him thinking you'd lost your marbles, you mean. Don't matter a lick, anyway, 'cause what you really want to know is something else: Is he headed my way?*"

"That's the gist of it, yeah."

"*Are you, bubba?*"

"Am I what?"

"*Heading my way, on account of the fact that you're looking at me here and now.*"

"No more than any other time in the past ten years or however long you've been visiting."

The ghost smacked his lips. "*Man, that is some fine root beer . . .*"

"Is that an answer?"

Leroy's eyes seemed to widen, looking sad and somber. "*Not him, no.*"

Cort Wesley could smell the sweetness of the root beer on the air between them, the beer he was drinking starting to turn his stomach sour. "What's that mean?"

"*What's one plus one?*"

"Two, last time I checked, champ."

"*You can do the math here just as easy.*" The ghost smacked his lips. "*Yup, this is some fine root beer. Anyway, you'll know how it adds up soon enough, bubba.*"

That's when Cort Wesley's phone rang, the number in the caller ID belonging to D. W. Tepper.

"You looking for Caitlin, Captain?" he asked, suddenly alone on the porch swing, foam having filled the drained portion of the Dad's Old Fashioned Root Beer bottle he'd left for Leroy.

"No, Masters," Tepper said, sounding like he was about to choke up. "I'm looking for you."

81

WASHINGTON, DC

Caitlin went straight back to the airport after her meeting with Senator Lee Eckles, even though she had three hours to kill before her flight was scheduled to depart. There was something about Washington that gave her chills as soon as she reached the city limit. She saw politicians like Eckles as the cesspool of humanity, faceless men whose features formed according to the moment, as pliable as Silly Putty and as changeable as a kid's Etch A Sketch drawing toy. She'd once heard that whatever a politico told you was likely to be ten percent true, and that might be generous.

She'd left her meeting with Lee Eckles certain that he was in league with Roland Fass on whatever it was she'd uncovered in Texas. If Jones was right, the CIA's illicit drug operations hadn't gone away at all; they'd just transferred to new regions, new drugs, new acronyms, and new players. She had pushed Eckles only so far because it was clear he was just one of those players, likely getting rich and solidifying his hold on power through his involvement in a drug operation of mammoth proportions.

As Caitlin read things, the senator and others must have tired of collecting whatever perks and cash lobbyists were able to pony up in return for looking the other way when it came to the drug industry. Sitting at the gate in the airport terminal, she even began to wonder if the congressional crackdown on Big Pharma had been bred of a desire, and a plan, to create a void that the group represented by Eckles could move in to fill.

It never ceased to amaze her how the Senator Lee Eckleses of the world inevitably retained the likes of lowlifes like Roland Fass, men whose skill sets were neither impressive, remarkable, nor even reliable. They'd always find a way to mess up somewhere, and Caitlin figured powerful men like Eckles naturally gravitated to those they could make utterly beholden to them. After getting out of prison, the only real work Fass could find was rumored to be with an underground, bare-knuckle fighting network that moved about various locations clustered around the border. She would have thought cockfighting to be more up his alley.

The likes of Eckles and Fass had united to form a network centered around the illicit production of opioids somewhere in Texas, which were then distributed nationwide. The amount of money they were making, under the circumstances, must be staggering, at the expense of taking, or destroying, tens of thousands of lives.

Caitlin imagined they had any number of canned excuses prepared to rationalize their actions, all easy to dismiss when she considered kids like Luke Torres getting snared in the web created by the most dangerous drugs in the world becoming so readily available. Those running the distribution and supply channels from the bottom up were acting with impunity, thanks to the blind eye being turned their way.

Until they ran afoul of the likes of Cort Wesley Masters, who was now determined to smoke them out. Literally, in this case, though Caitlin couldn't see him torching all of their distribution centers.

Her flight had just started boarding when a call came in from Cort Wesley.

"I'm just boarding the plane now after swabbing myself with Handi Wipes. . . . Cort Wesley?"

Nothing.

"Cort Wesley?"

Dead air.

"I'm still here, if you can hear me," Caitlin said, but the call had already ended.

82

Houston

Cort Wesley ended the call and pocketed his phone, having second thoughts about telling Caitlin what had happened when she was fifteen hundred miles away.

Matzke Park had been evacuated and closed to the public. Those remaining were all clustered about the soccer field where the shooting had taken place. There was a sea of uniforms and flashing lights as the Houston police continued trying to make sense of what had happened, even though it was painfully obvious that a sniper's bullet had done the trick. He did notice some Houston detectives checking trees that offered a clear view of the soccer field, though it was doubtful they'd be able to do a full reconnaissance, now that night had fallen, meaning crucial evidence might be lost.

"Be a good idea for you to keep yourself scarce," D. W. Tepper warned him, returning from a brief exchange with the Houston chief of detectives who'd taken charge of the scene. "As hard as that might be for you to manage."

Cort Wesley nodded, figuring he owed the captain that much for first informing him personally of what had happened and then arranging for transport for both of them on the Ranger chopper.

"After all, Mr. Masters," Tepper resumed, "it's not *your* son tucked inside a body bag. Guess you could call this your lucky day, all things considered."

"When I can see Luke?" Cort Wesley asked the Ranger captain, not feeling so lucky at all.

"As soon as the Houston police are finished with their Q and A."

"I'm his parent. Don't I have a right to be there?"

"I wouldn't push too hard on that. They're just trying to sort all this out—like why he was wearing the wrong uniform."

Cort Wesley spotted Nola Delgado lurking at the outskirts of the activity, fake press credentials dangling from a lanyard draped over her neck and carrying a camera to complete the disguise.

"Let's see if I can give them a hand with that."

"You switched the uniforms," Cort Wesley said, as soon as he'd drawn close to her.

"You're welcome," she said, her face devoid of expression.

"I didn't thank you for anything."

"You should have, since switching those uniforms is what saved your boy's life."

"What about the kid who took a bullet between his shoulder blades?"

"Close your eyes and picture your son wearing that uniform instead." Nola finally turned all the way toward him. "Think even Tide would get the bloodstains out?"

"You have any idea how much I'd like to punch you right now?"

She smiled at him. "Go ahead, Pops, take your best shot. And while you're at it, go thank the dead kid's parents over there for his standing in for your son."

"The dead kid's name was Ben Brussard. I met him the other day. He was the one who came clean about where he got the drugs from."

"Enabling you to burn down the place that was dispensing oxy and fentanyl like a gumball machine."

Cort Wesley cast his gaze toward the largest congestion of humanity, where he figured he'd be able to find Ben Brussard's family. "Maybe I *should* go see his parents."

"I'm sure they'll be comforted no end by the fact that it was your kid that was supposed to die instead."

Cort Wesley was left shaking his head, trying to make sense of how anyone could be this cold and indifferent, could give no thought to the fact that her actions had caused the death of a high school kid.

"You tell the Ranger, Pops?"

"None of your business."

"I'll take that as a no. Otherwise, she'd be here. What is she, taking some time off, maybe honing her shooting skills?"

"You don't want to take her on, Nola, believe me."

"We're sisters, remember? Why would I want to do a thing like that?" Nola asked him, seeming to mean it.

"You were baiting a trap," Cort Wesley realized in that moment. "You were expecting this to happen."

"Preparing for the possibility is different from expecting it, Pops. And if it was just about setting a trap, I wouldn't have needed to switch those jerseys."

"Did you spot the shooter?"

"All of a sudden, you're interested . . ."

"Just answer the question."

"I zeroed the tree he fired from as soon as the kid went down. But he was gone by the time I got there. In the wind, as they say, like he pretty much up and disappeared."

"What did he look like?"

"I just told you he was gone by the time I got there."

"No, you caught a glimpse, probably from afar. But you let him go."

"Now why would I do a thing like that?"

"Because you didn't want to leave Luke alone."

Nola forced a smile, pretended to fumble for her camera. "You don't know me at all, Pops."

"I don't think anybody does, not even your mother."

"The shooter was too far away for me to go after or risk a shot, with all the people around," Nola told him.

"You expect me to buy that?"

"Your son's alive. Can't you just leave it there?"

"Tell me about the shooter."

"He was big, I mean real big. Not as big as my sister's personal as-sassin, but close. And he was Native American, Comanche or Cherokee being my best guess. Sound familiar?"

83

HOUSTON

Cort Wesley felt a numbness settle over his spine as he recalled Caitlin's description of the killer she'd chased through University Hospital and ended up spilling a pipeful of oil on. He slid off to get some distance from Nola Delgado and called Caitlin again, but this time it went straight to voicemail, meaning her plane headed back from Washington must be in the air. He couldn't hold back from telling her that the pro who'd killed Lennox Scully and seven others at University Hospital had just shot a young man who was wearing Luke's uniform, which meant . . .

What *did* it mean, exactly?

Cort Wesley couldn't get control of his thoughts, beyond the obvious: the huge illicit drug ring he'd uncovered with Nola's help was somehow connected to what had happened in Camino Pass.

Which made no sense, no sense at all. Which was why he needed to talk to Caitlin. He tried her number again, with the same result.

He turned back to where Nola Delgado had been standing, but she was gone, having had enough fun for one day. She'd switched the uniforms, somehow, to set the shooter up, opting in the end not to go after him in order to stay with Luke. A study in contradictions, as if there was a little of Caitlin inside her, just as Cort Wesley was certain there was a little Nola in Caitlin.

He was about to try Caitlin yet again but, at the last moment, pressed the contact for Paz instead.

"I'm on my way, outlaw," the colonel greeted, engine and road sounds shadowing his words.

"You don't even know where I am."

"I'm headed north. That's right, isn't it? North, while waiting for your call."

Cort Wesley almost asked him how he knew even that much, then decided not to bother. "They're connected, Colonel."

"What?"

"The drugs and that town—the same force is behind both."

Cort Wesley could hear the road sounds again, before Paz's voice returned. "Do you know what Voltaire said on his deathbed, when a priest asked him to renounce Satan?"

"No."

"'Now, now, my good man, this is no time to be making enemies.'"

"I'm not going to bother asking what that means."

"If you need to ask, you wouldn't understand anyway, outlaw."

Cort Wesley spotted Captain Tepper moving fast toward a mobile SWAT command center, where a number of figures wearing flak jackets had just emerged.

"Masters!" Tepper yelled to him, as Luke followed the figures down the scant steps.

"I need to go, Colonel," he said to Paz.

84

HOUSTON

Cort Wesley didn't realize he was running until he nearly slammed into a pair of Houston uniformed officers inside the security perimeter. He thought he heard one of them yell "Hey!" after him, but he wasn't sure and didn't care. He was conscious of his own feet pounding the turf of the same field his son had almost died on—*would* have died on, if Nola Delgado hadn't switched his uniform jersey with another kid's.

In his mind, he called out Luke's name, but his stomach muscles were clenched so tight he couldn't muster the breath needed, so he just kept running until he swallowed the boy in his arms and felt the heat of his body and tears moistening his shirt.

"Ben was wearing my jersey."

"I know, son."

"Somebody switched them."

Cort Wesley let his words stand and hugged him tighter.

"It was supposed to be me."

Tighter still.

"I should be dead now, not Ben."

Cort Wesley eased him away. "But you're not."

Then he hugged Luke again, the tightest yet.

"You take the bird back home," D. W. Tepper said to Cort Wesley. "Rangers have been put in charge of the investigation, so I'm likely to be making my bed here tonight."

"Thank you, Captain."

Tepper stamped out his cigarette as if embarrassed to be smoking in front of a kid and turned toward Luke.

"How you holding up, son?"

The boy shrugged.

"We're gonna get whoever did this to your friend," Tepper said, his voice strained, sounding like he was speaking through a mouthful of gravel. "You can count on that, you hear me?"

The boy nodded, biting his lower lip.

Tepper looked from son to father, not needing to say any more. He half nodded, and Cort Wesley mirrored the gesture. He was reluctant to leave the scene, as if he hoped the killer might be somewhere about and he could still get a shot at him.

Supporting his son the whole way, he reached the Ranger chopper to find Nola Delgado standing in a dark patch untouched by the lights that had snapped on in Menske Park with the fall of night.

"Give me a sec," Cort Wesley said to Luke.

The boy was reluctant to let go of him but finally released his grasp. Cort Wesley walked backwards across the grass toward Nola so as to not have to take his eyes off his son. He reached her with his focus still trained on Luke.

"The shooter's name is Yarek Bone, Pops," she said to him.

"Yarek *what*?"

"Our paths have crossed a few times south of the border," Nola continued, instead of answering him. "Sometimes on the same side, other times on different ones."

"And yet he's still alive. Explains why you stayed with Luke instead of going after him."

"A man like that could've figured soon enough that he'd fucked up. Could've doubled back while I was giving chase."

"He that good?"

"I've known better, but not many."

Cort Wesley nodded, pondering her words. "Paz is on his way."

"Should make you sleep plenty easier."

"I'm going to turn him around to Shavano Park, in case Yarek Bone shows up to finish the job. Go home, Nola."

She grinned. "When things are just starting to get interesting? Not a chance."

"You need to find a hobby. Maybe origami or a Zen garden. Somewhere you can find some peace."

"Why?" Nola scoffed, face crinkling as if she'd just smelled something rancid. "You don't need a hobby when you love what you do as much as me, Pops."

"You're scared."

"Come again?"

"You heard me. This Yarek Bone has you spooked."

Nola didn't bother trying to deny that. "Like I said, our paths have crossed."

"You ever hear of Siamese fighting fish?"

"Sure. They go at it until one of them dies, even if it takes days."

"Like you and Bone. But you're both still alive."

"No one who goes up against this guy stays that way long, Pops."

"He hasn't met Guillermo Paz yet, Nola."

Cort Wesley's phone rang:

Caitlin.

Cort Wesley started walking back toward his son as he took the call.

"Luke's fine, Ranger."

"I'm shaking so much right now, passengers are complaining about turbulence. Somebody had the news feed on his laptop. You want to call Dylan or should I?"

"I'll do it. That way I can put his brother on the line. You've got other things to worry about," he said, and he told Caitlin about the connection between the drugs and all those deaths in Camino Pass, in the form of the man who'd shot Ben Brussard in the back.

"Yarek Bone?"

"That's who you went up against at University Hospital."

A pause followed, so long that Cort Wesley thought he might have lost her. "Ranger?"

"I'm still here. Just thinking on how best to wipe the floor with this Yarek Bone, Roland Fass, Senator Lee Eckles, and everyone else involved."

"I've already called Paz, Ranger."

"Stay clear of Nola Delgado in the meantime. Looks like we're going to need her before this is done."

PART EIGHT

FRANK HAMER

After Frank Hamer helped capture a horse thief on the ranch where he worked, the local sheriff recommended him to the Texas Rangers. Hamer joined the Rangers in 1906, and became part of a company that patrolled the South Texas border. He left the Rangers periodically over the years to take different law enforcement jobs, but by 1922 he had become a senior Ranger captain in Austin. In the 1920s, Hamer was a key figure in preserving law and order in Texas' oil boom towns. But it was in 1934, after he retired as a Texas Ranger, that Hamer scored his biggest triumph: Hired as a special investigator for the state prison system, he spent 102 days tracking the infamous outlaws Bonnie Parker and Clyde Barrow, finally ending their multi-state crime spree in a police ambush in Bienville Parish, Louisiana.

—Sarah Pruitt, "8 Famous Texas Rangers," History.com

85

Texas-Mexico border

The fights were being staged in a different location tonight, in a trench silo that had once held tons of grain. For the latest series of bouts, its huge, cylindrical shape was playing host to the hundreds in attendance, who lined the steel catwalks that Roland Fass had erected over the pit that looked an extension of hell itself. The whole setting had been retrofitted at considerable expense to serve as another in his network of clandestine locations where his bare-knuckle brawls were staged. There wasn't much he could do about the poor air quality or circulation, never mind the cramped confines. But the audience didn't care, so long as the open bars were operational and flowing with enough booze to get them through the night.

Attendance and revenue were sure to both be down, because Yarek Bone wasn't on the card. Too bad, Roland Fass thought, since a return engagement by his biggest draw, in the wake of beating five men to death in record time, would have led ɔ Fass having to close the doors early.

Fass charged a five-hundred-dollar admission plus a twenty percent vig on all gambling proceeds. He was not about to let his clientele complain, since he didn't expect any of them to pay taxes on their winnings. Local authorities in counties and towns where the fights were staged were given a "detail fee" for not showing up to work a detail or bust his balls in any way.

With four fights down and a dozen more to go, Fass surveyed the crowd that spiraled across five levels above him, whipped into a frenzy over the very real possibility of watching a man get beaten to death, secure in the notion that they were safe. He waxed whimsically on how long any of them could have lasted against Yarek Bone, doubted it would have reached a minute. He wondered what made a man willing to pay five hundred bucks to stand in a rancid pit where the stench of stale sweat owned the air and blood sprayed like dewy mist on a Gulf morning.

Fass's phone rang and he knew he had to answer it. He couldn't put off talking to Eckles any longer.

"Where the fuck you been?" the senator demanded. Then, after a pause, "You're not from Texas, are you?"

"What's the difference?"

"You already had the Texas Rangers breathing down your neck, and now Caitlin Strong's going to be crawling up your ass. What the fuck were you thinking, letting Bone take out a kid?"

"Pedal to the metal, like you said."

"No such shit ever left my mouth, Fass."

"No harm in scaring them off."

"Aren't you listening to me, you asshole? You can't scare off the Texas Rangers. Caitlin Strong's going to come calling, so you better make sure your affairs are in order. First you lead her straight to me, and now you authorize an Indian who could have wiped out Custer's army by himself to take out a boy who's as close to a son as she's got."

"Good thing Bone shot the wrong kid, then."

"And don't even get me started on the kid's father, dipshit. I finally got a peek at his classified military file. Does the name Rambo ring any bells with you? Man, you sure can pick them, can't you? Tell me, Roland, when you went up the river on that embezzlement beef, did you pick the warden's pocket?"

A commotion broke out and Fass spotted uniformed figures shoving their way through the crowd, having burst through the guarded entrance above, on ground level.

"I have to call you back, Senator," he said, ending the call and pocketing his phone.

Then he spotted Caitlin Strong advancing toward him.

86

Texas-Mexico border

"You're under arrest, Mr. Fass," Caitlin said flatly, her voice sounding tinny in the odd acoustics of the trench silo.

"Maybe you didn't hear, we're protected."

Caitlin froze on his stare. "Not from me or the state of Texas, sir."

Fass looked around at the crowd, which was taunting the police and making no effort to rush toward the exits. "You really want to cause a riot, Ranger? This is a pretty rowdy crowd, armed better than those state cops, in all probability."

"You know where our motto 'One riot, one Ranger' comes from?"

Fass shook his head. "And I don't care, either."

Caitlin ignored the commotion circling around her, figuring the state cops could fend for themselves. In that moment, as far as she was concerned, she and Fass were the only two people in this old grain silo that still stank of fertilizer.

"Goes back to 1896, maybe seven years after Texas outlawed prize-fighting. But that didn't stop promoters from trying to stage a heavy-weight title fight in Dallas, between Bob Fitzsimmons and Irish Peter Maher. Local officials got wind of the thousands of folks sure to be streaming in for the festivities and wired the Rangers for help. The mayor came down to meet the train that the reinforcements he'd requested were coming in on and out steps a single Ranger, no bigger than you. So the mayor comes up to Captain Bill McDonald and says to him, 'Are you the only one they sent?' To which McDonald replied, 'Hell, ain't I enough? There's only one prizefight.' You get the point, sir?"

"No."

"I'm shutting you down, just like Bill McDonald stopped that championship match. You, and Eckles, and whoever else is involved here. You can tell the senator that the reconstituted Air America is being grounded. And while I don't know the part you all played in the deaths of nearly three hundred residents of Camino Pass, I will soon enough. Speaking of history, did you know that the state of Texas was the first to execute a prisoner by lethal injection—Charles Brooks Jr., in 1982?"

"Thanks for the history lesson, Ranger," Fass said.

"There's a method to my madness, sir. You want to enjoy a different fate than Brooks, all you need do is start talking and don't stop until you've given me enough to nail the whole gang operating in the shadows, starting with Eckles."

Fass scratched at his head, the motion looking rehearsed and contrived. "I'm confused here, Ranger."

"Maybe I can help set you straight."

"What exactly are you arresting me for?"

"Suspicion of murder, sir."

If Caitlin's remark rattled him, Roland Fass wasn't showing it.

"And who do you suspect I murdered?"

"Does the town of Camino Pass have a phone book? Because if it does, that would be the perfect place to start."

"I've never been there and hadn't even heard of the place until news of what happened hit the airwaves a couple days after the fact."

"As in pretty much all the residents dying in their sleep."

"News reports continue to say the cause is still being determined. You plan on arresting me for the murder of all those people I never met, without even knowing what killed them?"

"There's always the eight people Yarek Bone killed at University Hospital. I make you as an accessory to that, just like you are to what happened in Camino Pass."

"What's a Yarek Bone?"

"Did you really just ask me that?"

"I never heard of the man."

"This would be the same man you may have sent to paint a bull's-eye on a high school boy's back," Caitlin told him, feeling the sweat starting to soak through her shirt and jeans. "Also the same man I have it on good authority is your star attraction at whatever you want to call this," she added, sweeping her gaze about the converted silo.

Fass tried to hold to his bravado, which was bred of the sweat and testosterone stink on the air of the silo. "And now you want me to talk, get my sentence reduced for something I had no part in. Is that it?"

Caitlin nodded. "You know the drill, Mr. Fass. And I believe you de-nied your complicity in that embezzlement beef, too, before you finally changed your plea to guilty."

"That's a lot different than murder, and you don't have a damn thing on me."

Caitlin gazed about at the audience for that night's bare-knuckle brawls, which was slowly filing toward the exits, grumbling their dis-satisfaction and protesting the loss of their admission fee after only four bouts had been staged. "Not much that I can prove at this point," she conceded. "Guess we'll have to settle for operating an illegal gambling venture and a sporting venue without a license."

"Are those even felonies?"

"The warrant I'm holding says they are." She took a step closer to Fass, catching the strange combination of peppermint and beer on his breath. "The thing is, sir, Yarek Bone killed the wrong kid today. That's lucky for you, since the real target's father would've gotten to you be-fore I could, if it was his boy whose funeral was about to be listed in the papers. But there's still a dead eighteen-year-old gunshot victim on your doorstep. Rangers don't take kindly to anyone getting murdered, but when it's a kid, we get taken back to our roots, when I would've put a bullet in you before slapping on the cuffs."

Fass extended his hands in appropriately dramatic fashion, forcing a smile. "Knock yourself out, Ranger."

"Where are those ingredients being stored in your warehouse end-ing up? Where's the drug lab, Mr. Fass?"

"Drug lab?" Fass smirked.

"Who besides your senator friend is behind all this, by way of Wash-ington? Where'd the money come to bankroll the whole thing? Tell me about the new Air America."

"It was a movie, starring Mel Gibson I think."

Caitlin took another step closer to him, feeling the heat of his rapid breathing on her face. "You're disposable, sir. How long you figure it'll be before Eckles sends Yarek Bone after you? Maybe he has already. Maybe me coming here tonight saved your life. Would you like me to describe what Bone did to some of the victims he took on behalf of an Indian resistance group called Fallen Timbers? Here's a hint: check out what a man looks like after he's been scalped. How about this judge who ruled against a tribe's petition to toss some frackers off their land? Bone skinned the man but made sure to leave him alive."

Fass started to swallow, then stopped, not wanting to do anything to expose a kink in his resolve or his story. Caitlin could see him working up his courage, a weak smirk displaying the upper hand he wanted to believe he was holding. She wasn't sure if the odor roiling her was lifting off him or the air in general. Maybe it was both, having soaked into his skin like odors stick to an old, worn carpet—until you roll it up and deposit it in a dumpster.

"If this crazy story of yours is even remotely true, what you're up against is bigger than you, bigger than the Rangers, bigger than this whole fucked-up state of yours," said Fass. "Might be wise to back off a bit, so nobody paints a target on your back, too."

"How'd you know he was shot in the back?"

"The dead kid you mean?

"His name was Ben Brussard, and that detail wasn't released in any of the press reports. Lucky guess, Mr. Fass?"

Fass made no attempt at a response. Caitlin watched him struggle with what to say, until her phone buzzed with an incoming text.

"Now how about that," she said, after checking the message. "Maybe you should use your one phone call on Senator Eckles so you can tell him our medical examiner just figured out something big about the deaths of all those folks in Camino Pass."

87

SHAVANO PARK, TEXAS

"You look a lot better sitting there than Nola Delgado, Cort Wesley," Caitlin said, resting her shoulders against the back of the porch swing.

Cort Wesley rocked it slowly. "Just like you look better in your spot than Leroy Epps."

"The two of us have been cheating, in other words."

"Nice to have you home safe and sound, Ranger, especially since it looks like we're fixing to go to war again," Cort Wesley said, toasting Caitlin with his bottle of Dad's Old Fashioned Root Beer.

She lightly touched the bottle with the extra-large coffee she'd picked up at 7-Eleven, still with another half to go after she'd warmed it up in the microwave. The night had turned cool for fall, crystal clear, with the stars battling each other for attention in the sky. Caitlin looked up and wondered what she would wish for if one of them fell from the sky.

"A new brand," she noted, looking at the remains of the bottle Leroy Epps had gotten started.

"What can I say?" Cort Wesley took another sip. "It brings back memories of my misspent youth."

"I thought you were trying to forget that."

Luke was upstairs in his room, asleep, thanks to a sedative a paramedic had provided at the crime scene up in Houston. Guillermo Paz was somewhere about, as well, although neither of them knew where exactly. He'd left to park his truck somewhere out of sight, after doing a thorough check of the house while Caitlin and Cort Wesley remained outside with Luke, and they hadn't seen the colonel since. But he was close by, watching the house even now, for sure.

"That would make more room in my mind to figure out what I'm going to do to Senator Eckles and company."

"The problem is, we don't know how high this network reaches and who exactly it includes, other than Eckles," Caitlin noted.

"How about giving me a few minutes alone with him?"

"I was thinking more along the lines of Paz."

Cort Wesley nodded, taking another sip from Leroy Epps's root beer. "I could live with that."

"Or maybe Nola Delgado."

"Tough to get someone to talk when they're dead, Ranger. And I don't know if your half sister has another gear."

They were due to meet Doc Whatley at his office early tomorrow morning, along with Captain Tepper, about whatever Whatley had uncovered about how cyanide gas had managed to kill an entire town. The circle would be kept small, understandably, until they had a better idea of what they were dealing with. The fact that Washington was involved to the level it appeared to be meant keeping things buttoned up.

Lee Eckles, as Texas's senior senator, could make all kinds of trouble for them, and even grind things to a virtual halt, unless they came up with something they could use soon.

"I invited Jones to join us tomorrow morning, Cort Wesley."

"What the hell for?"

"You want a rough count of the people in our corner? We're going to need him. He helps bring this whole thing down, he punches his ticket back to Homeland."

Cort Wesley's eyes told her he wasn't convinced. "Unless he gets a better offer along the way. This is Jones we're talking about, remember? The man has the loyalty of a cat. Comes home to whoever feeds him."

"What'd you tell Dylan?"

"Not to come home, under any circumstances."

"Because you don't want another son painted with a bull's-eye?"

"More like because Nola Delgado's here and she brings out the worst in him."

"She saved Luke's life, Cort Wesley."

"And got another kid killed in his place." He gulped down some more root beer and laid the bottle atop the swing between them, watching Caitlin ease the prescription bottle of Vicodin from the pocket of her jacket.

She twisted off the top, held it briefly, then twisted it back on.

"I thought you said your head still felt like there were fracture lines running through it, Ranger."

Caitlin stuck the bottle deeply into her jacket pocket, where she'd have to work to reach it. "It does."

Cort Wesley's eyes drifted to the slight bulge in her pocket. "Lowest dose, you said."

"Take four to six every day and it's not so low anymore. I think I can get by on aspirin."

"Taking what Jones said to heart?"

"He thinks I'm an addict, Cort Wesley."

"He was making a point, Ranger. The famous gunfighter pointing the barrel at herself."

"You agree with him?"

"Given my current thoughts on opiates in general, it's not a good time to ask me that. But no, I don't think you're hooked."

"Neither was Luke. First thing I've been doing every morning for months now is to pop a pill. First time the pain starts to get bad again, I reach for this," she said, pulling the prescription bottle back out from her pocket. "That needs to stop."

Cort Wesley nodded his approval.

"As a matter of fact," Caitlin started, handing the bottle to him. "For safekeeping, to eliminate temptation, so I don't end up in the emergency room too."

He left the pills in her outstretched hand. "Can you enlighten me on what Nola Delgado's taking to make her think the way she does?"

"Why are you asking me?"

"Because you share the same blood."

"And that's all we share," Caitlin snapped, sticking the pill bottle back in her pocket.

"It's like she's another species," Cort Wesley said, gnashing his teeth. "The kind of neighbor who fishes your newspaper from the bushes and drops it off alongside the paperboy's severed head for missing the stoop."

Caitlin rolled her eyes. "Nice image."

Cort Wesley drained the rest of his root beer. His hand was trembling when he set it back down on the swing, his eyes moistening with the start of tears.

"I got two images stuck in my head that'll probably keep me awake for the next year or so. The first is what that thirty aught six shell did to Ben Brussard. It was a through and through, meaning it likely tore the heart from his chest when it came out."

Caitlin swallowed hard. "Why don't you skip the second image, Cort Wesley?"

"Wish I could, but I can't chase away the vision of unzipping that body bag so I could identify Luke in the park." He swiped his sleeve across his eyes. "The fact that it didn't get that far hasn't stopped me from freezing the picture in my mind." He looked away. "Do you have any notion as to how a whole town killed by cyanide gas is connected to a drug enterprise being run by a cartel out of the Capitol Building?"

Caitlin waited for him to turn back toward her before she answered. "That's what Doc Whatley will hopefully tell us tomorrow."

88

Presidio, Texas

A big, well-dressed man Roland Fass had never seen in his life escorted him to a dark SUV with its windows blacked out, after securing his release from jail. Fass watched him open the rear door, not needing further instructions to climb inside, where Senator Lee Eckles was waiting.

"What took you so long?" Fass smirked. "I was in jail for all of three hours."

"I wanted to wait until I could fly back to Texas, so I could tell you to your face you're going to disappear for a while."

Fass turned his gaze out the window for a parting look at the tiny Presidio, Texas, jail where he'd been taken because it was the nearest town to where the fights earlier tonight were being staged. The basement jail boasted two rusted iron cells with old-fashioned key locks and smelled of must, mold, and mildew. The concrete walls were etched with thick water stains and the floor was discolored in patches, where more water had leached through.

"You'll lose the bail you just posted."

Eckles shook his head. "Know something, Roland? If you were any dumber, all I'd have to do is water you twice a week."

"What did I say?"

"Bail? You really think I posted your bail?" The senator shook his head again. "Leave a trail back to me for all the world, including that goddamn, pain-in-the-ass Texas Ranger, to see? You think that's the level I operate at?"

Fass had no answer, so he stayed quiet.

"The arrangements are being made now. You'll be in the wind in no time."

"Where to?" Fass managed, his insides tightening up the same way they did when he had figured he was going to federal prison for a stretch.

"Someplace where you can't give us up. I don't want to know, so I don't have to resist the temptation to kill you myself." The senator softened his tone. "There's one thing you need to do for me before you pack your bags."

"Anything, Senator," Fass said, realizing Eckles was the only thing standing between him and having to face Caitlin Strong again.

"When can we have the new production line up and running with the revised specifications?"

"'Revised specifications,'" Fass repeated. "You make it sound like we're changing how many milligrams we put in our aspirin tablets. Do I have to remind you we've got the Texas Rangers crawling up our asses?"

"*Your* ass, Roland, and your ass has nothing to do with the manufacturing plant. Next order of business is to get those contaminated pills out of there safe and sound. After that, we can cash your ticket to new beginnings, some promised land not named Siberia."

A passing car pushed high beams into the SUV, illuminating Eckles enough for Roland Fass to think he had fat, all-black marbles for eyes, which seemed to glow in the dark after the vehicle had passed.

"You need to rethink all that, Senator. You need to pull back on all this until Caitlin Strong backs off. I'm telling you, she's like a human bear trap, and right now she's got us snared."

Another passing set of high beams revealed Eckles grinning from ear to ear. "Then it's a good thing I'm hitting the Delete key on her. It pays to have the right friends, Roland—something you should keep in mind."

89

San Antonio, Texas

"Look at this," Jones said, leaning on his big sedan in the Bexar County Medical Examiner's Office parking lot. "The band's really back together."

"You were never more than a roadie, Jones," Caitlin told him. "And count your blessings we invited you to the show."

"I wouldn't be here if you didn't need me for some reason, Ranger," he smirked. "Taking advantage of each other is the basis of our entire relationship." Jones turned his gaze on Cort Wesley. "Morning, cowboy. Sorry to hear about your boy."

Cort Wesley nodded. "He's still alive, but that won't be true of the shooter once I get my hands on him."

"Yarek Bone, I understand, which means you're going to need some pretty big hands."

"You know him, Jones?" Caitlin posed.

"His Fallen Timbers group represents a genuine threat to the homeland. What do you think?"

"Sounds like a man you would've wanted in your employ," Caitlin noted.

"I'm not saying I wasn't tempted, Ranger. Hey, if Bone was killing for us, he wouldn't have been killing for anybody else."

"It's not 'us,' anymore, Jones, is it?"

Jones smirked again. "I'd say the rest of the government has finally caught up with me."

"Hiring psychopaths and running what might be one of the biggest drug operations ever seen," Cort Wesley said. "Remind me again how the government's using my tax dollars?"

Until that morning, Caitlin didn't even know the Bexar County Medical Examiner's Office had a conference room. It was cramped, barely enough room to accommodate the oversize table squeezed inside, which looked as if it had been salvaged from another county office.

Caitlin and Cort Wesley entered, with Jones right behind them, to find that Doc Whatley and Captain Tepper had been joined by the resident Ranger tech expert, Young Roger. Guillermo Paz, meanwhile, was guarding Luke back in Shavano Park. Caitlin had somehow half expected Nola Delgado to be present as well and was relieved to see that she was nowhere to be found.

"Well," Tepper said, rising from his chair, before which a pair of take-out coffees were set, "the gang's all here."

"Is one of those for me, Captain?" Caitlin asked him, as Tepper sat back down.

He laid his hands before the cups protectively. "Not unless you smoke a cigarette with it."

"I think I'll pass," Caitlin said, her head pounding at a tolerable level that nonetheless took four aspirin to reach. The pain was still preferable to the Vicodin, which was burning a hole in her pocket right now.

"Let's get started," said Doc Whatley, from the head of the table. "To recap, we figured out real early on that the deaths in Camino Pass were due to hydrogen cyanide poisoning. What we didn't know was how the gas could kill an entire town and where it came from, not to mention how two residents managed to survive."

"Their survival proved to be a vital clue in coming up with the answers we needed," Young Roger said, after Whatley looked toward him to pick things up from there.

Young Roger was in his midthirties but still didn't look much older than Dylan. Though he was a Ranger, the title was mostly honorary, provided in recognition of the technological expertise he brought to the table, which had helped the Rangers solve a number of internet-based crimes, ranging from identity theft to credit card fraud to the busting of a major pedophile and kiddie porn ring. He worked out of all seven Ranger company offices on a rotating basis. Young Roger wore his hair too long and was never happier than when playing guitar for his band, the Rats, whose independent record label had just released their third CD. Their alternative brand of music wasn't the kind Caitlin preferred, but it had grown on her, and hearing it live had given her a fresh perspective on the band's talent.

"I looked at the medical records for Lennox Scully and the kid, Andrew Ortega," Young Roger continued, "trying to see if there was something about their chemical makeup, something in their blood levels, that could explain their survival. I compared the results to a bunch of the autopsy reports, only to reach the conclusion that their survival wasn't due to internal factors but what could only be described as external ones."

He stopped and looked around the table.

"I spent hours and hours looking at pictures and schematics at Camino Pass. Scully survived in a converted supply closet and the kid survived in a fallout shelter. Anybody want to hazard a guess as to what those two locations have in common?"

"No windows," Cort Wesley piped in right away.

"Solid notion, Mr. Masters," Young Roger complimented, "and one I briefly considered myself. I knew I was close but still on the wrong track." He looked about the room again. "Anybody else want to try?"

"You mind stowing the classroom crap, son?" D. W. Tepper said to him.

"Water faucets," Young Roger said, after clearing his throat. "That's what was missing from those two locations and what killed the rest of the residents of Camino Pass."

90

SAN ANTONIO, TEXAS

"You know how they say the worst tragedies aren't the result of one bad thing happening but a conflation of several?" Young Roger continued.

"What did I just say, son?" snapped Tepper.

"Sorry, sir, I was just being rhetorical."

"Yeah, well, stop that too."

Young Roger cleared his throat again. "The first thing I discovered was that a water main break fifty miles away had led the Department of Water and Sewer to shut off service to Camino Pass on the night of the tragedy. So if residents turned on the water, nothing but accumulated gas would be released. That's important, because there's plenty of data over the years of people being sickened, or even worse, when sewer gases invade a home through pipes with no water flowing through them. That's the precedent for what happened here."

"Last time I checked," interjected Jones, unable to help himself, "there was a big difference between what you're describing and hydrogen cyanide."

"But they're both gases, and the cyanide managed to leach into the aquifer supplying Camino Pass with its water at the very time there was no water in the pipes. Because gas rises, the cyanide made its way through the water system into the pipes—just like sewer gas, only on a mass level—and emerged with sufficient potency to kill everyone a reasonable distance from any water faucet."

"Explaining how Lennox Scully and Andrew Ortega managed to survive," picked up Caitlin. "But where'd the cyanide gas come from exactly? As I understand cyanide, it's not a naturally occurring element, say like methane, so it doesn't collect over time."

"That's right," Young Roger nodded. "Cyanide enters water, soil, or air as a result of both natural processes and industrial activities. In manufacturing, cyanide is used to make paper, textiles, and plastics. You can find it in the chemicals used to develop photographs, not to mention the fact that cyanide salts are used in metallurgy for electroplating and metal cleaning. Cyanide gas is also used to exterminate pests and vermin in ships and buildings, but only by professionals with the training to understand the precise amounts required."

"Nice answer, Rog," Caitlin said, "but not to the question I was asking."

"Try this then," Whatley interjected. "Cyanide is also vital in the process of removing gold from its ore."

Caitlin looked around the table, finding everyone else except Young Roger as perplexed as she was. "What am I missing here, Doc?"

"We need to go back a ways in history to answer that question, Ranger," Doc Whatley interjected, taking the floor fully. "All the way back to William Ray Strong and Pancho Villa . . ."

91

Mexico; 1898

"Don't make me regret not delivering you to Presidio to stand trial, Pancho," William Ray said, firing at a pair of Wong's men who were coming straight for them, knocking both off their saddles.

"How about you let me take you to where Wong has those kids stashed first?" Villa asked him.

That turned out to be back north, toward the border. They were accompanied by the same gunmen who'd torn up Felipe Wong's camp. William Ray's initial thinking was it had been a rescue mission for Villa, undertaken by the bandits he'd been riding with after fleeing a murder charge. But reflecting on the way they shot and rode left him pegging them more as soldiers—or at least as men who knew their way around the gunfights more typically associated with combat.

"Think I get it now, Pancho," he said to the young man riding next to him. "One of the men with us now was following you the whole time, waiting for you to smoke out Wong's camp so these boys could make their move."

"You tell a great story, Ranger," Villa said, keeping his gaze fixed forward.

"I'm not finished telling it yet. When I started on this new thinking, I figured it must be about the poppies. But that didn't make no sense, because what good would a bunch of red flowers do gunmen like these? That got me figuring your whole ruse was about something else for sure: guns. I saw these boys toting crates full of rifles and more on their horses. You had wagons stationed somewhere nearby, the kind with those thick wheels that can handle mountain terrain, lugged by mules. Right or wrong?"

Villa grinned. "Why bother? You already know the answer."

"So what's a gang of bandits need with that kind of firepower?"

"'Bandits,'" Villa echoed, breaking out into a chuckle and then a laugh.

"Something funny about that?"

"You were hot as blazes before. Now you're cold as ice."

"What's that mean?"

"These men aren't bandits by trade. The bandits I've done my share of running with are led by Ignacio Parra. Maybe you've heard of him."

"There's wanted posters of him posted all over Texas, if he ever ventures across the border from his base in Durango." William Ray cocked his gaze at the cluster of two dozen or so gunmen riding north behind them. "So who are these boys, amigo, if not bandits?"

"They're soldiers, and we're preparing for war."

"Against who?" William Ray asked him.

"Porfirio Diaz."

"The president of Mexico?"

Villa squinted into the sun. "I know you Americans revere his efforts to modernize Mexico, prepare it for the coming twentieth century. But what he's really done is line his own pockets and rebuild the military to wipe out anyone who challenges his rule. The poor see him for exactly what he is: a tyrant who has plunged already desperate Mexican farmers and laborers into poverty. He's taken their land and enslaved them for meager wages that make it impossible for them to become anything but criminals, fighting for the opportunity to sell the opium and heroin produced by the likes of Felipe Wong."

"And yet Wong and those other Chinamen are operating right out in the open, where everybody can see them."

Villa was still looking at William Ray. "Of course. Because Porfirio Diaz is in business with them. The money they pay in bribes goes straight into his pocket, to be funneled to pay tribute to the provincial governors and others he needs to control to solidify his hold on power."

William Ray took off his Stetson, the burn of the sun enough to make him replace it immediately. "Doesn't sound like those guns you clipped from Felipe Wong are gonna do you much good, son."

"Revolution is inevitable. And when it comes, when the opportunity arises, we'll be ready. You're right about firepower, Ranger. Diaz has centralized the military under his total control. So, yes, we need to be patient, even if it takes until he's finally out of the picture to restore hope to the people."

"Spoken like a true revolutionary, Pancho."

"I've studied how Texas revolted with Mexico."

"And I ended up the bait for the trap you needed to set for Wong. I delivered you right to him—your plan all along, I'm guessing. You want to thank me? Tell me about what Wong put those kids he stole to work doing."

"They're not the only innocents he's enslaved, Ranger. There are hundreds of others, maybe even thousands, doing his bidding."

"I'm going to ask you again, Pancho," William Ray said. "What's this bidding they're doing for him?"

"It's better if you see for yourself."

Just as the sun began to cool, William Ray Strong and Pancho Villa climbed a hillside overlooking a work site dominated by tunnels and pits dug into the ground. Villa had been true to his word, and the Ranger spotted what could well have been the kids from Camino Pass lugging water buckets hanging from boards laid over their shoulders. They were bent over, struggling to stay upright. Chinese work foremen wielding bullwhips supervised the process, readying their whips any time a single drop was spilled. More of the kids were digging with shovels, while others cleared stone and rock from the ground to find reasonably soft earth through which to dig. There were adults about, as well—all Mexican, as near as William Ray could tell—who'd been similarly enslaved, or put to work for the lowest wages imaginable.

The workers had unearthed an underground stream that bubbled up to the surface from the pits dug amid it. A host of workers continued to dig trenches to rout the water in a crisscrossing design that made the camp look like the inside of an anthill. And there appeared to be some method to the madness, as another group of workers, soaked in water and clay-colored mud, sifted pails and deep-bottomed plates through whatever residue the waters had brought with them from below.

Looking down on that scene, the Ranger knew that whatever Felipe Wong was digging for was at the behest of, or at least with the cooperation of, the Mexican president. That made it easy to see why Pancho Villa felt revolution was the only card the Mexican peasant class had to play.

"You know the problem with revolutions, amigo?" William Ray challenged Villa. "Too often, the poor forget to show up."

"That won't be the case here, Ranger."

"How you know that, exactly?"

"Because they're going to have leaders."

"Well, the battle Texas fought for independence mostly started in the early 1830s, but it didn't end in victory until Sam Houston bested Santa Anna in April of 1836 at the Battle of San Jacinto. You're gonna need as much patience as bullets."

William Ray turned the binoculars on a pair of raised mounds of earth, hollowed out in the center, the likes of which he'd never seen before. He figured they must have been the brainchild of the likes of

Felipe Wong, the concept brought here all the way from China, along with those poppy seeds.

Each of those raised mounds featured a Gatling gun poking up over the earthen walls and aimed directly at the center of the camp to discourage any potential rebellion by the workers, along with any assault from the outside. As far as the Ranger could tell from this distance, though, these weren't ordinary Gatlings; they were the next-generation gun, which had been produced exclusively for the U.S. Army.

Already a formidable and fearsome weapon, the Gatling had been improved and adapted to take the new thirty-caliber smokeless cartridge and featured six barrels instead of the original five, but William Ray had heard they were working on a model that had ten instead. He'd also heard that Dr. Gatling himself was adapting this model so it could be powered by electric motor, with a belt to drive the crank. William Ray tried very hard not to picture what a weapon like that could do to men charging bravely forward with no more than rifles or pistols in their grasp.

"Those Gatlings aren't here just to keep the peace, amigo. They're also here to make sure nobody strays too close to whatever they're digging for."

Pancho Villa ignored his point and gazed down on the work camp with the naked eye. "If we're going to rescue those children, Ranger, we'll need to find a way to take the guns out."

"And what do you get for your part in that, amigo?"

"Isn't it obvious? I get the Gatlings, once you figure out a way to stop the gunners from mowing my men down."

"You let me think on that." William Ray lowered the binoculars so he could look Villa in the eye. "Right now I want to know what's so important here for Wong to have a pair of Gatling guns to make sure nobody gets in and nobody gets out."

"Gold, Ranger," Villa said, taking the binoculars from William Ray's grasp. "Felipe Wong is mining for gold."

92

SAN ANTONIO, TEXAS

"Gold? Now I've heard everything," Tepper said, when Doc Whatley finished his tale. "But I thought we were talking about how hydrogen cyanide ended up in those empty pipes that normally feed Camino Pass its water."

"We still are, Captain," Whatley told him. "Isn't that right, Roger?"

Young Roger nodded, his long hair flopping up and down. "It sure is. Cyanide, especially back then, was crucial to the process of extracting the gold from the ore contained in gravel. It was a painstaking process, but remarkably effective for the time."

Caitlin was starting to get the gist of where they were going with this. "How far was this gold mine from Camino Pass?"

Whatley seemed to be running the math in his head. "Best guess, as few as fifty miles or as many as a hundred."

"A long way for cyanide to travel, if that's where you're going with this, Doc."

"Ranger?" prompted Young Roger, waiting for her to turn toward him before continuing. "I believe I've identified any number of comparable mines from the same general period, some much larger and deeper than this one, far closer to Camino Pass then and now."

"But nobody's working them anymore, Rog."

"Doesn't matter," he said, addressing the entire table. "There must've been a sizable vein that pretty much rimmed this town on all sides from maybe a mile out. The seismic studies I was able to access indicate as many as fifty gold mines were active at various times in the general area, with varying results."

"And I'm guessing they all used cyanide," Caitlin said, "which means we're talking about an incredible amount of poison potentially collecting in the ground."

"The process is called gold cyanidation," Young Roger nodded, "a hydrometallurgical technique for extracting gold from ore."

"Sounds pretty advanced for 1898, from a technological standpoint," noted Captain Tepper.

"The beginnings actually date all the way back to 1783, but it was the slowing of gold mining in South Africa in the 1880s that proved to be the game changer. Turned out, the newer deposits being uncovered were something called pyritic ore, which resisted all attempts to extract the gold, until scientists led by John Stewart MacArthur figured out that by suspending the crushed ore in a cyanide solution, a separation of up to ninety-six percent pure gold was possible."

Jones whistled. "Beats my government pension, kid."

"Of course," Cort Wesley picked up from there, "back then, I don't think anybody figured what they were doing had the potential to wipe out an entire town."

Young Roger nodded. "The nature of tragedy, remember? The concentration of mines around Camino Pass is unprecedented. All those mines had closed down before a single resident who died five nights ago was even born. But pockets of cyanide deposits remained, more than enough to leach into the underground streams, bubbling up occasionally into the groundwater."

"Groundwater's not what killed all those folks," Tepper reminded. "You already told us that."

"I did, indeed. See, back then, there was no EPA or environmental safeguards of any kind, pretty much. And the predominant method of extracting gold from ore was known as 'heap leaching,' in which cyanide solution was sprayed over huge heaps of crushed ore spread atop giant collection pads. The cyanide dissolved the gold from the ore into the solution as it trickled through the heap. The pad collected the now metal-impregnated solution, which was stripped of gold and resprayed on the heap until the ore was depleted."

"How much cyanide are we talking about here?" Caitlin asked him.

"In 1982, at the Zortman-Landusky mine in Montana, fifty-two thousand gallons of cyanide solution poisoned the aquifer that supplies fresh drinking water to the town of Zortman. The accident was discovered when an employee of the mine, who knew they were using cyanide, detected the smell in his tap water."

"Did you say fifty-two *thousand* gallons?" Tepper asked, scratching at his scalp with one hand and holding a pen like a cigarette in the other, to the point where Caitlin thought he might take a match to it.

Young Roger nodded again. "I did, sir, and I use that example in particular because it's the closest we've got to a precedent for what happened in Camino Pass."

"What if Zortman's water had been shut off when that worker smelled cyanide coming from his tap?" Caitlin asked him.

"If the concentration was anything close to Camino Pass, he would've been dead before he sounded the alarm and the overall results would have been the same. And that near disaster in Montana was hardly isolated. Among just the ones we know about, there was the Kyrgyzstan Kumtor mine in 1998, the Aural mine in Romania in 2000, and the Proyecto Magistral mine in Mexico in 2014. Again, none of the conditions encountered in Camino Pass were in evidence for any of those. You might say that, up until last week, anyone living close to a gold mine has been dodging one big bullet that finally hit the bull's-eye in Camino Pass."

Captain Tepper kept starting to raise the pen to his mouth before remembering that it wasn't a cigarette. "So, son, altogether, how much cyanide would we be talking about with regards to that network of mines enclosing the town?"

"Conservatively, as much as five hundred thousand gallons."

Tepper's mouth dropped. The cigarette pen dropped from his hand.

"That figure," Doc Whatley picked up, "is a rough estimate based on the concentration of cyanide in the blood of the Camino Pass victims. Roger and I believe the variances were due to how far, exactly, each victim was from a water faucet. The cyanide gas originated at the source of the town's water supply, flowed up through the empty pipes, and permeated the air."

"In other words," Tepper said, finding his voice again, "we got one hell of a mess on our hands. But how is it this poison remained deadly for so long?"

"Cyanide doesn't break down or degrade like other chemicals or toxins," Whatley explained.

"And there's ample precedent for that, too," Young Roger added. "Cyanide spills into groundwater can persist for long periods of time and contaminate aquifers. Groundwater contaminated with cyanide can also pollute neighboring streams. For example, at the Beal Mountain Mine in Montana, which closed in 1998, so much cyanide seeped into the groundwater feeding neighboring trout streams that the toxicity levels were still in the red years and years after the mine closed."

"There's something we're missing here," Caitlin interjected. "Sure, disasters like Camino Pass do happen spontaneously sometimes. But I'm not one to accept that at face value."

"What else you got, Ranger?" Jones asked her.

"I'm not sure. But there must've been some kind of inciting incident, something that somehow freed up a massive pocket of that hydrogen cyanide gas to push upward into the homes of all those folks. I'm not sold on the fact it was random, an unlucky stroke of fortune. Somebody caused this to happen—not advertently, but they caused it all the same." Caitlin thought for a moment, something seeming to occur to her. "You have people you can still call to get satellite footage of the area encompassing that town?" she asked Jones.

"I still have friends and associates at Homeland who feel I got royally screwed and who should be able to serve our cause in any way they can."

"So you can retake your seat at the table next to them."

"And so long as it serves your cause, you'd be fine with that," Jones challenged. "What is it exactly you want to eyeball, Ranger?"

Before Caitlin could answer, the conference room door burst open and a parade of men wearing Windbreakers marked FEDERAL MARSHAL stormed inside, guns waving.

93

SAN ANTONIO, TEXAS

"Federal marshals!" a voice boomed. *"Nobody move, and keep your hands where I can see them!"*

D. W. Tepper looked at the man and finally wedged the pen into his mouth, as if it were a cigarette. "You're kidding, right? I believe you must've kicked in the wrong door."

"Sir, I have a court order here for you to vacate the premises and turn over all evidence pertaining to the investigation into the deaths in

Camino Pass immediately!" the lead marshal bellowed, sounding like he'd practiced the words in front of a mirror.

"Anybody got a match?" Tepper still hadn't moved, continuing to address the lead marshal. "Son, I got a news flash for you. I'm a Texas Ranger captain and this case is under Ranger jurisdiction."

"Not anymore, sir," the man said, sweating up a storm and looking like his nerve endings had been cut. "My orders come from Washington, where this has been declared a national security issue."

"Who in Washington?" Caitlin asked him.

"I'm not at liberty to say."

"You can't say or don't know?"

"All of you, please vacate the premises as ordered or you'll face federal arrest," the lead marshal said, instead of answering Caitlin's question.

Tepper still didn't budge. "Son, you realize if it came to guns you boys wouldn't stand a chance, right?" He surveyed the six armed marshals who'd fanned out through the room. "Any of you ever been in a real gunfight?"

None of the men responded.

Tepper chuckled and blew out some breath. "Yeah, that's what I figured," he said, finally rising. "When I find out who signed that order, maybe I'll shoot them instead."

"Eckles," Caitlin said under her breath, as yet more men wearing FEDERAL MARSHAL Windbreakers ripped the entire medical examiner's office apart, as much out of spite as to look for something.

"You snap at Washington," Cort Wesley told her, "Washington bites back. What did you expect?"

"I'm not used to being on the defensive. I feel stupid for baiting Eckles the way I did, trying to get a rise out of him."

"Well," Tepper said, drawing up even with them, "I'd say you achieved that much. But look on the bright side, Ranger: this wouldn't be happening if we didn't have the sumbitch nailed six ways to Sunday."

"Where's Jones?" Cort Wesley wondered, scanning the office floor for him.

Caitlin joined his gaze. "Beats me. My guess is he hightailed it out, so as not to run afoul of anybody with *F-E-D* in their title."

"Some things never change," Tepper groused, "and he's still a son of a bitch."

"That surprises you?"

"Easy there, Hurricane. Save your winds for the boys we're going to bring down."

"That's the spirit, D.W."

"That's why I still carry a good ol' forty-five. It might only take seven in the mag and one in the chamber, but I never saw anybody get up from the first."

They rode the elevator to the ground floor.

"What now?" Caitlin asked, as the cab door slid open.

To reveal Jones standing in front of them.

"What was it you needed, exactly, Ranger?"

Outside, Caitlin laid out for Jones what she expected the satellite photos of the area around Camino Pass, going back as far as possible, to show.

"Tell your contacts I need a radius of ten—no, fifteen miles around the town."

Jones rolled his eyes. "Anything else? After all, your wish is my command."

"Can they get drones up, too?"

"When?"

"Five minutes from now would be great, but I'll settle for as soon as possible."

94

TEXAS-MEXICO BORDER

Senator Lee Eckles hadn't been inside the manufacturing facility since it went operational. It had been no small trick, figuring out how to appropriate the hundreds of millions of dollars required for its construction, especially when cost overruns necessitated him finding even more. That's where the cadre willing to swap dollars for power came in. Even with so much Washington experience under his belt, it still amazed him no end how few people truly wielded actual power and influence— the kind of men who could make you jump with a simple snap of their fingers. And several of them were involved in this project in a big way. That said, he didn't believe a single one of them had ever spent a second inside this facility. They were content to stay clear until the return on their original stake started rolling in. They were faceless entities to him, dancing bar grids and talking snow globes. When push came to shove, though, they were the men really running this country, and now they could practically own it as well.

The presence of all the machines their money had paid for made the massive facility seem much smaller, even though it remained likely the largest pharmaceutical manufacturing plant ever constructed. Eckles had heard various estimates easily exceeding one hundred thousand square feet, though it was difficult to tell with the naked eye, given the structure's unusual contours, which were built to conform to the existing landscape.

The warehouses registered under shell companies owned by Roland Fass were operating at far below peak capacity. The last few months had mostly been about launching some trial balloons prior to the full rollout. So another section of the facility, virtually equal in size to the manufacturing section, was strictly devoted to storage. That area was the cause of the vast bulk of those cost overruns, given that even Fass's own meticulously detailed specs had greatly underestimated the required needs. As a result, construction crews, who thought they were building something else entirely, had to punch through vast amounts of soil, rock, limestone, and shale to erect the extension.

Looking back, Eckles now realized that the problems with water seepage from a punctured aquifer must have somehow leached cyanide into the production process somewhere along the way. He recalled commenting to someone that the walls and ceiling were, literally, dripping wet in the area of the production line where chemicals were cut and mixed. In retrospect, he figured that's what had done the trick, and the limited reach of the water dripping off the walls and ceiling explained why only a portion of the inventory of pills on hand had been contaminated, as opposed to the entire lot.

Eckles watched the pills come off the rolling, automated assembly line in a constant stream that emptied into similarly rolling vats that were whisked away atop conveyor belts as soon as they reached a certain weight. At last count, there were now five hundred million pills stored here in rectangular, state-of-the-art storage drums, with automatic temperature and moisture sensors rigged to an alarm that would sound if either exceeded the limits. That amount was staggering on the surface, but lawmakers like Eckles knew it was the same amount that had been shipped into Florida around five years back. As he recalled, that amount was the equivalent of twenty-five pills for every resident of the state, regardless of age, in a single twelve-month period, made possible by the Sunshine State's lax medical clinic laws, which had allowed hundreds and hundreds of pill mills to flourish unimpeded.

Putting the drug distributors and manufacturers responsible for such egregious behavior effectively out of business had created a void of opiates on the streets. The plan undertaken by the powerful group the senator had spearheaded was to fill that void and put the resulting profits to far better use.

The storage portion of the facility looked like something out of a science fiction movie, with those rectangular steel drums stacked upon one another like a bunch of kings in a checkers game. The light was overly bright in some places, practically nonexistent in others, depending on the height of the stacks and position of the LED bulbs recessed overhead.

"How is it none of the contaminant warning systems worked—not a single one?" Eckles asked Fass, looking forward to the moment where he'd say good-bye to the asshole forever.

"Our tech guys think the contamination occurred on the manufacturing line, not here."

Eckles looked toward those dripping walls and ceiling again, while judging their proximity to that line. "Then how come none of the work crews got sick? And cyanide has a smell, like almonds, right?"

"They were wearing respirators and suits designed for astronauts," Fass told him. "The storage containers, meanwhile, are airtight, so, once sealed, no smell can push out of them."

"So we never installed contamination detectors on the actual line?"

"On your instructions, remember?"

"No, Roland, I don't, because I never gave them."

"You said we needed to cut a few corners, that there was no more money coming. We had to cut pretty much everything from the original plans that hadn't been installed yet."

Eckles was left shaking his head, picturing his fist rammed down Fass's throat. "And you never thought to tell me?"

"You're a busy man, Senator. We had things under control."

"Is that what you call it?" Eckles gazed around him again, his mind fogging up when he tried to estimate the number of shiny drums glowing under the harsh light. "We need to move these out of here yesterday, not give the Texas Rangers any time to regroup."

"We'll need to find one mother of a structure to handle the load."

"Don't worry, Roland, it'll just be a way station. The contaminated pills won't be there any longer than necessary."

"Headed where?"

Eckles had stopped in a dark patch of floor where the light shining down didn't reach, leaving him shaded in darkness, so that he looked more shadow than man. But his teeth reflected what little light reached him, revealing the biggest smile Fass had ever seen the senator flash.

"Where do you think? Maybe I'll just throw a bunch of names of our worst enemies into a hat. Let fate decide which country's streets are flooded with opioids toxic enough to take down a bull."

"You'll have to get your would-be victims to buy them first."

The senator flashed another smile that chilled Fass to the core. "Who said anything about *selling* the pills, Roland?"

PART NINE

MANUEL "LONE WOLF" GONZAULLAS

He rode a black stallion named Tony and often sported two pearl-handled, silver-mounted .45 pistols. On his chest was a shining Texas Ranger star, recalled Wise, who moved to Texas in 1925 and founded several successful independent oil companies.

Wise said news about the wiry Texas Ranger spread; everyone in Kilgore soon knew Gonzaullas was in town. . . .

The 1930s East Texas oil boom brought all kinds of people to Kilgore as the town's streets sprouted oil derricks. Buildings were shortened to accommodate new wells—even the bank was torn down for one, recalled Engel in 1985. A petroleum engineer, Engel headed the East Texas Salt Water Disposal Company in Tyler beginning in 1976. He remained active with the company even after his retirement in 1989.

As Depression-era oil discoveries multiplied, Kilgore's population increased from 700 to 10,000 in two weeks. The nearby communities of Tyler and Longview also grew—located about an oilfield 43 miles long and 12.5 miles wide. The East Texas field remains the largest and most prolific oil reservoir ever discovered in the contiguous United States. . . .

According to Herman Engel, the lawman was highly suspicious of anyone without callused hands. To make his presence known, Gonzaullas paraded his suspects down Kilgore's muddy, crowded streets on a "trotline."

One evening, after two weeks of investigation and raids, Gonzaullas triumphantly marched more than 300 men before the town's law-abiding citizens.

"He chained them to a long steel cable," Engle said. "Their identities were checked. They were told they could go free—if they left town in four hours; most left in ten minutes."

—"Petroleum History Almanac," American
Oil & Gas Historical Society, aoghs.org

95

"Let me handle this, Cort Wesley," Caitlin said, when she saw Nola Delgado drinking a Corona in one of the parking lot's few shady spots.

"I was thinking we double-team her."

"Better I do this alone."

"Why?"

"Because we share the same blood."

"But not the same heart, Ranger. Yours is as big and strong as your name. Hers most likely resembles a spoiled peach pit."

"I'll keep that in mind. Head over to headquarters with the others. I'll meet you all there soon."

Cort Wesley held his gaze on her as they moved in separate directions. Caitlin looked back toward him once but found his eyes tilted toward Nola Delgado instead; he started to sidestep, as if he expected her to do something he needed to be ready for. Nola tipped her bottle of Corona at him and smiled, barely acknowledging Caitlin until she came to a halt, blocking Nola's view of anything else.

"Sorry, I didn't bring you one, sis."

"You keep showing up places where you're not welcome, Nola. And it's barely ten o'clock in the morning."

"Hey, go easy on all the judgment shit." The killer known as el Barquero rolled her eyes halfway. "I do something to upset you?"

"Plenty, but that's not all. You drag trouble behind with you. Seeing you lurking about has become like spotting the Grim Reaper in the area."

"You call this lurking?"

Caitlin held her ground—and Nola Delgado's stare. "Shavano Park, the park where the shooting happened, and now here."

"Yeah, well, the only reason you know who plugged that kid in the back is because of me. When Yarek Bone gets the death penalty, I should get a medal, sis."

Caitlin didn't bristle at being addressed that way today. Maybe she was getting used to the truth. Maybe that was part of what Cort Wesley was getting at, being strong from the heart.

"The likes of Yarek Bone don't get the death penalty, Nola. They cling to the fringes, only to disappear when the need arises, so they can live to kill another day."

"He shot a kid," Nola said, as if Caitlin needed to be reminded. "You trying to tell me you're going to let that go?"

"I was speaking in general. Men like Yarek Bone spend their lives crossing lines. But sooner or later they cross one they can't go back from. Before this is over, he's going down. Roland Fass and Senator Lee Eckles, too. My way, not yours."

Nola drained the rest of her Corona and smacked her lips as if thirsty for another. "You come over here to tell me that?"

"Maybe I just wanted to make conversation."

"How about some compliments for restraining myself when those feds showed up? They could all be stuffed in a trunk right now."

Caitlin stepped farther into the shade and took off her Stetson. "You want me to thank you for not killing federal officers?"

"That could've been a disguise. I could've taken them out just to be on the safe side."

"You kill with the ease most people drag their trash to the curb."

"And you don't, sis?" Nola's expression was trapped somewhere between derision and playfulness. "Face it. The only difference between us is you don't enjoy it as much as I do. Or maybe you're just pretending not to."

"For me, killing is a last resort, not a first."

"Sure, call it whatever you want, but you still end up in the same place I do. We've got the same blood pumping through our veins, the difference being the entire Strong family has been hiding behind that Texas Ranger badge for five generations."

"While you hide behind the myth of el Barquero."

Nola's expression turned smug, as if Caitlin had just made her point for her. "What myth was our great-grandfather William Ray Strong hiding behind at that gold mine in 1898?"

"Why don't you tell me?"

"Glad to, sis. Glad to . . ."

96

Mexico; 1898

"Right now, I want to know what's so important here for Wong to have a pair of Gatlings to make sure nobody gets in and nobody gets out."

"Gold, Ranger," Villa said, taking the binoculars from William Ray's grasp. "Felipe Wong is mining for gold."

William Ray took the binoculars back and pressed them against his eyes. "Those Gatlings are gonna be a problem, amigo. But I suppose they could prove helpful in your revolution."

Villa's eyes glinted. "Do we have a deal, Ranger?"

"I want to make sure I get what I came for out of this too."

Pancho Villa handed the Ranger the binoculars. "Look down there and tell me what you see."

"Those the kids from Camino Pass?" William Ray asked, watching a half dozen kids distributing food to the Mexican peasant workers, as rifle-wielding Chinese men looked on.

"Some of them."

"Since you, or your men, have obviously scoped this place out before, how many kids we looking at in total, amigo?"

"I'd say fifty, but this is just one of many mines Wong is working. There's likely another hundred in the area of the border."

"A lot of kids."

"And a lot of gold to end up in the hands of a man like Felipe Wong."

William Ray turned his body all the way around to look at Villa, as if he were still holding the binoculars at his eyes. "'Course, I imagine that gold ore might be even more helpful to your cause than those Gatlings."

"That's possible."

The Ranger turned his gaze downward, seeing all he needed to with the naked eye. "But this isn't just about guns and gold, amigo, is it? I could tell there's something else just by the way you kept eyeing Wong. Care to tell me what that is?"

Villa's expression turned utterly flat. "The man who raped my sister, the man I killed, I worked for him, Ranger."

William Ray trusted his horse as much as he did his gun, blessing the fact that he'd managed to ride out of Felipe Wong's camp on Jessabelle, just as he'd ridden in. He trusted his horse enough to lie limply across the saddle with arms and legs left to flop in rhythm with the horse's stride, knowing the animal would continue straight in the direction they were moving.

Toward the gold mine.

He didn't know if the children abducted from Camino Pass were still delivering food to the laborers, because he didn't dare move his head to look. He imagined the Chinese guards, maybe the gunners behind those fearsome Gatlings, had already spotted the horse coming with what looked a dead body splayed over the saddle. William Ray was actually counting on that, since it would command all the focus of Wong's men and allow Pancho Villa and his bandits to draw as close as they dared, to position themselves for a final charge, utilizing the fall of dusk to further mask their approach.

The problem was that such a charge would be suicide for all of them if the Gatlings were still up and running. Taking one out of the picture was doable, but William Ray still hadn't settled on a plan do take both down. That was the thing about plans, in his experience. The more they were rooted in your mind, the more up shit's creek you'd be if something unexpected entered the mix. He preferred to let his instincts guide him, convinced that his own father, Civil War and Ranger hero Steeldust Jack Strong, was among those putting stuff in his head.

William Ray figured this would be as close as he'd ever come to the kind of battle Steeldust Jack had experienced as part of the much-celebrated Texas Brigade during the Civil War—hopelessly outgunned and outmanned while walking straight into a hornet's nest.

He heard voices spouting off rapidly in Chinese as soon as he reached the outskirts of the mine, passing by the tents, lean-tos, and bedrolls tucked tight until night fell. He figured those bedrolls were likely intended for the enslaved children, and he was angered all the more by the thought of them being left to fend for themselves when the desert nights grew cold.

Jessabelle faithfully strode right up to the edge of the mine itself. The voices were louder in his ear. He couldn't understand shit, but he imagined they were discussing or arguing over what to do with the dead or wounded man whose horse had wandered into camp. William Ray felt strong hands seek purchase on his frame and then dump him to the ground. He landed hard, his face breaking his fall, leaving him dazed and bloodied where some rocks had split the flesh over his right cheekbone. The Ranger still hadn't determined his next move precisely, figuring that he needed to respond to whatever the Chinese did.

In this case, one of them grabbed hold of him, high on his right side near his shoulder, and worked to turn him over so he'd be face up to the sky. He was ready with one of the two Colts Pancho Villa had provided him, when he opened his eyes to the blinding sun and a trio of figures silhouetted by its glow.

He shot the man standing over him, then the ones on either side of him. He drew his second Colt in the same breath's length it took to lurch to his feet, firing both pistols as he angled for the nearer of the two Gatlings. He'd left seven men dead behind him by the time he'd drained both pistols. He held one by the trigger guard, with his teeth, while he reloaded the other Colt, then repeated the process, when more of the Chinese guards finally opened fire behind him.

This was where he was most vulnerable, where the whole plan could go to shit in a hurry. But William Ray managed to half leap and half climb over the mounds of earth protecting the nearer of the two Gatlings, already opening up with the fresh loads in his twin Colts at two Chinese guards who were mounting a bull rush for his position, the big gun they'd been manning forgotten.

At the edge of his consciousness, the Ranger heard the heavy thump of charging horses, indicating that Villa and his men were launching their attack. He'd taken out one of the big guns, but the other remained steady—that, and far more armed Chinese than he'd anticipated were coming from everywhere at once. No way he could get them all, given the time it would take to reload the Colts while drawing fire, leaving him only one option, which he hadn't fully considered until that moment.

As the thundering of Villa's riders made him feel like air bubbles were bursting inside his head, William Ray lunged behind the Gatling and grabbed hold of its dual handles, spinning the gun toward the center of the camp lying between the dug-out veins of the mine being worked.

The fact that the Rangers often found themselves working alongside cavalry regiments that toted Gatlings along by wagon had left William Ray familiar with the big gun's general workings and controls. The Gatling gun's operation centered on a cyclic multibarrel design that facilitated cooling and synchronized the firing–reloading sequence. Each barrel fired a single shot when it reached a certain point in the cycle, after which it ejected the spent cartridge, loaded a new round, and, in the process, allowed the barrel to cool somewhat.

This 1895 model featured an olive drab gun housing with the barrel and front components left blued. William Ray made sure the hopper was slammed home and then hit the trigger while clinging tight to the gun's handles.

He may have been familiar with its workings, but he had never actually fired a Gatling before, and the sensation was like nothing he had ever experienced. All his insides seemed to be shaking, as the big thirty-caliber shells exploded in a constant stream through the rotating barrels, each burst depressing the expanded thirty-round hopper further, until the distinctive *click* signaled it was time to slam another into place.

William Ray yanked a fresh hopper from the ammo box at his feet, ejected the spent one to ram it home, locked the bolt back in, and drew the slide toward him. Then he was firing again, finding an awkward, pounding rhythm to the effort that left his teeth clacking. The reports were deafening, drowning out all but the clang of the most recently expended shells smacking against those that had already scattered across the hard-packed gravel at his feet.

The gun's power literally launched Chinese gunmen airborne on impact. Something felt like it was kicking the Ranger's stomach from the inside as he continued to spray thirty-caliber shells toward targets who were eviscerated under their force. That left William Ray figuring he now knew what God Himself must have felt like on a particularly wrath-filled day.

With the field cleared of all but a gravelly mix kicked up into the air by the Gatling's fire, he rotated the heavy mount sideways, in line with the second gun, which was just then sighting in on Villa's oncoming riders. He had less than half the hopper left, which had to be good enough, since no way there'd be time to jam a fresh one home from the ammo box at his feet. So he sighted in on the gunner opposite him and let the Gatling rip again, imagining what it must have been like for those who had worked the original models with a hand crank. The rest of the hopper's shells not only blew the opposing pair of gunners apart but also tore the second Gatling from its mounts and dropped it out of sight before the Ranger both heard and felt the gun click empty.

By then, Villa and his men were firing their Colts on the remaining Chinese gunmen from horseback, taking plenty of fire in return. William Ray charged into the maelstrom with both Colts freshly loaded and blasting away. He hoped all those kids would have the presence of mind to seek cover, or at least to drop low beneath the sprays of gunfire.

With the gunfight still raging around him, William Ray rushed down into the warren of cratered earth, into the labyrinthine veins of the mine itself, gathering up terrified children and shooting the gunmen who impeded his path as he went. There was a twisted beauty to it all, and though he had long been a man who professed a distinct distaste for killing, something about these moments made him feel more alive than any other time he could recall.

The declining rate and frequency of return fire from above told the Ranger the battle was ebbing. Judging by the steady, regular thudding of hoof beats, Villa's bandits were on the verge of cleaning up what he'd left for them.

He shot two more Chinese and was down to his last ten shells when the final kids fell in behind him, grasping just enough of his instructions to get in line. William Ray then swung around and retraced his steps back to ground level, encountering not a single other gunman in his path, but more fearful than ever on account of having maybe four dozen kids in his charge. He emerged and reclaimed the surface with them tight on his heels, where he found Villa and his men rounding up and executing the surviving Chinese guards and work foremen. His first thought was to make the kids turn away, but then he figured they had a right to see retribution being enacted upon the men who'd so victimized them.

A handful of Mexican peasant workers had dropped to their knees, terrified and uncertain of the bandits' intentions for them. William Ray pictured Villa enlisting them in his cause, building that revolutionary army he figured to need someday. More of his men, meanwhile, were loading both Gatlings into separate wagons, and others had charged past the Ranger to gather whatever gold ore or nuggets had already been pulled from the walls or fished from the groundwater the trench had unearthed. William Ray caught the scent of almonds heavy on the air but didn't know why, unless it was the residue of some lost memories or senses thrown askew by the intensity of the past few minutes.

"What now, Ranger?" Villa asked, walking his horse up close to William Ray.

The Ranger realized that working the Gatling had scraped or burned both his hands raw, the skin already beginning to blister. "I take these kids back home."

"And then?"

William Ray held Villa's stare. "I think you know, amigo."

"Not a job for a man on his own."

"I suppose. But that doesn't mean I won't finish it or die trying."

"I don't like the 'dying' part. I'd like to do something about that, if I can."

"You're welcome to ride along," the Ranger told him, "but we've had our fill now, and I wouldn't ask you to do any more than you've already done."

Pancho Villa smiled at him. "What are friends for?"

97

SAN ANTONIO, TEXAS

"You see my point?" Nola asked, once she had finished.

"Why don't you spell it out for me?"

"Spilling blood is part of our heritage. We were born this way. All the Strongs were, and that includes a half Strong like me. When William Ray was firing away with that Gatling gun, you don't think he was loving every minute of watching the bodies drop in front of him? And beyond that, how many Indians did he bury in the desert? How many Mexican bandits did he put in a box? Compared to him, we're Sunday school teachers, sis."

"Stop calling me that."

"Me stopping won't make it any less true. And I'm guessing, from those federal marshals showing up at the medical examiner's office, that you can use all the friends you can get right now."

"You're not my friend, either."

Nola nodded, as if she'd already made her point. "You want to deny the truth, go ahead. It's still the truth. We are what we are because we were born that way."

"Your mother raised you to be a killer, Nola."

"Because she knew I had it in me, was born with it in my blood, just like you were. You should be grateful—proud even. I figure people like us are as rare as Einstein, except we deal in bullets instead of numbers."

Caitlin was left shaking her head. "I don't know what's scarier, hearing you say that or the fact that you believe it."

"Bodies fall wherever we go; that's our nature, sis. You can try to change that or temper it, but when the time and the need comes we go to guns the way some people go for a breath mint. Who we are is what we do. It's time you accepted that. You'll be happier, trust me."

Caitlin was about to respond when what felt like a lightning bolt struck her head, dead center, a throb settling behind her eyeballs that was too painful to disguise.

"Headache, sis?"

"It comes and goes."

"Don't forget, I was there when it started. A blast percussion like that one scrambles your brains worse than dumping them in a blender. I've got another beer in my car, if you want to take a pill or something."

"I'll pass."

"On the beer or the pill?"

"Both." Caitlin grimaced, fighting down a wave of nausea. "Maybe I should arrest you for public drinking," she managed, hoping to change the subject.

"Better make it fast."

"Why?"

Nola Delgado frowned. "Federal marshals just stormed your medical examiner's office. Do you really think it stops there, sis?"

As if on cue, Caitlin's phone rang with a call from D. W. Tepper.

"I'll be there shortly, Captain," Caitlin greeted, having lost all track of time.

"No, you won't, Ranger. Headquarters and any other public space is off-limits to you for the foreseeable future."

"Come again?"

"Federal marshals just arrested me. You're my one phone call."

"They did *what*?"

"You heard me. The charge is violation of the Alien and Sedition Act, kidnapping the Lindbergh baby, or some other made-up bullshit. I can't even pronounce some of the shit they're slinging, but it's got something to do with your dressing down of ICE at that elementary school."

"Like what?"

"Like obstruction of justice or some shit like that."

"Eckles," Caitlin hissed.

"I'm running out of time here, so I need to make this fast. Keep your head low and stay out of sight, Ranger, because Washington's gunning for you."

"They better check their aim, Captain."

98

CAMINO PASS, TEXAS

Senator Lee Eckles initiated the call from his car, repeating the process that would once again conceal the identities of the call's participants. Participants would speak into their phone and the app would transfer spoken words to text for all to follow.

"Things are under control," Lee Eckles said into his phone, after confirming all participants were on the line and activating the app.

OH, IS THAT WHAT YOU CALL IT WHEN THE TEXAS RANGERS ARE COMING FOR US? came the first response, identified by a five-number sequence: two numerals followed by a hyphen, and then three more.

"They're just cops who wear fancy hats."

JUST COPS, from another, similarly unidentified participant. DOES THAT INCLUDE CAITLIN STRONG?

"She's no longer a problem. Neither is Camino Pass. We're going to make it like that never happened. Rangers don't have shit anymore, because we just took it out of their hands."

SO THINGS CAN CONTINUE AS PLANNED, from another five-number sequence.

"They can indeed," the senator reported. "But another opportunity has presented itself, one I raised in our last call about how a large portion of the pills manufactured at our facility have been contaminated by the same toxin that wiped out the population of Camino Pass. I can now confirm that portion numbers in the area of several hundred million of sufficient toxicity to make the ingestion of one pill fatal."

WHAT ARE YOU GETTING AT?

Eckles didn't bother reading the number designation this time. "What I hinted at during our last call. There are two things too much of the world has in common: a desire for drugs and a hatred for America, at least on the part of foreign governments."

THERE'S NOTHING NEW ABOUT THAT.

"What's new is the ability these contaminated pills provide us to do something about it. Forget a couple hundred million. Picture two *billion* of these pills distributed through China, Russia, the Middle East—take your pick from our many enemies."

WHAT YOU'RE DESCRIBING IS MONSTROUS.

"I'm not convinced that's the case. What do you call dropping bombs? What do you call war in general? Because we're at war now and we all know it, even if we don't call it that."

I HAVE NO DESIRE TO GO DOWN AS THE BIGGEST MASS MURDERER IN HUMAN HISTORY.

"Except no one will ever know it's us. And by the time the cause of all the deaths is discovered, it'll be too late to warn anyone. And remember, we're dealing with multiple languages and, often, closed societies. Anybody want to hazard a guess as to what a billion deaths would do to our enemies?"

NOT ALL THOSE BILLION ARE OUR ENEMIES.

"Maybe not," Eckles responded, glad the literal transmission of his words wouldn't capture the impatience in his tone, "but their governments are. And are we really able, or in a position, to make that distinction? I don't think so. We're talking about the future, my friends. We're talking about securing it. Forget running the country; we can own the world."

There was a pause, so long that the senator wondered if the secure connection may have been broken.

AND ASSUMING WE DECIDE TO GO AHEAD WITH THIS, 66-534 started, leaving it there.

"We'll need to build networks, distribution channels. An ambitious effort, for sure, but we have the necessary resources and personnel to make this happen."

WE STILL NEED TO GET THEM TO BUY THE PILLS.

"No, we don't. Because we're going to give them away."

99

SAN ANTONIO, TEXAS

Caitlin couldn't resist driving by Ranger Company F headquarters, feeling her skin tighten at the sight of the convoy of black, supersize SUVs rimming the front of the building. She wondered where the federal marshals, or whoever had come in those vehicles, had taken Captain Tepper. She imagined it was some intake center and resolved to find out for sure. She pictured Cort Wesley and her breaking him out in a blaze of guns and glory.

Maybe Nola Delgado's right about me . . .

It was a strange thought to form, under the circumstances. But that said nothing about how watching the scene transpiring at company headquarters made her flesh crawl—almost as much as the mere consideration that a man like Lee Eckles, United States senator or not, could have orchestrated something like this. Clearly, he wasn't alone in building the biggest drug operation in U.S. history. She imagined it likely was all aimed at lining plenty of pockets and securing or enhancing power. Money might not be the root of all evil, but in her experience it came pretty close.

Caitlin swallowed down two more aspirin with a lukewarm water lingering in the cup holder, hoping they'd make some dent in the pain in her head, which felt like a fault line had ruptured along her skull. With the outline of the Vicodin bottle still protruding from her jeans, she wished she'd insisted that Cort Wesley keep hold of them, to eliminate the temptation she was feeling now.

She didn't want to linger too long where she or her vehicle might be spotted, so Caitlin forced herself to drive off, even though a part of her nature wanted to enter the building and see how good these men were with a gun. Anger and frustration inevitably made her think that way, violence being a place her mind went for displacement, or even comfort.

Spilling blood is part of our heritage. We were born this way. All the Strongs were, and that includes a half Strong like me.

Nola Delgado's voice resounded in her head anew. Caitlin was not in the mood to consider the insight in her statement.

Instead, she focused on the matter at hand, driving from headquarters across town to Stone Ranch at Westover Hills, one of San Antonio's most luxurious apartment complexes. Funny how, when Jones was working for Homeland Security, Caitlin had never considered his living situation. He existed only as an annoying phantom who popped in and out, with no more physical form, for all intents and purposes, than Casper the Friendly Ghost. Given that he was no longer based in Texas, she had no idea why this was the address he had provided, or what he was still doing here.

Stone Ranch offered units of varying sizes and layouts, which were known for their luxury and style. The apartments featured floor plans that had been written up in *Architectural Digest* and featured private-entry garages, patios, a private gym, and a lavish pool rimmed by cabanas. It was like living at a country club—hardly something she could picture being right for Jones. She wondered if he'd signed the lease under his own name.

She found herself checking her rearview mirror constantly during the drive over to Westover Hills on the I-410, looking for more of the black SUVs she had spied outside Company F headquarters, never imagining she'd be wanted by forces inside the United States government. But she had more important things to worry about, starting with Jones.

"You decent?" Caitlin asked, as the gated complex came into view.

"I'm out by the pool."

"I'll take that as a yes."

"I don't have good news, Ranger."

"It's been that kind of day."

"So I've heard. We can have lunch if you want. I'll order something from the clubhouse."

"I'm on an asshole-free diet."

"I'll give your name to the guard at the front gate."

Caitlin found him alone, halfway along the curved pool, the sun gleaming off the crystal blue water. Jones was seated in one of the beige fabric chaise longues that featured an attached red, rectangular pillow. A wrought iron table by his side held an empty plate.

"How's the head?" he asked her.

"I'll live," she told him, the aspirin having barely made a dent in the pain.

"Hope you don't mind I ate without you," he said from behind his sunglasses, not so much as budging or appearing to regard her.

"I'm not hungry anyway, Jones. By the way, I seem to remember you being in shape, once upon a time."

Jones budged only to gaze at his flabby stomach, moving his eyes from one love handle to the other. "You mean back when it was important, when it mattered."

"You're still here. Seems a waste of rent money to me, under the circumstances."

He took off his sunglasses and squinted into the sun at her. "We have Homeland Security to thank for that. After they dumped me, they forgot to cancel the lease or ask for my keys back. Your government at work."

"I've seen far too much of that already today."

He sat up, his stomach protruding farther over the waistband of his bathing suit.

"You going for a retro look in that thing?" Caitlin asked him. "Like James Bond or something?"

"More like Burt Lancaster in the movie *The Swimmer*. You should check it out. Looks like you're going to have plenty of time to do so, given that I drew an utter blank."

Caitlin sat down on the chaise next to his, the sun raising a thin layer of sweat beneath her shirt. "As in those satellite photos I asked you for?"

"Based on your theory that this secret drug manufacturing facility is somewhere under the desert in the area of Camino Pass."

"I thought it made sense."

"Except it's not there, Ranger. I spent enough time to feel like I worked for Homeland again, looking at overhead satellite shots of the area going back ten years."

"And?"

"And nothing. Not a truck coming or going. Not a construction vehicle, which you figure these assholes would've needed to build something like this. Absolutely nothing other than normal vehicular traffic, none of which fit anything close to what you'd be looking for." Jones studied her, his expression neither gloating or empathetic but a strange combination of the two. "You're not wrong often, but it looks like this is one of those times."

Caitlin shook her head. "That doesn't make sense."

"It is what it is."

"Civilian life has made you philosophical, Jones."

"Cheer up, Ranger. My company is hiring. I'm sure they can find a place for you. Your boyfriend, too."

"You're a true pal."

"I do my best."

Caitlin started to look away, then fixed her gaze back on him. "The facility has to be there, Jones. My great-grandfather uncovered the fact that Felipe Wong was mining gold all across that stretch of the border. And you heard Young Roger's estimate that those mines clustered around Camino Pass used something like five hundred thousand gallons of cyanide to separate the gold from ore. I figured constructing that facility must've let it loose, one mother of a pocket that ended up killing the residents of Camino Pass when their pipes went dry and hydrogen cyanide gas took the water's place."

"A great theory, if it wasn't so damn wrong."

"I'm not buying that, Jones."

"No, you and reality never did have much of a relationship. But this time you've boarded the crazy train with a one-way ticket to nowhere."

"Train," Caitlin muttered, the perspiration beginning to blanch her shirt turning cold and clammy.

"You look you just saw a ghost."

Caitlin was on her feet, with no memory of standing up. "I believe I just did."

Jones pushed himself forward atop his chaise longue and crossed his legs. "Anything I should know about?"

But she was already striding off, pace quickening with each step. "Thanks for lunch, Jones."

100

Shavano Park, Texas

Cort Wesley sat parked in his truck, down the street from his own home. A big SUV was parked directly before his house. He was too far away to see how many men were inside, but he thought he glimpsed a pair of shapes in the front seat.

He had opened the windows, the slight breeze doing little to relieve the heat that had built up inside, as well as around him. He could even feel it in his ears, as if his rage at being unable to approach his own home for fear of being detained by federal marshals was boiling his brain. There were times when Cort Wesley would have just rammed their SUV and dealt with the men inside up close and personal. But he couldn't risk getting picked up just when Caitlin needed him the most. Luke was safe under the protection of Guillermo Paz and, he reminded himself, this was all about bringing down the largest drug operation that had ever permeated the planet.

"Know how I knows you're not yourself, bubba?" Leroy Epps asked, appearing suddenly in the passenger seat of his truck. *"You didn't stop off and pick up a couple of root beers to keep us cool in all this heat. Love the new brand, by the way."*

"Thanks."

"That all you got to say on the matter?"

"What else were you expecting?"

"Oh, I don't know, maybe something about no longer being able to tell the good guys and bad guys apart."

"That's nothing new, champ."

"Really? I must've forgot all the times you couldn't go home on account of federal marshals taking a shit on the lawn."

"You get testy when you don't get your root beer."

"I didn't know what 'testy' means when I was alive, and I still don't, now that I ain't."

"I've been reading more."

"Not much up my alley these days. It's not like they got lending libraries where I be now."

"Life without Amazon, too."

"You mean the river?"

"No, the internet shopping site."

"Believe I'd have a tough time establishing credit with them in my current state."

Cort Wesley glanced across the seat. Leroy's shape seemed to fade toward translucence before sharpening again. "Maybe they're selling the wrong stuff."

"Oh?"

"They should be selling a pill that makes people do the right thing."

"Still have to get folks to buy it, bubba, and from where I'm sitting, plenty of them are real happy being assholes. The ones you're up against now being a prime example."

"Lee Eckles has turned the U.S. government into the world's biggest drug dealer."

"Some would say it's been that way for a good long time."

"There's a difference between turning a blind eye and looking at the situation through a telescope, champ."

"You lost me there."

"Politicians have never been averse to padding their own pockets, but this is about running a drug operation bigger than anything the cartels or anybody else has ever pulled off. They've made the old Air America into the Apple of the drug business."

"Apple?" the ghost raised.

"The company, not the fruit."

"You've lost me again, bubba." Leroy turned his gaze up the street, toward the same SUV Cort Wesley had been staring at for over an hour. *"So what are you gonna do about them and their bosses in particular?"*

"I'm going to sit here roasting in the heat until the call comes from Caitlin that it's time to fry some ass, champ."

His phone rang, CAITLIN lighting up in the caller ID.

"Ask and you shall receive, bubba," Leroy Epps said, grinning.

IOI

SAN ANTONIO, TEXAS

Caitlin had pulled into a parking garage on the campus of Northwest Vista College, just a few miles from the Stone Ranch apartment complex. The security camera she passed under triggered something in her mind, which faded as quickly as it had come.

She wanted to get off the street in case she was being followed, and she figured the garage was a safe place from which to make a call and follow up on something Jones had triggered in her mind.

But this time you've boarded the crazy train with a one-way ticket to nowhere.

Train, indeed. The fact that Jones had shot down her theory about using satellite footage to track down Senator Lee Eckles's drug manufacturing facility had triggered a memory of something that Captain Ben Hargraves of the highway patrol had said to her at the command post outside Camino Pass. She called his cell phone number and he answered after the first ring.

"Hargraves."

"Caitlin Strong here, Captain."

"I'm off duty, Ranger."

"This isn't about Camino Pass. It's about that train you used to hear."

"Come again?"

"You mentioned that you heard it when you were a little boy, mostly at night. Your parents sent you back to bed, insisted you were imagining things. But you told me you were convinced they were lying. You were right, Captain, because I believe that train was real. I think your parents heard it regularly too, along with everyone else around where you grew up."

"You don't say . . ."

"Where precisely was it that you grew up, sir? And tell me everything you can remember about this train."

Caitlin called a second number, which she'd strangely committed to memory, as soon as Hargraves had told her what she needed to know.

"I thought you would've lost my digits by now," Nola Delgado greeted.

"Where are you, Nola?"

"Why do you care?"

"Because I'm getting the band back together. I need you."

"Me or my gun, sis?"

"Is there a difference?"

102

Shavano Park, Texas

"They still out there?" Luke asked Guillermo Paz.

Paz continued to gaze out the window on the right of the front door. "I was thinking of mixing them up some drinks that would glue their lips together," he said, without turning.

"You're standing in just about the same place where my mom died after one of your men shot her. Remember?"

Paz turned at that. "All too well. But I'm not that man anymore. I needed to be here then, just as I need to be here now. Back then, I didn't know how much my encounter with my Ranger would change my life."

"I was here," the boy reminded. "You look pretty much the same to me."

"In appearance, yes, but in no other way."

"And that's supposed to make me feel better?"

"You ever hear of Heraclitus?" Paz asked.

"I studied him in school," Luke said, trying to sort through his feelings about being alone with Guillermo Paz for the first time since the big man had drowned two gunmen in his tropical fish tank at school a few years back. "He was a Greek philosopher. We covered him in AP history."

"Then you should know Heraclitus believed that all things are characterized by pairs of contrary properties, like something that can be both hot and cold at the same time. Results in a constant push-pull, a battle for dominance that ends in harmony as the concepts grow organically closer to each other until they merge."

"What's that have to do with you killing my mother?"

"I hadn't accepted the other part of my consciousness yet. I didn't, until that day changed me and made me realize I was two men instead of one. The man I used to be killed your mother, that's true. But the man I became saved your life and the life of your brother. That's the man standing before you now."

"And if those guys outside decide to come through that door?"

Paz started to grin, then stopped. "They won't get very far."

Luke smiled. "You read Nietzsche, Colonel, or Schopenhauer? Because they had plenty to say about redemption."

Paz nodded, impressed. "You studied them, too?"

"Yes, sir."

"That must be a good school you go to. Maybe I could be a guest speaker. I've read everything Schopenhauer ever wrote. He believed redemption was a release from the very need to exist, liberation from life itself. I've read all of Nietzsche, too, and he believed it was more like personal affirmation, taking control of one's own fate. But I don't believe either of those principles. I don't believe redemption exists. I believe it's a word we made up to make ourselves believe we can change our natures. But we can't; we can merely adjust them to better suit our needs."

"You ever think of giving teaching a try?" Luke asked him.

"I already did," Paz told him, thinking back to his failed stint teaching English to immigrants. "It didn't work out very well. More recently, I taught gym at an elementary school. That didn't work out too well, either. I also audited college classes for a time, until a professor quit on account of me."

Luke sighed, and in that moment he was again the little boy Paz recalled from ten years ago. "I wish I could just go back to school."

"T. S. Eliot once said, 'Sometimes things become possible if we want them bad enough.'"

"And what if they don't?"

"You find someone who can make them possible."

Luke nodded. "In my AP class, we covered Nietzsche's writings on

Ariadne, Theseus's lover, who provided the thread that allowed Theseus to find his way back out of the labyrinth after slaying the Minotaur."

"What does that mean to you?" Paz said, feeling like his recently departed priest and understanding better what he must have sounded like all those times he'd visited Father Boylston in the confessional.

"That a person can venture anywhere on their own but they need help finding their way back and are forever striving to find the right thread. And you still haven't told me why you drowned those two guys in my fish tank a few years back, when you could have just knocked them out and tied them up or something."

Paz shrugged. "I thought they looked thirsty."

Part Ten

JOAQUIN JACKSON

As much as any Texas Ranger who served in the last half century, Joaquin Jackson knew well what fellow Captain C. J. Havrda meant about being a part of history. That was surely the case up until the day Jackson died of cancer on June 15 in Alpine, Texas. He was 80. The lawman was a part of history from 1966 to 1993, working thousands of cases across the Lone Star State.

Jackson might have done as well at another point in history—say, in the real Ranger heydays. James L. Haley, who helped write Jackson's second book, *One Ranger Returns*, says, "His love of open country, and horses, the thrills of chase, danger, adventure—he was aware that all those would have been heightened in the Old West. However, he certainly accepted that those days were over."

Jackson himself never made that comparison, at least so far as we know. But he believed that modern Rangers could have done the job back then: "The storied Ranger heroes of days gone by, Leander MacNelly and John B. Jones and Bill McDonald and Frank Hamer, still have their equals today. To paraphrase Gloria Swanson in *Sunset Boulevard*, it is the times that have gotten small."

The times, and maybe a bit more. Jackson remained a Ranger private his entire career so he could work in the field, not behind a desk. . . .

He knew that he'd done his job, done it well and he took pride in it. "I was an active officer in the oldest and most legendary law enforcement agency in the United States," he said. "As a Texas Ranger, I have always understood that I was part of a rich, proud tradition. I'd drain the last drop of blood from my body to uphold it."

—Mark Boardman, "The Lasting Influence of Texas Ranger Joaquin Jackson," *True West*, November 18, 2016

103

SAN ANTONIO, TEXAS

"You're blocking my sun, Ranger."

"How'd you know it was me?"

Jones took off his sunglasses. "It was either you or the manager of this place telling me I've been evicted."

"Knowing the way Washington works, you'll be able to retire here."

"Back so soon?"

"You were right, Jones."

"You came all the way back to tell me that?"

"I thought it made for a good conversation starter. See, you were right about nothing being built beneath the Texas desert within spitting distance of Camino Pass. You were right because it was already there and had been since the Cold War."

Jones sat up, his once flat stomach rolling out over his bathing suit, his voice lowering to a whisper. "You're talking about the underground railroad."

"Is there a reason why you're whispering?"

"Force of habit, Ranger. There was time when speaking of the mere existence of the underground railroad could have gotten you sent to Guantanamo—or something comparable for the time."

"I'm guessing there's a reason for that."

"That reason being the government spent the equivalent of a hundred billion dollars today fulfilling a paranoid fantasy. A roughly thirty-year project that began in the 1950s and picked up speed again under Reagan. Forget the Star Wars lasers-in-space project, Ranger. This one was the ultimate boondoggle."

Caitlin remained standing. "Keep talking, Jones."

He pulled his feet off the chaise longue and set them on the concrete. "Picture a nationwide, interconnected, underground network of railroad tunnels connected to department store–sized command and control centers where chosen elites could ride out a nuclear holocaust for a century or so. Moronic minds—the same minds who had students practicing to hide under their desks to survive a nuclear blast—actually saw this as a viable plan to maintain the government so it could ride herd on the survivors above ground. I've seen the studies, Ranger. Know how many Americans would survive an all-out nuclear war with all major population centers attacked?"

"No."

"Want to take a guess?"

"I'm not in the mood."

"Somewhere between fifty and seventy-five million, though some estimates were in excess of a hundred million. Between a quarter and a third of the total population, generally. The same studies reported that the biggest problem at that point would be governmental infrastructure. Who'd be in charge exactly? Not answering that question would be to accept *The Road Warrior* or *The Walking Dead* as the state of things, pretty much."

"Sounds like you've been watching a lot of television, Jones."

Jones put his sunglasses back on. "My new job doesn't come with the demands of the old ones."

"Or the gym time, obviously," she said, looking at his stomach. "So they build this underground railroad to maintain command and control."

"They never finished it, of course. The project died with JFK, was reborn with Nixon, and then was pursued full-bore by Reagan before George H. W. Bush killed it for good when it had already gone wildly over budget."

"There's a surprise," Caitlin frowned.

"In the end, they got maybe a third of the thing done. Care to guess where most of that was?"

"How about right under our feet?"

Jones glanced down at the polished concrete at his feet. "Maybe not literally, but Texas for sure."

"I talked to a highway patrol captain who claims he used to hear an invisible train regularly."

"Invisible only because it was probably rumbling a hundred feet or so beneath his feet, carrying men and supplies to one of the command and control bunkers they were building."

Caitlin took a step closer to Jones, angling to the side so the sun reached Jones again. "I think the people we're after turned one of those command and control centers into a drug manufacturing facility that belongs in the *Guinness Book of World Records*, and I'm betting it's a stone's throw from Camino Pass."

"And who might these people be, Ranger?" he asked her, clearly interested.

"You take them down and you can write your ticket back to Washington. You'd be a hero, Jones. Homeland would welcome you back with a red carpet."

Jones weighed the prospects of that, nodding. "And what about you?"

"I'm a federal fugitive, remember? Better I lay low and let you take the credit."

"And who would I be getting the credit for taking down?"

"Among others, Senator Lee Eckles. Know him?"

"He was always quick with a buck when it came to national security. The kind of man, after he shakes your hand you go looking for Purell."

"That much hasn't changed, although a shower might be more appropriate."

Jones nodded again. "You nail him and I get the credit."

"That's the idea."

"And what do you need from me in return, Ranger?"

"The original plans for this underground railroad. And something else."

"What's that?"

"How the story of my great-grandfather, Pancho Villa, and Felipe Wong ended."

"What makes you think I know?"

"The way you were gloating after you told me a part of it, Jones. Even a blind man could read you."

Jones slid a neighboring chaise longue closer to his. "Take a load off and make yourself comfortable, Ranger. This may take a while . . ."

104

Camino Pass, Texas; 1898

"You're welcome to ride along, amigo, but we've had our fill already and I wouldn't ask you to do any more than you've done."

Pancho Villa smiled at him. "What are friends for?"

Villa rode alongside William Ray Strong back to Camino Pass, the town where he'd been jailed just two days earlier. Delivering home the children Felipe Wong's men had taken was joyous and bittersweet at the same time, given the massacre of so many fathers and brothers at the hands of Wong's gunmen in the aftermath of the abduction.

William Ray watched the reunions transpire under lanterns and torchlight in the center of town. Word spread fast, and more of the townsfolk rushed to be reunited with their children; pretty much everyone else gathered to join in the subdued celebration.

"We could stay here tonight, Ranger," Villa suggested. "Pick up more of my men and set out to make our move on Wong at first light."

"I'm not waiting until first light. There's some work needs doing under darkness, and tonight's as good a time for that as any."

Villa nodded, even though it was clear he didn't agree with the strategy. "We'll need to gather some supplies for the trip first."

William Ray nodded slightly. "Supplies and something else, amigo."

The metal storage containers were normally used for cow's milk. There were four of them, with two hanging from each man's saddle. The extra weight slowed the ride south and necessitated an occasional dismount to allow the horses to regain their strength.

"Don't want to have a horse die on us in the middle of the desert night, do we?" William Ray challenged Villa, when he protested the time it cost them. "Now, I know you got yourself a revolution to run, but I believe it can wait until the sun's burning up the sky tomorrow."

Villa eyed the four cow milk cans, which looked like giant rusty cylinders for a steam engine. "When I was a boy, I flew kites."

"Glad to hear that, amigo."

"I'm getting to something here. You need to trust me."

"Last man I really trusted was Steeldust Jack Strong, and you don't look nothing like Steeldust Jack."

"I'm not *su padre*, Ranger, but I'm still here, still with you."

"That warrants an exception," William Ray said to Villa. "Now, tell me what you got in mind with these kites?"

They stopped in a town to which several of Villa's men had fled with the gold ore and Gatling guns. The process of stitching the six kites Villa figured they needed took time, but not so much that they couldn't reach the Las Bajadas territory claimed by Felipe Wong while there was still enough darkness left ahead of the dawn.

"We could wait another day," Villa suggested.

William Ray shook his head. "He could regroup by then, amigo. I figure he's already gotten word of what happened up at the border. On top of your boys riding herd over his, he's gonna be scrambling to get things settled down. I figure, on top of everything, that he's scared, and there's no worse feeling than something a man hasn't known before, at least not lately."

Villa nodded. "We'll need to take a couple of my men with us."

"Suits me just fine, so long as they don't mind dying."

"Like you?"

"Some things are worth it. Plenty, in fact."

"Like this, Ranger? Why? Is it Wong himself? If that's the case, it should be me doing the killing, not you."

"Not who he is as much as what he does. See, Pancho, you got your feeling about this revolution that's coming to Mexico. Well, I got a feeling about this opium that's coming to Texas and other places across the country. I done enough reading to know what it did in China, and now men like Wong and his compadres are fixing to do the same thing to your country and mine. I can't abide that; I can't allow it. That's what makes what we're doing worth it, and, if I haven't told you already, I'm damn appreciative for your help."

The young man's eyes glistened, looking in that moment more like a boy's. "Wait until you see my kites in action, Ranger."

Villa chose four men he trusted the most, men who'd also done the most soldiering and killing of any in his bandit bunch. They were still a three-hour ride from Wong's stronghold in Las Bajadas, and William Ray figured dawn was five hours away, meaning they'd be cutting things close.

The ride to Las Bajadas was made longer by the need to bypass the rolling hills and mountain range that held the actual camp of Felipe Wong and to keep to the fertile lands of his poppy fields instead. William Ray expected there'd be guards, and he accepted the notion that he'd have to take them out with the quiet of his knife; he was not about to expect anyone else to perform that task.

Until Pancho Villa volunteered the men who'd accompanied them.

"I chose them for a reason, Ranger. This is what they do," the young revolutionary said flatly.

William Ray nodded, scratching at his beard and believing for the first time that Villa might truly overthrow the Mexican government someday. His tone was that of a man as sure of his principles as he was of his actions, and also a man who forgot neither his friends nor his enemies. The Ranger had witnessed that firsthand numerous times in the days they'd been together. He was no kid, for sure, in any way besides age, enjoying both ambitious scope and the singular vision required to realize it.

"Then let's get to it, amigo," William Ray told him.

He and Villa made their way into Felipe Wong's fields, toting those milk cans of kerosene, two each, dangling from straps slung over their shoulders, as soon as Villa's men returned, breathless and covered in the blood of the men they'd just killed. They took up guard posts of their own, against the chance that replacements for the dead men, or reinforcements, came down from Wong's camp up in Las Bajadas.

William Ray knew four cans and two men weren't even close enough to cover the entire scope of Wong's poppy fields. But the dry conditions meant the contents would catch quickly once the fires started. The night was moonless, an additional blessing, which, along with the camouflage provided by the endless rows of high-climbing red flowers, would keep them totally out of sight.

In all, it took twenty minutes for the Ranger to drain his two cans of kerosene. Then he abandoned the cans and hurried through the fields toward the rendezvous point, where he found Pancho Villa already prepping the four kites. The smell in the air indicated that Villa had used one of the remaining cans of kerosene to soak the tightly knotted fabric strung between the thin sticks of wood that formed the frames of the kites. Villa had already strung spools of string to the ends of the kites, just enough to control their initial flight until he released them seconds later. By that time, it would be obvious to anyone looking down from the mountains and hills of Las Bajadas what was happening.

They were racing the coming daylight by the time Villa, keeping one kite for himself, dispensed the other three to his men, who immediately fanned out to preselected positions around the field.

"How do they know when to strike their match?" William Ray wondered.

"When they see my kite rising."

"How'd you know there'd be enough wind tonight to pull this off, amigo?"

Villa grinned broadly, looking like a boy again. "I didn't."

The next few minutes left an indelible mark on William Ray Strong's memory, which he was certain would remain vivid until the day he took his last breath.

First, Pancho Villa's kite rose into the air, already fluttering from the flames consuming it. It spun wildly, even as the three others followed its path into the air in a perfect rectangle around the perimeter of Felipe Wong's poppy fields. The first kite to rise plummeted like a falling star moments ahead of the other three.

Almost instantly, a huge plume of flames shot into the air, spreading faster than William Ray's eyes could keep up with. A sound like crickets chirping resounded through the night as the flames climbed high toward the sky, even as a trio of more audible *poofs* sounded and curtains of flame sprang up from the three other corners of the field. They converged on each other rapidly, and the Ranger saw, in the bright amber glow superheating the night, that Felipe Wong's entire field of poppies would be an inferno soon.

A stench that was bitter and sweet at the same time filled the air, thickening to the point that William Ray had to soak his kerchief in water from his canteen and wrap it tightly over his nose and mouth to ward off the sickening odor. The crackling ebbed, sounding more like wood being eaten by a hearth fire, and the Ranger was silhouetted by the blistering flames, next to Pancho Villa.

William Ray took off his Stetson and mopped the sweat from his brow and cheeks with a swipe of his sleeve.

"Kites," he said, his smile even broader than Villa's had been. "I'm gonna remember that one, amigo,"

The young revolutionary turned his way. "It's just one field, Ranger. You can't burn them all."

"Not in one night, anyway. Maybe when you're running things in this country you'll drop the likes of Felipe Wong into the ground and plant daisies over their graves, amigo."

"He'll be coming after you, Ranger," Villa said, as the sun peeked over the horizon. "You know that."

"You bet I do. Matter of fact, I'm counting on it."

William Ray was standing in the middle of the trail he knew Wong and his men would be taking to give chase. The sun was high enough to burn the sky by then, shining in the eyes of the riders who ground to a halt and squinted to see the man ahead of them. He was holding in one hand a twelve-gauge shotgun, provided by Pancho Villa; the other hand was clenched into a loose fist.

Felipe Wong rode at the head of the group, a mix of befuddlement and amusement stretched over his features, as if he was unsure what to make of finding the man whom he sought lying in wait for him, instead.

"You killed my men. You took my gold, my guns. And then you burned my fields. Tell me, Ranger, was that worth dying for, all this that was none of your concern?"

"Why don't you ask those children I returned to their homes, Mr. Wong? You can do anything you damn well please down here or in

China or on the moon, for all I care. The mistake you made was crossing into Texas. That made it *my* concern. And if you set even one foot over the border again, the Texas Rangers will be waiting."

"But not you, William Ray Strong, because you'll be dead."

"We'll see about that, sir. Right now, I'm going to give you a chance you never gave all those kids you been stealing. Tell your men to turn tail and get gone from here so you and me can finish this between us."

The riders clacked thirty guns into position, all trained on the Ranger.

"I think I'd rather watch them gun you down instead."

"Suit yourself, Mr. Wong," said William Ray, opening his fist and, in the same motion, flicking the cigarette lighter he was holding.

The flame fluttered in the breeze as he dropped the lighter, igniting the line of kerosene that darkened the ground at his feet. The fire caught like a fuse and ran toward the much thicker pool he'd left almost directly where the riders were stopped. Horses reared in panic and weapons that only a moment before had been ready to fire launched into the air as the riders struggled for control.

William Ray had never heard worse screams than the ones that came from the men tossed from their saddles into the flames. Their horses burst from the fire, the pounding of hooves on the hardpan sounding like thunder. A second crescendo of piercing shrieks followed, as the fire caught some of the desperate horses ablaze. The scene of flaming riders galloping atop fiery steeds made the Ranger think of something bred of hell itself—the ultimate destination of the men who were dying before him.

The Ranger glimpsed a single rider who seemed to shed the flames and surge sideways off the trail, chancing a steep dive into an adjacent valley. He knew it was Felipe Wong even before the next wave of coarse smoke cleared to show that the man was nowhere in sight.

William Ray had insisted that Pancho Villa ride on without him, but there he was, when it was over, waiting with his men near the scab tree where the Ranger had hitched Jessabelle.

"Thought I told you to get riding."

"I wanted to see this to the end, Ranger," Villa told him, glancing at his men. "We decided to hang around in case you needed our help."

"And now you got yourself a country to save. Let me tell you, amigo, from my experience, you got a ton of work ahead of you."

Villa joined his men on horseback. "You may have dealt Felipe Wong a setback, Ranger," Villa said, clearly aware that Wong had managed to survive, "but he's got more gold mines, more poppy fields, and more Gatling guns, too."

"That's what Mexico needs you for," William Ray told Pancho Villa. "To make the likes of Felipe Wong and his compadres realize their business isn't welcome."

Villa grinned, turning to look toward the north. "Be careful what you wish for; they may end up in Texas instead."

William Ray looked back toward the smoke rising over the trail where he'd set his trap for Wong and blocking a measure of the sun, now burning high in the sky. "You happen to cross paths with him again, Pancho, you tell him I'll be waiting."

105

San Antonio, Texas

"Wong lived to become Mexico's biggest drug dealer of the time," Jones finished. "As for Pancho Villa, I guess you could say 'Better late than never' when it came to his revolution. . . . Ranger?" he prompted, when Caitlin remained stoic and silent.

She rose from the chaise next to his, trying to stretch out the tightness that had settled in during Jones's completion of the story. Her head felt like someone was trying to drill a hole in it from the inside out. Maybe she should have waited until all this was over and done to make the switch to aspirin. What difference would a couple more days make, anyway? Her hand dipped into her pocket and closed around the familiar shape of the pill bottle, but that's where the bottle stayed.

"I need those plans for this underground railroad," she told Jones, hoping the pain would subside on its own.

Jones looked up at her in the shade, the sun having moved on. "You don't find the way things finished for William Ray Strong more than a little ironic, under the circumstances?"

"Why, because he burned a poppy field?"

"Because in the long run it didn't matter, didn't even make a dent in what was going down in Mexico even then. You really think you can win the war on drugs by taking down some corrupt politicians?"

"I'm not trying to win the whole war, Jones, just this particular battle. Eckles and company made the mistake of basing their operation in Texas. Would it bother you if I said I was just doing my job?"

"Not at all, except for the fact that it's bullshit. You're doing this for the same reason you always do: because it's personal. Because drugs came close to hitting the Off switch on a boy you've spent the last ten years mothering. Even if those drugs in particular didn't come from that underground plant, it's a target you can hit, and I can't remember the last time you missed the bull's-eye, a gunfighter through and through."

"My ancestors were the gunfighters, Jones."

"Sure they were. Gunfighters for their times, just like you are for yours. And now you've got yourself a brand-new target."

"That's why I need those plans, so I know what I'm shooting at."

Jones looked down, sighing deeply. "I can get you the plans for the underground railroad, Ranger, but I can't get you an army, and you can't rely on me to call in the cavalry this time."

"You haven't met my sister, Jones."

Jones narrowed his gaze. "If this were the Old West, you and Masters would have your faces on wanted posters, with bounty hunters on your ass instead of federal marshals."

"I'm surprised you haven't turned me in for the reward money, by the way."

"Don't tempt me, Ranger. I could use the cash in case Homeland finally figures out they're still paying for this place."

Caitlin met his stare, suddenly having trouble sizing him up. "You want to come along for the ride, we'll save you a seat, Jones."

He took his love handles in either hand and shook them. "I think I better sit this one out, Ranger."

"Suit yourself."

"Just remember who was there for you when it counted, once you put these assholes out of business—or in the ground, whatever comes first."

"Get ready to head back to Washington, Jones. Homeland Security will be calling before you know it."

106

Texas-Mexico border

"How many people can you kill with this shit?" Yarek Bone asked Roland Fass, inside the underground facility's cavernous storage chamber.

"One pill does the trick," Fass told him, gazing around at the endless stacks of shiny steel drums. "Do the math."

Bone joined his gaze. "How about I take one of these barrels instead of my fee?"

"You've already been paid."

"True enough, but my men haven't. We haven't discussed the fee for *their* services."

On Fass's instructions, Bone had brought with him a dozen more members of his Fallen Timbers group to provide security until the massive shipment of the contaminated pills was safely on its way.

"Since we're handling the loading chores, which I've got to figure brings its own share of danger," Bone continued, "one of those barrels is the least you can do. Come on, Roland. It'll save me the trouble of stealing it. My people have a lot of enemies whose names belong on those pills."

"If I don't see you do it, nobody will ever know."

Bone smiled. "You know, you're not as big of an asshole as I thought you were."

The barrels needed to be loaded onto pallets and then moved a hundred yards to the tunnel, where a fully refurbished diesel-powered train was now operational again after all these years. From there, it would be a straight shot to the north, where the tracks terminated and the steel drums full of deadly tablets would be loaded onto waiting trucks. The instructions came down from Senator Eckles himself, the goal being to separate the contaminated lots from the rest of the batch while at the same time getting those two hundred million-plus deadly tablets some-place where Caitlin Strong and company would never find them. There was too much at stake now, Eckles knew, to leave them in place, even with the Texas Rangers removed from the scene for a while.

With everything running smoothly and on schedule, Yarek Bone and his Fallen Timbers fighters guarding against any potential attack or incursion, Fass called the senator to give him a progress report.

Eckles ended the call while Fass was still talking, having heard enough. He couldn't stop picturing the chaos that dropping a hundred million or so pills on the streets of Moscow or Beijing would wreak, a society collapsing right in front of his eyes. And that was just for starters. Eck-les looked forward to watching countries that were worth shit to him going to shit right before his eyes.

The pills contaminated with cyanide almost made him forget the remainder of the current stockpile, which ultimately would lead to up-ward of five billion dollars in profit. That money would help fund the manufacture of more pills, both standard opioids to put on the streets and the toxic ones reserved for America's worst enemies, once they fig-ured out how to replicate the process that had thus far developed all on its own.

Eckles's group had certainly dodged a bullet here. He not only had arranged for transport of the contaminated pills for safekeeping but also had eliminated the Texas Rangers and their associates from the equation. Maybe he'd invite Caitlin Strong to the White House, once he was president, and serve up a good old-fashioned Texas barbecue in honor of the Texas Rangers—for their failure to stop him from becom-ing the most powerful person in a world he had helped remake.

Wouldn't that be something?

107

Texas-Mexico border

The map Jones came up with for the underground railroad as it had been constructed beneath Texas contained the structure's original schematics, looking more like architectural or topographical layouts. And, sure enough, one of the massive command and control centers lay just a half mile to the south of Camino Pass, practically straddling the border. Caitlin had no corresponding map of Felipe Wong's gold mines from back in her great-grandfather's day, but the seam of ore that stitched its way along the border would've carried almost directly over the facility that the likes of Lee Eckles had turned into a drug factory.

According to the plans, one of the access points for that particular command and control center was located inside the mouth of a camou-flaged man-made cave. After plenty of rummaging about, which left her wondering how accurate the map really was, she found a submarine-style hatch built into a set of carved earthen walls. The hatch opened onto a long, steep set of stairs that may have descended to hell itself for all she knew.

"Once we get down in the tunnel, Colonel, Nola and me will smoke them your way," Caitlin told Paz. "Leave you and your men to take out the trash."

Paz looked toward the men on either side of him, former members of the Venezuelan secret police, who'd stayed with him to work freelance, along with the two he'd left to guard Luke Torres.

Then his expression tightened. "I look forward to meeting Yarek Bone, Ranger. I look forward to meeting any man who shoots children in the back."

Caitlin wondered what Bone, a man who had never met anyone even close to his match, would make of Colonel Guillermo Paz.

"You and your men follow us down and base yourselves here. Shoot anything we flush back your way, Colonel." Then she moved to her ear the high-tech, military-grade prototype walkie-talkie that Jones had provided. "We're headed down, Cort Wesley. Stand by."

"We're close," Doyle Lodge said.

Cort Wesley was just pocketing the fancy walkie-talkie after talking to Caitlin, who was around a half mile away and about to descend into one of the tunnels that made up the underground railroad.

"I can feel it," Lodge continued.

The old man been a demolition specialist during the Korean War, assigned to the Fifty-Ninth Bridge Company Combat Engineers. His job had been to build floating bridges for US and South Korean troops to cross the Imjin River, and then to blow the bridges up before the enemy could follow. Once deployed, his team would be transported into combat-infested areas ahead of the infantry and had to seek cover over and over again when enemy shelling drew close. The man, who went on to become a Texas Ranger, had used a crude form of plastic explosive that looked and felt just like Silly Putty, which he'd wire under the corners of the bridge, sometimes with enemy troops within earshot or even sight. Cort Wesley appreciated the fact that this meant Doyle Lodge was the last man across, after he'd set the explosives and rigged the detonator.

And that was what Lodge was doing now, planting and layering explosives with as much expertise as any Cort Wesley had seen during his own military service. In this case, that meant packing the plastic explosives in such a way that the unstable ground would collapse downward, forever entombing the drug manufacturing plant directly beneath them.

"How'd you get the explosives?" he asked the old man, who was toiling away without a drop of sweat showing anywhere on his face.

"They're mine, son."

"Come again?"

"Confiscated them from some drug lord and, wouldn't you know it, I forgot to turn them in."

"So how old does that make the stuff?"

"I don't rightly remember. A few years, ten maybe."

"You've been storing this plastique for ten years?"

"It was the tail end of my career. I was already old. Better make that twelve years, as a matter of fact."

"This stuff better not come with an expiration date, Doyle."

The old man looked up from his labors, finally dabbing the first specks of sweat from his brow. "No more than I do, son."

108

TEXAS-MEXICO BORDER

The stairs ended in a tunnel that reminded Caitlin of something out of a science fiction movie. All sleek and shiny, dominated by a set of barely worn train tracks showing no rust. She pictured them curving beneath Ben Hargraves's hometown to the west, where he'd heard the train's grinding howl as a young boy—a ghost that was very much alive, as it turned out.

That town had been wiped out by a flash flood from the Rio Grande a few years back. Camino Pass, meanwhile, was located a mere half mile or so to the northeast, likely within spitting distance of the remnants of a host of Felipe Wong's gold mines. Caitlin imagined all that cubic tonnage of hydrogen cyanide gas from those mines leaching into the aquifer supplying Camino Pass its water. She figured that all the construction work required to get Lee Eckles's underground drug lab up and running must have somehow punched a hole in the earth's crust, releasing the hydrogen cyanide gas, which ultimately made its way into the pipes serving Camino Pass. And when the town's pipes went dry, that gas had seeped up and emerged through the water faucets to wipe out the entire town—except for Lennox Scully and Andrew Ortega.

There was another wild card here, though: the effects of the cyanide gas. Jones had told Caitlin he was after the means by which the cyanide had wiped out an entire town, in order to weaponize it. Now, she figured, he must suspect that someone associated with Lee Eckles had already figured that out and that the men she was after had found themselves with a weapon of mass destruction on their hands. Not a good thing for a cadre that had already shown no compunction about killing Americans with an endless flow of drugs. That meant the stakes were even higher than before—and they had been pretty high to begin with.

"How many you figure we'll be facing, sis?" Nola wondered.

"You know Yarek Bone better than I do. Why don't you tell me?"

"Those Fallen Timbers brutes follow him around like puppies."

"In other words, Bone has an army at his disposal. You just answered your own question, Nola," Caitlin told her.

"The more, the merrier," her half sister came back, unruffled by the prospects.

The process of loading the first lot of steel drums onto the train cars was coming to an end. Four hours into the job, six entire freight cars, hitched to old diesel engines on either side, had been packed with steel drums containing the opioid pills contaminated with cyanide. That left another half to go, which would leave Fass in the company of these whack job Native American terrorists far longer than he would have preferred.

"We're just about ready to roll with the first batch, *kempai*," Bone said, suddenly by his side and towering over him.

"Kempai?"

"It's a Shoshone word."

"I thought you were Comanche."

"I am, but my mother was Shoshone and the language is similar." Bone turned his gaze on the ancient steel behemoth, its old idling engine snorting up a storm. "How far we have to go before we unload?"

"End of the line, fifty miles to the north. The trucks will be waiting."

"They better be," Bone said, glaring down at Fass.

"What's *kempai* mean, by the way?"

"'Gopher.'"

"What now?" Doyle Lodge asked Cort Wesley, having finished planting in the ground two hundred pounds of plastic explosives he'd been storing for safekeeping for some unknown period.

"We wait for Caitlin's signal."

"Then we scramble some eggs?"

"So to speak."

"Means killing a bunch of folks."

"Something neither of us is a stranger to."

The old man's gaze turned distant, as if the exertion and the heat had taken their toll on him. "In Korea, sometimes I imagined I could hear the boots of enemy soldiers clacking against the bridge plate sounding directly over me. Sometimes they drew so close I could almost look them in the eye. Sometimes their gunfire sounded as the bridge blew. I can't even count how many times Chinese troops were shooting at us while we wired floating bridges to blow across the Imjin River. I remember a friend of mine named Ernie falling under one of our heavy transport vehicles when it overturned, his legs crushed as bullets whizzed around him with a bunch of us trying to pull him free. We managed to save his life and he was medevacked out. It was the last time I saw him, though I heard later he'd gotten hooked on pain meds and never really got off them." His gaze sharpened again and retrained on Cort Wesley. "He was the first man I ever knew who became an addict—just a kid, really, like my boy and yours."

Cort Wesley considered the contents of the mammoth facility he could only hope was directly beneath them. "We pull this off, Doyle, we'll be keeping an awful lot of kids from following him."

Guillermo Paz wished he could have stopped off at San Antonio's famed San Fernando Cathedral, where Father Boylston had been headquartered, and seek the priest's blessing for this mission, as he'd done with so many others. For a time, after his priest's death, Paz had spoken out loud to him, but Paz abandoned the practice when Father Boylston showed no signs he was listening. Since the day that Paz's eyes had met Caitlin Strong's and his transformation had begun, he genuinely believed the feats he found himself performing on her behalf were the result of some cosmic bargain he'd made with God, with his priest serving as the conduit. Now, with that connection broken, he feared that God would no longer be watching over him to guide his efforts, no matter how holy this mission might be.

For the first time in longer than he could remember, Paz felt vulnerable, questioning his place here as well as the universe as a whole. He prayed in his mind for his priest to give him a sign from the great beyond, something that might assure him that his transformation had lost no ground.

Then he heard a rumble, the tunnel around him beginning to shake, as if an earthquake had taken hold of the area, helping him to do God's work.

Thank you, Father, Paz almost said out loud.

He quickly realized that it wasn't an act of God that had descended upon him, though. It was a speeding train, coming fast and hard.

109

Texas-Mexico border

Caitlin and Nola Delgado shrank back against the wall as the train's lights blew a hole through the darkness in the tunnel beyond.

The construction of the tunnel was remarkable. All curving, tubular, and sleek, formed of once shiny steel that had dulled over the years and rusted in patches where groundwater had soaked through when the area above them flooded. It was a technological marvel built by men with an open-ended budget and a mandate based on a paranoid delusion. Jones had called it a hundred-billion-dollar boondoggle, which nonetheless left Caitlin picturing comparable warrens and track networks scattered all across the country. Unfinished and never joined up, much like the Cold War master plan to assure the maintenance of command and control in the event of a nuclear war.

"Showtime," Nola said, pulling a backpack containing more of Doyle Lodge's long-stored plastic explosives from her shoulder.

"What are you doing?"

Nola began wedging bricks of the plastique against the finished walls, which were topped with a gritty surface. "Making sure that train's got no place to return to. Man, this shit goes back to prehistoric times . . ."

Nola wedged a detonator-triggered blasting cap into the mound. "You couldn't come up with something that doesn't look like it came from a high school chemistry lab?"

"The Texas Rangers don't include plastic explosives as part of our arsenal."

"So long as the shit works," Nola said, going back to work on a fresh mound.

Roland Fass was watching loaders ease into position more of the pallets crammed with the squarish steel storage containers when he heard Bone's voice over his walkie-talkie.

"There's something wrong."

"What?"

"I don't know. We need to rethink the plan."

"As in . . ."

"I'm bringing this heap back."

"The hell you are," Fass said, in a tone he never would have used to Yarek Bone's face.

"There's something up ahead."

"Could you be more specific?"

"Trouble, kempai," Bone told him, above the racing sounds of the train chugging along at thirty miles per hour.

And that's when Fass heard the blast that turned everything on Yarek Bone's end to static-laced garble.

The ground rumbled beneath Cort Wesley and Doyle Lodge, and thin plumes of dust were kicked into the air.

The old lawman cupped a hand over his eyes and squinted into the desert beyond. "A couple miles that way, by my estimate."

"Paz," Cort Wesley figured. "Putting this underground railroad out of business for good."

"You read me, Cort Wesley?" he heard Caitlin's voice hail over the walkie-talkie.

He unclasped it from his belt and drew it close enough to feel the heat of the plastic and metal. "Loud and clear, Ranger."

"Nola and I are approaching the facility now. Get ready to make things go boom."

Cort Wesley watched Doyle Lodge pushing finger-size steel triggers into layered mounds of the plastic explosives at strategic intervals, drawing on his experience blowing bridges during the Korean War. "Just waiting for the word."

"We got lights and men in our sights, Cort Wesley, lots of both."

"This is going to be fun," he heard Nola Delgado say in the background.

Paz watched the back of the train whipsaw from side to side, anchored by a rear engine facing back toward where it had originated. It looked like a giant snake, slithering quickly one way and then the other.

The explosives he'd set and triggered farther back had done their job, just as planned, tearing the track beds apart and leaving no rails for the train to gain purchase. But the plastique that should have blown beneath the front engine and the cars must have misfired, because all he saw was white smoke. The train wobbled as it ground past him, continuing to sway from side to side.

In that instant, the rear coiling cars tore free and toppled over, skirting forward on their sides and showering sparks as they rode fast down the tunnel. Paz's men just managed to avoid them, as Paz himself ran alongside the surviving cars, with the onrushing spilled cars gaining ground on him.

The front half of the train started picking up speed again, almost past Paz, when he leaped out from the narrow platform and grabbed hold of a ladder on the last car.

"What happened?" Bone heard Roland Fass's voice demand.

"We're being attacked, that's what happened, kempai. Lost half the train cars."

"*What?*"

"You heard me."

"Who, goddammit? *Who?*"

Bone could feel the presence of an enemy, whoever was behind this, drawing closer. "Let you know when I find him. Over and out," he finished, tossing the walkie-talkie aside as he moved for the engine compartment door.

110

TEXAS-MEXICO BORDER

Roland Fass watched Bone's Fallen Timbers fighters fan out into position, guns poised and steadied toward the darkness in the curving train tunnel beyond.

Caitlin Strong . . .

He had no idea what made him form that thought. But who else could it be?

How did she track us here? How did she find this place?

It didn't matter. Until that moment, his biggest concern had been how to explain to Lee Eckles the attack on the train bearing the first batch of the contaminated opioids. Now he realized that the entire facility was under attack and there was nothing Eckles could do to help him. He figured Caitlin Strong was in for a surprise when she came up against Yarek Bone's gang of stone killers, figured he'd have at least some good news to report when she finally proved no match for the opposition.

Worst-case scenario, they still had more than half the deadly pills, and another half billion or so regular opiates, to distribute. Of course, those warehouses strategically located near major population centers across the country would have to be abandoned and replaced with others. A setback, for sure, but one they could survive if Bone's men got the job done here.

And that's when Fass heard the fresh blasts from closer down the tunnel. A cloud rolled out of the darkness, toward the light of the platform, as chunks of the ceiling dropped at his feet, dragging dark, rancid dirt behind them.

———

Cort Wesley felt the fresh rumble, closer this time, the ground seeming to lift up before settling down again. It was enough to make Doyle Lodge lurch backwards from setting the final detonators in place, as if searching for firmer ground.

"You sure know how to throw a party, son," he said.

Cort Wesley's GPS started beeping, and he yanked it from his pocket to find a flashing light already close and soon to be almost directly beneath their position.

Caitlin!

The maps Jones had provided of the underground railroad had proven to be spot-on, indeed, allowing him to breathe easier, given that he now was sure that when Doyle Lodge blew his ancient plastic explosives, the largest drug manufacturing facility the world had ever known would be put out of business for good. All he had to do was wait.

This was not something he was good at, though, especially when it came to Caitlin shooting it out with who knew how many gunmen below, whether Nola Delgado was with her or not.

"You got this?" he asked Doyle Lodge.

The old lawman cupped a hand over his ear. "What was that, son?"

He flashed his walkie-talkie for Lodge to see. "Keep yours at the ready. I'll call you when it's time to hit the switch."

Lodge lowered his hand and smiled. "Kill a couple for me, will ya?"

The ceiling was still collapsing when Caitlin pocketed her GPS signal indicator. She was in range of the platform, which was lined everywhere with shiny steel drums, a few of which had toppled on their sides and were rolling about. Workers moved to get them steady, while men she took for Fallen Timbers fighters fanned out with weapons steadied into the rolling cloud of dust and debris that camouflaged her and Nola Delgado's approach forward.

"You know the biggest difference between us, sis?" Nola asked her suddenly.

"What?"

"When you gun men down, it's legal."

"What's your point?"

"Maybe I should join the Texas Rangers."

Then she charged down the platform ahead of Caitlin.

Paz clung to the side of the train. *Thirty miles an hour doesn't seem fast until you're hanging on to ridged iron with your fingertips,* he mused. Beyond that, the slats on this car must have bent in the blast, because the train wobbled as it rolled on, shaking up a storm and threatening to dislodge him.

Built decades ago to conform to the natural contours of the topography, the tunnel dipped and darted its way along, the wobbling seeming to worsen as Paz mounted the ladder. He was almost to the top when he glimpsed a pair of shapes literally fastened to the train's top. He saw them just in time to duck back down beneath their twin streams of pistol fire.

They could only be a pair of Fallen Timbers killers lying in wait. He'd encountered more than his share of such paramilitary groups back in Venezuela, trusting neither those that professed to support the government nor those waging war against it.

Paz settled on a strategy to use the superior position of the Fallen Timbers fighters against them, easing the shaved-down M4 assault rifle around from behind his shoulder and flak jacket. He then remounted the ladder as high as he dared, steadying the barrel up and well forward, pointing ahead toward the tunnel ceiling, which was little more than concrete layered over cut-out rock. Adjusting his aim further as instinct directed, Paz let loose with a spray the gunmen must have figured was wildly off target.

Until the train rolled under that section of ceiling, a moment after it began to collapse in a thick shower of rock, concrete, and other debris. Paz heard grunts, groans, and what might have been a scream, though the roaring of the big diesel engine made it difficult to tell.

By the time he mounted the roof, the train had shed most of the debris that had crushed the gunmen, who'd chained themselves in place. They were either badly wounded or dead, and either way they weren't about to offer any further resistance to him, Paz thought, as he crouched and then stood all the way up on the train's roof.

Just as the massive figure of a man who could only be Yarek Bone climbed atop the first of the three remaining cars.

Cort Wesley found the camouflaged entrance to the underground drug plant exactly where his GPS locator indicated it should have been, according to Jones's map. He twisted open the hatch and yanked it open.

A set of steep steel steps with matching railings dropped down a good hundred feet, accessing the facility beyond.

Thank you, Jones, he thought. The man formerly with Homeland Security was seemingly much more helpful to the cause now that he wasn't part of Washington anymore.

Almost to the bottom of the stairs, Cort Wesley heard a rumble he first took to be a fresh explosion, until he spotted a flood of several dozen workers charging in panicked fashion toward the stairs he was descending. Some had fled so fast that they had yet to shed outfits that resembled something between a hazmat and a space suit, respirators dangling from their necks as if they'd forgotten to discard them as well.

The rush surged past Cort Wesley, paying him no heed at all. The direction from which they had come was the direction in which he had to go.

"Cort Wesley!" he heard Caitlin's voice crackle from his walkie-talkie.

"I'm down in your neighborhood now, Ranger, and on my way."

"A good thing," she told him, "because I'm trapped."

III

TEXAS-MEXICO BORDER

Caitlin had caught up with Nola and found her pinned behind a pillar, bleeding from the face. Loose flecks of concrete from ricocheting bullets had pricked her like a dozen pins.

"You need to learn patience, Nola," she advised, taking cover behind a separate pillar as more gunfire rocketed their way.

"Never my strong suit, sis."

Nola peeked out from the pillar, steadied her aim with the M4 assault rifle, and fired in the same motion. Her spray was instantly returned by what felt like a dozen bullet streams, chasing Caitlin back behind a curve in the tunnel. The pillar she'd been poised behind looked like somebody had taken a jackhammer to it.

Bone's Fallen Timbers gunmen must have figured they had nailed her, because they now concentrated the whole of their fire on Nola Delgado. That freed Caitlin to spin outward, firing her M4 on full auto in the open. She lacked real shooting experience with the weapon, aware as all gunmen were that cardboard made a bad substitute for blood and bone. From this distance, the best she could hope for was to keep the Fallen Timbers fighters at bay, to serve as a distraction and free up a fire lane for Nola.

Nola seized the opportunity, spinning out from the pillar she'd been using as cover, with a fresh magazine jammed home. Ahead on the platform, Caitlin glimpsed shapes being chewed up by the fire as Nola charged forward to shrink the distance between her and her targets. Others retreated for cover behind an impenetrable wall of what looked like steel storage drums, probably containing the latest shipment of drugs—or, to Jones's point about something weaponized, maybe something even worse.

Caitlin surged forward in Nola's wake, enemy fire spewing bursts of concrete and floor tile, the sting of impact against her skin and clothes feeling like pinpricks poking home. She took cover behind another pillar, immediately behind the half sister her father had never known existed.

Nola was breathing hard, clearly far more rattled than she was accustomed to. "How many strips of plastic you got left, sis?"

"Two bricks," Caitlin told her, picturing them inside separate pockets of the cargo vest she wore over her flak jacket. "A trigger for each."

"Give me one—no, both."

Caitlin tossed the twin mounds across the platform and Nola snatched them out of the air, molding the claylike compound into a shape slightly bigger than a softball and perfectly round.

"How old you say this stuff was?" Nola asked her.

"I didn't."

Nola finished balling the plastic explosive up. "Fire in the hole, sis," she said to Caitlin, wedging a finger-size detonator into the center.

Then she hurled the softball-size mound into the air the way she would a grenade. It soared as if catching some kind of underground wind. It landed close to the enemy gunmen firing upon them, and then Nola hit the detonator.

The explosion pushed a flood of air through Caitlin's ears, the vibration deafening her as much as the sound, bringing with it the original scorching pain she'd felt months before, after triggering the blast that had almost blown her eardrums to smithereens. That pain had made her a hostage to the same kind of pills that had almost killed Luke and that had taken nearly eighty thousand lives last year.

She needed a pill—make that a whole bottleful—if she'd been able to spare the time needed to reach into another pocket for the Vicodin she'd brought along for the ride.

A rumbling she could feel at the pit of her stomach came next, as the airburst ruptured the walls at the far end of the train tunnel. Concrete and the rock formations layered behind it crashed inward in a massive pile that climbed all the way to the ceiling.

When the dust cloud thinned, most of the rectangular steel drums behind which the Fallen Timbers fighters had taken cover had toppled over, a few continuing to teeter upon their perch. The blast had torn holes in plenty of them and turned still more into twisted metal good for nothing but scrap. White, oblong pills were scattered everywhere, covering the platform and tracks with what might have been snow.

"Oops," Nola said, spotting the mound of concrete that had collapsed onto the platform, cutting off that way forward.

Paz drained the rest of his magazine toward Bone's position, the man's massive shape dropping down between the first car and the engine as if anticipating the action perfectly. He was sure to be timing his next move, keeping in mind the precious seconds it would take to reload.

So Paz didn't reload. He tossed the submachine gun aside and ran, leaping from one train car to the next and reaching the head of the front car at the very moment when Bone remounted it, pistol in hand. His presence seemed to confuse the Comanche, taking him by surprise, enough for Paz to knock the pistol from Bone's grasp.

He was still ready when Bone lashed out with a knife that looked as big as a sword. Its dulled finish was testament to its age; it likely had been passed down from previous generations of Bone's family and thus was a weapon that had killed before. Bone worked it like an extension of his arm, side to side, jabbing and thrusting forward to keep Paz back-pedaling and retreating until he had no more space to go.

The fierce intensity and confidence gleaming in Bone's eyes told Paz that this was the plan, and he let the Comanche think it was working. Briefly. Then he lurched forward suddenly, a blur of motion that had him first knocking the blade-wielding hand aside and then snatching the man's wrist and twisting until it audibly snapped and went limp like a broken doll's arm.

The giant's eyes flashed uncertainty, but not pain. Paz was lunging for the kill when those eyes changed again, enough to tell him he'd walked straight into Bone's trap, even before he caught the blur of a second blade jerking forward in Bone's other hand.

"I'm on my way!" Cort Wesley said into his walkie-talkie, rushing against the flow of the last of the fleeing workers.

"Not a lot you can do," Caitlin warned him. "Nola triggered a blast that left a debris pile too big to blast through. And we can't go back because Paz blew up the tunnel that way, too."

Cort Wesley ran through the sprawling assembly line of the massive drug manufacturing plant, charging through breached airplane hangar–like doors that led into a storage chamber piled from floor to ceiling with the rectangular steel storage drums he recognized from that warehouse in Houston. They contained the very kind of narcotics that had almost killed his son, enough pills to cause who knew how many more overdoses.

Then something else caught his eye.

"I've got another idea, Ranger," he said into his walkie-talkie.

Paz twisted at the last minute, so Bone's knife blade dug into his side, scratching up against his rib. Fiery pain burst through him, but he'd been spared the fatal blow that otherwise would have resulted.

He clamped his hand over Bone's, pinning the blade in place to keep him from either jerking it in, deeper and around, or yanking it out. Their eyes met, and Paz saw in the Comanche's a realization that the tables had turned, that he'd missed his best chance. He tried to surprise Paz by hammering him with the hand attached to his broken or dislocated wrist, the pain somehow still not registering. The resulting blows, though, had little or no effect, Bone unable to make his fingers work themselves in a way that otherwise would have done real damage.

Still, Paz felt himself growing weak, his purchase atop the speeding, swirling train growing more precarious, as he began to lose feeling in his legs and feet from the shock of his wound. Bone seemed to sense that, and he pushed the blade in all the way to the hilt, spilling more blood in what was now a steady stream that dripped down onto Paz's combat boots. Paz pretended to try using his other hand to help yank the blade out, a distraction meant to allow him to push Bone off the train car. But the Comanche was ready for the move, his mouth open in what looked like a black hole, which gave Paz an idea for his last chance.

Risky, indeed, yes, but as his priest once told him, quoting T. S. Eliot, "Only those who will risk going too far can possibly find out how far it is possible to go."

Thinking of Father Boylston was all Paz needed to find the strength to yank the final half mound of plastic explosives from his pocket and force it into Yarek Bone's gaping mouth. Paz pushed a trigger stick into the puttylike mixture and, as Bone's eyes bulged in panic, used all his strength to launch the big man backwards across the top of the train car.

Paz felt his balance waver, but he managed to dip a hand into his pocket for the detonator and found the plunger. The blood was still leaking from his side when he depressed it and watched Yarek Bone's eyes bulge before the plastique wedged inside his mouth exploded.

The blast threw Paz off the train as it shredded Bone's torso and eviscerated everything above his sternum. The train shed Bone's lower body around the next curve, the dangling legs making it look like the remains of a department store mannequin.

Paz hit the platform hard, just in time to see the last three cars of the train and the engine spin off the tracks, folding up like an accordion. The old locomotive had completed its final ride, with what was left of Yarek Bone painting the ceiling above it.

"Ouch," said Paz.

"When are you ever going to learn, Nola?" Caitlin said. The two of them were trapped, with the tunnel blocked off in one direction and the train platform blocked in the other.

Nola looked unfazed. "What are you worried about? Pops'll come to our rescue."

"Pops?"

"I call him that on account of he's Dylan's dad. You know, like family."

"No, I don't know."

That's when they heard a rumbling, followed by the crackling of the walkie-talkie Caitlin had clipped to her belt.

"Stand clear, Ranger," Cort Wesley said over the roar of whatever machine he was driving.

Caitlin had no chance to respond before the pile of earthen debris and concrete was split right down the center by the shovel of a massive front loader with tires as tall as Guillermo Paz.

"Hop on," Cort Wesley called down to Nola and Caitlin, waiting until they were on board to reverse.

They rode the loader as far as they could, plowing a path through any and all debris that had been shaken loose by the explosions. The ceiling was shedding swaths of tile, concrete, and earth, maybe ready to collapse altogether.

It was time to speed up that process, as they drew close to the still intact stairwell that provided their only escape route.

"You read me, Doyle?" Cort Wesley said into his walkie-talkie, and they started up the spiraling stairs he'd taken down from the surface.

"I was getting ready to take a nap, son."

"Wait another a minute and let's see if you still got what it takes, Ranger."

"Be somewhere else in sixty seconds," Doyle Lodge told him. "That's all I got to say."

Roland Fass emerged from his hiding place behind the steel drums packed with opioids, inside the expanded storage area. He'd proven himself to be many things over the years, but mostly a survivor, content to continuously remake himself into something else. Someone had once accused him of having a spine made of Jell-O, which Fass took as a compliment, since it meant he could adopt any shape.

Something he was clearly going to have to do here.

The operation was finished, and so, eventually, would be everyone involved in it. Senator Lee Eckles may have thought himself immune to the efforts of the law, but that didn't include the likes of Caitlin Strong, as evidenced by her laying utter waste to a facility deemed impregnable. A bunch of explosions were all it had taken to bring it down. How exactly was it supposed to survive a nuclear war?

Fass felt a rumbling that he first mistook for originating inside him, because that's what it felt like. Then he realized it was everywhere, around as well as within him. His last conscious thought was of a wall of darkness dropping toward him from above, before his breath was punched away and the world was swallowed in a single gulp.

112

Washington, DC

Senator Lee Eckles banged the gavel hard to bring to order the public hearing before a packed committee chamber. It was wall-to-wall people, spectators, and press. Goddamn standing room only, and nationally televised on the major news networks, to boot. He could barely remember what this hearing before his Senate health committee was about, he was so excited.

Since Roland Fass was the only man who could link him to the drug business that had ended in a spectacular debacle, Eckles felt like he'd been granted a mulligan, coming out of the whole mess with his reputation enhanced. In absurd counterpoint, he'd called this hearing to excoriate the parties behind the massive drug network that had been toppled by a mysterious, unidentified force—rumors ranged from the Navy SEALs to Delta Force, the marines, the spirit of John Wayne, and ghosts from the Alamo. He was one of a select few to know the truth, which was fine, since there was no evidence of his actual involvement or that of the cadre of power brokers who'd backed his play from the beginning. He'd already deactivated the network they'd used to communicate, rendering everyone associated with the operation untouchable.

"I hereby call this hearing to order," he said, again banging the gavel dramatically.

Today's hearing was about the shutdown of the drug distribution warehouses scattered throughout the country, which had been set up under his auspices. The only paper trail, though, led straight to Roland Fass, who, as best he could figure, was buried under a million tons of rubble. That meant his connection had been wiped out; he was untouchable, as well.

Eckles had actually come to believe that today was going to mark the unofficial opening of his presidential campaign. Though he didn't have the support of those well versed in placing their men in and around the White House, it didn't mean he needed to abandon the effort. He didn't need them, didn't need anyone, was popular enough to gain the presidency on his own.

"Anyone having business before this committee today, please come forward so you may be heard," he announced, repeating the Senate's boilerplate, ceremonial committee greeting.

"I'd like to be heard, if I may," a voice boomed from the gallery, and Eckles watched Caitlin Strong rise and start forward.

"You are out of order, Ranger," Eckles said, hammering his gavel over the murmurs sifting through the crowd. "As far as I know, you have no business before this committee and are not scheduled to testify."

"I've got business, all right—not with the committee but with you, Mr. Chairman. See, sir, I'm here to place you under arrest for murder."

The murmurs rose to a heated pitch of voices, silenced by Eckles banging the gavel so hard and so frequently that he broke the handle. "This isn't Texas, it's not the Old West, and you can't just barge in here and do your typical grandstanding on national television."

"Guess I should've remembered to wear some makeup, Senator," Caitlin said, holding a manila folder in her hand, halfway between the hearing table and the raised dais where Eckles sat, dead center.

"And who are you alleging I killed, Ranger? Don't tell me . . . John F. Kennedy?"

"No, sir," Caitlin told him. "Thomas Janeway. And I've got the warrant right here."

Eckles closed his fist over what remained of the gavel.

"You recall the name, Senator?"

"Tommy was killed in that car accident on the Sam Houston Parkway I managed to survive when I was little more than a boy in 1989."

"You were almost twenty-five years old at the time, sir. You may recall he slammed into a station wagon and killed an entire family, in addition to himself."

"Exactly. Because *he* was behind the wheel. *I* was in the passenger seat, lucky to survive, and I have blessed my stars ever since."

"You were even luckier to get away with it, Senator, because your friend 'Tommy' wasn't driving that car at all. You were."

Eckles waited for the audible gasp to subside before responding; the gavel was no longer in any shape to pound on the table.

"I'm afraid you have your facts wrong, Ranger."

Caitlin approached his desk, removed an eight-by-ten photo from the manila folder, and slid it before him. "Then I'm guessing this picture, taken a half mile back at the tollbooth you ran, must be wrong too, sir, since it shows you, and not Thomas Janeway, behind the wheel," she said, producing proof of an idea that had first been triggered in her mind when she had spotted the security camera at the Northwest Vista College parking garage.

Eckles tried very hard to not regard the photo, but he couldn't resist a glimpse. "It's obviously doctored," he said smugly. "I once served as a county commissioner in Texas, so I know full well that, back in those days, toll systems dumped violators' photos every six months. What you've got here has all the value of one of those pictures taken inside an arcade concession booth for a dollar."

Caitlin stared straight up at him. "Here's the thing, Senator. I didn't get this photo from some old bin or archives in the Department of Public Safety. I got it from Thomas Janeway's family."

Eckles swallowed hard.

"He was dead, of course, by the time the ticket for the toll violation, and the picture proving it, got there. So his parents put it with the rest of his things, where it remained until I paid them a visit. They never knew you were behind the wheel, Senator, that your family put the fix in to pin the blame for the accident on their son. My guess is your family's people destroyed all trace of the film, but they must've forgotten about the violation that had already been mailed. So the original photo that's been gathering dust for thirty years or so is the only sure proof there is left that you're a murderer. You killed Thomas Janeway and that family of four because you were drunk behind the wheel. No statute of limitations on that, back home, last I checked."

Eckles summoned enough bravado to wave the photo before her. "It's the back of two heads, Ranger."

"With yours in the driver's seat and Tommy's slumped to the side next to you. If you look closer, you can see a reflection in the windshield, thanks to those big road lights overhead. Your reflection, Senator. Your face. You can keep that copy."

Eckles managed to rap the remains of the gavel down once, over the murmurs that had again begun to pick up through the crowd. "The committee will take a fifteen-minute recess."

"Fine by me," Caitlin said, reaching for the handcuffs clipped to her belt. "The state of Texas has waited thirty years to see justice done in this matter. We can wait a little longer."

EPILOGUE

A Ranger is an officer who is able to handle any given situation without definite instructions from his commanding officer or higher authority.

Texas Ranger Captain Bob Crowder, quoted by the
Texas Department of Public Safety

Caitlin got the bad news on the morning Luke would be graduating early from the Village School.

"Lee Eckles is dead," D. W. Tepper told her over the phone.

"How, Captain?"

"Heart attack, by all accounts."

"My ass."

"I'm surprised he lasted this long, Ranger."

"But not long enough to give up the identities of those at the top of the food chain. Guess I shouldn't be surprised, since word is he was getting ready to start identifying the real power behind this whole thing. Men like that have enough money to bribe Saint Peter to get into heaven."

"Where a whole bunch of folks won't be headed, thanks to you burying the rest of their stash."

"Small consolation."

"It'll have to do for now, Caitlin. Sometimes patience makes for a better weapon than bullets. Meanwhile, go have a good time at the boy's graduation. You got plenty to celebrate."

Luke had decided to graduate early from the Village School, having amassed enough credits to don a gown in January instead of waiting until June. With all that happened, he hadn't gotten his college applications or his campus visits nearly finished. Better to spend the next few months focusing on that, he believed, and Cort Wesley agreed. So did Caitlin and his older brother, Dylan.

And, apparently, so did Guillermo Paz, who arrived only slightly late, taking a chair alongside them on the aisle instead of one way back in the rear, as was his normal custom, to avoid drawing attention. A few hushed whispers spread through the crowd when Paz took his seat, but he seemed unperturbed and didn't so much as cast the crowd the kind of look that would have either silenced them or sent them heading toward the exits.

Luke leaned in toward Caitlin. "I invited him," he whispered.

His hair was combed beneath his tasseled cap and his graduation gown fit him straight out of a picture. A decent crowd filled the Village School auditorium, though nothing like the primary spring graduation, which was held outside to manage the overflow. Luke likely would have been named valedictorian, if not for the drug incident that had tarnished his reputation, though not his academic record. As it was, he'd submitted an essay along with other early graduates, a portion of which might be read from the stage by Head of School Julia De Cantis to showcase the direction in which the early graduating class saw its future heading.

Caitlin sat in silence, occasionally squeezing Luke's hand, while Dylan blew the hair from his face on the other side of his father, looking like he'd much rather be somewhere else. Nola Delgado hadn't shown up, but Caitlin figured Dylan would be meeting up with her later, the two being generally inseparable.

As the head of school read excerpts from the submitted essays, Caitlin listened for Luke's, knowing when his came even before he squeezed her hand.

"The future ain't what it used to be."

"You learn that one from Paz?" Caitlin asked above a sprinkling of laughter through the crowd, glancing at the huge shape tucked into the end of the row.

"Yogi Berra," Luke corrected.

"Well," Caitlin said, exchanging a smile with Cort Wesley next to her, "it's still about as true as it gets."

———

On the way out of the auditorium, Caitlin stopped by a trash container. She took the Vicodin from the pocket where she still tucked it and jiggled the pills that were left inside. Then she looked toward Cort Wesley and cast Luke a wink before tossing the orange prescription bottle into the trash can.

"Don't believe I'll be needing these anymore."

Author's Note

I love penning these pages to finish out another Caitlin Strong adventure, love giving you insight into the crazed mind of a writer and how this particular book came to be. Fortune, as they say, is the residue of design, and *Strong from the Heart* was born of a combination of both.

First, the design. I knew I wanted this book to follow the lines more of a traditional high-stakes, high-action thriller. More Steve Berry and James Rollins. A big story featuring a big McGuffin, to use the term Alfred Hitchcock coined to describe what everyone is after. Well, when in doubt, turn to the headlines, right? I wanted to base a story on something current, something people were talking about and fretting over. A genuine crisis.

Like opioids.

Yup, that was where *Strong from the Heart* started, with this magical question: What if Caitlin Strong took on the opioid crisis? What if that crisis hit painfully close to home? What if Caitlin herself realized she might have a problem, too?

Then I was off and running. But, as all of you know, that's never enough for me. So I had this vision of a prologue centering around a small town wiped out in a matter of minutes or even less, a kind of homage to the classic opening of Michael Crichton's *The Andromeda Strain*, something that's stayed with me since I first saw the film when I was maybe twelve years old. The problem was I had no idea what killed the town of Camino Pass and how it connected to the opioid crisis that would define the book's central focus.

Now we come to the fortune. Turned out that hydrogen cyanide was the ideal toxin to get the job done. Turned out cyanide was used heavily in the process of extracting gold from ore. Turned out there were gold mines at one time stitched along the border with Texas and Mexico. See what I'm getting at here? Anyway, I had my book.

Next came the historical thread involving Caitlin's great-grandfather, William Ray Strong, who'd already kept company, in past books, with the likes of Judge Roy Bean. I'd started writing the scene where he rides into Camino Pass, the very same town that gets wiped out in the present, to pick up a prisoner, only to learn that the town's children have all been kidnapped, before I realized that prisoner was none other than a young Pancho Villa. Somewhat historically accurate as far as Villa's background was concerned, but mostly I thought it would be a blast to team the two of them together. And the trail they end up following leads straight to another historically accurate fact: that Chinese immigrants to Mexico brought poppy seeds with them, giving birth to the very drug trade roiling the United States today.

How about that?

The thing I enjoy most about writing the Caitlin Strong books is probably the very same thing you enjoy most about reading them: watching the pieces of the story slowly come together. Kind of like assembling a jigsaw puzzle. And if I don't know how those pieces are going to fit when I start the book, it makes it that much harder for you to figure out the various twists and turns that spring up along the way. Call it the fun of writing spontaneously and not working off an outline. The best stuff I came up with in *Strong from the Heart*, and all the other books in the series, is the stuff I wasn't aware of when I first put fingers to keyboard.

That's what makes the Caitlin Strong books such a blast to write. And the more fun I have writing them, the more fun you're going to have reading them. So it should come as no surprise that I have no idea what the story I'll have for you at this time next year is going to be. I just know I'm going to love writing it, which means you're going to love reading it. That's a promise.

So be well until next we meet, and feel free to reach out to me at www.jonlandbooks.com. I enjoy nothing more than hearing from my readers—well, except for writing the books in the first place!

Acknowledgments

Stop me if you've heard this before, but let's start at the top with CEO Tom Doherty and Forge's publisher Linda Quinton, dear friends who publish books "the way they should be published," to quote my late agent, the legendary Toni Mendez. The great Bob Gleason and Natalia Aponte are there for me at every turn. Editing may be a lost art, but not here thanks to both Natalia and Bob, and I think you'll enjoy all of my books, including this one, much more as a result.

My friend Mike Blakely, a great writer and musician, taught me Texas firsthand and helped me think like a native of that great state. And Larry Thompson, a terrific writer in his own right, has joined the team as well to make sure I do justice to his home state along now with his son-in-law, a Texas Ranger himself. And special acknowledgments to Bill Miller who helped me smooth out the geography of the Lone Star State. Thanks, again also to Terry Ayers for making my scientific jargon sound at least somewhat credible.

A final thanks to Dan Addario, on whom I based the Doyle Lodge character you just met. For more of Dan's incredible story as a legendary DEA agent who's been fighting the war on drugs as long as there's been one, check out the book *Chasing the Dragon*, which I wrote with him. Like Doyle Lodge, Dan lost his own son to the scourge of opioids. And the fight he continues to wage is aimed at ensuring not another parent need experience such a tragedy.

Check back at www.jonlandbooks.com for updates or to drop me a line, and please follow me on Twitter @jondland. Thanks to all of you who've already written, tweeted, or emailed me your thoughts on any or all of the first ten books in the Caitlin Strong series. You are truly the wind beneath this particular author's wings and I genuinely hope you enjoyed this Caitlin Strong adventure as much as the others.